Praise for Judy Sheehan's

. . . AND BABY MAKES TWO

". . . *And Baby Makes Two* is real life, real love,
real romance in the city."
—Monica Horan ("Amy" on *Everybody Loves Raymond*)

"Rife with suspense and whip-smart prose."
—*Brain, Child*

"Filled with touching and funny insights into the ups and downs of
the adoption process. Recommended for all libraries."
—*Library Journal*

"[A] warm, poignant, humorous adventure of a woman who
wanted a child . . . a happily ever after story."
—armchairinterviews.com

"A warm, funny look at foreign adoption and single motherhood."
—*Kirkus Reviews*

ALSO BY JUDY SHEEHAN

. . . And Baby Makes Two

WOMEN IN HATS

WOMEN IN HATS

[a novel]

Judy Sheehan

BALLANTINE BOOKS · NEW YORK

A Ballantine Books Trade Paperback Original

Published in the United States by Ballantine Books,
an imprint of The Random House Publishing Group,
a division of Random House, Inc., New York.

LIBRARY OF CONGRESS CATALOGING-IN-PUBLICATION DATA
Sheehan, Judy.
Women in hats: a novel/Judy Sheehan.
p.   cm.
ISBN 978-0-345-48008-8
1. Mothers and daughters—Fiction.   2. Actresses—Fiction.   3. Broadway
(New York, N.Y.)—Fiction.   I. Title.
PS3619.H439W66 2008
813'.6—dc22   2007043770

Printed in the United States of America

www.thereaderscircle.com

2 4 6 8 9 7 5 3 1

Book design by Mary A. Wirth

for Bob

WOMEN IN HATS

Prologue

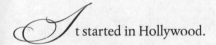t started in Hollywood.

BRIDIE IS A BRIDE

A rising starlet at Warner Bros. is set to make good on the promise of her nickname. Late yesterday, the studio announced that Bridget "Bridie" Donnelly will be tying the knot with her charming beau, the much older John Hart of the studio's legal department. So, it looks like this "Bridie" can turn to her "Groomie" to iron out any contract disputes! Not that she's in need of much assistance. At the tender age of eighteen, Bridie is as poised and authoritative as the big stars she dines with at the commissary. That must be why she lands bigger and bigger roles in each new picture.

Bridie and her fiancé were all smiles as they discussed their future plans. Says he, "I'm looking forward to our happy home life together. I want lots of kids!"

Says she, "Yes, and I've got a plum part in Bette Davis's next picture! I play her daughter, and I've got the absolute juiciest scene with her. Wish me luck!" And for that plum part, she'll be billed as Bridie Hart. Meanwhile, we'll send our good luck to Mr. Hart. He's got himself a genuine firebrand!

Variety June 1957

Their wedding photos appeared in every movie magazine that Bridie could name. The publicity boosted her career, but it failed to sustain the marriage. Years later, Bridie made a habit of regaling cocktail party guests with complaints that her attention span just dwindled away from poor John Hart. Eight months into the marriage, Bridie was bored silly. After all, she was so young, so full of life, dreams, and ambitions. She shouldn't have been tied down like that. So she left him, and life went on. Bridie dramatically denied all the rumors about the marriage ending because of a fling with Tony Curtis.

Edgar Threadwell was the surprise second husband for Bridie Hart. Gossip columnists were unanimous in their assessment of the couple: Bridie had once again married her opposite. They turned to their egg timers to calculate just how long the marriage would last.

And for the unlovely aspects of the recent Academy Awards ceremony, we must turn to Bridie Hart. Nominated for Best Supporting Actress for her dazzling comic turn in *Telephone Tango,* Bridie arrived in style, sporting an original Oleg Cassini gown. "Everyone tells me I look exactly like Jackie Kennedy! But with red hair! And a bustline!" Bridie modestly proclaimed as she strolled the red carpet. But her happiness was short-lived. When the Oscar went to Rita Moreno for *West Side Story,* Bridie was in no mood to be a good loser. Our sources tell us that she strode to the bar at the first opportunity and opted to vent her spleen to anyone within earshot, and a few who weren't. Her terribly English, terribly quiet, and brand-new spouse, noted architect Edgar Threadwell, seemed mortified by Bridie's capacity at the bar, and by her invective against the Academy.

Judy Garland, who had also been nominated for Best Supporting Actress for the stirring *Judgment at Nuremberg,* approached Bridie to offer solace to the younger actress. To our eyes, Bridie was too soused to listen that night. But perhaps, by now, she has had time to reflect. And if she's reading this, let us simply say: Bridie, when you're getting sobriety advice from Judy Garland, you are not having a good night.

Moviegoer March 1961

When retelling her life story at her many cocktail parties, this would be the point in the tale when Bridie announced that she and Hollywood were simply not meant to be. Her voice would change, as she seemed to visibly rise above Hollywood and her second marriage. So, she had quit Los Angeles and offered herself to New York, as a kind of Christmas present, and the city welcomed her. Those party guests who remembered the rumors of Edgar's stormy departure, or a certain studio head's refusal ever to hire Bridie again, tactfully refrained from interrupting her tale.

Barely 25 years old, Bridie Hart is already a Broadway stalwart, forever showcasing her beauty, her brains, and her big fat voice. Last Saturday, between the matinee and evening performances of her new musical, *Jezebel,* Bridie lived up to her nickname once again. She married her director, Frank Majors. The Bride, or should we say, the *Bridie,* was dressed in tasteful yellow organza, this being her third wedding. "Third time's the charm!" she declared to her bevy of chorus boys, who served as surprising and rather noisy bridesmaids.

Majors, a veteran of two marriages himself, feels that he

and his star are a match made in theater heaven. "We fight like the devil, but we always make up. Hell, enough scotch and you can forget what you started fighting about in the first place. We're perfect together!"

Playbill October 1964

That's how the good years began. At first it seemed that Frank and Bridie *were* made for each other. The papers carried photos of the two of them dining in a quiet corner of a West Village Italian restaurant, holding hands over red wine and spaghetti. Bridie's voice was at its softest when she painted those pictures for her guests.

Bridie and Frank were so much more than the sum of the parts she played. Together, they fought more, drank more, and worked more than they ever could apart. No, not every play was a success. When they tried to set a Greek tragedy in modern times, their *Helen of Flatbush* was the most notorious flop of that season. And their nasty fight on the air, during an interview with Jack Paar, offered a glimpse into the volatility of their marriage. But none of that mattered. Bridie and Frank were bruised, but they were never broken. A golden couple, they rose above the petty details of their days and enjoyed their lives. They did it for themselves. They did it for everyone.

Should a couple like that have children? No, they should not. They should drink and fight and work and sleep and get up and do it again. But they didn't know that, and soon the papers were reporting Bridie's pregnancy. First, they had Lilly. Born with dark eyes and a shock of dark hair, Lilly must have been wise to her parents' childishness right from the start, since it usually seemed to amuse her. She outsmarted all of her nannies and waited until she was eight years old before informing her parents that they really needed to enroll her in some sort of school.

Then, Leigh was born. Leigh Majors. She was a serious child. Bridie often told her that she didn't smile until she was three, and that was a smile she gave herself for making her bed ever so perfectly. She may have been the first three-year-old to achieve hospital corners. How could she have known that her birth would signal the start of the tough years in her parents' marriage?

· · ·

"Lilly, what are they fighting about now?" Leigh asked her sister.

"Same old thing, kid. Don't let it bother you."

But it did bother Leigh. The angry voices couldn't be smoothed down or tucked away. How did Lilly sail through these storms unscathed, and could she teach Leigh to do the same?

"Hey, Leigh! Look at all the makeup I stole from Mom." Lilly displayed her treasure—a miniature suitcase filled with Max Factor and Revlon. Before Leigh could give a halfhearted smile or offer the expected "Neat!" response, she flinched at the sound of her father's voice roaring in their parents' bedroom.

"You wouldn't fucking dare! I'd break you! I'd ruin you!" It was Frank, but it didn't sound like Frank. That was not the voice he used with Lilly and Leigh.

"Hey! Kid! Come here!" Leigh obeyed her sister's command. "I'm gonna make you a movie star!" Lilly promised.

With that, Leigh settled on the floor, tried to tune out the shouts from Bridie and Frank, and let her sister apply a faceful of cosmetics. It was soothing to focus on the lipstick, the soft brushes against her cheek, her sister's fingertip as it smudged eye shadow across Leigh's brow. The false eyelashes were taking an extraordinarily long time, and Leigh nearly drifted to sleep while her sister glued and unglued Leigh's eyelids. But she bolted awake when Bridie's voice penetrated her makeup fog, shrill as ever.

"GET OUT OF MY HOUSE! THE GIRLS AND I DON'T WANT YOU HERE!"

There was more, some sort of response from Frank, but Leigh couldn't hear it, since Lilly began to sing. She found herself giggling as Lilly chirped, "Midnight at the Oa-a-a-asis! Send your camel to be-e-d!" Leigh had no idea what it meant, but it had to be funny. She tried to open her eyes and see the hip-swinging dance that she knew accompanied Lilly's song, but her eyelids were once again glued shut.

Bridie's voice was closer now. "HOW DO YOU EVEN KNOW THEY'RE YOURS?" Was she in the room with them? Lilly wasn't singing anymore, so Bridie must have come in. Leigh tried to pry her eyes open. Lilly said nothing, but she gently moved Leigh's hands away from her glued-shut eyes, and Leigh didn't resist. Bridie kept shouting, "LILLY'S SO GORGEOUS AND TALENTED, SHE CAN'T BE YOURS. AND LEIGH, WELL, THAT WAS WHEN I WAS DOING THAT PLAY WITH JACK CASSIDY! REMEMBER?"

"Don't do that, Bridie. Don't use them like that. Just don't." Frank's voice registered fear, or was it sadness? Leigh needed to see his face to put it all together, but she was sealed into darkness. Lilly let go of her sister, who groped in the dark like Patty Duke in that movie. Lilly's voice rang out, from up high.

"Okay, you guys, you're all done now. Bridie: go get ready for your show. Frank: go take a shower, you stink."

Leigh began to peel the glue from her eyelids, now that there was no one to stop her. She couldn't follow the argument in the room without seeing the players. They were too loud, too fast, too complicated.

"Mother!" Lilly used that term only to reprimand Bridie. "It's seven-twenty. You're going to be late for your call."

Bridie hesitated, then affected a kind of dignity as she said, "I've never missed a curtain in my life," and walked away. Frank stumbled into the room to hug his daughters. His voice was small and muddy as he said, "I love you girls more than the world. You know that, don't you? You're more than the world to me. I fucking love you girls."

Lilly was right, he really needed a shower. Leigh was about to tell him so when Bridie's voice pierced the room with, "AND YOU BETTER NOT BE HERE WHEN I GET BACK!" punctuated with a door slam. Leigh pried one eye open just enough to see that Frank was crying now, and somehow smelling worse. Lilly patted him on the back and said, "You'll feel better when you don't stink so bad." His walk was slow and unsteady as he headed back to his room. Within a few minutes, they heard the shower running.

Leigh closed her eyes to cry, and glued them shut once again.

WEDDING BELLS

We are pleased to announce the blessed union of our school's financial adviser, Barton Glumm, and Bridie Hart, the mother of our own fifth-grader, Lilly Majors. Miss Hart, a popular stage actress, met Mr. Glumm at the Saint Philomena fund-raiser during the Feast of the Holy Assumption. And we all remember her rendition of "Hey, Big Spender" that night, don't we. Mr. Glumm, a lifelong bachelor, was smitten from the first chorus. The happy couple had a quiet civil ceremony, due to Miss Hart's previous forays into marriage. And so, Mr. Glumm is transformed from solitary investment manager to husband, father, and perhaps even Stagedoor Johnny! But will Miss Hart now deign to join us for the occasional Parent-Teacher Association Meeting? Time will tell. Meanwhile Miss Hart's younger daughter, Leigh Majors, will enroll in Sister Mary Michael's kindergarten class next

September. We will have quite the family affair here at
St. Phil's!

Newsletter, St. Philomena's School for Girls May 1975

Even Bridie had to know that she and Barton were a mismatch.
Leigh thought that Bridie was seeking some sort of antidote to
Frank's passion, and Barton was it. As an investment manager
Barton never made anyone spectacularly rich, but never saw anyone lose more than twelve dollars in a year. Not if he could help it.
Bridie praised his blue suits and encouraged him to grow his side-
burns. Leigh was relieved that she wasn't going to be asked to call
him "Daddy." Lilly spent hours erasing tiny numbers from his
ledgers and replacing them with new tiny numbers.

* * *

"It's Saturday and it's twelve o'clock and Daddy should *be here by
now.* Where is heeeeee?"

Leigh knew she was whining as she collapsed against the refrigerator door. But if she hit just the right note, she could make Bridie
wince and stop clopping around in her platform shoes long
enough to notice that her children hadn't eaten breakfast yet. It
was Frank's weekend with the girls, and Leigh didn't want to waste
a minute of Daddy-time on boring things like food.

Clop-clop-clop. Bridie was in pursuit of coffee, one eye squinted
open, the other still shut. Why was she wearing platform shoes
with her pajamas? What was wrong with her?

"He's not here yet because he doesn't love you. Not like
Mommy does. Do you have to block the refrigerator? You know I
can't drink my coffee without milk."

Leigh moved as slowly as she could, just to torture her coffee-
deprived mother. Frank did love her. Frank did love her. Frank did
love her. So there.

"Hey, kid," Lilly called out from across the kitchen table. "Cheerios. Twelve o'clock."

Lilly had poured out a full box of Cheerios into two overflowing bowls. Leigh smiled but then Bridie shrieked, "Jesus Christ, that's IT? There are only three drops of milk left? That's not enough! Now how am I supposed to drink my coffee? Goddamn selfish brats, you think everything is for you." She slammed the refrigerator closed, poured the pitiful remnants of milk into her cup, and threw the empty carton across the room. Leigh decided not to duck, not to flinch, not to move. Bridie wasn't done with her diatribe.

"You two finish off the milk and never consider the fact that your mother needs some fucking milk for her goddamn coffee in the morning." *Clop-clop-clop.* Bridie was headed back to bed with her precious coffee, containing the last of the milk. "I'm putting a lock on the refrigerator, I swear to God. And anyway, you girls could stand to lose a few pounds. Barton! Wake up! You need to go out and get milk. NOW!"

•   •   •

Barton Glumm died. Maybe it was the wide ties and plaid pants that Bridie insisted he try. Maybe it was the shock of married life for one who was too set in his ways. Maybe it was the way Bridie burned through his money. Officially, the cause of death was a stroke. Unofficially, Leigh thought the real cause was Bridie.

WHO WILL BUY MY OVERPRICED JEWELRY?

Faithful chickens, you know that we are never ones to delight in the misfortunes of others. Even when the others are loud, drunken actresses who bully columnists as if all were locked in a Stepmother-Cinderella cycle with no glass slipper in sight. Oh, no. Far be it from us to point out that a certain redhead (well, formerly redhead, we suspect, but only her hairdresser knows for sure) is undoubtedly having financial woes. Why don't we doubt it? Because said redhead is selling off her furs, her jewels, and her overdecorated apartment at bargain-basement prices, and with impressive speed. Now, Red has been married many times, most recently to a financial whiz who invested her fortune in—get this—a show. A show, my little chicks, a show! I couldn't print it if it weren't true! It was called *Wild on Wall Street* and it was about the crash of 1929. Doesn't that sound like fun? It gets better. He declined to invest in *A Chorus Line*. Instead, he put all of wifie's money into a show that closed in New Jersey, just to add insult to insult. What's to become of poor, obnoxious Red? Will she work in this town again? Not anytime soon. One of her ex-husbands used to direct her into reasonably tolerable performances, but he is gone from her life, never to be admitted back in. And so are the reasonably tolerable performances. Red came to us, hat in hand, from Hollywood, and to Hollywood she shall return. At least that's the word we hear from those who have ventured into her Fifth Avenue garage sale. And Hollywood can have her.

But for now poor little Red is penniless and thirty-six. Oops! Did I do a meanie thing there, revealing her age? Not to worry, my chicks. She can't afford to buy a newspaper today.

Broadway Beat September 1977

Frank was always late for everything. But today? Why today? This was a painfully wrong day to be late. This was the day that Bridie was moving herself and the girls to Los Angeles. And Frank had sworn that he would be there to say good-bye to his daughters. Did Bridie choose an early morning flight on purpose? She knew that Frank wasn't good at mornings. Did she work hard to make it more difficult for him?

"We have to go to the airport now, Leigh." Bridie was counting suitcases while she spoke. She snapped her fingers at the crew of movers, who took this cue to start loading the luggage into the car.

"He'll be here. We can't leave without saying good-bye."

Stupid Bridie had gotten herself cast in some stupid situation comedy in stupid Los Angeles. Leigh read the script, and thought it sounded amazingly stupid on paper. It would probably sound even stupider on television. *Mother Love.* Leigh had snuck the script with her on her last weekend visit with Frank.

"Insipid," Frank declared as he reached page seven. "Inane. It'll be a hit. Mark my words. Your mother will finally conquer Hollywood. God bless her."

"But I don't want it to be a hit. I want it to fall off the air and I want us to come right back to New York and be with you."

Frank's career had cooled—even Leigh could see that. He kept moving into smaller and smaller places, while dating less and less attractive actresses. Leigh stayed awake nights worrying about him, and how she might never get to escape from Bridie to go live with him.

"Kiddo, I'm fine." He sat her down and studied her sad, serious little face. "In fact, I'm clean and sober for the first time in my life. Don't you worry about me. Let *me* worry about *you*. Okay?"

"Okay," Leigh answered reluctantly. "And you know what, Dad? You smell a lot better than you used to." She intended that as a compliment, so she couldn't understand why Frank was laughing so hard. After all, it was true. He seemed to be showering on a regular basis these days. He was getting out of bed like a person, even if it was late morning when he did. And now he was directing a new play in a new theater downtown. He was far from Broadway, but he really was okay.

"Now, Leigh, this play I'm directing—it's not going to be a hit," he explained. "Well, it'll be a success, but nothing like what your mother's going to have with that TV show."

"Then don't do it," reasoned Leigh.

"But I love it. I do. I love this script, and I think the actors are first-class, even if nobody's ever heard of them. They're working their asses off, and I'm proud of them."

"Then it'll be a hit." Leigh wanted to reassure him.

"No. It won't. But it'll be better than that. It'll be good," he answered quietly.

"And then we can come back to New York and live with you." Leigh added her happy ending and waited for Frank's answer. He opened his script and began scribbling more notes.

After a while, Frank explained that he was about to start tech week, which involved late nights of setting what few lights this theater had, and working with the outdated sound equipment, the shabby costumes, and the broken props. It sounded awful. He used no positive adjectives, but he looked so engaged, so satisfied and awake. Leigh wanted to skip packing up her life for L.A. and stay with him to curse at the rotten speakers and fuss with lights.

"Maybe someday you'll help me with one of these plays." Frank smiled as if he knew, and Leigh believed him.

Maybe tech week was keeping him from showing up now, before they left for L.A. But he needed to get here. Now. He needed to tell Bridie that he'd be taking custody of his girls soon. Soon.

"Leigh," Bridie chirped. "Your father's probably in a bar with some gullible young girl. He's not going to get here. Not in time."

Leigh sat on the floor, frozen in a perfect picture of stubbornness. The luggage was loaded into the car, and Bridie was tapping her nails impatiently against the door frame. Leigh shut her eyes tight.

Lilly joined her on the floor and whispered, "We gotta go. It'll be okay, Leigh. You'll see. I'll take care of you."

"You really should get over him, Leigh," Bridie said as she jangled her keys. "You're setting yourself up for a helluva miserable love life in the future. That's a daddy complex that's set for doom. Mark my words."

Leigh unfroze long enough to look at Bridie and mutter, "Oh, shut up." This prompted Bridie to snap her fingers again, which cued the movers to hoist Leigh into the car.

Not since Lucy Ricardo has TV been so in love with a red head! You know who I'm talking about—Bridie Hart, aka Bridie Love of *Mother Love,* the widowed mother of five rambunctious kids on NBC. From her achingly beautiful rendition of the show's theme song to her closing chat with the kids in the TV audience, Bridie is charming, warm, real, and full of, well, Love! For this reviewer, that closing chat with the kids is something that only a real star could pull off. In these cynical disco days, it is a revelation to see a genuinely kind and loving person look right into the camera and make us feel that she is talking only to us. This woman, this wonderful woman, has used a silly medium to improve the lives of children and families everywhere.

I understand that she has two lovely daughters, Lilly and Leigh. Lucky, lucky girls.

"TV Time—Views & Reviews" Peoria Daily Press September 1978

Fame. At last, true fame. Bridie was the center of attention wherever she went. She worked extraordinary hours and made personal appearances at everything from the opening of movies to the uncrossing of ankles. Leigh tried to enjoy Bridie's absence from the grand house, but it was hard to wrap her arms around nothing.

For the first time, Lilly seemed to be struggling, too. She was expelled from two very pricey schools, but no one minded. And that just seemed wrong to Leigh. People should mind. It should matter. After all, it mattered when it happened on *Mother Love.*

When Bridie Love caught her oldest son plagiarizing a paragraph in his term paper, it launched a dramatic two-part, very special *Mother Love*. Bridie Love minded. So, Leigh Majors decided to mind.

"Lilly, you've got to go to class at this next school. And do your homework, at least once in a while. Okay?" Leigh couldn't muster the stern voice she had practiced, at least not when Lilly was so sunny, so easy and happy.

"Okay, Leigh. I promise to try. But I think you do enough homework for both of us. Mom was saying that I could drop out of school and be a singer. I think I want to be a singer." Lilly was smiling, but Leigh struggled to maintain her serious scowl. It was the same scowl she used when Bridie gave her daughters martini-mixing lessons.

"Oh, Lilly," she sighed. "What if you turn into Bridie?"

"Ewwww!" Lilly answered through her laughter.

Well, who would have thought the old man had so much blood in him? Remember Frank Majors? He directed all those really gay musicals with his wife, Bridie Hart, who dumped him and moved on to become a TV Mom / Weekly Annoyance. For a while there, he was majoring in scotch with a minor in every other brown liquid, and no one would back his latest gay musical. But we hear that he got sober and realized that he actually had some talent and some blood flowing through his veins. And holy shit is he good. But somehow, Majors got the playwright of his latest production, *Purr*, to remove his head from his large intestine and do some rewrites. Then he cast the play with the absolute perfect genius cast, even if they're all unknowns. How did he find them? How did he make this play so much better? How did he stage a fight scene with no violence, and still scare the living shit out of the audience? This guy has got it. That's how. He got out from under the Bridie Hart/brown liquid anvil, and found his inner director. And let us all say a big fucking THANK YOU.

The Village Voice January 1986

Frank visited Los Angeles when he could, which amounted to twice during the seven year run of *Mother Love.* He had planned many more visits, he called, he scheduled, but he canceled a lot. His life was not his own, somehow, and forces beyond his control stepped in and trapped him in New York. Leigh didn't pretend to understand, but she did play the good sport. Bridie wanted to see Leigh turn her anger against her father, but Leigh just wouldn't give her that satisfaction. When he did visit, he stayed at the nearby Holiday Inn. His income was so much smaller than Bridie's, and it showed. It never seemed to bother him, and it bothered Leigh only because she knew that this was what stopped him from visiting, from taking her away from Bridie. He stopped talking about custody, and every time Leigh mentioned it he looked away, opened a script, or changed the subject.

But when Leigh was sixteen, and Frank canceled yet another visit to L.A., she packed her bags. She would go to New York herself this time, and she wasn't asking Bridie for permission.

"Leigh," Lilly pleaded when she saw Leigh's bags on the bed. "Mom will freak big-time. You can't just disappear."

"Why not?" Leigh asked as she folded her shirts into perfect squares. "You do it all the time. You scared the crap out of me when you disappeared for three days last month. Now it's my turn."

"Sorry." Lilly closed the suitcase, interrupting the flow of precision packing. "I told you, I was just in the Valley, doing a gig with the band. Mom doesn't seem to mind when I go. I didn't get that you worried so much."

Leigh tried to roll with Lilly's absences, tried not to be her older sister's scold, but she was bad at faking it. Lilly had dropped out of school and joined a local band as their lead singer. Her gigs often turned into all-night parties. Bridie seemed to think that this was delightful. It was as if Lilly were giving some adolescent stamp of approval to her mother's bad behavior.

"Hey, Leigh. I have a great idea. Why don't you come with me tonight. With my band. That would be so cool. You can be my first groupie. And that way, you'll know that everything's okay. And who knows, maybe you'll have a little fun."

"That's okay." Leigh shook her head. "You go ahead. I've got stuff to do here."

"But you can't just leave." Lilly wasn't letting go of that. "It's one thing if *I'm* gone all night," Lilly argued. "She expects that. But you—if you just vanish, she'll have a stroke and then we'll have to feed her through a straw and give press conferences about how brave she is. You don't want that, do you?"

But Leigh didn't care. Then she broke her promise. This would be one of the rare occasions when Leigh lied to her sister, promising to leave a note for her mother explaining this sudden absence. Leigh pushed Lilly out the door, and soon after, left the house herself. She silently refused to leave a note for their mother. Now Bridie would have to worry about her younger daughter for an entire week in the middle of the school year.

Leigh arrived in New York with no trouble. She confidently took a cab from JFK to the Off-Off-Broadway theater where she knew she would find Frank. Her father was postponing the opening of a new play so that he could fine-tune the writing, coach the actors, and, finally, perfect the technical cues. This was the reason he had given for canceling this particular visit to California. Leigh entered the theater just as Frank was being especially tough on his lighting designer.

"No, no, no! I want SOFT light, you fucking idiot!" he was yelling from his seat in the middle of the house. "SOFT! SOFT like your dick!" And the lights onstage miraculously softened. Leigh approached him carefully.

"Now, who the hell is walking in the house when I'm trying to hear sound cues?" He rose from his seat, ready to kill. But when he saw Leigh, he scooped her up and swung her in the air. "What are you doing here? Does your mother know you're skipping school?" She fed him a neat series of lies: this was Bridie's idea, school is out for the week, and all is well. When he looked thoroughly convinced, he sat her next to him and said, "Tell me if you think this music sucks."

The yelling and adjusting of cues continued into the middle of the night. Leigh forgot all about how her mother must be sick with worry. Her father was busy ruling the world, and he wanted her opinion.

• • •

Leigh returned to Bridie's house a week later, walking through the door with her suitcase and sporting an I ❤ New York T-shirt. Her mother greeted her with, "Oh, hey, Leigh. Want to make Mommy a martini? That's a good girl." Leigh froze, then realized that Lilly must have told Bridie about the trip to see Frank, must have explained and alleviated her mother's worries.

Lilly found her sister upstairs and asked, "Did you tell Mom where I was going?"

"No. Actually, it never came up. I only saw her for about four minutes this whole week, and she never asked me where you were. So I figured she must have read your note."

"I didn't leave a note. She just didn't notice," Leigh answered, then added, "or she didn't care."

Leigh wanted Lilly to argue with that, but she could see that

Lilly was coming up empty. Maybe it would take a full month's disappearance to earn Bridie's notice. Maybe longer.

"Girls! Come here! I need you!" Bridie was shrieking from her bedroom. What could it be now? Did she discover a new wrinkle on her face or did she need help lifting a glass to her lips? The sisters exchanged a dramatic roll of the eyes and went off to attend to their mother, who was carrying on, bellowing and weeping. It was just like the day she found out that *Mother Love*'s time slot was being moved into direct competition with *MacGyver*.

Bridie was holding the phone against her heart, the receiver dangling off the hook. She was hovering over her bedside radio, tuning in some news station.

"It's true! It's all true! He's gone!" Bridie was wailing. "My love, my lover, my soul mate. He's gone. He's dead!"

Soul mate? Leigh checked in with Lilly for the identity of the mystery man, but Lilly shrugged. Ever since her success on television, Bridie had given up on being a bride, though she had a revolving door of lovers. But who among that gallery would be a soul mate?

Bridie threw the phone across the room. It clipped Leigh on the elbow, so she sat on the floor to nurse her wound. Lilly was frozen to the spot, not even acknowledging her sister's injury. The static of the radio moved to the center of the room.

". . . but later, Majors found a new career Off-Broadway, where he acquired a reputation as a tough director who really delivered the goods."

Bridie picked up her wailing again, and Leigh's elbow was throbbing. Were they talking about Frank on the radio? Why? Lilly moved slowly to the floor, and put her arms around her sister. That was how Leigh figured it out. Yes, it was Frank. Bridie's publicist had phoned to tell Bridie that the news was breaking on the radio: Frank collapsed on his way to work that morning, and was dead on the spot. They think it was an aneurysm. Bridie's lover and soul mate. Their father.

* * *

Necessary Evils. Didn't we all just dismiss them as one more band trying to suck the life out of the reggae beat? Admit it. You did. And their first album, *Death by Chocolate*, was very, very medium. But their latest, *Nightfall*, is very, very good. The songs themselves are leaner, the arrangements more pointed. Lead singer Lilly Majors sounds like a modern-day Patsy Cline, with a lush, round voice that's got a huge reserve of emotion behind it. But she doesn't claw and tear at the songs like she used to. Her singing is a thousand times simpler than it was on her first album, and through that simplicity, every thought and feeling tumbles from the songs effortlessly. At least that's how it sounds. They're going on their first national tour this summer. Be there, so you can tell your grandkids that you heard the coolest new band when they actually were the coolest and the newest.

Notes and Tones April 1992

Leigh grew quieter and Lilly grew louder. The band was on the brink of everything, and Lilly was voraciously hungry for it all. She partied, she experimented, she raced up the coast on her shiny black motorcycle. And she laughed off Leigh's soft-spoken concerns.

After Lilly's accident, Leigh relived those scenes, but with much more volume. What if she had yelled at her older sister? What if she had been strict and forceful? Could she have convinced Lilly to slow down?

LILLY MAJORS IN CRITICAL CONDITION

Lilly Majors, daughter of Bridie Hart, remains in critical condition today, following her motorcycle crash over the weekend.

Majors was speeding along the Ventura Highway when she lost control of her motorcycle and crashed into oncoming traffic. There were no other injuries. Bridie Hart has been at her daughter's bedside since the accident. Hospital spokesmen hold out little hope for Majors' recovery.

Lilly Majors was about to start her first national tour with her band, Necessary Evils, and had been receiving rave reviews for her vocals on their latest album. The 25-year-old singer is the only child of Bridie Hart and the late director Frank Majors.

cnn.com   July 1992

Correction: Lilly Majors has a sister, Leigh Majors, also the daughter of Bridie Hart and the late director Frank Majors.

cnn.com   July 1992

They moved about the house silently all through the morning of Lilly's funeral. Leigh would duck behind a door to cry into her hands, and then keep moving. She checked on the caterers, and cursed her mother for not hosting the funeral reception at a restaurant. She sorted through the condolence greetings, and cursed her mother for sobbing and keening so loudly all night. She hoisted flower arrangements around the living room, and cursed her mother for moving the family to L.A. in the first place, for being such an inadequate mother, for encouraging Lilly to sing with a fucking band, for telling Lilly she looked so hot on a motorcycle, for all the stories she ever told about Lilly on television that seemed to give away bits and pieces of the lost girl. She cursed her mother as often as she breathed. Fuck Bridie. Leigh dropped the flowers and went upstairs, past the room where Bridie's crying was down to a soft whimper. She packed her suitcase perfectly.

LEIGH MAJORS DIRECTS

Okay, folks, we'll try, really try, to skip all the bionic jokes and Farrah Fawcett references and get right to the point: Leigh Majors is a good director. Not the Lee Majors guy with the fake-looking everything that you secretly loved as *The Six Million Dollar Man*. No, this is a girl—her mom is Bridie Hart, her dad was Frank Majors, and her sister was the Lilly Majors that all rock-and-roll purists still worship. Now, that's one weird-ass pedigree. But somehow, out of all that mess, the girl can direct. She has staged a *Medea* with what may well have been a budget of seventeen cents, but she made it so damn interesting that I actually had my mouth hanging open like a big white fish. The play was part of the Greek Geek Marathon at the Wonderland Theater downtown. That place is always kind of an acid trip for me, and the artistic director, Kendall Epstein, has a reputation for scaring her directors as much as her audiences. And, by the way, the seats are hard and there's no air-conditioning, but who cares? It was fucking brilliant. It was clear and strong, and Majors didn't let her actors get away with anything. And, oh yes, I think she understood the play, and wanted the whole audience to understand it, too. And we did. And I say that as someone who didn't want to go, didn't want to like it, and still doesn't want to. But I couldn't help it. Hey, folks, I laughed, I cried, it was a part of me. Two dismembered thumbs up.

Downtown Press August 2000

$$\left[\; 1 \;\right]$$

*H*er name was Leigh Majors and she was never going to change it. She would not even discuss switching to any of her mother's names, especially not Hart. So, she endured the same exhausted bionic jokes the press loved to make over and over. But these days, smart critics stopped shoehorning in references to six million dollars, and even stopped padding their word count with her family history.

She was Leigh Majors. She was no longer the daughter of Bridie Hart, America's most beloved TV mother—Bridie Love, better known as Mother Love. No one seemed to notice that the show had been off the air for fifteen years. The endless reruns were airing somewhere in the world at any hour, keeping it alive for its many fans. Space aliens capturing our satellite signals must assume that we are a warm, nurturing species with questionable fashion sense. And they probably all worship Bridie, the mother of all mothers.

Leigh was no longer the daughter of Frank Majors, the late

Broadway director, who was famous and notorious in equal parts. Once a director of glitzy commercial successes, he drank himself into failure after Bridie left him. But he came back for a second act that surprised the New York theater world: he finished up his life in sobriety, doing small-scale, intricate work that bore no resemblance to his boffo box office with Bridie.

No one thought to classify her as the kid sister of Lilly Majors. Lilly, the burgeoning postpunk rock star. Lilly, whose motorcycle spun out of control on the Ventura Highway and broke her. Lilly, who died in the middle of her twenties, just as Leigh was starting hers. No one had tied Leigh with Lilly since their school days, which felt like a shadowy dream.

That was over. Now she was Leigh Majors, for good and ever.

Sometimes actors attempted jokes about her name when they auditioned for her, and when they did, she would smile politely as she wrote "No" on their résumés. She was a good director, but she couldn't direct past stupid. Over the years, well-intentioned people suggested name changes to her. Perhaps she could use her middle name, Eunice? No, she doubted that she could learn to answer to a different first name. But she did like to point out that her middle initial made her name look, at first glance, like LeighE Majors. And she was damn sure that she would never dishonor her father's memory by removing his last name. She was Leigh Majors. Done.

And she wasn't going to hyphenate her name, either. She wasn't opposed to hyphenated names, as a rule, but her husband's name was Michael Payne. No hyphenations here. Bad idea.

Her own name felt like such a shallow thought right now. Isn't that what her actors would dwell on? Isn't that what her mother would do? Leigh shuddered and went back to work, dismantling the set of her latest show, *I Love You, Motherfucker!* It was a musical about Tourette's syndrome, and had been a great success here at her downtown home, Wonderland Theater. But it closed, as all shows do, so Leigh and her cast had to break down the set.

Leigh had been the director-in-residence at Wonderland Theater for three years. The job came to her following a smashing success as Wonderland's guest director for *Medea*. She won the hearts and minds of her actors, local critics, and the notoriously hot-tempered artistic director of Wonderland—Kendall Epstein. Most of the people who passed through Wonderland muttered about Kendall's impossible personality. Leigh found Kendall to be difficult, but very possible.

Striking a set was usually such messy, strenuous work. But not today, not for Leigh. She wasn't going to lift anything heavier than a coat. She tried to gauge exactly how far along her pregnancy was. Five weeks? Six? Her brain turned to lint when she tried to do math. Maybe it was only four weeks.

She had known almost immediately that she was pregnant. The physical tenderness, the vague queasiness. She knew before any stick could turn blue. But that morning, as a birthday gift to herself, she indulged in a quick trip to the drugstore and a long visit to the bathroom (the nice one for the audience members, not the icky one for the actors). And when the little stick confirmed her intuition, she allowed herself to be happy. She allowed herself to hope. She allowed herself to whisper, "I'm pregnant." The joy of that sentence danced over her skin.

She carefully wrapped that blue stick in plastic, then in paper, then in plastic again, and hid it in her large canvas bag. She had been pregnant once before, and too many people had found out entirely too early. Leigh closed her eyes when she remembered how they hid from her after the miscarriage. People were afraid of her, she knew. Afraid of watching that much grief walk through the door. Leigh worked hard to make it okay for them, since she knew that she could never make it okay for herself.

"Are we done? Is everyone going to O'Malley's?" a tenor called out, to a chorus of approval. But Leigh noticed that her cast and crew had gotten carried away, pulling down the red velvet drapes upstage that they were supposed to leave alone. Leigh found them in a heap, across the lime-green plastic chairs in the front row.

"Leigh? Are you coming?" A needy chorus girl tugged at her. Saying good-bye to her actors was always a wrenching experience that Leigh dreaded. Setting that scene in a bar would only exacerbate the pain. But how could she escape it? Leigh couldn't think, so she just kept looking at the drapes, calculating how long it would take to rehang them. Someone was watching her, and doing that same calculation. It was James, her stage manager.

"Leigh?" James asked. "Are we rehanging these drapes?"

"Right. Yes." Was he some kind of mind reader? Throughout rehearsals, he always seemed to know what she needed—a coffee, a sandwich, a break—and now he offered her a way to say good-bye to her actors. By the end of the first week, James recognized Leigh's early signs of frustration and burnout. Whenever they surfaced, he'd call an extra rehearsal break and take Leigh outside, where they would talk about anything but the play. He had a way of drawing her out that made her feel like telling him too much. After all, he trusted her with stories from his own life, so why shouldn't she return the trust? Leigh could also think of several times when James called those breaks without any signs of stress or burnout from Leigh, but just so that they could continue their conversation from the previous day. Leigh smiled, remembering how they talked their way through Russian literature and modern politics.

"I'll be along in a while," Leigh called out to her actors. She hugged each of them in turn, and kept herself from crying by forcing an extra-broad smile. She would miss them all, even the pain-in-the-ass actors who fought her at every turn. She felt it already. She watched them file out, but her bangs were getting so long, soon they would block her view. Note to self: cut bangs. She looked up at the wisps of hair and still couldn't determine if her hair was light brown or dark blond. It was a no-color color. She didn't approve of her hair's indecisiveness, but she couldn't bring herself to pay that much attention to her hair, so she blew a gust of breath to push the bangs away from her eyes.

The actors were looking back at her for one last wave goodbye, and Leigh reminded herself to stand up straight. She had always been a tall, angular girl, and was determined not to hide her height by slouching, as so many tall girls did. As a child, she had been so proud that she could reach things all by herself. And besides, James was still here. Was it her imagination, or was he standing up a bit straighter these days, too? Was that because of Leigh?

"Leigh?" James asked. "The drapes?"

Leigh turned and wow. James was right there, so close. He was three inches away from her, which forced her to look into his eyes, such a deep, searching brown. And his hair color matched. Very decisive. Every now and then she got lost in those deep, dark eyes. And she was in serious danger of getting lost just now.

"Let's get to work," she answered as she pulled a drape from the front row. The cheap velvet left a blanket of red fuzz all over her black T-shirt and blue jeans, her uniform. James pulled two ladders into place, and they worked together in cool quiet. Their movements synchronized: smooth the drape, hold, staple-gun, smile; smooth, hold, staple-gun, smile.

They both turned as they heard the familiar *click-click* of boots walking down the center aisle and onto the stage. Kendall always stepped like she meant it. She clucked and sighed when she saw what Leigh and James were doing.

"I knew you people would take the drapes down," Kendall said. "You don't have to stay and put them back up. Go home."

Kendall smiled and shook her head. She was a tiny woman, until you got to know her. She kept her gray and white hair cropped close, and rarely wore makeup on her heart-shaped, feline face. Every year, Kendall's body got a little rounder, but she squeezed into the same combinations of denim and leather every day.

"It's your fucking birthday, Leigh." Kendall's voice was a throaty rasp. "Go home."

James smiled, stabbing Leigh with a pang of guilt. She hadn't told him or anyone in the cast about her birthday. Big hypocrite. She baked cakes for every one of her actors' birthdays, but concealed her own. And here she was, carrying bigger secrets than her birthday.

"Go on!" Kendall insisted. "Get out of my theater, already. Go."

Leigh and James left a final drape and headed to the back of the house to retrieve their light coats and heavy bags.

"And Leigh," Kendall called out. "Happy birthday."

Leigh smiled, saluted, and gave a quiet "Thank you." She stopped to check her date book, where the next day's to-do list was nearly empty. How would she fill the post-show void without a to-do list? Oh, but it was nearly time to reorganize her closet. Leigh cycled through the different closets and storage areas in her apartment as a preventive measure against chaos. The theater kept her busy, but she made the most of the downtime between plays, rehearsals, and production meetings. As she replaced the date book in her large canvas bag, James caught up with her, and the two walked together down Wonderland's long dark hallway and squinted like vampires against the remains of the early September sunset.

"Walking to the train?" James asked. They had walked together to the train after every rehearsal and performance. He never needed to ask, but he always did. They boarded the train and found two bright orange seats together. James reached into his backpack and handed Leigh a small, flat gift-wrapped package. Curled ribbons had been bent to funny angles in his backpack.

"Hey," he said. "Happy birthday." Leigh wished she could stop herself from blushing. "Don't open it until you get home, okay?" he added.

"You didn't need to do this. I'm too old for birthdays anyway," she replied with a mix of flirtation and demure honesty. And with that she lifted her chin and angled her face in a way that she knew would make her look younger. She had learned that trick from her mother.

"That doesn't sound like you." James looked genuinely confused.

Was that the first time he had seen her channel her mother? Leigh really wanted to know what *would* sound like her, but she knew better than to ask that. She spoke to James as if they were at a rehearsal surrounded by gossip-hungry actors, steering away from personal topics. Now she changed the subject and told him what a good job he had done with a complicated show, a challenging cast, and a script that was in a constant state of revision (thanks to her).

The trained lurched forward, pressing Leigh against James. They were minutes from his stop, and Leigh still had everything under control. That tiny secret, that swimming creature in the center of her, helped to put her at ease with James. He was a harmless crush, a by-product of hormonal madness. Any other thought was now, officially, impossible.

"Listen, James. You've been absolutely gorgeous." OH MY GOD, she didn't really say that, did she? Maybe he hadn't heard her over the rattle and bang of the moving train. He raised his eyebrows and smiled. Oh, Christ, yes, he had heard her. "I mean, great. You've been absolutely the greatest stage manager I've worked with. And believe me, I've worked with lots." Leigh thought she sounded like an aging madam at a bordello. "You're organized, you're clear, you're right on time. And that all sounds so pitifully small compared to what I really want to say."

James stood up. The train was nearing his stop.

"What do you want to say?" he asked.

Leigh shook her head, and James matched her.

"I don't know," she answered. "I wish . . ."

She stood up, wondering if she could actually kiss him good-bye. They smiled and balanced as the train slowed to a stop. Anything could happen. When the train doors opened, she dared to reach out for his hand. He squeezed her hand, then reached past her hand to touch her cheek. He let his hand rest there while he said, "Me, too." He kissed her on the forehead, then dashed through the closing doors.

Leigh ordered her pulse to slow down. She should take some time away from Wonderland and let these crazy feelings fade. Let them transform into something more productive. She sat down as she and her fellow passengers hurtled through dark tunnels under the city. Right away, Leigh opened his gift: a box set of Ella Fitzgerald CDs. When did she tell him that Ella was her favorite singer? She couldn't recall saying it, but she must have.

She found the small note that James had taped to the gift.

To Leigh Majors,
   So glad you use your superpowers for good instead of evil.
   I'd pay six million dollars to work with you again.

                                        Best,
                                        James

He waited until now to stoop to a joke on her name? Leigh happily noted that James lost points in her universe for this. So much for James.

By the time her train was above Fifty-ninth Street, Leigh was officially relieved that the production crush on James was going to be brought to its proper conclusion, which was a whole lot of nothing. This was the worst temptation she had endured in her six years of marriage, but it was just a crush, and she didn't act on it. It began as nothing, developed into nothing, and ended as nothing. Done.

Leigh folded his note into ever-diminishing squares, pressing each edge sharply and neatly. Good-bye, James. What would her father have said about James? He would have said, "Beware. Don't mess around when you've got a good thing at home." That's what he would have said. Leigh was at least 80 percent sure of that.

It was dark when Leigh finally reached her building. Some days, traveling up and across town felt like traveling to Alaska, and this was such a day. She unlocked the door, and was surprised to find the apartment dark and empty. Michael was out? On her birthday? On her closing night?

She kept the lights off, enjoying the spare simplicity of her home, which was decorated in shades of white, off-white, and eggshell—neutral tones that Leigh found very soothing in a frantic city. The off-white sectional sofa offered the only seating, in clean geometric lines. It was as smooth and perfect as the day she and Michael bought it.

This was her oasis of emptiness. There were no magazines, no newspapers, no plants, no pillows, no souvenirs from trips, no objets d'art. In fact, the only decorations in the living room could be found on top of the fireplace mantel. There, a gallery of family photos sat, all the same size, all in silver frames, each spaced an inch and a half apart. Leigh believed that this spacing gave the eye time to rest and experience each picture. She slipped out of her shoes and padded over to the mantel. One of the pictures appeared to be crooked. Was it crooked when she left for the theater that morning? Impossible. Leigh had to remedy this crookedness immediately. She reached for the offending photo and studied the family parade:

Frank in a tense standoff while directing Brian Dennehy.

Bridie and her third Emmy Award.

Bridie and Lilly on the set of *Mother Love*. Lilly was only thirteen, but she was so pretty already. Did Lilly ever have any awkward years?

Bridie having a very uneasy luncheon with Nancy Reagan.

Bridie drunk at Leigh's wedding.

Leigh had too many pictures of her mother because this was Bridie's favorite Christmas gift to anyone—a framed photo of herself. Bridie. Leigh could lose her smile at the mention of that name. But tonight she kept her smile as she quietly promised the tiny bump in her belly that she would be a better mother than old Mother Love ever was. Not that this was saying much.

But then there was the sepia-toned wedding photo of Leigh and Michael. She looked so serious, while his smile was blinding, even in the artfully yellowed photograph. Instead of flowers, she was holding a checkbook. The photographer caught them just as she was writing the last check to the caterer. Leigh Majors paid for her own wedding, declining any of Bridie's Hollywood money.

But where was Michael now, on her birthday? Oh, why hadn't she gone to O'Malley's with her cast? That had to be a better birthday celebration than this empty apartment. This felt pathetic.

Leigh picked up the picture of Bridie and Lilly. It wasn't her favorite picture of her sister—the favorite wasn't displayed out here for all the world to see. She kept the best one in her bedroom. That one was a photo of Lilly, age fourteen, with her fingers splayed over cheeks and circling around her eyes. She was Junior Birdman, with ten years to live. Lilly was laughing at the photographer—Frank. That was a much better picture, and somehow it captured Leigh's father as well as her sister. But Bridie had framed this shot of herself and Lilly for Leigh because it was a damn good shot of Bridie's own face and legs. Leigh reframed it in silver to match the other photos on the mantel. But yes, Bridie had been a true beauty; even Leigh couldn't begrudge her that. Leigh shook her head and zeroed in on her mother's lip-glossy smile, then put the picture down and said, "Yes, but you're losing your looks, old woman." She was louder than she had expected to be.

And then, *BLAST!* The lights came on full and bright, followed by a loud chorus of "SURPRISE!" Entirely too many people had been hiding in the dark of her apartment, waiting to scare her like this. Leigh dropped the picture, and didn't even register the pain when it landed on her foot.

Michael stepped forward from the crowd. "We gave up on you turning on the lights! We just had to go!" Leigh smiled and shook her head. Everyone must have heard her, but at least her mother wasn't at the party. No harm, no foul.

"Your mom's in the dining room!" Michael said quietly in Leigh's ear.

Shit. Leigh kept fake-smiling as she searched for her shoes. They were hidden behind the crowd. But Michael smiled his blue-white smile, and Leigh had to smile back. Ah, well. Leigh had insulted Bridie. Again.

"Should I go in there?" Leigh asked.

"Have a drink first," Michael advised. "She's way ahead of you." He retrieved the fallen picture, and before Leigh could find a glass or anything to drink, she heard Bridie's respectable contralto sing out, "Happy birthday to you! Happy birthday to you! Come visit your mother! Before she loses her looks!"

· · ·

It was a full-fledged party. Wow. Now that the lights were on, Leigh saw flowers and silly birthday decorations. She saw a crazy collection of friends that might never have been in the same room but for Michael inviting them to this full-fledged party. She caught a glimpse of a catered spread in the dining room, and suddenly realized that she was famished. The gorgeous food smells woke her to the full extent of the party. Michael must have been planning this for weeks. She never suspected.

Leigh decided to ignore her mother's summons while Michael led the guests in a rousing chorus of "Happy Birthday to You." Michael, sweet Michael, did everything for Leigh. Caution be damned, she had to get him alone and tell him that she was pregnant. But when? How?

Michael had gentle, curved features where Leigh was sharp and angular. His hair insisted on curling up, despite all efforts and salon products to smooth it down. He planned surprise parties while she planned rehearsal schedules. Michael invited Bridie to their home, while Leigh could barely e-mail her mother.

Michael escorted his wife as she worked the room, greeting, hugging, kissing everyone, recycling the same greetings again and again.

"Are we late?" asked Michael's mother, Sylvia, a tiny silver-haired sprite.

"Of course we're late," said Michael's father, the senior Dr. Payne. Leigh still called them Dr. and Mrs. Payne, and, as badly as they wanted to be called Mom and Pop, they had given up trying to change her ways.

"Happy birthday, dear!" They hugged and kissed Leigh. "Is your show still running?" Mrs. Payne asked. "My book club wants to go. We're trying to branch out more. What's it called again?"

Michael interrupted. "The show is over. Sorry!" No one wanted to say *I Love You, Motherfucker!* to this sweet little woman. "It closed today, Mom."

All of Michael's friends and colleagues recognized Dr. Payne immediately, and vacated the comfiest seats for him and for his wife. Dr. Michael Payne Sr. may well have been New York City's first famous cosmetic dentist. Defying convention of the time, Dr. Payne Sr. bought a series of advertisements on subways and buses, displaying his grinning face and his slogan, "The Payne-Free Smile!" Everyone in town knew Dr. Payne. In fact, he had bought a new series of ads to announce his retirement the previous year, and to promise that "Junior Will Keep New York Smiling the Payne-Free Smile!" He clearly owned the gene pool his son swam in, and he knew it. Dr. Payne even joked that they didn't need to change the photos on the "Payne-Free Smile" subway ads. "Same name, same face, same great service," he had crowed. Leigh was certain that Michael must loathe being known as Junior, but she understood why he said nothing. His father had bequeathed him a very lucrative practice, and a built-in reputation for success. Michael kept smiling.

Back in the dining room, Bridie loudly called out, "Who wants to make Mother Love a manhattan?"

Wait a minute. Bridie was ready for a refill so soon? That could be a bad sign that Bridie was either wallowing and sulking or bravely medicating herself against some emotional injury, probably committed by Leigh. Unless, of course, it was a good sign that she was in a party mood, ready to be the belle of Leigh's ball, which, once Leigh thought about it, was a worse sign than the first bad sign. Bridie was just a bad sign all by herself. Leigh was longing once again to be with her cast at O'Malley's.

Every partygoer fell under Bridie's spell, and Leigh watched her mother's magic settle like pixie dust over the living room. The guests giggled and watched one another to determine who would get to bring Bridie her beloved drink. Who would make her happy and receive an extra dose of her charm and maybe even a Mother Love chat? Seven people tried to find a polite way to elbow one another away from the bar. An aggressive orthodontist won the battle, while the rest of the party grinned with envy. Ah, yes, look at them: they were in Bridie's thrall. Even Dr. and Mrs. Payne craned their necks to see Bridie Hart in the next room. Leigh had married their son six years ago, but Bridie's presence was still a thrill.

Leigh replaced the scotch her husband had brought her with ginger ale. Ha-ha, see? She was already a better mother than Bridie, who often posed for pictures with a cigarette in one hand, blowing smoky air kisses to her children. Leigh remembered the photo of her with a martini, drinking a toast to a soon-to-be-born Lilly. She often thought about framing that photo, or, better yet, sending it to the *Enquirer*. Michael blasted pop music to keep the party lively. Soon, there was a great deal of bad dancing in the room.

"Someone should stop them. For their own good. And mine." It was Maddie, Leigh's dearest friend, and possibly the one person immune to Bridie's charm. Maddie was cover-girl pretty, though she didn't seem to have a clue about that. She had chiseled features that held crystal-blue eyes, framed by blond Botticelli curls. She was a knockout even when she tried to look awful. Actually, she was incapable of looking awful. She could smudge her face with paint and lock herself in a scowl, but she was still beautiful. Maddie painted and had her own distinctive style—the old masters of oil paint if they had decided to depict the seedy underside of Manhattan. She created elaborate, detailed portraits of pimps, homeless people, hot dog salesmen, and dog walkers. All of her paintings had an Old World feel, and showed an enormous amount of respect and affection for her subjects.

But whenever she spoke, Maddie mangled the English language, and she knew it. "I don't talk good because I'm visual. Not vernal," was how she defended herself. Yes, she probably meant "verbal," but Leigh almost never corrected her.

Michael joined the bad dancing, offering a strange hybrid of hip-hop and seizure. He looked terrible, but he looked happy. His parents smiled and clapped for him until two dentists tried to pull them to the dance floor. They giggled and declined.

"Maddie? Do you think my dad would have liked Michael?"

"Whoa! What prompted that? And, just by the way, I never met your dad. He would have liked me, though. I'm pretty sure of that."

"Me, too."

Would Dad have liked Michael? Leigh liked to imagine that she always knew what her father would think, that she was so in tune with him, she carried him around with her. But when she was very tired, she didn't have the energy to create her father's likeness, his opinions, his bristly chin against her forehead. If it required so much energy, there was a very real possibility that she was manufacturing her memories and images of him from scratch. Leigh rejected that notion. Of course she knew her father. She closed her eyes and imagined the scene where she tells him that she's pregnant. How he'd lift her in the air and howl with joy. That's what he would do.

She was 75 percent sure that her papa would have been glad that she had married a "civilian," as he would have put it. After he and Bridie divorced, he knew better than to marry another actress. Oh, sure, he slept with a few dozen, but that was different. His last girlfriend was a veterinarian who seemed to care for him as tenderly as she did the stray dogs that she was always adopting. Yes, Frank Majors would certainly have been pleased that his daughter married a dentist. During his sober years, he extolled the virtues of associating with audience members, rather than artists. "They matter more," he would say. "They're the whole damn point of what we do." Leigh was more than 90 percent sure he had said that.

Michael always seemed to be smiling with those perfect, luminous teeth. Leigh smiled herself when she pictured his gentle, calm features. Whenever Leigh's energy level reached the manic level, usually during tech rehearsals, Michael was the perfect antidote. He didn't know how to worry, and his neck was incapable of going rigid with tension and anxiety, the way that Leigh's did. He was her cure. Of course, she hadn't needed him to cure her anxiety for *I Love You, Motherfucker!* James had kept her calm throughout that production. Leigh wondered if Michael knew that.

In their two years of dating and six of marriage, Leigh and Michael never had any of the venomous separations or public explosions that Leigh had witnessed in her mother's marriages. Michael didn't seem to want drama. He wanted to be happy, which, by definition, included wanting his wife to be happy, too. Best of all, Michael understood the burden of famous parents. True, Dr. Payne wasn't written about in the tabloids, but Michael was under the parental microscope that Leigh knew so well. He was expected to perform as his father had.

"Hey, Leigh, look around. Every man on the dance floor is wearing khaki pants and a blue shirt," Maddie observed, and it was true. There were slight variations in the shades of khaki and blue, but absolutely every man was wearing the same combination. Even Dr. Payne Sr. wore the uniform.

"Is there some kind of Banana Republic cult taking over?" Maddie continued.

"Yes."

But then they spotted Cameron, Leigh's favorite set designer. He was wearing a purple paisley blouse, skin-tight pink pants, and a fringed red scarf wrapped around his waist like an unnecessary sarong. His fabulous hair must have been set with hot rollers, and he was wearing lip gloss. He looked so pretty. He danced through the sea of khaki pants, an interpretive modern ballet, maybe. The rest of the theater crowd followed in Cameron's wake and appeared to be teaching the dentists how to dance. Michael had invited a strange cross-section of actors and designers from Wonderland. Leigh wondered if he had tried to invite Kendall, or if she still scared him. He hadn't invited James, of course, because he didn't know James. Leigh tried to recall how often she may have mentioned James to her husband. Had she talked about him at all? Had she talked about him too much? Before she could work out an answer, Cameron did a show-stopping triple spin, garnering applause from everyone. Leigh made a quiet bow of thanks to Cameron, now that everyone at her party was having actual, visible fun.

"Leigh! Come dance with me!" Michael pulled Leigh toward the dancing dentists. "One dance." Dancing against the pop tempo, Michael held Leigh close and moved slowly. "Having a happy birthday?" he asked.

"Definitely." She angled her head against his, and it looked as if she were trying to hear his thoughts. Despite the crowd around them, perhaps she could tell him about her pregnancy (she didn't allow herself to think the word *baby* yet). She looked up at him, which prompted Michael to kiss her on the forehead. Just as James had done.

James. No. A woman who was in possession of a blue stick wrapped in two layers of plastic and one layer of paper should never think about a man whose dimples cast as deep a shadow as those around James's perfect mouth. She shouldn't even think about James's mouth. Not right now. Not ever. She should never be alone with James again. She should tell Michael everything. They would laugh and cry over the hope of a new baby. He would touch her stomach so gently, and she would silently realize that her hormones had driven her temporarily crazy. Of course she would never cheat on Michael. Of course she would forget all about James. Michael would tuck her into bed and hold her, ignoring their party guests, ignoring Bridie. Leigh wanted this little scene for her birthday. It was all she wanted. She took his hand and tugged gently, to take him away from the party.

"Derwood! Is this all you have to eat?" Bridie called out. Leigh flinched.

"Excuse me, honey." Michael left his wife on the dance floor, to tend to La Bridie.

"Hey." Maddie tapped Leigh on the shoulder. "This music sucks. Let's run away." Leigh and Maddie smiled conspiratorially as they grabbed the necessary provisions of potato chips and ginger ale, and found a quiet corner.

"Ginger ale?" Maddie sounded disgusted. "Get the good scotch!"

"Open the chips," Leigh answered.

"So, how was the closing?" Maddie looked like she really

wanted to know, so Leigh tried to assemble an answer over the wail of whatever boy band was being blasted.

"It was good, and it was weird and it was wonderful. I miss them all so much. And I'm proud of myself, because some of today was genuinely weird. I'll say that much." Leigh wanted so badly to tell Maddie that she was pregnant, pregnant, pregnant. She was pregnant! Only two things stopped her: she couldn't tell a soul before she told Michael, and she remembered how hard Maddie cried after the miscarriage. Don't tell her yet.

"You should be proud," Maddie continued. "Even *Kendall* said it was good. And that's a lot!"

Leigh wished that Kendall were at the party. Not that Kendall would be gooey sentimental about Leigh's birthday, but her presence always made Leigh feel stronger. For years, she had fantasized about standing in a small room while Kendall and Bridie fought over her. It was right out of a Godzilla/Mothra movie, where the monsters duke it out for rights to the puny humans. But the two had never fought, had never even met, since Bridie consistently missed Leigh's Wonderland productions. All of them. She had stopped manufacturing excuses years ago.

Bridie's laugh carried over the pop music. Say what you like about her, the woman could project.

"Oh, my God. She's still waiting for me in there," Leigh remembered out loud.

Maddie gurgled out a laugh as she nodded in agreement. Leigh started to move toward Bridie, but when she caught a glimpse of herself in the mirror over the mantel, it slowed her down. Her hair was a limp shadow around her head, accentuating the dark shadows under her eyes. She wore no makeup and her clothes were dirty from the day's destruction. Leigh was about to confirm every criticism her mother ever made to her. Happy birthday.

"Courage." Maddie was right behind Leigh as she spoke quietly but much too earnestly.

Leigh would have to work her way through a thicket of dancers to get to her mother. She made a faint first attempt, then backed away. A second attempt, with much louder "Excuse me"s and "Pardon me"s, failed, too. She wondered if she wanted to reach her destination enough to work this hard. She couldn't project over the music like her mother could.

"Darling! Yoo-hoo! Happy birthday, my baby!"

The sea of dancers parted on cue, the music lowered, and Leigh half expected the guests to sing a chorus of "Hello, Dolly!" as Bridie took center stage and found the most flattering light. Everything stopped as Bridie stretched her arms forward to welcome her reluctant daughter into her embrace. Leigh made sure that she forced her grimace into a smile as she crossed to her mother and hugged her.

"She's so lucky," someone in the crowd whispered. Someone who didn't know Leigh very well.

Still embracing her daughter, Bridie held an empty glass forward and stage-whispered to one of the dentists, "Lookie, lookie, sweetheart, Mummy's empty!"

The aggressive orthodontist jumped forward, looking ever so grateful for the chance to refill the glass, and Bridie addressed the crowd. The sparkle of her black sequined jacket put Leigh into a trance. The music stopped, as if Bridie had arranged it so that she could have her little scene.

"Everyone, I'd like to tell you about how Leigh came into this world. First, I had nine months of the most drastically awful morning sickness, and my doctor made me *beg*, absolutely *beg*, for medication to stop it. Unbelievable! When I finally went into labor, there was a dreadful rain and hail storm, and I simply could not get a taxi. It was impossible. So I flagged down a police car and made a grand entrance to the hospital, siren blaring. But, get this, the nurses told me to go home, I kid you not, because the baby would not be forthcoming anytime soon. Thus proving that the entire medical profession delights in making us beg for relief! The nurses must have been in league with that doctor!"

Bridie was fanning her attention out among the rapt audience. Her voice shifted musically to build the story to its obvious conclusion. Leigh's fake smile was hard to maintain.

"So I was soaked to the bone and rather upset, as you can imagine. But even I couldn't persuade the evil head nurse to see reason, let alone compassion. She was about to call me a cab—what an angel of mercy!—but I asked if I could please use the restroom. I could, and, well, how can I put this delicately? Leigh's first view of the world was the inside of that toilet. I looked down and there she was, staring back at me."

The whole party howled with laughter, even though most of the civilized world had heard this story at least once. Bridie had told it to Johnny Carson on *The Tonight Show* and it was replayed a lot when he died. For Leigh, the humiliation would live forever on videotape.

"Obviously, I couldn't walk, so the evil nurse had to come into the bathroom and help me. We delivered her right there on the bathroom floor. And when I was done with my part, I sat up on my elbows, looked that nurse in the eye, and said, "*Now* you can call me a cab."

Cue the laughs. Follow with applause. Leigh smiled and nodded, noting how her mother had deleted any mention of her father's presence that day. He was the one who flagged down the police, brought the nurses into the bathroom, and said the punch line about calling the cab. Bridie could cut him out of family stories, just as she had cut him out of family photos.

"I give you Leigh Majors!" Bridie called out, as she led the party in rousing applause, stronger than the scattered hand she'd gotten just before. Leigh took a modest bow. She hated bowing, but she used it to punctuate an ending for the little scene. Perhaps she couldn't hide anymore, but she could at least use some domestic activity to keep her mother at bay. She found it quickly—at least a half dozen glasses and beer bottles sitting on tables without coasters, which was forbidden in Leigh's home under any circumstances. Once the water-ring crisis was averted, Leigh hoped to find a lot of tasks at the food table.

"Why are you doing that? Let Derwood do it." Bridie was still projecting loudly, although her audience had resumed dancing.

Back when Leigh and Michael first announced their engagement, Bridie jokingly cast herself as Endora, disapproving of her merely mortal son-in-law. Michael had laughed at it, even after Leigh explained that the joke was at his expense. "She's pretending she can't remember your name because you're not significant enough for her." But he disagreed. "It's *Bewitched,* honey, and she's being the mean mother-in-law. Don't you get it?"

Privately, Bridie described Michael as "much too pedestrian to join our family tree," but she promised her daughter that there would be no serious objections at the wedding since "this will make such a lovely first marriage for you."

Leigh ventured into the dining room. Michael had opted for a rainbow of colors for the paper goods, whereas Leigh would have chosen her favorite cream and ecru. She looked away from the color to focus on food that needed to be replenished and detail-level messes to be cleaned. Between her dirty clothes and the work she made for herself, she looked like an unhappy caterer.

She overheard Cameron in the kitchen, confessing, "I never missed that show. It was like church for me. And Bridie Love was a better mother to me than my own mother, which, okay, isn't saying much, but still. I adore her. I worship her. It's killing me that she's here at this party and I can't talk to her. I'm so afraid I'll cry, and I wouldn't want to make a scene."

"I wanted to marry her," said one of the dentists.

"I wanted to *be* her," Cameron replied.

* * *

"Time to open the presents! Everyone gather round!" Bridie's voice carried throughout the apartment and into other hemispheres.

Maddie found Leigh in the dining room and grinned. "Guess what? Your mom wants you to open your presents. Now. So, she sent me to find you. Did I find you?" Before Leigh could answer, Cameron and the aggressive dentist appeared and began pulling Leigh by her elbows into the living room, where her gifts were stacked and ready.

"Okay, so, I found her!" Maddie called after them. "I'll just have another drink here. Seeing as my job is done and all." Maddie's voice faded into the background.

When Leigh saw the mountain of presents and the audience waiting to watch her open them, she realized how bone-tired she really was. Was she having a late bout of morning sickness? Didn't she begin the day with a show and a set and a production crush, and wasn't that a lot to let go of in one day? Couldn't she stage a retreat somehow?

"Honey," Leigh half-whispered to Michael, "shouldn't I open these tomorrow?"

"Boo! Boo!" the guests called out. Michael shrugged and told Leigh to "Have fun!"

"Open mine first, sweetie," Bridie said. "A mother's prerogative."

Leigh saw that Cameron was staring at Bridie, and that his cheeks were blotched with pink and his eyes were wet. Was he about to throw himself at her?

Leigh ripped into her mother's offering. It was a small, flat rectangle, encased in paper that felt as heavy as leather, with four different cloth ribbons. A professional job. Before Leigh completely uncovered it, Bridie shouted out, "It's a picture of me with the Dalai Lama!" The crowd oohed respectfully and Leigh held up the framed photo for all to see. Bridie gushed, "He's a darling little man. So short, but he really looks good in orange, and that's a tough color to wear, don't you think?"

Cameron nodded in vigorous agreement. Leigh lifted a heavy gift, but Michael snatched it away. "That one's from me. Open it last." He took it and hid it somewhere behind the crowd.

"Nothing X-rated, I hope!" Dr. Payne chuckled.

Mrs. Payne shook her head and said, "Here, honey. Open ours next."

It was a cute stretchy outfit—no, it was a series of outfits. Leigh sifted through the package and saw a mix-and-match set of clothes in black, white, pink, and blue. Everything was made of the same comfy stretchy material—three tops, a skirt, and a pair of pants. Her in-laws had never bought her clothes before. Bridie used to impose designer couture on Leigh, but she had given up on that years ago.

"It's called Mama-Garb!" Mrs. Payne explained. And then Leigh noticed the picture on the tags: a pregnant woman, looking oh-so-happy in her stretchy clothes. These were maternity clothes. Leigh was fighting back the crowd's applause, registering her mother's stony expression, and trying to acknowledge Mrs. Payne's cry that "This is the latest thing for city mothers!" More applause.

Somewhere in the back of the crowd, she heard Michael shouting, "No! Mom! What the hell?" or something like that. If only Leigh could tell him that this was the perfect gift.

"Try it on!" Mrs. Payne suggested, as she pulled the shirt over Leigh's head, over Michael's objections.

"Now, now, now. I know this girl," Mrs. Payne continued, waving her hand in Michael's direction to stop his protests. "You two are going to try again, and when you do, you'll have these lovely clothes to slip into." Mrs. Payne primped the shirt into place, and Leigh looked down at the large blue shirt that circled her middle. "See?" Mrs. Payne cheered. "Not too big, but it will stretch as you get bigger!"

Leigh imagined her body expanding to fill the space that the shirt offered.

Bridie took over with her trumpet-voice. "Michael says she's not pregnant! Now, everyone hush!"

Michael was whispering fiercely into his mother's ear, and poor Mrs. Payne looked so guilty and sad. Leigh stepped in to hug her and thank her for the gift anyway.

"Leigh, honey, I'm sorry," Michael whispered in her ear.

"It's okay," Leigh said in full voice. "I love these clothes. Thank you." But he stood by her side, ready to defend her against any other potentially hurtful birthday gifts. Leigh scanned the crowd and saw Bridie, laughing a little too hard as she leaned on Cameron, who seemed close to fainting with joy.

Should she be dramatic and tell him right there, in front of everyone? In front of Bridie? Would Bridie make an announcement like that? Probably. But should Leigh miss this moment just because it was Bridie-esque? Would a whiff of Bridie Love bring bad luck to Leigh's impending motherhood? Wrapped in her pregnancy costume, Leigh realized that the party had gone silent. Everyone smiled and waited for Leigh to say something— preferably something about babies, but she didn't dare jinx it. So the silence continued. Where was Maddie? Why didn't Bridie ask for another drink? The silence was thick.

"And what's in *this* box?" Leigh busied herself with the next present and the next. A clear and present theme emerged from the gifts: a set of relaxation tapes, a self-help book about how to relax, relaxation bath salts, relaxing herbal teas and candles, a certificate for a spa relaxation treatment, accessories to relax her eyes, feet, and hands. Why did everyone think she needed these things?

"Thanks, everybody! So much! This looks so . . . relaxing!"

And the gifts were done. Good. Leigh loaded her arms with gift paper, ribbons, and scraps of tape that had stuck to the rug. Did they think it was funny to make her look like a person in need of remedial relaxation? Did they think relaxation was the solution to all her problems?

"Leigh, honey, don't you want to open *my* present?"

She looked up from the papers and saw Michael presenting his gift in both hands. She hesitated, and then dropped the papers from her arms, letting them scatter at her feet. She acted as if she didn't mind the mess. And wasn't that the sign of a person who needed no help relaxing?

Michael's gift was the heaviest thing she had lifted all day. Inside, she found a three-ring binder. She took a dramatic pause before opening it. What if this was the detailed justification for her need to relax, in book form?

She opened the cover. On the first page, neatly typed in the center, she read:

WOMEN IN HATS
A PLAY IN TWO ACTS
by Michael Payne, D.D.S.

Leigh turned the page and saw

ACT ONE
SCENE ONE

(The set is a chic New York hat shop in 1962. There are elegant hats on the shelves and in display cases.)

Leigh stopped reading.

"End the suspense, darling. What is Derwood's gift to his beloved wife?"

"It's a play?" Leigh didn't intend for that to come out as a question.

The news seemed to electrify Michael's parents and the party guests even more than the maternity clothes and herbal candles did. Michael wrote a play!

"Let me see that!" Dr. Payne Sr. had the script in his hand and was scanning it like an Evelyn Wood graduate. Michael was on fire with delight. It was as if the whole party had been leading to the unveiling of his masterpiece. Leigh was still gnawing on the please-relax birthday theme. Michael must have told them what to get; they couldn't all see her as Tension Girl. And now he gives her a play? What kind of gift was that?

"Look! Look!" Dr. Payne Sr. called to his wife. "It's about my mother. It's about her hat shop, back in the old days. Oh, God, she'd love it. She'd be so proud, she'd be so . . . Come here!"

Leigh stepped back as father and son hugged. She smiled and bit her lip just until it hurt. It was a mild punishment. How dare she stand here seething at the man who threw her a birthday party and wrote a play about his dead grandmother? Clearly, Leigh was a terrible person, full of tension, who needed to relax.

"My son, the Renaissance man!" Dr. Payne declared.

Leigh was alarmed to find that Bridie had disappeared, and it was always wise to track the movements of a natural disaster like her mother. Time to end this scene.

"Everyone." Leigh was addressing the cast of *Her Birthday Party*. "Thanks for the wonderful gifts. I'm going to be so relaxed, I might melt through the floorboards! And thanks for coming here, and keeping this big surprise. And thanks for being our friends. Just being in our lives is the best present anyone could ask for. Thank you."

And curtain.

2

Leigh was alone in her bedroom with *Women in Hats*. The late-remaining guests partied on in the living room. She wished that she had some sort of ritual or juju to ensure that the play would be good. Bridie seemed to have a superstition for every occasion, so, naturally, Leigh had none. What could she possibly say to Michael if she hated his play? The muscles in her neck twitched and tightened. This would be a good time for one of those breaks with James where he told her how wonderful she was. But no one was offering her a break now. Instead, Michael was giving her a gift with built-in pressure and demands. Happy birthday. She glanced at the door when the partygoers let out a loud whoop, then she hugged the script to her chest and said, "Be good, be good, be good."

MARGARET

Mothers are always smarter than their sons. That's a law of nature.
My poor dope of a son wants to be a dentist. Can you imagine any-

thing more stomach-turning? Please, don't try. But I'll show him what's what. He needs to run my hat shop, find a nice girl who can afford a hat from the pricey shelf, and give me grandchildren. And then send me to Paris every spring. Oh, and be happy. Of course.

Margaret Rayne was a thinly disguised version of Mildred Payne, Michael's grandmother. Leigh never met her, but knew that she did run a hat shop, did have a dentist son, and did go to Paris every spring. And the dialogue did sound like some sort of 1962 comedy. He had gotten that right. What had he gotten wrong?

Never mind. She didn't need to critique the play. Isn't that what a Very Tense Person would do? Not Leigh. She decided to find seven nice things to say about it. Or five. She thumbed through the pages, not really reading them. Did Michael write this play to be performed? By actors? On a stage? Probably. Oh, how had this happened? Somehow, her husband had written a play that would have been popular forty or fifty years ago, but who would want it now?

"There you are. You're a terrible hostess, hiding from your own party guests—even if they are as exciting as a pencil. I think Cameron wants to marry me and have my babies. He's a sweet boy. A tad emotional."

Bridie was standing in the bedroom doorway, smoking, which was verboten in Leigh's apartment at all times, by all people. And Bridie knew it. Would she put the cigarette out if she knew about Leigh's pregnancy?

Leigh climbed off the bed and dropped her mother's cigarette into the remains of her ginger ale, then scrubbed her hands energetically against her jeans to remove the tobacco and lipstick that lingered on her fingers. By the time she finished, Bridie had already lit another cigarette.

"I'm in the middle of act one," she talk-smoked. "It needs work, but it's damn cute. Don't you think?" She didn't wait for an answer. "Well, you sort of *have* to think it's good, don't you? Who knew little Derwood had such hidden potential? Well, you sort of *had* to know that, too, didn't you?"

"You like the play?" Leigh asked as she opened a window and waved the smoke away.

"You don't?" Bride brought herself and her cigarette closer.

"Can't I just finish reading it first?"

"Are you going to direct it?" Bridie was revving up.

"Where could I possibly do it?"

"Do you hate it that much?" Bridie used her meow voice.

"Why don't you answer my question?" Leigh reverted to TV-movie prosecutor tones.

"Which one?" Bigger meow voice.

Leigh took a deep, smoky breath. Bridie was enjoying this.

"By the way, Leigh. Nice blouse." She took a long, victorious drag on her cigarette.

Leigh looked like a little girl playing dress-up in Mommy's shirt. Not that she had ever done that herself, but the maternity blouse seemed to be swallowing her. She pulled it over her head and tossed it on the bed while Bridie prowled the room, inspecting the furniture, bedding, and drapes. She didn't need to say a word, but she did anyway.

"This beige-on-taupe color scheme—it's like living in a bowl of oatmeal."

"We like it. By the way, Mom. Don't you ever knock?"

Bridie smiled and batted her eyes. But then she found the framed photo of Lilly as Junior Birdman. She picked it up and asked, "Why haven't I seen this one before? Who took it?"

Leigh took the picture back. "Who do you think?"

And Bridie understood that it must have been taken by

Frank, or, as she called him, the Frankenmonster. She nodded and acquiesced. Within two years of Frank's death, Bridie had returned to hating him, which was her way of demonstrating how well she had worked through her grief. These days, a reference to Frank was an easy way to silence Bridie. So, she wouldn't get to talk about Lilly. Not today. Some things were still sacred.

But Bridie was still here, and she was much too resourceful when it came to tormenting her daughter. Leigh urgently, desperately needed to find Maddie. Had she left the party? Just as she started toward her bedroom door to begin the search, Bridie stopped her by saying, "I look *fabulous* in 1962 fashions. Did then, do now. But does the Margaret character have to be forty years old? I can't play forty anymore. There. I admit it."

Leigh stopped moving, but said nothing, and just let her mother continue. Why hadn't she anticipated this? She must have been so tired, so off her game.

"But I can still play fifty," Bridie insisted as she primped in the mirror. "And fifty is the new forty. And old is the new black. And yes, yes, yes, it would require some minor changes—but it's a first play. It's going to need work anyway. They all do. And we can help him."

"We? No. Not we. *We* are not helping him."

"Yes, we. Of course, we. We have the experience and the understanding. It's in our genes." Bridie continued primping.

"No." Leigh blocked the door, although she didn't know why.

"He married into a theatrical family and he wrote a play. A play that centers around a woman. A woman of a certain age. Of course we're going to help him."

"No."

"And we'll start by changing Margaret to a fifty-year-old. Or fiftyish. Yes?"

"No."

"You'll see, she'll have more maturity, more richness of character. And she'll have more monologues."

"No."

"Can you imagine what people would say if you didn't direct this play?" That fucking meow voice again. Bridie was done primping. For now.

"Bridie." Leigh went with the older-wiser voice to control her mother.

"Leigh." Bridie went with the singsong brat voice to undo her daughter.

"Hey, wait a minute. Where did you get that script?" It took Leigh this long to realize that there were two scripts.

Bridie clutched her script with both hands as she replied, "Much as the boy loves you, I didn't think he'd given you the only copy of his masterpiece. It was right there, sitting next to the computer. Didn't you ever see it? He must have been working on it for months, sweetheart. Don't you two ever talk?"

Leigh moved closer to her mother (and her mother's mirror), and knew that she had also moved a few inches closer to admitting defeat. She had lost all control of the day, and had no friend, no ally, no stage manager to help her. And that was what she sorely needed right now: a stage manager.

"You stole it. Give it back, Mother."

"Fine, fine. Here. I relinquish the script." And she did so with a grand flourish. Bridie paused in the doorway, a good effect for dramatic pronouncements. "Derwood! I need a copy of your script. I have a feeling it's delightful."

Michael's response was muffled. Leigh sat on the bed, looking at the script her mother had dropped there. She had already dog-eared the first few pages. Leigh tried to smooth them back to perfect, but they wouldn't go. She kept smoothing and kept smoothing and kept smoothing. She was wearing the paper away.

How much time passed before the door opened again?

"Hey! Where you been?" Maddie, drunk Maddie, was tumbling onto Leigh's bed. "Your mother's trying to get the dentists to play strip poker!"

Leigh stopped smoothing long enough to ask, "Do they know she cheats?"

Maddie laughed too long, then slipped into quiet. She took up more than half of the bed as she smiled up at Leigh and quietly said, "You're so lucky."

. . .

Leigh woke in the middle of the night and couldn't find sleep again. She had given up on telling Michael about her pregnancy while the party lasted. But it lasted longer than she did, and she fell asleep while Michael showed out the last few guests. Now, unable to sleep, she roamed the living room, searching for small messes or items out of place.

Maddie was sleeping on the couch. She had such fine, delicate features and such a loud, honking snore. Leigh found a blanket and covered her friend, who then snorted in her sleep. Leigh tried not to laugh out loud as she tiptoed into the bedroom and retrieved Michael's script, then slipped into the kitchen with it. She hooked her feet up on a chair and thought her tummy felt ever so slightly fuller. She and her secret baby settled in for a good read.

And it was good. Or, at least, it wasn't bad. Except for the fact that her mother had poisoned the play a bit by assigning her face and voice to the mother character, Leigh liked it. It was a sweet story, and the characters were believable. After all, these were real people. Sort of. They were Michael's people. And Michael was an amateur. *Amo amas amat.* Amateur. Lover. Someone who does something because they love it. He must have written this play out of love. And it showed. It was sweet and old-fashioned and full of love.

Leigh was drooping back into sleep and let herself slip back into the room, then bed, where Michael was smiling in his sleep.

. . .

When Leigh awoke for the second time, Michael had already left for work. He'd left a note on the bedside table:

Leigh,
   Call me when you finish reading the play. I hope you like it.
   Happy Day After Your Birthday.

                                        XO Michael
PS: Maddie is passed out on the couch. Again.

She was smiling at his note, at Maddie on the couch, at her easy schedule for the day—just organize the kitchen cupboard. An easy day. It was the day when she would tell Michael about the pregnancy. No. About the *baby.* At last.

It was when she shifted her body up in bed that she felt it. She pulled back the sheets and confirmed it. She was bleeding heavily. She didn't jump out of bed and start screaming, the way she had last time. She froze and stared at the mass of blood until she couldn't look at it anymore.

"No. No, no, no." She shaped the words through her sobs.

. . .

"Dr. Griffin says she'll see you in five minutes."

Leigh was pale and still. Maddie sat next to her in the waiting room, rubbing her back, her arm, her head. That didn't actually help, but the fact that she was trying to help helped.

"Thanks for coming with me." Leigh managed a half-smile.

"Shouldn't I call Michael?" Maddie asked, and this was especially selfless, since she had never liked Michael.

"No." Leigh didn't want him to hear this misery over the phone. She didn't want him to hear this misery at all, come to think of it.

"Leigh? I can come in with you, or do you want me to wait here in the waiter room? Whatever you like."

Leigh smiled at "waiter room." The smile gave her enough strength to pretend that she was strong enough to see the doctor alone, so off she went, alone with one less secret.

She peeled herself down to the paper gown and gripped the little table while her doctor confirmed it all. Yes, it was a miscarriage. Yes, it was just like last time. Yes.

"Leigh." Dr. Griffin did her best maternal voice, which was very, very good. Dr. Griffin had frizzy auburn hair that created a warm halo around her head. She had a vertical worry line between her eyes that ran deep and cast a shadow sometimes. This was one of those times. "You've mentioned that your mother had severe nausea during her pregnancy with you."

Yes, and Leigh would have accepted that gladly, easily, and not complained about it for thirty years, as Bridie had done. Why was Dr. Griffin focused on that, of all things, in the midst of all this blood and loss? Leigh looked up and realized that her doctor was waiting for her to start listening to her again. She nodded and said,

"Yes. I gave you her medical history. It's all there. Her doctor said it was just morning sickness. She didn't have any miscarriages."

"Yes, and it says here that her doctor gave her DES." The little wrinkle between her eyes was a dark fault line. It made her look like she had even worse news than the miscarriage.

"What's DES?" Leigh didn't actually care. She had yet to experience morning sickness herself.

"Diethylstilbestrol. It was a popular antinausea medication for pregnant women. It cured the mother's morning sickness." Leigh could see that the shadow on Dr. Griffin's face was ready to reveal itself. "But now we know that DES left daughters infertile."

The shadow leaped across the room. It was locking itself around Leigh's body, pinning her arms down, pushing her to the floor, but she resisted.

"But I got pregnant. I didn't have any trouble getting pregnant. Both times."

"Yes, but both pregnancies terminated the same way. And, Leigh. They always will. If I had seen this history before, I would have advised you against getting pregnant again. I'm sorry."

Dr. Griffin resorted to a model of female reproductive organs to show what was wrong, what was damaged and malformed inside Leigh, and why any future pregnancies would all deliver this early, bloody mess. But the shadow masked Leigh's ears and blurred her vision. It reached down her throat and silenced her.

"And that's why I have to advise you"—Dr. Griffin was reaching her point—"Please, please, don't put yourself through this anymore. Don't try to get pregnant anymore. Physically, emotionally, this is going to take an awful toll. And I've seen marriages, people, crumble under the pressure this can bring. You have to learn to accept this."

Oh, God, the finality of that little statement sliced Leigh open at the chest. She needed to cry, and, what the hell, Dr. Griffin could handle it. She cradled Leigh, who cried into her hands, onto the doctor's shoulder, into a mass of Kleenex. She cried as much as she had bled.

.   .   .

When they first met, Leigh barely noticed Michael. All she could see or care about was the script she was directing at the time for Wonderland. Even when she put it away, it played in front of her eyes. It teased her with its thorny plot and requests for impossible special effects. Leigh studied it in the air. It was a wonder she didn't walk into oncoming traffic.

She was waiting tables at a popular Mexican restaurant on the Upper West Side (no one could call her a spoiled trust-fund baby, no, sir). Michael and his dental-school alumni pals arrived for the restaurant's infamous brunch, which offered unlimited margaritas with its bland huevos rancheros. It was always a raucous, messy shift. Leigh had her customers point to the menu to place their food orders, since no one could be heard over the din. She barely noticed the customers themselves. She just brought their food and cleaned up the bathroom after the women who couldn't hold their tequila. She certainly didn't pay special attention to the dental-school contingent, but Michael sat up straight when Leigh walked over to the table and pointed to a list of specials. He was smitten at first order. He mimed a request for her phone number, but she pretended that she didn't understand. The unlimited tequila had been known to inspire marriage proposals from her customers. Wasn't this guy just another drunk ex–frat boy? She brought him his food and thought about that play some more.

When her shift was done and she had mopped up the unfortunate mess in the señoritas' bathroom, she packed up her script and headed downtown where she could really get to work.

Later, Leigh would learn that Michael had dropped a pile of cash on the table, abandoned his friends, and followed her outside. She didn't notice him stalking her all the way to her usual table at her favorite dive. There, she could settle into a well-worn velvet Queen Anne chair, and study paintings by local artists whenever she lifted her gaze from her script. A Jackson Pollock wannabe was particularly helpful whenever she got stuck. Trying to untangle the collections of colors dripped on the canvas would relax her mind, and her work could continue. She was in her spot. She looked around the room to ask for coffee.

"You're not Maddie," she said to the grinning ex–frat boy holding the coffeepot. "Where's Maddie?"

"I'm Michael," he answered.

Maddie, whose long legs could walk a city block in four steps, was at the table before Michael could explain himself. At almost six feet tall, she insisted on wearing high heels. The height advantage allowed her to stare Michael down.

"That's my coffeepot, buddy. Give it."

"Let me just explain. I was at the restaurant—"

Maddie turned to Leigh and asked, "How much tequila did you bring this guy?"

Leigh could see that Michael was blushing. He didn't seem to know how to hand over the coffeepot safely. He insisted on pouring coffee for Leigh first. She couldn't hold back her smile. This was not a drunk ex–frat boy. Who was he?

"I'm sorry," he finally said. "I just had to meet you. And believe me, I've never ever done anything like this before. But with you, well, what can I say? I had to. You're special."

Leigh closed her script and invited him to sit with her despite Maddie's wildly signaled objections. Maddie passed Leigh a note: "Maybe he's a crazed stacker."

Stalker. Maybe. He sat a little too close. So Maddie was never very far away, either.

Michael seemed to be a man in a job interview, applying for the role of Leigh's Boyfriend. He wanted that job and was selling himself energetically. He pointed out his strengths and qualifications and owned up to a few weaknesses, and Leigh half wondered if he was going to offer references.

Finally, he asked her about her life, and the evening became a lot less fun for Leigh. How many times was she going to tell her life story to some guy who would fall out of his chair with the words "Your mother is *Bridie Hart*?! I love her! You're so lucky!"

Michael was no exception. He gushed over his boyhood memories of watching Mother Love, and, oh, the impact she had had on his formative years. It was a familiar melody. Leigh hummed along until it was done. When his Mother Love rhapsody was over, Michael returned to the current object of his affections: the taciturn waitress with sad eyes. Leigh Majors.

"Hey. You know what? Even when you smile, your eyes still look sad. I wish I could change that."

"How?" Leigh actually believed he had a cure for what ailed her.

"You shouldn't be waiting tables, Leigh. You should be doing these plays, or whatever else it is you want to do. You need someone like me to make that happen."

How could he know instantly that he wanted her? That they were right for each other? That this would work? How did he come by such a huge store of confidence? Michael seemed born knowing the important things. He knew that he had to marry Leigh—

and she admired him for coughing away his laugh at her name. He knew that he had to be a dentist, of all things. They shared the common bond of famous parents in the child's profession of choice.

"People think I want to be a dentist because of my dad, but it's just not true. I'm good at it. It makes sense to me. I always wanted to be a dentist."

He sounded like the wayward elf in *Rudolph, the Red-Nosed Reindeer*, and Leigh smiled at the association.

"Hey, look! I made you smile!" He glowed with delight. She smiled more, though her eyes still looked sad. He wanted only to make her smile. Michael Payne, D.D.S.

*   *   *

Maddie brought Leigh home from the doctor, cleaned up, made tea, fluffed pillows, and left only when Leigh pretended to be asleep. Even though Maddie had insisted, "You don't have to play brave with me," Leigh couldn't help it. She played brave so well.

Real sleep finally did overtake her, ending when she heard Michael open the door. She sat up in bed and waited for him to find her.

"Leigh? Are you okay?"

"Yes." That was a reflex answer. Anyone could see that she wasn't okay. "I mean, no. I'm not okay."

Michael sat down on the bed and Leigh actually felt afraid to tell him, afraid to walk through this one more time. She looked down at his hands, they were so clean and pink.

"I was at the doctor today. I should have called you. But I didn't." Why hadn't she rehearsed this speech? Because it was too frightening? Probably.

"What happened? Are you sick?" Leigh still wasn't looking at his face. His hands were smooth.

"I was pregnant, and . . ." The dark shadow locked itself around her throat once more, and she couldn't fight it off. She had said "was." She let Michael put a few thoughts together until she could speak again. "I had a miscarriage. It was this morning. It was so . . ." Her throat was set to explode. "It was so bad."

Michael reached for her and rocked her. He smelled a bit like antiseptic. Leigh was done being the brave little patient and bit against his shoulder as she cried. She felt his chest convulsing. He was crying, too.

"Why?" he was asking. She couldn't understand any other words he said.

"Bridie. It was Bridie. She did this to me." Leigh's voice was raw. "She took this drug when she was pregnant with me. And now I can never have children. I can get pregnant, but I'll always end up like this."

Michael had been hit by a glacier. He separated his body from Leigh's by a few precious inches so that he could study her face. No, she wasn't raving. This was the truth. He got them both tissues and offered Leigh some of the water Maddie had left on the nightstand. But he kept his body on its own turf.

"What do you mean?" he asked.

Leigh did her best to recapture Dr. Griffin's words about DES, about female reproductive organs, about Leigh's fate.

"Was this a legal drug?" Michael asked, as if he were planning some sort of lawsuit.

"It was then. It isn't now."

He nodded, but didn't say anything. Leigh watched and waited while Michael paced the room. Leigh slowly realized that this was happening to him, too, after all. She waited for him to come close to her again, but he didn't do it.

"Is she sure?" he finally asked. Yes, Dr. Griffin was sure.

"But why didn't she say anything like this last time? She told us to try again. I remember."

"Last time was my first miscarriage. It took them a while to get all the medical history. All the Bridie history. Now they know. It's definite, Michael. It's real."

When he sat down again, he was even farther away from her. "Are you okay?"

The brave little patient nodded yes, then no. But he was still over there, not here with her.

Leigh watched the sun rise the next morning and decided that she wouldn't wrap herself in a cocoon, as she had done the last time. This time, she made herself go to work. Yes, work would offer structure and distraction. It would take her far from the scene of all this misery. But the subway ad offering affordable health insurance for kids ruined her perfect escape to work. Infants in angel costumes broke her down. She had to leave the train three stops early and walk the rest of the way.

"Jesus, Leigh. You shouldn't be here. What could you be thinking?" Kendall rose from her desk and found a chair for Leigh. Kendall knew. But how?

"Maddie told me." Of course. The two became friends when Leigh brought Maddie in to usher at Wonderland and paint the occasional set. From the look on Kendall's face, Maddie must not have spared any details. "Oh, honey. You don't want to be here at a time like this."

"Yes, I do, actually. I want to be anywhere but home. I want to be with people. If that's all right. I know it freaks everyone out to be around someone who might spontaneously burst into tears, but I don't want to sit in a blank apartment staring at the walls and thinking sad thoughts. That doesn't help me."

Kendall smiled and the lines in her face overpowered her. "Cry whenever you want to. This is a theater, remember." She hugged Leigh, which she had maybe done six times in all the years they had known each other. Kendall was never a hugger.

"Well. What would you like to do while you're here?"

Oh, in between plays was such a nasty limbo place to be. There was everything and nothing to do. Leigh had concentrated on getting herself to the theater, but hadn't thought about what to do when she got there. She trolled around for a task when Kendall took pity on her and offered, "Would you like to read some plays that have been submitted? They might make you laugh. Unintentionally."

Kendall herself had given up on reading new plays until at least three people she trusted praised the texts to the sky. Prior to that resolution, she was famous for saying the most ego-crushing things to first-time playwrights. There was that time she told a young woman to lose everything but the first seven words of the second act, and defended this as constructive criticism. There were so many times that she said, "You've accidentally written a comedy," to a playwright who thought he was sitting with a tragedy.

Leigh had to bear that in mind when she said, "Michael has written a play."

"About what? Bicuspids? Root canals?" She was starting to laugh. Hard. "What's it called?" she managed to ask. "*Molar Express*?" Leigh tried to smile politely while Kendall came up with "*One Chew Over the Cuckoo's Nest? Twelfth Bite?*"

Leigh slowly (she was doing everything slowly) pulled the

script from her worn backpack and handed it to Kendall. "It's about his grandmother. It's hard for me to be objective, but I think it's kind of sweet. It's an old-fashioned drawing-room comedy. A well-made play. I think people might actually like it."

She should have planned this speech before putting the script in front of Kendall. She had accidentally damned him with faint praise.

Kendall took the script, looked at Leigh to gauge how serious she was, then began reading as she walked back to her own chair.

"*Women in Hats.* Okay, I'll tell you what. You read something from the slush pile, I'll read Michael's play. And you have to go home early today, too. Get some rest. Do we have a deal?"

Suddenly, Leigh felt protective of Michael's work, his pride, his grandmother. Kendall's blistering critiques must never be passed along to Michael. Maybe she should stop Kendall.

"Go on." Kendall was already waving Leigh away. Leigh grabbed a stack of bound scripts from the tall stack in the corner and set her course for the garret above the theater.

Leigh had perfect privacy here in the garret. The Wonderland company tried for years to use it as a rehearsal room, but no one liked this space above the costume shop. Too cold, too creaky, too full of ghosts of the Lower East Side. The walls sloped in at sharp, dramatic angles, like a Parisian garret, which gave actors the hopeless feeling that they were all starving artists, which made them order more pizza, which made them gain weight, which made them more unhappy. So Wonderland's rehearsals were transferred to its basement, while the upstairs space became Leigh's private garret. She came up here to read scripts, make notes, think, rehearse difficult things to say. Leigh loved the garret because it was clean and spare. It had no clutter, no fuss, no Diet Coke cans left by thoughtless actors or assistant stage managers. For her, it wasn't cold, it was cool and quiet, and it was all hers.

Leigh first discovered the garret when she was an intern at Wonderland. Kendall's rigid schedule had forced her to work a month of lunch shifts, so that she could assist at evening rehearsals. Her budget suffered, but a month with Kendall was like a free doctorate program. After a few weeks, she came to understand that Kendall yelled at everyone, not just at her, and it was not to be taken personally. Alone in the garret, she could sort through Kendall's over-the-top list of demands and understand the artistic vision her mentor was pursuing. Other interns may have complained, but Leigh saw the value in each day there. These days, Michael subsidized her life in avant-garde theater so well, she had to avoid any and all conversations about money. The other staffers would undoubtedly resent the comfort and security Leigh experienced. She reminded herself to be thankful that she had Michael in her life as she settled into the first script, *Coming Out,* the story of a young man coming out to his family. He worries for a few pages, then tells them the truth. They surprise him by being unfazed by this revelation. They have dinner. Blackout. Curtain. Done. Leigh fought to stay awake.

The next play, *Your Sacrifice Is in Vain,* involved a volcano eruption that destroyed the lives of the island natives who gave yearly sacrifices to angry volcano gods. It had thirty-two speaking roles and a live volcano center stage. It was a stunning combination of expensive and impossible.

The third play, *His True Self,* concerned a man who was growing a twin out of his left arm. In each scene, the twin became larger, more mobile. Eventually, the twin could speak. Finally, it killed the man.

No, Leigh hadn't read each line of each play. She couldn't. She shouldn't have to. She headed back to Kendall's office and found James on the way there.

"Hey," he called. "How are you doing?" He smiled and had a warm sawdust scent to him. She breathed it in.

"I'm good," she lied.

She hadn't listened to those Ella Fitzgerald CDs yet, but was getting ready to pretend that she had when he said, "You don't look good. Are you okay?"

She had to look away from him. Maybe he could read her mind if he saw her eyes. Maybe she was mixing up body parts. Anyway, she didn't want to talk about or even think about it. *It.* She had to push *it* from her mind.

"I've been reading these plays and they're just terrible, terrible, terrible."

James was looking into her eyes and, oh, no, could he see the true terrible behind her eyes? Leigh was losing her polite smile, fading into sad rather quickly.

"You don't want to tell me what it is?" he asked. She couldn't answer, but only shook her head.

"Okay." He held his arms open for an embrace. She hesitated and his eyes took on that large, round Stan Laurel expression that made him impossibly charming. She ducked into his arms for a quick hug. When quick turned into lingering, she looked up at him and stepped back.

"Gotta see Kendall." She clutched her scripts and kept her head down until she reached Kendall's office.

Leigh found Kendall on the telephone. From the sound of her voice, she was arguing with one of the many unions she tangled with.

"Don't tell me he gets hazard pay for that. . . . What if I lower the platform? What if I remove the platform and he hops in place? What if I just take him home and make him chicken soup? Jesus Christ, I'm sixty-four years old and *I* can make the damn jump. Why can't a healthy, active twenty-three-year-old actor?"

Actors Equity. Kendall would lose this battle, Leigh was certain from what little she heard, and Kendall should have known that, too. But that never prevented her from fighting anyway. Leigh sat down across from Kendall, who acknowledged her with a wave while listening intently to the person on the other end of the line. After a minute, she held the phone at arm's length and stared at it as she shook her head. She was losing the battle.

"Hey!" Kendall shouted. "I remember when unions *helped* people! I remember when people like me marched and picketed to get unions like yours *more power*! My God, I was young then!"

She slammed the phone down, and Leigh actually thought she saw smoke coming from Kendall's ears. Optical illusion. It was dust, launched into flight by the phone slam. Leigh waited for Kendall to slam a few drawers before attempting a conversation with her. *Slam! Throw! Bang!*

"Kendall?"

"Idiots."

Let her throw a few more things. Kendall was pacing an intricate pattern around her small office. She managed to slam drawers on two of the elderly file cabinets near her desk.

"People are idiots. Especially actors. One day, I'll do a whole evening of plays without actors. Or playwrights." Kendall found Michael's script on her desk. She lifted it up, just to drop it back on the desk.

Leigh wondered if she was going to pass out. She had no feeling in her hands. That probably wasn't good. She was busy thinking about her numb fingers when Kendall said, "Okay, so I read Michael's play. Good news, bad news. Which do you want first?"

"Bad news." Always.

"Tough. Here's the good news: it doesn't suck. It reminds me of the kind of crap they do at those corporate theaters in midtown, the ones that all the tourists fight for tickets to go see, and then they fall asleep."

"That's the good news?" Leigh was thoroughly confused.

"The bad news is, honey, it's a dinosaur. It doesn't belong here. Even if we could put together the kind of posh production values this play needs—it wouldn't fit in with anything else in our season. Or in our history, for that matter. And by the way, you know this season is completely booked, and next season is halfway there."

Leigh saw a glimmer of hope there, and seized it.

"Tourists would like it?"

"Would love it," Kendall confirmed.

Kendall may not have meant that as a compliment, but Leigh took it as one anyway.

"Okay, enough about *Women in Hats*. I'm tired, so you should go home. We're not doing your husband's play. Done."

Exit.

. . .

Michael opened cans of chicken soup and warmed them up. That was the extent of his cooking skills, and it was all so well intentioned, it was delicious, especially when he crumbled oyster crackers into the mix. They sat at the table, where he could watch her eat her soup. He spoke in quiet tones about benign subjects.

"I thought it was going to rain today," he said. "But it didn't."

"Good soup," Leigh answered as she hovered over the bowl and sipped it slowly.

She knew that this was his way of taking care of her. This cottony environment would act as a bandage around her until her wounds didn't hurt anymore. It was hopelessly naïve, but Leigh couldn't bear to tell him that. And he didn't touch her. Ever. Even when she said, "Michael, your play is good. It's very good."

Michael sat up and had more energy in his voice than he had dared show since Leigh's miscarriage. He was bordering on loud when he cried out, "Really? You like it?"

"I do."

Michael gushed about his story and his characters and how "they all love each other, even when they don't show it." He said this as he retrieved his script from the office. He held it open to the minor skirmish between mother and son in the second act. He read the beginning of the scene surprisingly well. He angled his body back and forth to inhabit each character fully as they confronted each other. And that was passion, wasn't it? It was endearing, in its own way. But Leigh had no other homes for any plays beyond Wonderland. She couldn't bring this play to life, but she couldn't leave it alone. In her mind, she mapped out a list of theater companies she might call on his behalf, but then she pushed it aside while he finished the scene.

Fade out.

. . .

It was wrong to compare one miscarriage to another, but Leigh did it anyway. The first one was the most nightmarish. It was the biggest shock. Leigh spent a week in bed, in the dark, mourning her loss. Michael was as devastated as Leigh was. They both cried spontaneously throughout the days and weeks that followed. And they clung to each other. They avoided Central Park for months. Too many babies and children. After a while, though, they were drawn by the energetic hum of the city around them until one day they were laughing at the way Maddie complained about the summer's oppressive "heat and humility." Leigh put the miscarriage away, as part of her past. She was ready to move into the future.

But the second miscarriage wouldn't let go. It carried into the future with the word *never*. The finality of that word shut Michael down. Never. No. Not ever. Never-never land.

A week had passed, and each morning Michael left the apartment earlier and earlier. He began running in Central Park.

"Good run?" she always asked when he returned.

He raced to the shower, calling out, "Great! But I gotta get to work!"

At first, Leigh would trail him to their front door, insisting on a kiss. After two weeks of insisting, she let it go. She wanted him to kiss her without any insistence. But Leigh would give him time, buckets of time, to cope.

*   *   *

Leigh and Maddie were in their usual coffee shop, across the street from Leigh's apartment. A whole month had passed since she had closed her last play. Since her birthday. Since *it*. Kendall seemed to be forgetting *it*. She swore at Leigh, just as she always had. Maddie was clearly on the fast track to normal, or whatever term she would use for it. She gossiped over coffee as they always had. But being in between plays was not getting any easier for Leigh. She tried to make it more fun by giving herself projects she termed "life maintenance." She returned to her closet cleaning, book alphabetizing, and Tupperware lid matching.

"When's your next play?" Maddie asked.

"Not until next season. Kendall hasn't chosen it yet, so I can't even get started. I'm going crazy. And it's a whole year away. I might actually lose my mind before then."

"You need to do something," Maddie advised. "There's nothing else for you to organize or clean. Honey, you need a play, or else. You sound like you're going to turn yourself into a real basketball case."

Leigh's coffee went down the wrong way. She coughed herself to right again.

"I'm okay," she said at last.

"See? It's true. You need to relax." Leigh's mind flashed back to her birthday party and those gifts. "You need a project that's going to take your mind off what happened." True, Maddie never used the word *miscarriage,* but it was still as shockingly close as anyone had come to talking about it. Her eyes went large and she stopped eating. "I'm sorry. I shouldn't talk about it."

"It's okay. I mean, it's not okay, but it's okay. You know?" Leigh was squirming in her seat. She needed to change the subject and fast, but her mind wasn't working today.

"If you need a play, why don't you direct Michael's? I mean, would Kendall be okay with that kind of nespotism?" Maddie asked.

"You mean 'nepotism.'" Leigh didn't mean to correct Maddie, but it just came out.

"No. I mean when you're in charge and you're the only one with any power, and you show special favors to your family. You know. Nespotism."

"Oh." Leigh sipped her coffee slowly.

Maddie was now devouring the breakfast as if it were her first meal in a while, or, perhaps, her only meal for the day. Maybe it was. She hadn't mentioned selling a painting in a long while. Not everyone had the luxury of a dentist-husband to float them along during the in-between times that happened for most artists.

"Rico's leaving for Japan next week," Maddie announced as she pulled on her bagel. Okay, so if Leigh wasn't going to talk about Michael's play, Maddie would just change the subject.

"Good," Leigh declared. Rico was entirely too on-again, off-again to be considered a decent boyfriend in Leigh's book. And when he was in on-again mode, he made a cruel art of correcting Maddie's invented vocabulary whenever he could. Leigh had a hard time seeing what Maddie saw in him.

"And yes, I slept with him, and no, I don't care that you don't approve. I'm not even going to be able to talk to him after he leaves, so I'm not going to pretend I don't want him. The band is booked all over Kyoto and some other Japanese-sounding places. This could be really big for him." Maddie was smearing a thick layer of cream cheese and gobs of jelly on a bagel while she spoke. How did she stay rail-thin with this kind of appetite?

"Good for Rico." Leigh didn't try to sound sincere. Maddie scowled as she vacuumed more food into her body. Rico would not be back in New York for at least six months. He would not be reachable by phone or by e-mail. Leigh secretly hoped that Maddie would forget him and find a nice dentist instead.

· · ·

After breakfast, Leigh dropped in at the theater. She hauled another stack of scripts up to the Wonderland garret and dove in. She didn't like the play about a race of underground bug people whose story closely resembled *Richard III*. She hated the play about the man whose ex-wives conspire to kidnap him because he's such a fantastic lover, he ruined them for anyone else. She despised the play about two teenagers who find Jimmy Hoffa's body, then try to auction it on eBay. It was all so stupid and thin and unsatisfying. It was a bowl of soy protein when she really wanted a steak. She wanted something more. She began to dream that her next play would have a longer run than six weeks, have a better cast than the actors willing to work for subway fare, get reviews and recognition beyond *The Village Voice,* and include a budget that exceeded her yearly shoe expenditures. She wanted to see actual smiles as patrons left the theater, not just the thoughtful looks they wore after her Wonderland productions. She wanted to direct *Women in Hats.* If not here, somewhere.

[3]

hen Leigh finally told Michael that she wanted to direct his play, he seemed confused.

"Well, yeah," he said quietly. "I thought you already wanted to direct it. Do you mean you didn't want to direct it before?" He paused en route to his post-run shower and moved closer to Leigh, who was perched on the sofa.

"Oh. Yes. Yes, I did. I always wanted to direct it." No, she hadn't, but he was moving closer and might be able to detect a lie. She stood up and explained, "But now what I want to do is work on finding a place where it can be done. That's not the same as directing. That's something more. Else. Something else."

He came even closer and didn't seem to notice that she was making this up as she went. He very nearly hugged her as he clutched her at the elbows, which counted as physical contact. She shook her head and tried to smile.

"The thing is, I'm not a producer. I don't have money or space or anything. But I want to find a way. I really need a project like this. I need to throw myself into my work."

He looked at her cautiously and said, "Maybe your mother can help?"

"No." She sat back down, throwing away an opportunity to be close to her husband.

"Think about it," he called as he jogged to the shower. "Just think about it!"

. . .

Maddie sent a text message to Leigh's phone:

12 u no wear.

It took Leigh a minute or two to figure it out. Maddie wanted to meet at noon at their usual coffee place across the street. She found her friend at their usual table, wearing an unusual hat and sunglasses, indoors.

"Maddie!" Leigh called out, but her friend shushed her. Leigh slid into a chair and asked, "Okay. What is this? Are we hiding from someone?"

Maddie looked all around the restaurant, like someone in a bad spy movie. Leigh tried not to laugh, because Maddie wasn't laughing.

"I never told you this," Maddie began. She looked around again, and let her voice drop low. "I don't pay taxes," she said without moving her lips or unlocking her jaw. Leigh couldn't make out the words.

"You don't hate Texas?"

Maddie leaned in and energetically whispered, "I. Don't. Pay. Taxes."

"Ever?" Leigh wasn't sure how she felt about that. Taxes were a rule, and rules were meant to be followed. Then again, her friend was being so courageous and interesting.

"Why are you telling me this?"

"Because. I've been hearing these clicking sounds on my phone. It's all weird and crackly. Maybe that's because someone is listening in on my calls."

"No, honey," Leigh answered. "You just have a cheap phone. That's all it is."

Maddie looked disappointed that Leigh wasn't putting this together. "It's the IRS. They're finally on to me. They've found me and I'm going to end up in Alcatraz or something. And then Rico freaked me out and said how these are the guys who got Al Capone, so now they're going to get me. I really think they've got a tip on my phone. That's why we had to meet here. They're after me."

Leigh wanted to ask her why she didn't pay taxes, how she had gotten away with it for so many years, and why she believed that the IRS had a *tap* on her phone. But she didn't.

Instead, she said, "You have to do a preemptive strike. You have to go to them."

She outlined a plan for Maddie to throw herself on the mercy of the IRS, if they had any. First, get a smart lawyer. Second, bring the smart lawyer to the IRS and work out a payback plan with them. Leigh was going to move on to explain "third," but a tear began to slide down from behind the sunglasses. Tough, tall, beautiful Maddie looked frightened and small.

"I can't. I hardly ever sell a painting, and when I do, it all goes for paint, rent, and food. In that order. I don't have the money they're going to want. I don't have a regular job, and the IRS is all about regular jobs. The last time I did my taxes, the tax guy told me that I'm not really an artist because I don't sell enough paintings. To quote the guy, 'It's your *hobby*, but not your *job*.' So they say that I can't deduct the cost of my materials. They'll expect me to wear sensible flats and a watch and go to a cubicle. That's not me. Do you remember what happened when I worked at that insurance company last month? How I shredded all those claims and made a sculpture out of the paper strips?"

"I'll help you. I'll get you through this." Leigh sounded like a superhero who could actually help her friend and get her through this.

"I've been off the grid for so long, and I've liked it that way. I don't want to be a grog in some corporate wheel. That's what they'll want, and I can't, I just can't can't can't." Maddie hid behind her coffee cup.

"Right. We'll work on that. Maybe you can get a regular job that isn't corporate. And then you can go to the IRS and work all this out."

"No way, no way, no way." Maddie peeked around the side of her coffee. "I can't go to the IRS. I'm too scared. They're going to have me thrown and quartered."

"I'll get you a job. At Wonderland."

. . .

That was easy. Leigh barely had to make her case for hiring Maddie when Kendall agreed to it.

"I didn't pay my taxes for twelve years," Kendall boasted. "So I get what she's going through. Those people invented the payback-as-bitch scenario." She sat back at her desk and rubbed her face with both hands, erasing the memory of the IRS. "She can be our house manager, she can do some box-office work. But we don't pay much. Your shows do great, but we're just not a sellout kind of place."

Leigh thanked Kendall as much as Kendall would allow, and

left, even though she was itching to stay. She remained by the door outside Kendall's office, staring at the warped and dirty floorboards, trying to detect a pattern in the wood grain, trying to figure out how and when to say what she wanted to say. She leaned against the wall and tried to rehearse a speech in her head.

"Holding the building up?" It was James, who was standing very, very close to Leigh, just as he did when he was her stage manager.

Okay, she needed to avoid looking into his eyes. She ended up looking at his shoulders, and that was almost as bad. She brought her eyes back to the floor.

"Hey!" he said as he moved away from her. "Guess what I'm going to do?" She couldn't guess. "I'm going to use the typewriter. The *electric* one!" He pointed to it proudly.

"Use the computer," she grinned as he rolled paper into the typewriter.

"No, thanks. I'm good. So, what are you"—he pressed a key—"up"—he pressed a key—"to?" He searched for the last key and pressed it.

Good question. What was she up to? And why was she so nervous? Was it James? No, much as she might like to blame him, he really wasn't a source of nerves for her. He was generally a source of calm and organized (if old-fashioned) work.

"I have to ask for something." Leigh was piecing it together as she spoke. "And I'd rather not."

"Still," James said as he found one more key to press, then looked up. "It's okay to ask. Even if she says no."

He smiled that smile that forced her to smile back. She spun on the ball of one foot and returned to Kendall's office.

"So!" Leigh's voice was higher than usual, and she felt certain that James was listening from the door. "So!" she chose a lower pitch this time.

"So?" Kendall was peering over her half-moon reading glasses.

She was working on budgets; Leigh could tell from the spreadsheets scattered over the desk. But it was okay to ask. Even if Kendall said no.

"So. What if we did something different? What if we did something that could run longer, say, on a minicontract? What if we did something sort of, you know, commercial?"

Kendall took off her glasses, sat back, and cued Leigh to continue. She did.

"Look at the Public. They do small shows, big shows, and shows that are commercial successes. Those shows get to move on for bigger runs. And those bigger runs bring in money to fund the experimental work. We need something like that. A profitable play would be better than any fund-raiser we've ever done." The argument she had been forming in her mind sounded so smart, so coherent. She really liked it, and, from the look on her face, so did Kendall.

"True. The hard part is finding the right play. But yes, if we could find it, I'd love to stop having to cannibalize the lobby furniture to build the next set. But how do we find it? It didn't sound like you liked that play about the underground bug people."

Holy shit, this just might work.

"Women in Hats." Leigh left it at that to be fun and theatrical.

Which prompted Kendall to say, "Jesus, Leigh, when did you turn stupid?"

"I'm not stupid. It's good. Okay, it needs a little work, but it can run. You're crazy to turn your nose up at this."

Leigh's cell phone rang, and the display warned her that the caller was Bridie, the walking saltshaker in search of a wound. Did she have to answer this call? No. No, thank you. She shut off the phone and put it away. It wasn't the first time she'd screened her mother.

"Hey, Kendall. Last year, my mother made a cameo appearance

on some stupid-ass TV sitcom. And guess what role she played? Bridie Love. No shit. It was just one short scene, and she was seated at a kitchen table for the whole thing. Never got up."

"What the fuck does this have to do with your husband's play? Jesus, Leigh, are you high?"

"The director didn't like the Jimmy Choo shoes that wardrobe had purchased for Bridie, so some lucky intern was promptly dispatched to Prada to pay full price for a new pair. And, of course, the new shoes were perfect. The director was happy. *But the shoes were never seen on camera.* Bridie wore that pair of shoes all the way home. She still wears them."

"Stupid TV shows spend stupid money on stupid shoes. I still need your point, Leigh."

"The cost of those shoes exceeded the entire budget for any production any of us has ever done at Wonderland. That's wrong. And we have to change that."

"Hey, James!" Kendall called out. "Could you come in here a minute? Leigh's having a mental collapse. It's kind of fun." James entered and looked around for the punch line, not realizing that Leigh was it. His eyes, his shoulders, his smile, the ink stain on his fingers from some sort of typewriter struggle—these didn't distract her this time. He was sending her a current of electricity across the room, and it fed her courage.

"You're making a mistake, Kendall." Her voice sounded so calm.

"James, do you think we should do creaky, old-school commercial stuff that doesn't fit in with our season—and it's written by a dentist, by the way—just because it *might* make money? Or should we have some sense of our mission and our artistic integrity?"

Leigh kept herself steady. It had taken her five years to stand up to Kendall, so she might as well enjoy the scene.

"You have to be true to your theater. And it is your theater."

James was addressing Kendall, who raised an eyebrow in triumph. "But," James added, "I like those old plays. They're fun. I think there's room for every kind of play. I think it's a sign of health when there's every kind of play being done."

Kendall shook her head and slammed her feet to the floor. "What the fuck is wrong with you people today?" She looked at James, then Leigh, then James, then Leigh again. "Okay. Maybe I should think about it," Kendall conceded.

It was working. Unbelievable! Wonderful! Leigh's mind was racing ahead, weeks and months past this conversation. She was mapping it all out in her head: the production, the rehearsals, the success. Her heart was thumping, and she wished she were holding on to the furniture to keep her from bouncing out of the room.

Just then a big noise in the stairwell interrupted the best scene Leigh had played since her show closed, since *it*. And she knew, long before anyone else, that her mother was the source of the noise. She could make out her mother's voice shouting, "I *did*! I *tried* to call her, but God knows if phones even work in hovels like this one. Maybe the rats chew through the phone lines."

Leigh found the words "I need to sit down," and noticed that James rushed a chair over to her. She must have looked sickly and pale. Bridie often had that effect on her.

There was a man's voice alongside Bridie's. Leigh didn't recognize it, and she didn't care. Her mother was coming up the stairs like grim death.

"Are we there yet?" Bridie was laughing. Leigh wanted to disappear.

James was hovering over her protectively and every cell in her body wanted to merge with his, hide with his. No. That was unacceptable. Sit up straight.

"Leigh! There you are!" Clarion voice, arms outstretched. Another classic Bridie entrance.

Leigh stood up, pretending to be strong and confident. It was too late to fool James. Kendall looked uncertain, but Leigh could always dupe her mother. She just needed to position herself so that she couldn't see James anymore. Then she'd be fine.

"Mother. What are you doing here? We're in the middle of a meeting." Leave it to Bridie to kill the momentum. "Why didn't you call first?" Leigh remembered too late that she had screened her mother's call. She spoke over Bridie's response. "And who have you brought with you?"

As soon as she asked, she recognized him, and felt foolish for asking.

"Leigh, this is Harry Greenwald." Bridie, Leigh, and Harry managed introductions around the room, but Harry was one of those "needs no introduction" legends in the theater. Even Kendall looked impressed. Harry Greenwald had been producing Broadway plays and musicals since 1957. He had more hits and misses in his career than most people saw in a lifetime of theatergoing. Age had slowed him to the point where many people just assumed that he was dead. And now this icon was being led about town by Bridie Hart, who said, "Harry, darling, sit down before you fall down."

He answered, "You don't have to tell me. Stairs are bullshit."

"Leigh, for heaven's sake. What are you doing?" Bridie smoothed Leigh's neckline down. Leigh didn't realize that she had been pulling the neckband of her T-shirt over her mouth. It was an inadequate way to hide, but it was all she had. She fought hard to remember that she was strong and, what was the other word? Confident. Oh, yeah.

"I was adjusting my shirt," Leigh said confidently.

"Of course you were." Bridie reached over Leigh's shoulder to touch James, probably on the face, as she said, "Hello, I'm Bridie Hart."

She paused as if waiting for an audience to give her a round of applause. James didn't clap. He just said, "James McGovern. I stage-managed Leigh's last show."

Bridie purred a little "Mmm-hmm," and turned to her daughter. Bridie had a million questions. She wanted to know why Leigh's office was so small, what the dressing rooms were like, what sort of improvements they were planning for the building, did they have decent lighting equipment, and where was the man in charge, anyway?

"That would be me. We haven't met. I'm Kendall Epstein, and this is *my* office."

"Oh. Of course. I should have known. Anyway, how wonderful to meet you." She reached across the desk and gave Kendall a quick handshake.

"Harry, this is Kendall Epstein and this is her office. Isn't that delightful?" Bridie was walking a busy lap around the room, happily brushing away dust motes. "She runs this place, I believe. Doesn't it remind you of that little place on Forty-fifth Street where you used to test out nightclub acts?" Bridie giggled and hovered over Harry protectively. "Most people don't know that Harry worked with nightclubs, too, but oh, that was such a long time ago. I auditioned for him myself, back in my salad days. And you were so handsome then, you devil. I still see a bit of what I saw in you that day—and that night. Remember, Harry?" She dug at Harry with her elbow and giggled demurely. Leigh felt completely justified in rolling her eyes. Bridie didn't notice; she was still working the room. "But let's not talk about the past. Let's talk about the present and this lovely little theater you've got here. It's absolutely charming. Do you add the dust in the lobby for special effect, or does that happen naturally? Well, whatever the method, the effect is like a walk through time. It's like gossamer. It's simply magical."

Bridie ballet-turned around Harry and returned her gaze to Kendall.

"What do you want?" Kendall's voice sounded sharp. Leigh sat back and let Kendall be strong and confident while she herself got her bearings on this new configuration. She could handle this. She started by pretending that James was not standing behind her. That eliminated a lot of complications for her, so that she could catch up with Bridie's diatribe.

"Miss Epstein, oh, please let me call you Kendall, you have no idea how excited I am to meet you at last."

"Can you cut the shit already?" Harry asked.

"Yes, please," Kendall added.

Godzilla, meet Mothra. Mothra, meet Godzilla. Now fight.

"So, Kendall." Bridie perched on Kendall's desk, crushing a few dozen spreadsheets. Kendall noticed them right away. "I've only just met you and I'm already a great admirer. Here you are, running a charming, quirky little theater company, against all odds. You must be so plucky! You understand what that means because, and I think it's all right to say this, you're 'of a certain age,' aren't you? You can admit it. I'm there, too, and it's stunning how the body rebels once you pass fif—forty. It's simply awful, isn't it?" Bridie was leaning into Kendall now, but Kendall was focused on pulling her spreadsheets from underneath Bridie's rump. "How do you maintain your energy? Yoga? Clean living? How much longer are you going to run this darling place? Hmm?"

Tug! Kendall successfully retrieved her crinkled spreadsheets. But Bridie's voice was so big, so vibrant, so high-octane, the silence that followed her question felt like a plane landing in the ocean. The passengers checked themselves and their belongings, in case they had shifted in flight, then hung on for dear life. Leigh took some comfort in seeing Kendall struggle to keep up with Bridie. Leigh was in good company.

"Actually, I know I can't do this forever. Not at this pace." This was the first time Leigh had ever heard Kendall hint at retirement. She wondered if Kendall had ever spoken about it before.

"Of course you can't, my dear," Bridie purred. "It's an unreasonable burden, and you've shouldered it so well. There must be endless repairs and such, which have kept you from replacing the front carpet, yes? Let's take a look at the theater itself. Harry! Up, Harry, we're going to look at the theater." Bridie slipped off the desk and started for the door.

Harry looked up. "You're done bullshitting?" he asked. He took some time to pull himself out of his chair, and it was James who leaped forward to help him.

Bridie led the way, and it took Leigh a minute to realize that Bridie didn't know how to find the stage from Kendall's office. She was leading them all toward the scene shop. Finally, Leigh twisted her way around in front of her mother and brought the whole group to the stage. While they walked, Bridie told one of her favorite stories: the one about Harry going on a bender with Bob Fosse in 1967.

"And then Fosse said, 'And all this time, I thought there were *two* girls!'"

Bridie laughed as if she were both telling and hearing the punch line for the first time. Leigh admired her mother's technique: the story sounded spontaneous, and she finished it just as she crossed to center stage, basking in what little light was available. Even Kendall looked impressed.

"Hey! Hi, everybody!" It was Michael, sitting in the front row. He crossed to Leigh, kissed her, and then hugged Bridie. "I thought I was late, but then you weren't here. Weren't we supposed to meet here?"

They stood in a loose circle: Harry, Bridie, James, Leigh, Kendall, and Michael. It was bad blocking, and Leigh wanted to move them into a better stage picture than this. She managed to see James checking out her husband, sizing him up. She shifted and turned her back to him once again. Maybe her superpowers were in the back of her mind.

"Excuse me, Miss Hart, just one question." This was it. Kendall was going to take on Bridie. Leigh could tell from the fake calm in her voice. "What the hell are you doing here?" Mothra was going to smack down Godzilla. "I'm sorry to be so blunt, but this is my theater and I have work to do."

"Of course you do. I imagine you'll be replacing those interesting seats any day now." Bridie gestured toward the lime green chairs, but never looked at them. "And Harry here has to catch a flight to Paris this evening, don't you, Harry. People think he's dead, but actually he's working on a new musical about Jerry Lewis. Doesn't that sound fascinating? Our Harry has staying power, don't you, Harry." She wrapped her arms around him and cooed, "Oh, yes, I remember that about you, Harry. Who could forget?"

Bridie's giggle was still girlish, and it made Harry smile.

Leigh spoke to Kendall, deliberately making her small voice such a contrast to her mother's that it captured everyone's focus. "Don't try to rush her, she'll only drag it out more to spite you. She'll tell you why she's here when she feels like it. I know. She's my mother."

Kendall shook her head and said, "Fuck your mother," and turned on her heel for what would have been a dramatic exit, but Bridie wasn't done yet.

"Of course, of course," Bridie said as she let go of Harry. "You're tired. You're overburdened. I certainly understand. I'm a terrible person for overtaxing you like this and making your difficult day even more impossible for you to complete. So, I'll come right to the point."

Kendall stopped and waited, which was a tactical error, in

Leigh's opinion. Finishing the exit would have had more impact. Oh, well, she couldn't coach Kendall through every moment of a Bridie Hart scene. Kendall would have to work this out for herself.

"Sorry," Michael called out, "but I wasn't able to cancel my four o'clock veneers, so I'll have to get going soon." His voice didn't carry very far. He broke up their circle, sinking into one of the hard green plastic chairs in the house.

"Oh, Michael, of course," Bridie purred

MICHAEL? She called him MICHAEL? That was almost as disturbing as watching Bridie say, "Michael, this is James." Bridie announced brightly to James, "Michael is our playwright," then turned back to Michael and loudly whispered, "I'm not sure what James does here, but here he is, and isn't that nice?"

It took Leigh this long to realize her mother's evil plan for that afternoon. She kicked herself for not seeing it already, and dreaded watching it unfold.

"Mother, if this is about *Women in Hats,* you're too late. I've already taken care of it. It's done. And now you can go."

"In a bit, in a bit." She waved Leigh away. "Now, Harry, as you all know, is a great producer, and what do great producers do? They raise money! Lots of it! And Harry here could squeeze dollars from a turnip, believe me."

Now it was Harry's turn to look worried.

"Why are you so full of shit today, Bridie?" he asked. Bridie patted him on the shoulder.

"So here is my proposal: Michael's play should be done here at Wonderland, with Harry producing, Leigh directing, and yours truly in the lead."

"Bridie, listen to me." Leigh made sure her voice carried across the stage. "I've got this play under control. You're too late. I'm directing it. You're not in it. Not. Repeat *not.* We're already going to do it. Done."

"You would take this play, Michael's baby, his only child, and drop it into this little nowhere place, like an orphan on a doorstep?" Leigh missed the rest of the speech. She felt as though a baseball bat had just landed on her head. Michael's baby. Bridie didn't know about this latest miscarriage. Did she? Leigh fought to keep herself standing. Bridie kept talking. "This would be a win-win-win. Michael's play would get the loving, caring launch that it deserves, our little family would collaborate on a project for the very first time, and Wonderland Theater could have its first profitable venture in . . . ever, from the look of things." Bridie ventured a look around the theater and smiled charitably. Kendall raised one eyebrow, folded her arms, braced for battle. Bridie's smile expanded as she said, "Now, of course, your cute little company couldn't afford to hire quality actors like myself, so that's where we bring in Harry. You two could coproduce. Like some charming old couple! A play like this one could pay for a lot of dismal artsy plays that only four people go to see and even they don't enjoy themselves."

Still silence, until Bridie added, "And you're welcome." Her voice was much lower, less bright. She lowered her energy level, so the sales pitch must be over.

Kendall looked like she was still processing it all. She must not have seen it coming the way that Leigh had. And now that it was here, center stage, it was Leigh who had to make it all right, all by herself. But Kendall finally did speak up, and she trained all of her shock and anger at Leigh.

"Did you plan this? Did you stage it? Is this what you had in mind all along? Upstairs just now, you knew your mother was going to show up and try to take over my theater?"

Kendall had completely eliminated Bridie from her line of vision, zeroing in on Leigh. "No," Leigh's voice cracked. "Kendall, look at me and believe what I say: I didn't plan this. I didn't know she was going to come here. I don't want her here. Or anywhere. And hey, it's not like she ever came to see any of our plays here, so why would I expect her to show up on some random afternoon?"

"Jesus," Bridie stage-muttered. Leigh pushed on, moving closer to Kendall, who didn't back away.

"The awful truth is, my mother and I must have both thought of the same thing. And that sentence kind of makes me want to throw up, so let me just ask you to think about this play. Give it a chance. I had some problems with it at first, but it really grew on me. So think about it. Don't dismiss it out of hand because this terrible woman has invaded Wonderland and made it seem like such a bad idea. She could make a sane person turn against breathing and sunlight."

"Excuse me?" Bridie tried to interrupt, but failed.

"This could be great." Leigh stayed focused on Kendall. "And it could help Wonderland."

Kendall turned her back on the crowd, a sure sign that she was working it through. She never liked to have people watch her change her mind.

"We could workshop it. Next season. Late. Maybe." Clearly, Kendall was softening, just a bit.

Michael gasped and was the poster child for joy. Leigh was ready to grab this small half-offer, but Bridie spoke first.

"No. Darling, we don't wait that long when we have a money-maker. We do the play now. As in *now*. Neither of us is young anymore. I don't need to get a minute older before I play Margaret. But Michael, sweetheart, you'll let her be just a wee bit older, won't you?"

Michael nodded vigorously. He was too busy winning the lotto and moving into the Playboy Mansion. He was pure happiness. But then Kendall swung in the other direction.

"Even if it is a good idea, and I'm not saying that it is, I don't have space for it. I have a full season booked. I have signed contracts and marketing materials printed. I can't undo my season on a whim."

Poor Michael was waving good-bye to Hef and the grotto. And then it was James, of all people, who spoke up. "Does Mr. Greenwald have any space available to him?"

Harry was half-smiling, as if he had been waiting for someone to catch up with him and his space.

"I do. But it's not here in the city. Property's crazy expensive here. I have a nice little place. Perfect for this play."

"Where is it?" Leigh asked.

"Jupiter," Harry replied.

"Florida," Bridie added.

Bridie started describing the receptive audiences and good press they'd find in Florida, not to mention the chance to retreat from a New York winter. Of course, if things went well in Florida, they could beat a path directly to Broadway.

Harry rolled his eyes, but her words sent Michael back to Fantasyland. He missed Bridie's lengthy tale of a torrid weekend in Jupiter with Burt Reynolds. Leigh tuned it out. She was strangely calm for someone who had just turned her life inside out. Harry was staring at the floor, waiting for Bridie's story to end. When it finally did, he said, "After the Florida run, we look at what we've got. Broadway's not out of the question, but it's a wait and see."

"Wait. So, then, I'm out," Kendall said. She sounded about 10 percent disappointed. Maybe 20 percent. "If Harry has the money and the space, you don't need anything from me. So you can all just take your little meeting to Harry Greenwald's office. I'll bet it's a lot prettier than mine."

"It is," Bridie assured her. "You heard the woman. Let's go."

Bridie took four long strides toward the exit. So that was it? Leigh was just supposed to turn her back on Kendall, on Wonderland, on James? No.

"No," Leigh commanded. "If you want me, you have to include Wonderland. Kendall's still a producer."

Kendall was shaking her head. "Half an hour ago, I wanted nothing to do with this play. So don't do me any favors. Go. Be a big Broadway hit. Be happy." That was all the time Leigh needed to click it all into place.

"Harry gets the backers and the space," Leigh commanded as she took center stage. "Kendall hires the staff and serves as an adviser. It's a joint venture between Greenwald and Wonderland or I'm out." Oh, shit. Bridie had that sphinx smile that might mean that she had another director in her pocket. Leigh quickly added, "And Michael, you'll go with me, right?"

Michael was choking, strangling, unable to breathe. He finally said, "I . . . I have a four o'clock. Veneers . . ." and shifted in his uncomfortable chair.

"Done." Bridie spoke for Harry, Michael, and Kendall.

Michael's incandescence returned. Leigh turned her gaze to Kendall, but her peripheral vision caught a happy Bridie slipping her arm through Harry's. No one spoke for a very long minute. Finally, Bridie began babbling about Harry's musical about Jerry Lewis, which was entitled *Monsieur Goofy*. Harry didn't appear to be listening until Bridie said, "I think it's going to be a smash! Don't you, Leigh?"

"It better be," Harry mumbled. "Working with you, I'm going to need shitloads of money."

"Oh, hush," Bridie ordered, and another long minute of silence hung over the room, broken only by Michael's tiny joyful noises.

"Look at us," said Bridie. "One big, happy theatrical family."

But then she took James by the arm and said, "Please tell us that you'll be joining my daughter as her stage manager. Clearly, she needs you."

James said yes, of course, and Leigh finally looked at him. She couldn't read him. Was he sad? Worried? Happy?

Michael finally burst out of his lime chair and shook James's hand. "Welcome aboard. Look, I've got to get to my four o'clock, and I'm so late." He made the rounds. "Harry, you're my hero. Bridie, you're the best. Kendall, you rock. And Leigh, I love you." He kissed Leigh, and then shook James's hand again. "Welcome aboard," he repeated. He was almost out the door when he turned and said, "I wrote a Broadway play!" He strutted out of the building. Leigh realized that she had been smiling for the last three minutes. Smiling.

"Leigh," Kendall interrupted her reverie, "you and I have a lot to discuss. If I'm the adviser, I'd better start advising now."

Harry looked at his watch and cried out, "Bridie! I thought you said this would just take a minute. You're so full of shit. Let's go!"

Bridie started to follow, but stopped when she was face-to-face with Kendall. Leigh stayed just close enough to hear her mother.

"That's right, you're her adviser," Bridie said quietly. "And I'm her mother."

[4]

$\mathscr{S}$itting on the sofa was a challenge for Michael, who was evolving into a plugged-in power generator. His right leg bounced and vibrated enough to spread tremors throughout the room. Leigh pressed a hand to his knee to stop him. The stillness lasted a few minutes, then resumed, full blast.

"Sorry. I'm too excited," he explained when Leigh tried to still his bouncing leg for the fourth time. "I'm sorry, but you get to do these plays all the time, and this is my first. How do you stand it? I think I'm gonna have to up the morning run."

And he did. He ran farther distances every morning to burn off his extra energy. When he returned to the apartment, he sang off-key in the shower, then tossed an odd collection of fruits and yogurts into the blender.

"Wow," Leigh said as she made coffee in slow motion. "You went running in the rain?"

"Is it raining?" he asked, as he peered out the window. "Oh, that's nothing. It felt great. You should try running, too. It actually *gives* you more energy."

"I get my energy from coffee, the way God intended." She slouched over her cup, while Michael stretched his calves.

"I've got four new patients from the Road Runners Club. It's great. They all floss!"

Leigh watched Michael retreat to the bedroom to get dressed. He didn't lose any momentum, and called out to her, "Oh, you know what I was thinking about while I was running? The Tony Awards. Are they just all political? Do we even stand a chance? I mean, Bridie, yes, for sure. But what about the play?"

"I don't actually know. If—and it's a big *if*—but, if this play goes to Broadway, it'll be my first Broadway play, too."

That sentence propelled Michael into the kitchen, where he kissed Leigh on the cheek and said, "Right, sorry. Oh, so when I was at the reservoir, I was thinking—what about the film rights?"

"What film rights?" Leigh was too sleepy to remember that her husband's play had rapidly spun into the center of the universe.

"What if somebody makes a movie out of the play? How cool would that be? Would you still get to direct? You'd be a big Hollywood director! But would we have to keep Bridie in the lead? Could we maybe get Meryl Streep? Did I ever tell you about the time I saw her in Whole Foods? Man, she was hot. And, let's be honest here, your mother isn't a movie star, and Meryl Streep is."

"Michael, honey. Let's just get the play on its feet first. Then you can start thanking the Academy. Right now, it's just you and me." She moved close to him, pressing her body against his, untying her robe. "And you don't need to be at work this early. Come here."

She reached for his face, but he turned away. She tried not to feel scared.

"Michael, it's okay. We're adults. And we're married."

She wrapped her body around his, but he took her by the shoulders, a bit more forcefully than necessary. "Sorry. I have a lot more patients now, Leigh. Early appointments. I have to go. Sorry." He kissed her quickly on the forehead and left.

Leigh tried not to be angry, hurt, or insulted. She tried not to feel so stupid with her robe hanging open like that. She tried not to worry that he only ever touched her the way he'd touch a dear cousin. She tied the robe fast and tight.

•   •   •

In her imagination, Leigh cast the play with the finest actors she had ever seen, even though some of them would have to be brought back from the dead. She envisioned an elegant set, magical lighting, and top-notch costumes. She let herself indulge in the fantasy that Bridie would be professional, respectful, and cooperative, and that the play would be transformed into a witty, heartfelt family saga. It could happen. Her left brain noted that James was omitted from every one of these fantasies, and Michael barely registered in any of them. This was not a point either side of her brain felt safe exploring.

Maybe those happy delusions protected her from spontaneous combustion. She clutched them tight, and then relaxed enough to loop just a pinkie finger around them, but she never let them go. Two days had gone by since that Big Bridie Scene at Wonderland, and Leigh was still wearing this false armor when she met Maddie at the usual place, at the usual time. First, Leigh saw the expensive bottle of scotch on the table, then she saw the tear streaks down her friend's cheeks.

"Well, I did it. I came clean to the IRS." Maddie sniffled.

This statement dropped Leigh into a chair. Maddie had followed her advice. Leigh was locked in fear. What if she was wrong? Maddie should have gotten a second opinion.

Maddie continued. "I walked into the IRS office, no appointment or anything, and just started confessing to anyone who would listen. It felt good. I mean, hey, I figured that they already knew everything about me anyway. But now they know that I knew that they knew. And I know you followed that. So now they don't have to bug my phone anymore. Only it turns out they weren't actually bugging my phone. Remember the crackling noises that were making me so crazy? Turns out I have a cheap phone."

Leigh didn't let herself have any variation on an I-told-you-so expression, but just let Maddie continue. "So then I went to Wonderland and said, you guys are going to get a call from the government, and Kendall was all 'whatever.' "

"Never mind. Tell me about the IRS." Leigh helped herself to the scotch.

"So they get a nice taste of my paycheck, which, hoooo baby, is small enough already. I thought the pay sounded okay when I started, but I had no idea the government was going to slice off so much of it, and that was before Confession Day. How can I get promoted already? How do people live like this? It's criminal. Rico says that that's what justifies the way he always cheated on his time card at the store. Don't tell anybody I told you that. He'd kill me."

"Are you okay?" Leigh's voice was a bit raspy from the scotch, which was shocking her system into submission.

"No. I'm not okay. These people, they're all over me. They call me and write to me and they're even calling Kendall all the time. Just imagine how well she's coping with that. And Rico left this morning for Japan and I feel shitty, so don't even start on him. It's over. I don't think he's coming back from Japan. Ever." Maddie said more, but Leigh couldn't understand her when she was 70 percent crying and 30 percent speaking.

"Let's have more scotch," Leigh offered.

"When he said good-bye he was so calm, so done, so sapathetic. I wanted to hit him." Maddie collapsed over the table. "My life sucks. Why does my life suck?"

Leigh rubbed Maddie's back and made soothing sounds aimed at the top of Maddie's head. Even when she was upset about her sucky life, Maddie was still so pretty. She looked like a sad top model. Why didn't she know she was beautiful?

Maddie jerked her head up so quickly, it startled Leigh.

"I don't believe in crying over bastards like Rico." Maddie blew her nose loudly and continued. "So I won't. And anyway, the world didn't end, so yeah, I'm actually okay. I'm ready to do this tax thing now. I'm on the grid. I'm trying like mad to find another job for more money. Between Kendall's temper and the measly pay, I can't afford to stay there very long. I need something real. That's it, isn't it: I'm now officially a grown-up. Next thing you know, I'll have health insurance and I'll be yelling at kids to get off my lawn."

Leigh's smile was genuine. The muscles around her eyes were relaxed. She sipped her scotch and wondered if she should eat something. Yes, she probably should. Maddie clutched Leigh's arm and kept talking. "I'm really grateful that you got me this gig, so don't be offended that I seriously have to find another one. I need a job with more dollars behind it. So if you hear about anything, you'll remember your bestest pal, Maddie, right?" She smiled through the mascara circles around her eyes.

Leigh hugged her friend and whispered, "I'm so proud of you. You went to the IRS, and you're working it out. That's impressive." Her tongue was thick, and it was hard to say "impressive."

Maddie wiped her eyes and blew her nose loudly.

"What about you? Tell me something good, please."

"I need coffee."

"Why?" Maddie asked.

"Because I'm directing *Women in Hats*. And you're going to

help me. That'll be your promotion. You'll get a higher slala . . . salala . . . pay."

Leigh related the tale of her mother's triumph at Wonderland in exact detail. Why just describe Bridie's over-the-top gestures when you can also reenact them? It was a long story—possibly longer in the telling than in the original living of it—and it made her very thirsty. She lost track of just how much scotch she was consuming. It was such an appropriate prop for the Bridie parts of her story, it kept her going. Whenever she struggled to remember the next detail, she repeated her promise to Maddie that the pay (salary) with *Women in Hats* would be significantly higher than her current pittance.

"No one was ever meant to work with their family," Leigh said to her scotch. "It goes against all the laws of Darwin. And no one was ever meant to work with *my* family. And *I* was never meant to work with my family. You know what I mean?"

Maddie may or may not have had an answer to that, but Leigh put her hand over her friend's and said, "I'm drunk. Are you drunk? I'm drunk. Wow. Hey. Where are we going?" Leigh sniffled. "And when did it get dark out?"

Maddie was escorting Leigh home. It was only across the street, but it was challenging. As they entered her quiet apartment, Maddie asked, "So, what do you think, Leigh? Coffee or nap? Which one's going to help you out more?"

Leigh managed to say "Coffee" as sleep overtook her. She was sprawled on her bed, she knew that. And she suspected that she still had her shoes on. Maddie would never think to pull her shoes off, so she might end up getting dirt on the really expensive white duvet. Oh, well. Nothing to be done. Sleep won.

When she woke, late afternoon sunlight was changing the blank colors in the room to a dusty rose. Maddie was seated in a chair, holding something. A small book? A picture frame? The picture of Lilly. The one that Dad had taken all those years ago. Leigh hoped that Maddie didn't want to talk about Lilly. Not today.

"How's your head?" Maddie asked.

"Large," Leigh answered, and it felt true. Her head felt much bigger than it was supposed to be. It was hard to lift it. She looked to her nightstand, and saw that Maddie had set out an array of vitamins and a tall glass of water. Leigh tried not to grunt as she sat up and, one by one, washed the vitamins down.

"Leigh, I think that's the most polluted I have ever seen you. It was weird. I wish you could have been happier, but I'm kind of honored that you chose to get so drunk with me, of all people."

Leigh wondered if all of her track records were due to be destroyed: never gets drunk, never wears her shoes to bed, never directs a failure, never cheats on her husband with a handsome, remote stage manager. She sat very still.

"You never talk about her," Maddie said as she turned the picture of Lilly to face Leigh. It was true. Leigh didn't want to cheapen her sister's memory with silly conversation. So she said nothing, not even to Michael. And she really didn't want to say anything now.

"I miss her. She was . . ." The catch in her throat threatened to mature into a full sob. Leigh felt the muscles in her cheeks twitching. Maddie brought tissues and comfort, which only made it worse. Finally, Leigh finished what little she wanted to say about her lost sister.

"She was fun."

• • •

Harry was back from Paris. Leigh wasn't clear about how long he had been back, but his assistant summoned all the key players to a meeting in his office. Michael took special pleasure in rescheduling patients so that he could meet with "his producer." And his patients either didn't mind rescheduling dental work or anticipated seeing their dentist on an *E! True Hollywood Story* where they could supply pointed commentary. Whatever the reason, there were no complaints.

Kendall's face was frozen in her trademark half-smile, which meant that she was kicking into prime bemused mode. She laughed at herself, at the whole situation, but she didn't complain. Which was fine, because Bridie complained enough for everyone. She didn't like being anywhere at nine AM. There were precious few people for whom she would appear so early in the day, when her face was still puffy.

"Harry must still be on Paris time. Otherwise, he'd remember the kind of hours we usually keep in this business," Bridie grumbled. Leigh opened her mouth, but closed it right away. It was too early to argue with Bridie.

Harry lived and worked out of a grand town house on Fifth Avenue. Leigh felt like she was stepping into an oil painting of Edith Wharton's New York. What must it be like to be surrounded by so much splendor every day? Could anyone ever get used to it? She was irked to note that Bridie fit right in. She was even basking.

"Mr. Greenwald is expecting you." A beautiful young receptionist led them past another beautiful young assistant into Harry's beautiful office. Clearly, Harry was a man who appreciated beauty. He looked so small, compared to the massive antique chinoiserie desk, littered with papers.

"G'morning, kids," Harry growled. "Anybody want coffee?" Leigh and Michael both declined, but Bridie insisted on it.

"Of course! I require coffee! Why, in heaven's name, would you call me in here at such an ungodly hour?"

"Been talking to backers, and they're a little skittish. I'm at the halfway point. So, Kendall. You? You can cover the other half?"

Michael appeared to be the only person in the room who didn't understand. He turned to his wife and wordlessly gestured for a translation.

"He's only been able to raise half of the money we need," Leigh explained quietly. "He wants . . ." But she didn't need to finish that sentence. Kendall was cackling already. Half the money for this play would be more than she had spent in all the years she had run Wonderland. Her belly laugh echoed in the room. She didn't need to give an actual answer.

Leigh looked away before she could see Michael's devastation in full bloom. His voice broke as he turned to Harry and pleaded, "I didn't realize you had started trying to raise money." Harry didn't offer to keep raising funds. He cleaned his glasses for a long time and then continued.

"Look, we need to be realistic here. Not only do we not have enough money, we don't even have a Broadway house. And I seriously doubt that we're going to get one this late in the season. But here's the thing: if a Broadway house opens up, we have to have the cash to grab that chance by the balls. You understand?"

Wasn't it time to leave? It sure felt like leaving time.

"Well, Harry. Thank you for trying," Leigh said. "I'm sure I speak for everyone here when I say that we truly appreciate—" She was reaching across the table, extending her hand for a classic, strong, good-sport kind of handshake. Harry looked at her hand, but didn't take it.

"Whoa. Where you going so fast, kiddo? Sit, sit, sit. We're not done here."

Leigh looked to Michael, who might be trying to salvage his Oscar speech, to Kendall, who was wiping her eyes as she wrapped up her laughing fit, and Bridie, who looked too Bridie for Leigh to look at for long. Leigh sat.

Leigh, Kendall, and Bridie all seemed to understand that it was time to hand the floor over to Harry. But Michael pointed to Harry and shouted out *"Monsieur Goofy!"* which came across like name-calling at a little old man's expense.

"Beg pardon?" Harry asked.

"You're going to raise the money from your Jerry Lewis show, aren't you? That's what all this is leading up to. Right? Am I right?"

"No. I won't see any money from that for at least two years. At least. And when I do see money from that, I'm using it to go to Acapulco before I put it in another show. No offense." Harry had completely undone Michael, who dropped his head into his hands. Leigh absently patted her husband to give comfort, while she tried to get a read on Harry.

Harry stood up, increasing his height by inches. He walked the room and worked the crowd like a TV lawyer. His audience followed him around and around.

"We need another investor."

Kendall played off him, like the good prosecutor. "New plays are notoriously difficult to launch. Even with a name like Bridie Hart above them. If *you* can't find the investors, no one can."

Now it was Harry's turn.

"But I look at the four of you, here in my office, and I don't give up. I think this could still happen—because of one person, and I only need to say her first name: Bridie. Everyone knows who you are, what you've done. Kendall's absolutely right, your name will sell tickets. You're a star. And that's no bullshit."

Leigh wondered why Bridie wasn't gushing. She was quiet. She was squinting at Harry and pursing her lips. It wasn't like her to reject a compliment.

"Oh." Bridie had figured something out. Kendall let out a small laugh. She got it, too. Whatever it was, neither one of them liked it.

Michael wasn't watching his mother-in-law. He was craning around, watching Harry give his speech. Finally, he said, "So? Are we doing the show or what?"

Harry circled back to his desk. "That's up to Bridie. My dear, *you* can back this production. You've got money socked away in Swiss banks and Cayman Islands, I'm sure of that. You could back it and make a fortune if it runs. Meanwhile, I'll help you. I'll still act as producer, and make the whole thing run smooth. What do you say, Bridie? I think you could be sitting with a winner here."

Kendall looked shocked and disgusted. She covered her mouth as if she were nauseous. Leigh wondered why Michael looked so happy. Didn't he know that Bridie was going to say "No. Sorry. I will never put my own money in a show. Not even a sure thing. Never."

Michael let out a strangled "aargh" kind of noise. It didn't sound healthy, and it forced Bridie to direct the rest of her answer to him.

"I invested in a show once and I lost everything. Harry knows that perfectly well. I will never make that mistake again. Don't even start, don't even try. I will never, ever put my own money in a show." She turned back to Harry, lowering her voice to a growl. "You should know better than to ask." Harry retreated to his desk.

"But, Bridie," Michael pleaded. "You love this show. You have to do this show. Please," was the best Michael could argue.

Bridie took his hand and used her softest Mother Love voice on Michael. "Michael, dear. I can't. Besides, do you know what they call a production where the star is paying for everything? A vanity production. That doesn't sound like a very nice term, does it?" She lifted his chin to ensure that he was listening. "I, for one, don't take a star seriously once she does a vanity production. And besides, being the investor—it confuses her role with everyone involved in the production. Is she part of the team? Or is she everyone's boss? It's too hard to say. I'm sorry, Michael. But I can't do it. It would be wrong."

Leigh hated how impressive her mother sounded. It actually worked. No one, not even Michael, could argue with the warm, wise witch at the center of them all. Was she quoting from some old *Mother Love* chat? No. Impossible. Kendall rose and looked ready to shake hands and bid farewell. Leigh copied her.

"Michael, let's go home. Sometimes you just have to cut your losses. And I don't think there's anything more that Harry can do for us today. Am I right, Harry?" When Michael stood up, he looked as if he could beg for the life of this play. Harry shook his head as he stood up. His standing up looked like a punctuation mark. They were done. Period.

"No. Not if Bridie isn't opening her checkbook and Kendall's overdrawn. No. I'm sorry, kids. This is some tough shit."

Harry was escorting Leigh and Michael out the door, but Bridie sat atop Harry's antique desk.

"I'm still waiting for my coffee. Do the bunnies who work for you have short-term-memory issues, Harry?" Ah, that was Bridie's real voice.

Leigh tried to rush Michael along, but somehow Michael couldn't make himself leave the magnificent town house to face the gray New York morning outside. He lingered in the front room and complained, "I was so close. This was my dream and I almost achieved it. I can't believe she wouldn't back the play."

This was his dream? Really? How many other secret dreams did he have? Did they all involve raising large sums of cash and trying to force Leigh to work with her mother? Leigh gulped down her resentment and tried once more to move Michael closer to the door.

"You wrote a play. And that's really impressive. You should be so, so, so proud of yourself." Leigh used both hands to make sure he was looking into her eyes. "Lots of people talk about doing things like that, but you actually did it. Don't let this stuff undermine your achievement. Hey. Let's get some coffee and talk about it."

Michael was listening closely, and seemed to be formulating one big thought from Leigh's words. When the big thought was ready, he said, "I'm going back in there."

The beautiful assistants were not quick enough to stop Michael as he opened the door to Harry's office. Leigh followed him, and managed to hear Bridie yelling at Harry, "... and if you ever put me in that position again—"

"*I'll* do it!" Michael announced. "I believe in this play, and I'll back it."

Leigh tried not to panic. She knew that they didn't have half the cash they'd need to back a Broadway play. Maybe he didn't realize just how much would be needed. Harry must have had the same thought, because he smiled, leaned back in his chair, and looked so tickled. He put his feet up on his desk and said, "Okay, kiddo, how much you got?"

Michael crossed to the center of the scene.

"Five hundred thousand dollars." He sounded so proud, Harry was shamed into swallowing his laugh. Leigh was quickly doing arithmetic on their retirement funds. Michael was planning to bankrupt them, wasn't he. Fortunately, Leigh knew that this sum wasn't even close to being enough for a Broadway play.

"Come. Sit." Harry looked like he was ready to teach Michael a mathematics/life lesson. Michael sat on the edge of a side chair near Harry's desk.

"Let me teach you a little something." Hah. Leigh was right. She lingered in the doorway while her husband sat attentively by Harry.

"You can put your hands on half a million. Good for you. That'll get us going for the rehearsals and the run in Florida. But you'll need to do that six times if you want to rent a Broadway house, hire Broadway-level actors, build the sets, costumes, all those fancy hats, put lights on them, what am I forgetting?"

Leigh wished that Michael looked more defeated. Instead he looked happy. Why? Harry kept talking, and none of it was good.

"There's insurance, of course. That's a chunk of change. Did you want to add music? Sound? Want the audience to hear your actors? Then there's advertising. Do you want people to know your show is opening?" Harry took his feet off that nice desk and leaned in to Michael, as if they were alone in the room. "Son, I've run the numbers on this show. You're going to need a good six million dollars just to get started. I've raised three million, and I'm stumped."

Michael seemed to have been the only person in the room who didn't have that ballpark figure in mind. Still, his face glowed with happiness as he asked, "Is that all that stands between us and our production?"

Harry raised his eyebrows, and was a lot more obvious as he swallowed this laugh, saying, "Yes. Just a measly three million bucks between you and Broadway, kid."

"I can get it. I can raise it."

"Michael?" Leigh's voice squeaked as she ran to pull him out of this nightmarish mistake. "Where are you going to get three million dollars?" She shouldn't have asked him that. She should have just pulled him out of the beautiful town house and back to reality.

"I'll mortgage the practice."

Even Bridie blanched. Even Bridie didn't want to see her son-in-law ruin his life for this group ego excursion. Even Bridie.

Kendall called out from the other side of the room. Her deep barking voice took everyone's full attention. "Don't gamble money you can't afford to lose. And you might. There is no such thing as a sure thing. Do you understand me?" Michael didn't respond, but Kendall continued. "Okay, so you have a room full of old theater folk saying that this play of yours is commercial-commercial. But life's funny. Things don't always go the way the experts call it. It happens all the time. You could lose this money. You could lose your practice, your home, everything you own, your work, your father's work. Everything. This is an insane risk. Don't do it."

"Hey, it's been done before," Michael said as he offered the tale of how his father mortgaged the practice in 1983, following a nasty lawsuit that didn't go his way, although it should have. "And the practice is worth more now than ever. It's mine to mortgage if I want to. And I want to. And this is my play. It's my money. This is what I'm doing with it."

His baby. Leigh bit her lip hard.

"I agree with the boy," Bridie announced suddenly. "I think Michael should do it. We should all have such faith in our work. Bravo, Michael."

Michael bowed to a grinning Bridie. Leigh tasted blood on her lip.

"Fine," Harry said. "But. You gotta do one thing. Go home. Sleep on this one before you talk to any banks. Because this, my friend, is the biggest gamble you'll ever play. The odds are against you, and I don't want you and your nice little life on my conscience if this goes bust. I'm too old for that shit. Understand? You promise me you won't do anything for one whole day. Just calm down, sleep on it, see how you feel tomorrow."

Michael rose and shook Harry's hand.

"You got a deal, Harry." He walked out without even checking to see what Leigh was doing. She was frozen in the moment, then raced outside to catch up with her husband.

"Michael! Wait!" she called. He waved to her and shouted back, "I'm late! I'll see you at home! I'm so happy!" And with that, he ducked into a taxi and disappeared into Central Park.

Kendall sidled up beside Leigh and quietly said, "Talk him out of it."

Leigh didn't cook him dinner, because that would have been too obvious. No, she had to keep this simple. She would tell him, calmly and clearly, why it was ridiculously stupid to mortgage his whole life for a play. Leigh ordered Indian food, confident that she could ply him with curry. She ordered too much food, hoping to give Michael that overwhelming sense of plenty. Why would he want to risk all this plenty? She changed her usual jeans and T-shirt for a clingy black dress that was cut so low, she always worried she'd fall out of it. When she sat in a kitchen chair, the cool of the chair reminded her that the back scooped down to the point where you couldn't actually say it had a back.

When her intercom buzzed, Leigh assumed it was her food, and threw a chunky sweater over her dress. But she opened the door to find her motherfucking mother. Maybe Leigh could dismiss her before Michael or the food arrived.

Leigh couldn't deny that Bridie looked like a star, though she wanted to deny her everything, including entry to the apartment. She looked better at the end of the day, as if she had finally had enough time to settle into her face, her body, her clothes. She was a daily late bloomer.

"Is he here? Did he talk to the bank yet? Has he gone completely mad? What do you think?" As if Bridie wanted to hear Leigh's opinion. Of course, she unwrapped herself from a half mile of silk scarf, draped it over a chair, and continued right over Leigh's clumsy beginnings of an answer. "It's been on my mind all day. I went back and forth: Was I wrong to encourage him? Should I make some calls? Not everyone I knew is dead, you know, I still have connections. But they're all in television." Bridie settled herself in the center of the couch, arms outstretched, crucifix-style. It was her I-have-nothing-to-hide pose. Leigh knew it well. "That reminds me: do you think this should be a Lifetime movie? Oh, I just don't know. What time does he come back?"

Bridie leaped from the couch to the liquor cabinet, drawn to it like a moth to cashmere. "Can I help myself to the bar? How would he manage the practice while we're in rehearsals? How does one go about mortgaging a practice? Where are your olives?"

Leigh buzzed in the Indian food deliveryman and let Bridie continue to continue.

"That's what you're feeding your husband? Takeout? Honestly, at least I had cooks giving home-cooked food to my husbands. How do you manage to keep him happy? No, wait, don't answer that." Bridie hid her face demurely behind perfectly manicured hands and cried, "There are some things a mother doesn't want to know. Clearly, he loves you and he trusts you, because he's trusting you with his play. It's his baby, and it's in your hands, right? Are you sure you're ready for this? It's not just a play anymore, honey, it's so much more than that. It's a very big deal. I think he'd be really upset if it failed."

Leigh got as far as letting her mouth fall open when Bridie cut her off with her continued, continued continuing. She waved her fuchsia nails at her daughter as she said, "You know what I mean. It's not just the money, although this morning, I thought that it was all over." Bridie waved a half-full, half-empty bottle of vodka at Leigh and asked, "Is this all you've got?" But she didn't wait for an answer. She poured it over ice and continued. Of course.

"But this boy really, really, really believes in this play. He's a risk taker. Who ever heard of a risk-taking dentist? I mean, a successful one. Remember Barton? My fourth husband? That poor sap never took a risk in his life until he met me—and then he dumped all of our money into a turkey musical about 1929. If he hadn't died, I'd have killed him. Anyway. Your hubby is full of surprises, that's for sure. I always said he'd make a good first husband, and I think that I'm being proved right." She looked at Leigh over her glass, then lowered it and asked, "What? Why are you looking at me like that? It's a *compliment,* for God's sake!"

Leigh could hear Michael opening the door. She took the opportunity to tell her mother, "Will you please now shut up? For at least ten seconds? Please?"

Bridie swallowed the rest of her drink in wounded silence. Leigh stashed her chunky sweater over Bridie's silk road and greeted Michael, who seemed to need no curry, no drink, no nothing to lift his spirits. He kissed Leigh, obviously unaware of his mother-in-law's presence.

"I did it! I called the bank! You wouldn't believe how much money I can borrow against the practice!" And another kiss that made it obvious that he was still unaware of his mother-in-law's presence. Leigh jumped as she felt a cold bottle of champagne against her back.

"Sorry!" He laughed and put the bottle on the table. "Hey, you ordered Indian? Oh, God, I love you!" This time, Bridie interrupted before Michael could kiss his wife again.

"Are we celebrating? Fabulous! I'll get the plates and forks and put it all on the table." Bridie made it sound like quite a task. "We've got a lot to talk about, we three. Leigh, you should have invited Kendall and Harry. What were you thinking?"

Bridie exited for the kitchen, and Leigh seized her chance to say, "Michael. I thought you were going to give this a day." But Michael was too busy pouring champagne to hear her. She waited for him to look, to speak, to stop celebrating, but it didn't happen. She put her sweater back on and watched Bridie labor over the setting of plates.

"Let me help!" Michael bounced over to Bridie and helped lay out silverware and paper napkins. When the table was set, he opened all the food and took in the spicy smells with a theatrical inhale. Leigh realized that he had missed, or chosen to miss, her words. Maybe she should let it go, and give him a day to wake up.

They sat to eat, with Bridie cooing, "This kind of dinner makes me feel like a kid again! We used to stretch a dinner of spaghetti and meatballs for days and days." Michael and Bridie traded stories of youthful penny-pinching, while Leigh saw a pile of money ($3 million, to be exact) hovering like a storm cloud over the dinner table. She said nothing. The money reshaped itself into a large elephant, climbed into the center of the table, and crushed the tandoori chicken as Leigh realized that Michael was saying, "And Leigh—be sure you call James tomorrow. I'm not trying to tell you how to do your job, but hey, we don't want to lose him, he seems fantastic!"

With that, Leigh dropped her fork loudly against her plate, while her face registered disbelief and horror. Bridie and Michael stopped their conversation for a dramatic beat in Leigh's direction, then returned to each other.

"So. As I was saying . . ." Bridie launched another speech, another story, another opinion. It continued past Leigh's exit, collapse into bed, and forever.

$$\begin{bmatrix} 5 \end{bmatrix}$$

$\mathcal{L}$eigh?" Michael called from the kitchen. "What time do we need to be at the auditions? Sorry, I think you told me that already, but I forgot."

"Ten o'clock," Leigh called from the bedroom as she pulled her good jeans on, the dark ones with no paint stains. As she pulled her head through her black T-shirt, she realized that these days, Michael wasn't even in the same room with her if she wasn't fully dressed.

"Ten o'clock. Right. Sorry."

Leigh entered the kitchen and foraged for some breakfast. Michael nearly choked on his food as he said, "Oh! I took the last bagel. Sorry."

"It's okay. I'll get something on the way."

"Sorry."

"Michael. Stop apologizing. It's just a bagel. Right?"

"Right. Sorry."

* * *

Tilden Associates Casting had many rooms, and today one of them was dedicated to the auditions for *Women in Hats*. The room was a large neutral space, with a few simple pieces of furniture for actors to use: chairs, tables, a small platform that served as a stage area. There was a concentration of bright halogen lights above the stage area. There were professional-looking cameras in the back of the room, ready to videotape the auditions, and an enormous plasma screen where recorded auditions could be viewed.

Less than three weeks had passed since Leigh, Michael, and Bridie had signed contracts with Harry Greenwald. Leigh tiptoed through an attempt to slow Michael down, but he signed anyway, and she followed suit. Leigh hired James immediately, at her husband's insistence—at his energetic insistence—so she had no reason to feel guilty. Meanwhile, every agent in town had already received the cast breakdown and scenes to give their actors. The play was no longer a family discussion. It was out in the world. Like a virus.

At Wonderland, Leigh was accustomed to open calls that resembled *American Idol* nightmares. She became very accomplished at working the phones to finesse real actors into working for laughable pay in a run-down old theater. There was something permanently high school in having to beg favors like that. But Harry Greenwald played only with the grown-ups, and that was why Leigh, Michael, and James were sitting in Tilden's posh offices. Three different interns brought them cucumber-flavored water. It was so delicious, Leigh wished she had dressed better.

"I feel like I should have gotten a haircut before I came here," James confessed.

Leigh did her best to dismiss any such worries on his part while she primped her own hair. Her overgrown bangs were starting to impede her line of vision.

"You guys! Look!" Michael was exploring the video equipment at the back of the room.

"What's that for?" James asked as he joined the exploration.

"Okay, this—this is for videotaping." Michael pointed to the large camera on a tripod and James nodded along. Michael picked up a heavy silver rectangle with wires attached to it. "And this— this is for, um, I think it has to do with sound. Or color. Anyway. So, we get to tape the actors in their auditions?"

"Why do we need to tape them?" James asked. "Why don't we just look at them?"

"We'll look at the *tapes*," Michael explained.

"Why don't we look at them while they're right here. In the room. With us."

Michael looked genuinely angry. Leigh turned to watch them, and wondered why she couldn't step between them. Maybe it was best to let the boys fight it out.

"We should be able to review the auditions afterward if we want to," Michael reasoned in a reasonable voice.

"I've never done that." James shrugged.

"It's not that complicated. Pretty basic technology."

James raised both hands in a don't-shoot-me pose and sat in the front of the room, next to Leigh. Michael stayed behind the camera to explore the techno-toys.

Joseph Tilden, former-male-model-turned-accomplished-casting-director, entered. He still looked like a male model, and there was no way he didn't know that. He was silver-haired, golden-throated, and designer-dressed. He sailed to the front of the room and found Leigh and James examining the perfectly coiffed heads smiling up at them from a pile of headshots. Leigh suddenly realized that she was patting her own hair into submission again.

"Ah, you're looking through the headshots, I see. I'm Tilden. Joseph Tilden. You must be Leigh Majors, and you've got all my sympathy over that name, my dear." He squeezed Leigh's hand as if he were testing for bionic parts. Leigh took her hand back and quietly checked for broken bones while Tilden grinned and reached for James's hand. "And you must be our playwright, Michael. And you two are married, are you? Say, it takes some nerve, working together like this. You must really be in love."

"I'm James. McGovern. I'm the stage manager."

Tilden shook his head and laughed. "You're a stage manager? Somebody told me you were a dentist. I guess it makes more sense for a stage manager to write a play than a dentist. That sounded so absurd, I should have known it was wrong."

"Hey!" Michael called out from the back of the room.

Leigh nursed her injured hand and did her best to explain Tilden's faux pas: James = stage manager / friend; Michael = playwright / husband.

"Well. Don't I feel foolish?" Tilden said with no hint of foolishness. "And is this play going to move to Broadway?"

"Yes!" Michael declared.

"Maybe," Leigh said, more to Tilden than to Michael. "Depends on how things go with the out-of-town run."

"Pressure!" Tilden smiled at Leigh as he said it. "Listen, my staff has been handling everything for me. Can I get a quick look at your cast breakdown?"

Leigh looked around her. She had the sheet in her canvas messenger bag, but before she could grab it, James was shuffling a stack of papers he had attached to his clipboard, and Michael was reaching for his briefcase. They raced to deliver the sheet of paper to Tilden. Michael won, but Leigh suspected that James let him win.

Tilden studied the sheet for half a minute at most, while Leigh and Michael read over his shoulder:

WOMEN IN HATS
CAST BREAKDOWN

Margaret: *This role is cast. Bridie Hart.* 50-something female. She is matriarch of the family. Glamorous, outspoken, strong, but loving. Margaret is a survivor who landed on her feet and created a successful business after her husband left her. She insists on her son taking over the business, but must learn to let her grown son make his own choices in life.

Maxwell: 18-year-old male. Handsome, gentle, a bit too mild for his own good. He reveres his mother, feels greatly indebted to her. But his heart's desire is to become a great dentist. By the end of the play, he has become his own man.

Sarah: 18-year-old female, romantic interest for Maxwell. She is physically petite, but strong-voiced. She is wise beyond her years, as she heals the rift between mother and son, and takes on the mother's business.

Grace: 55 to 65-year-old female. She is the best friend and confidante of Margaret. Very warm and maternal. She is gentler and softer than her friend, but can stand up to her when necessary. She is funny and wise. Could be played by an older actress who is overweight.

Ted: 50-something male. Maxwell's father. Supportive and helpful. But finds himself in over his head when he takes on Margaret. Bit of a country bumpkin in the big city, but good-hearted.

"Yes. That makes sense." Tilden handed the sheet back to Michael and returned his attention to his wayward cuff while he said, "We've got a busy day ahead of us, so let's not waste time with anyone who isn't right, okay? They're all professionals, so just cut them loose and let them move on."

Leigh was in the middle of agreeing, of enjoying the professional atmosphere, when she heard the elevator doors open and that Ethel Merman voice call out, "Where should we go? Do you have the sides? Come on, darling, chop-chop! You can coast for just so long on that pretty face. Eventually, someone's going to want you to *do* something. Start now!"

Oh, God, Bridie was in the lobby. Who else would say "chop-chop!" in the twenty-first century? Leigh sank down in her chair while James rose and opened the door to their little haven, letting the devil in. Noisy Bridie took a quiet hug and kiss from Michael. She wore reds, golds, and pumpkin tones, perfectly coordinated with the new fall season. Kendall was trailing after Bridie, looking out of place and completely sick of Mother Love.

"Are we late? My fault entirely." She was wearing fur, even though the weather didn't call for it and she knew Leigh hated fur. She wore it over trendy jeans and some sort of silk wrap top that was so complicated, it must have come with directions. She draped the fur casually over a chair and talked to everyone and no one in particular. "I had a late start and then I bumped into Charles Cairo. And before you start lecturing that he's too young for me, I know that already. But *he* doesn't seem to know it. He flirts shamelessly, just outrageously. Of course, I told him that he needed a shave and a haircut, not to mention a new shirt. All the money that boy makes, and he seems to think that dirty hair and old clothes are chic. It's absurd. Nothing beats Armani on a man. Nothing."

Kendall took a seat halfway through the speech and took a stack of scenes and sides from James. They whispered to each other and Leigh would have given a major organ to hear what they were saying. James nodded and smiled. Kendall looked pleased.

What did they say? Leigh couldn't hear over Bridie's ongoing blather.

"Hello, you must be Joseph Tilden. I think we met years ago, didn't we? At a party in L.A.? If we didn't, we should have. I'm Bridie Hart." Bridie took his hand and held it close to her complicated top. "We're so delighted to be working with you today. I do hope you've got the A-list actors coming to read today. We have so many parts to cast, and we want only the best—right down the line. Isn't that right, Michael? This play represents such a wonderful opportunity for so many actors. It's exciting, isn't it?" She finally relinquished his hand and looked around the room, impatient and confused. "Well, Leigh. What are we waiting for? Let's get started."

Tilden seemed so entertained, but Leigh reacted as if she were down one quart of blood. She pulled herself up and said, "Take a breath," a bit louder than she should have. Leigh knew that she was advising only herself, but she soon realized that everyone had to think that her instructions were aimed at Bridie, who truly should have stopped for a breath. But Bridie didn't receive it well.

"What did you say to me?" Bridie asked in her lower register.

"I was talking to myself."

"Well, don't. People will wonder about your upbringing." She left her daughter no time to select a tangy, sarcastic response. "Let's get to work. Where do you want me?" Bridie asked.

"Gosh." Leigh batted her eyes at her mother. "For years I've dreamed of answering that question for you." She smiled, grateful for the renewed shot at sarcasm.

"Hi. I'm Kendall Epstein. You're Joseph Tilden? I've heard a lot about you." They shook hands, and she didn't register any pain from it.

"I've heard even more about you," Tilden said. "Why haven't we worked together before?" He sounded like a spurned lover.

Kendall smiled demurely and answered, "I can't afford you."

He bowed graciously as Kendall found herself a seat at the end of the second row. Tilden escorted Bridie to a seat at the other end of the front row. He made sure that everyone had the scenes that Leigh had selected for the auditions and plenty of cucumber water. In exactly ten minutes, they would begin.

Leigh sat in front of Kendall, right between James and Michael in the front row. She kept herself centered and aligned, consciously trying to avoid leaning toward either man. Such a professional.

Tilden paced behind them all. As each actor entered the room, he rose and greeted them, made introductions, and occasionally chatted with actors he knew personally. Leigh felt that the first three actors were shockingly good, while Bridie offered direction to each of them.

"Show me more colors! This is entirely too autumnal, darling. Warm it up to summer."

Or: "Can't you be more fluid with your face?"

Or: "Read it again, sweetheart, and this time—be interesting."

Leigh started with a subtle "Please, Bridie. Just let them read." Then she tried a simple "Shhhhh," and ended with a "Don't listen to her," aimed directly at the actor who responded by rolling his eyes toward the ceiling, and Leigh clutched James's arm. He nodded, and she knew that he had seen it, too.

Kendall thrust a small note in front of Leigh that read, "Make your mother STOP."

"Everyone?" Leigh called out. "Can we take a ten-minute break before the next actor?"

"Sure." Tilden seemed so casual, so everyday about this. He unfolded his lanky body and brought news of the delay to the receptionists in the lobby.

Bridie rose, indignant. "Leigh, we've got to get to the *good* actors soon. We don't have time for you to sulk."

Kendall leaned and whispered so close to Leigh's ear, her lips touched it as she said, "She will scare the good actors away. What are you going to do about it?"

Leigh had no idea how long she stood and stared at her mother, and wondered if it looked odd to anybody else.

"What? Do I have something in my teeth? Why are you staring at me?" Bridie asked. "Can we get back to work now?"

Leigh broke her stare when she heard James say, "I have an idea, Bridie, I'm obviously not reading Margaret very well." This brought an actual snort from Michael, who added, "I'll say."

James must have heard that, but he continued. "So why don't *you* read it, Bridie? I think that would just make every difference in the world."

Leigh might have kissed James, except that she must never kiss him. Ever. She returned to her seat and smiled at him as professionally as she could. Bridie strode to center stage and purred, "Let me show you how it's done."

Bridie became so caught up in her own performance, she didn't manage to direct any other actors. Oh, sure, when they auditioned the Maxwells, Bridie managed to break out of her performance long enough to make the same Mrs. Robinson joke to each actor. "Maybe we could do *The Graduate* and I could seduce you. Do you want me to seduce you?" Each actor laughed uncomfortably.

When they auditioned the Sarahs and the Graces, Bridie's demeanor changed entirely, but Leigh had anticipated that. Bridie needed to have a Sarah who was short and, ideally, flat-chested. She needed a Grace who was at least fifteen pounds heavier than herself, and refused to permit the role to be cast younger than sixty. "Sixty-*looking*. I don't care about their damn birthdays. I want them to *look* sixty."

By the time they saw the last actor, Bridie was showing clear signs of wear and tear. Her makeup had faded and her voice was hitting a much lower pitch. She looked older than usual.

"Michael?" Leigh had nearly forgotten that he wasn't just part of the furniture. "Can you take Bridie home? James and I need to sort through the pictures. I want to make decisions about the actors while they're still fresh in my mind."

"Yes, Michael." Bridie snuggled into her fur. "Take me home, but first let's pick up my dear friend, Mr. Johnnie Walker. Okay? I'll just freshen up a bit. Meet me in the lobby."

It took Leigh this long to notice that Michael looked like he had been hit by a city bus. His eyes had sunk deep, and the dark circles under them were the only color his skin retained. She didn't even realize that she was hugging him, then checking his eyes for signs of life.

"Michael. Don't let my mother take you drinking. Drop her off and go home."

"Sorry, Leigh, but I can't just leave her at some bar!" he insisted.

"I mean it. Don't be a gentleman. Don't be her escort. She knows how to drink all by herself. Believe me. Drop her off and go home. Drop her off and go home. Drop her off and go home." Would a three-time repetition be magic? Leigh was 60 percent certain that it would work.

Bridie danced into the room, a new woman, revived by a bright lipstick that must have been named Red Bull.

"Leigh, sweetie, before I steal your husband, let me help you out." With that, she tried to pull the actor headshots Leigh was clutching. She pulled. She pulled. Leigh studied her mother's lipstick and pretended that no one was pulling at her actors.

"Leigh. Will you for heaven's sake let go?" Leigh had to close her eyes as she handed the headshots to Bridie. "Honestly, I'm just trying to save you a little time. You look awful, you know. You should go straight home, and don't wait up for Michael and me. Meanwhile. Here."

And inside of twenty-three seconds, she assembled a stack of photos that represented "the perfect cast, well, actually, the best cast from what we saw today. Here. Have one of the little front-office chippies phone them tonight. We don't have any time to waste. Come along, Michael. I want to introduce you to some friends of mine. You'll adore them. They'll like you. Good night, all. Lovely working with you today!"

Bridie was out of the room, and Michael looked jazzed and ready to follow her. Leigh pulled on his arm.

"Drop her off and go home, drop her off and go home," Leigh urged. She reached up to kiss him, but Bridie called out, "Michael!" and he jumped forward at the electric zap of her voice. Leigh's kiss fell in the air.

The room was hollow and quiet after Bridie's departure. Kendall had been sitting and watching all this time. She rose from her chair slowly, letting her joints adjust to the new position in their own time.

"Leigh. Can you handle one more opinion, or is your head going to explode?"

"Opinion me," Leigh answered.

"You know how to cast this. You saw a lot of good people and a handful of duds. But you have plenty of actors to choose from in each role. Okay, don't hire that aging hippie chick who read for Grace, but other than that, you'll be fine. Your only casting problem will be Margaret."

"But Margaret's already cast," James ventured. "It's Bridie. Isn't it?" James may have been a little slow on the uptake here, but Leigh understood. She explained to James, "Bridie's poison. She's got the potential to poison the cast."

"Don't be so dramatic, Leigh." Kendall laughed. "She can undermine your authority. Nice save from your stage manager today, getting her to read. But when rehearsals begin, it'll be on *you* to get her in line. She may be your mother, but you're her boss now.

You're her director. Say it every morning in the mirror ten times. Carry a gun and a whip to rehearsals. Do whatever you have to do. Don't let her take over."

Kendall pulled on her worn leather jacket, looked warily at the elevator, then said quietly, "Do you think they're in a cab by now? I've had my fill of Bridie Hart for today."

.   .   .

It was dark outside and Leigh and James were alone. They sat in the front row, sorting photos, and somehow Leigh didn't feel tired anymore. She made a proposal.

"If we leave the building, we can't get back in, and then we'll have to come back tomorrow to finish. So, I say, let's stay here tonight and cast this thing. We've got enough good actors. We can do it."

"They say that seventy-five percent of directing is casting. So, let's get to work." He agreed.

"Let's not try to do seventy-five percent of my job on an empty stomach. Let's order dinner first."

She made it sound like they'd be up all night building a science fair volcano. But he had to know that this wasn't going to take very long. The best actors were obvious choices, and none of them landed in Bridie's pile of actors.

James took the headshots and made a series of piles on the floor, one for each role to be cast, while hungry Leigh ordered enough sandwiches and side dishes to feed all the actors.

Leigh picked up the headshot for Harmony Hecht, the aging hippie chick who had been reading the role of Grace and massacring it. She held the photo like a mask and impersonated the fake British accent that Leigh had been unable to talk her out of.

"Oh, Maaaahgaret, how aaaaah you managing this loverly hat shawp?" Leigh giggled.

. . .

They ignored the furniture and made a picnic for themselves on the small stage. They both wolfed down their sandwiches. Leigh wanted to ask him all manner of inappropriate questions. Was that a fleck of gold in his iris? Did he get that strong jaw from his mother's side or his father's? Why did his hair look perfect, even when it was a mess? Did he notice that she touched his arm too much? Did he have a girlfriend? What was his history? Could she touch his arm again? She started with, "So why don't you like technology?"

"That's an exaggeration, I'm okay with technology."

"Do you have a computer?"

He shook his head.

"Cable?"

He shook his head harder and was starting to laugh.

"A cell phone?"

"I don't need one. But hey, I know how to use the fax machine at Wonderland. Most of the time. I think I just move a hell of a lot slower than all this technology allows."

"Most stage managers love gadgets and contraptions and labor-saving devices. You're different." Leigh posed that as a question, and he took it as one.

"I don't like things that are designed just to get between me and real people. Why does anyone e-mail when they could call or go over and talk to the person? Why do we need a thousand television stations? If we really need entertainment that much, why not go see some live theater? I sound like an old fart, I know." He was offering to share his potato chips when he said, "When I was married, I felt like my wife kept me at arm's length the whole time. Like she knew how it was going to end. Like she was protecting herself right from the start. Machines can help you do that. I don't like it. I prefer actual people." He stopped to laugh at himself. "I can't believe I'm going on and on like this. You cast a spell on me, Leigh Majors. Do I sound like some kind of blast from the past?"

"You sound sweet." Leigh wanted so badly to kiss him, to keep him that close all the time. Hey, wait a minute. He had been married?

"You're lucky," he continued. "You and Michael."

Leigh held her breath for a minute. The "lucky" line had never ended that way before. She couldn't answer it, so she ate and ate and ate. So did James.

Leigh came up for air and managed to ask, "So, what were you and Kendall discussing?" He didn't seem to remember. "Before we started? You and Kendall? What was up?" He was still jogging his memory, and Leigh hastily added, "Sorry, I thought it was about the show. You can tell me it's none of my business."

James finally remembered. "Oh, yes. We were talking about the house manager that you hired to be my assistant stage manager. Anyway, Kendall said her name was Maddie, I think, and she wanted to make sure I was okay with it. And I am. She sounds like a fantastic girl."

Leigh put down the last few bites of her sandwich. "Did I step on your toes by hiring her? I meant to tell you—she really needs the work. And you'll love her, I promise!" Leigh said quickly.

"I'm sure I will."

· · ·

"Okay, so we've got the men cast. That was so painless." Leigh selected a first, second, and third choice actor for each role. If none of these actors accepted the role (Leigh didn't like to think about why they would reject it/her), she would hold further auditions. The rest of the actors she deemed unacceptable.

"Here. I'll put your first three choices at the top of the pile for each role." James was organizing everything. He had to know this was the fastest way to Leigh's heart. "Now we've got to cast Sarah and Grace." He dumped the two piles of photos on the floor between them.

"Here comes the pain," Leigh sighed. "It's like a seventeen-way tie for both roles."

"Maybe not. You've only got a handful of actors who've done this kind of play before. That experience should tip the scales, right?"

When did James find the time to read each person's résumé so thoroughly? They sifted through the women until, once again, they had a first, second, and third choice for the roles, followed by a stack of no-way-do-we-hire-them actresses relegated to the bottom of the pile. It was done. It was late, and even though Leigh wanted to linger awhile with James, she couldn't deny how tired he looked and she felt. He gathered the pictures and left their little sanctuary.

"This was the easiest casting session I've ever had. I have to remember to e-mail Tilden with a big thanks," Leigh said as she strode to the lobby, deserted except for James, who was already handwriting a note to Joseph Tilden.

"Not me. I don't have e-mail, remember?" He shrugged and returned to his pen and paper. "Thanks for a terrific casting session," his note began.

Leigh disposed of the last crumbs of their dinner, while James left handwritten instructions for the receptionists:

> *The first three headshots for each role are the director's first three choices for that role. Please contact the first choice, offer the role, and move through to the second and third choices, if necessary.*

Leigh had him add:

> *If none of the top three are available for the role, don't call any*
> *of the others. We'll hold another casting session, if necessary.*
> *Thanks for the use of the hall.*
>
> James McGovern

"Oh, my God. Where are the Sarahs? I have everyone else. I don't have the Sarahs!" James sounded as if he had lost a puppy.

"Right here!" Leigh rushed them over to James and added them to his giant picture stack.

Oh, God. He was looking into Leigh's eyes as they stood toe-to-toe. This was The Moment. She wished he would put down the pictures because, after all, this was such a Moment. If he pulled her close and kissed her the way that he so obviously wanted to, he'd drop the pictures and make a mess. That would ruin the moment. Put down the pictures, already. She looked up and knew that his height gave her that flattering good-angle pose. So perfect for . . . The Moment. He inched closer to her.

"Wait." It was Leigh speaking. She couldn't believe herself.

"You changed your mind?" He was still holding the damn pictures.

"Yes. No. I never made up my mind."

"But I thought you did. I thought—"

"You thought wrong, and I'm really, really sorry. Let's just say this all right now and get it over with. I'm so attracted to you, and I like you way too much. It scares me." She noticed that James took a step back, but her words were still tumbling out. "I'm scared because it's wrong and because it's what my mother would do, and that's pretty much the litmus test for wrong. And my poor husband, Michael. I think we can make it past this little bump. As long as you and I don't . . . you know . . ."

"What?" Poor James. He looked so confused.

"Not that you're a little bump. You're James, and you're so wonderful. And I really hope that you'll still want to work with me, even though I can't do this."

"Can't do what?" It took Leigh all this time to realize that James had no idea that he was supposed to be having his heart broken. He looked like he was trying not to smile at the deluded woman standing too close to him. She wilted as she faded back to the door.

"Oh, no. Oh, no. Oh, no." She was unable to move back in time and undo this. "Oh, my God. I have to go. Now."

"Wait! Leigh! It's okay, please don't be embarrassed."

Why did he have to say that word? Now she was a walking, brainless blob of embarrassment. She held the elevator button, hopeful that this technique would summon the elevator faster. She kept her back to James as she instructed, "Please, just take care of the headshots and I'll see you at rehearsal. Please. Leave me alone."

"Come on, Leigh. Talk to me."

Leigh had been holding that damn button for a month when the elevator door finally opened. She had to turn and face him until the door closed again. He wasn't smiling anymore. He moved toward the elevator, and bravely reached in to stop the closing door, but then he pulled his fingers back from near amputation. Leigh watched the door close on the sight of James clutching the headshots. He had no business looking so sad. That was Leigh's turf.

Leigh was crying before she reached the sidewalk. She walked home to cry herself out before Michael could see her. When she walked into an empty apartment, she let herself cry a bit more.

6

There was only one thing to do: pretend it never happened. Pretend she never semi-sort-of threw herself at her stage manager. Pretend she never wrecked their working relationship, contemplated betraying her husband, and humiliated herself beyond redemption. Leigh had never suffered through adolescent crushes when she was an actual adolescent. Was it coming back to haunt her now? No, no, no. Just pretend it never happened. That was the mature, grown-up thing to do.

Leigh resolved to avoid saying the name "James" at all costs. Fortunately for her, Michael spent the day after the auditions nursing a Bridie Hart hangover. She waited until he had been up for a few hours to say (very, very quietly), "I asked Harry for a few days with the cast here in New York, so that you have a chance to hear the play out loud."

Michael twitched a bit. He had been a statue on the couch for so much of the day, the twitch stood out. Something bothered him about "hear the play out loud." What was it? She decided to explain why she was disrupting his painful quiet.

"When you hear the play, it's easy to find where you might want to make changes. Then you can e-mail them or fax them to me in Florida."

Michael found a surge of energy to turn to her and ask, "When did we decide that I'm not going to Florida?"

"We never did." Leigh waited for Michael to state a preference; but he stayed silent. "But that's okay. Let's decide now. Can you leave New York and keep the practice going?" She sat on the arm of the couch and combed through his hair with her fingers. "If you could go, it could be so wonderful for us. What do you think?"

Michael lifted his empty coffee cup to Leigh and asked, "Can you bring me more?"

. . .

That evening, when the phone rang in her living room, Leigh let the answering machine pick up. It was Tilden.

"Leigh, Joseph Tilden here. Good news. We've heard back from all of your first-choice actors and they all accepted. Now, how often does that happen?"

Leigh was happy enough to reach for the phone and talk to him. Before she got there, she heard him say, "Of course, I should add that I was more than a little surprised by some of your choices."

Leigh stepped back from the phone.

"But you're the director. And they say that casting is what—eighty-five percent of the job? You must know what you're doing. Well. Waiting to hear from Greenwald about schedules. Keep me posted if you hear anything, and again—congratulations. Yes."

Tilden didn't like her casting choices? Well, then he should have stuck around with her and Ja—the stage-manager guy—so that he could contribute to the casting decisions and maybe even prevent an awful ending scene that still haunted and humiliated her.

Her fax machine let out an ominous series of beeps and buzzes, and then hummed some paper through. It was from Harry Greenwald. The first page promised that the second page would offer Leigh a tentative schedule. Harry had scribbled "SUBJECT TO CHANGE" on his note, and underlined it three times.

In mid-December, Leigh would have three days of New York rehearsals, mostly table reads. She'd meet the cast, have Ja—the stage manager—take care of travel logistics, and get to hear the play for the first time. It was four weeks away, but it felt like it would be here in a blink.

The cast would go their separate ways for the holidays, then regroup in January to travel to Florida for six weeks of rehearsal, one week of previews, then six weeks of an actual run. Somewhere during that run, Harry and Kendall would decide whether the show was worthy to open on Broadway.

Leigh read all the dates on the fax and just put the paper down, like it was any piece of paper. She flipped through the desk calendar to get a handle on the time frame, and still was unafraid. She made mental notes for time to meet with designers, deadlines for Michael's rewrites. She had it. She owned it. It was a tangible project and she would conquer it.

Michael trudged by on his way to the kitchen. Leigh heard the faucet run, and saw Michael return to bed with a glass of water.

Then she flipped the calendar backward. She wanted to remember the last time she and Michael had had sex. She already knew that if she needed a calendar for that, the answer was bad. Still, she wanted to know.

She flipped the pages back, back, back, before it. They hadn't had sex since before it. No, stop calling it it. The miscarriage. Back to the miscarriage in September. Two months now. If she hadn't bled that morning, or any morning since, where would she be now? Just starting a second trimester. Starting to show. Starting to tell people. How big would the little creature in her belly be?

Leigh slammed her calendar shut and promised that she'd never do that to herself again.

• • •

Michael took it upon himself to make Thanksgiving reservations at Indigo. He was going to spend a disgusting amount of money to feed an excessive amount of food to his parents, his wife, and himself. And Michael would not be dissuaded.

"Don't eat too much breakfast," he warned, which stopped Leigh in midbite. "We're going to have quite a Thanksgiving feast tonight. After all, we have so much to be thankful for."

"But the money, Michael. You've tied up everything in the play. We can't afford anything too lavish."

"It'll be fine. After all, once the play runs and the money starts rolling in, it will all be worth it."

Leigh retreated to the bedroom, where he was sure not to follow her, and took a nap.

• • •

"Leigh? Honey? It's three o'clock."

"AM or PM?"

"You need to get dressed for dinner."

Leigh looked around the monochrome bedroom. Just a minute ago, she had been immersed in a dream of bright colors where she was moving very fast, wanting to move faster. Where had she been exactly? The images flew back to their colorful home, leaving no traces. Michael had laid out Leigh's slinky, low-cut black-on-black dress at the foot of the bed.

* * *

Leigh and Michael were the first of their party to arrive, which was the way Leigh usually did things. Before she was seated in her chair, before the champagne was popped, she noticed that their table had a fifth seat. Who was going to sit there?

"Bridie's coming?"

"Well, yes. Sorry. I thought I told you." He absolutely had not told her. She knew that he knew that she knew he never did.

"About your mother," he continued. "Mom and Dad don't know anything about me investing in the play and how I got the money and all. And I really, truly, don't want you to tell them. Can you make sure your mother doesn't spill the beans? I'm sorry. I know that's a lot to ask."

It was difficult enough to tell Bridie what to say, but it was impossible to tell her what *not* to say. Usually, any forbidden words danced before her eyes until she had to blurt them out. Leigh had a catalog of bad childhood stories where Bridie spoke the most inappropriate words she could find. The time she explained her divorces to Leigh's kindergarten class. The time she told a good-looking waiter that Leigh and Lilly were growing up in Hollywood as children of divorce, and were therefore destined to be promiscuous, according to the latest magazines. The time she told Leigh's prom date that Leigh had her period. The time she gave a stomach-churning description of her hangover on parent-teacher night. The time she offered lurid details of the casting couch on Career Day.

Michael was pouring two glasses of already overpriced champagne, for which they would pay even more because it was Thanksgiving. Leigh tried not to do the math, but she couldn't help it. She didn't want any champagne. But Michael raised his glass, so Leigh raised hers, too. Michael said, "You're what I'm thankful for.

I'm sorry that I never understood before just how brilliant you are, how hard your work is, and how much you care. I'm so lucky."

All of a sudden, the room was brighter, warmer, safer, better. Leigh put down her glass and kissed him and kissed him. She felt his hands brush her back and she was so glad she had worn a dress with so little fabric to it. She was still kissing him when she heard her father-in-law shout, "Hey, you two! Get a room!" from across the restaurant.

Michael and Leigh giggled and cheered and toasted his parents, and wasn't it glorious since Bridie was not there yet? They finished the champagne, then switched to wine, and Bridie was still not there. Hungry and a little drunk, they ordered dinner without Bridie. Leigh had an appetite appropriate for a bear just out of hibernation. She ate her own dinner and enough of Michael's to have fed Bridie, who was *still not there,* so Leigh had extra reason to be thankful. She sat back and watched her husband joke and parry with his father, but no one talked about *Women in Hats* or any other play. Sylvia rolled her eyes and made them stop, already. She told embarrassing childhood stories about Michael (why did he like to paint himself with Magic Marker so much?).

"You know," Dr. Payne Sr. said, "he got his artistic talents from my side of the family. My paintings are still hanging in the reception area."

"And they're classics!" Michael lifted his glass. They praised his father's paintings until it was time to order dessert. Leigh couldn't choose from among the three desserts offered in the prix fixe menu, so she requested all three, and yes, she understood that there would be an additional charge, but she wanted pie, sorbet, *and* cake, please.

"Atta girl! Have your pie and eat cake, too. Or something like that." Michael had been laughing throughout dinner. He looked like a sweet boy.

"HAPPY THANKSGIVING TO YOU ALL!" Bridie called out from the front of the restaurant, making a bold cross to the table before turning to the restaurant crowd and projecting, "GOD BLESS US, EVERY ONE!" Entirely too many people applauded.

Bridie sat down and began lengthy apologies and far-fetched explanations for her tardiness, but she brought them to a tidy finish just in time to order two manhattans from a waiter at a nearby table. "One for now, one for a New York minute from now."

Leigh didn't tense up, didn't sour, didn't slow down on her desserts, didn't scowl at her mother, didn't start an inner speech about the burden that is Bridie. She did fade in and out of Bridie's monologue, however.

"And then George, of course, with those eyes that look like he's looking up at you, even though he towers, absolutely towers, over everyone in the room, and it's just sexy beyond words, especially when he's smiling, because he has the perfect laugh lines, and, well, what was I saying? Never mind. He's a sexy beast. Enough said." Bridie inhaled a manhattan and smiled suggestively at Dr. Payne Sr. She clutched his arm and asked, "Have you ever been to Tahiti?" He hadn't. "Oh, you should go immediately. Book a flight tonight. It changes your view of your body. One month in Tahiti and you'll live in your body for the rest of your life. Do you know what I mean? Live in your body?" Bridie crossed her hands across her chest, then pressed her hands against her thighs. "You must learn to live in your body. It's essential, especially as you get older. It's why everyone thinks I've had work done, which, by the way, I haven't."

Leigh made a point of choking on cake. Michael and his parents howled with laughter, until Bridie slammed her drink to the table, letting it spill. Leigh watched it soak into a gray shadow on the linen. Bridie's fingers snapped a gunshot sound, and another drink was on its way.

Dr. Payne signaled for coffee, and Sylvia recounted a story about when Michael was a toddler and he drew giant eyeglasses around his baby eyes, using laundry marker. Bridie seethed over more manhattans as Sylvia's story got more and more laughs, and Leigh kept eating.

After dinner, Leigh and Michael giggled their way into a cab. But the cab ride lulled them into a drowsy state. The effervescence of the evening evaporated quickly. Finally at home, they yawned into bed, finishing the night with a quick kiss and a heavy sleep.

•   •   •

It was December 16, the date of the first rehearsal for *Women in Hats*. Leigh had been awake for hours when she finally saw some sunlight slicing through the darkness. Michael was smiling in his sleep. Did he always smile in his sleep? As his wife, shouldn't she know that already?

She gave up trying to fall back to sleep, and headed for the kitchen and embraced coffee as her new best friend for the day. She stayed there while Michael showered and got dressed so that he could clear out of the bedroom in time for her to shower and dress as well. He would wait in the living room. He'd probably apologize for a few dozen things that were not his fault, and smile sweetly at his wife. Just like yesterday, just like the day before that.

•   •   •

Leigh watched the actors walk into the rehearsal hall and had to wonder if she had fallen back asleep and was having a classic director's nightmare: she had the wrong cast. Oh no no no no no. This had to be a cruel prank. Where was the hidden camera? They were all bottom-of-the-pile actors, Leigh was absolutely sure. At this point, she was actually able to make eye contact with James and give him a standard *What the fuck?* look. As upset as she was over the hellish parade of actors, she was happy that she didn't have to use any actual words with her stage manager. Yet. She sat down and wondered if the coffee had burned a large hole in her stomach. Something was burning.

Michael was greeting the actors and chatting with them. Bridie was waiting in the building's administrative office so that she could make a proper entrance after all the actors were seated. Maddie saw Leigh's horrified expression and was completely confused. She turned to Leigh and asked, "What could have gone wrong already?"

"Can't say. Tell you later," Leigh whispered. "Can you loan James your cell phone? Tell him to call Tilden." Leigh watched Maddie hand over the phone to James, who nodded to Leigh from his position by the door across the now crowded room. He stepped outside discreetly to ask Tilden the obvious *"What the fuck?"*

Leigh kept chatting carefully with the arriving actors. She had to make sure that she didn't say anything about actually having hired them. She imagined a host of lawyers recording her every word. Maddie could be her witness today. Michael shook hands with each actor in turn.

She looked around for a camera, but she had to admit that she wasn't famous enough for that. James returned rather quickly and he looked like he was now suffering from Leigh's stomach-hole syndrome. He pulled Leigh aside and whispered, "This is my fault. I reversed the pictures."

"What? Why? Why would you do that? Do you hate me so much—"

"It was an accident. I put the stacks upside down, because I was feeling sort of flustered and confused, because of, well—" *If he said anything here, Leigh swore to herself that she would strangle him with the nearest piano wire.* "It doesn't matter why. This is my fault."

Hey, he didn't say anything to humiliate her further. She was measurably grateful for that. Now he just needed to set things right.

"Okay, so we're losing some rehearsal time here, but we'll have to roll with that. Meanwhile, you're the one who got these people hired in the first place, so you can tell them what went wrong, but be gentle, and I'll go to Tilden and get the right—"

James was shaking his head, looking ready to give a really dire prognosis.

"We can't. We're stuck with them. We've made official offers to them. We can't rescind the offers. They can quit, but we can't fire them without due cause. Equity rules."

Leigh looked at her potluck cast. She pushed James aside (was that the first time she had touched his chest?) and slammed herself into a chair. She covered her face and heard two actors whisper sentences with the word *diva* in the middle. Was this better or worse than having them intone "She's so lucky"?

"Leigh? What's the matter?" Michael was asking. But Leigh couldn't say it in front of the cast, so she just let her head fall to the table while the milling chitchat centered on her bad behavior. Why should she care? She was ruined. Wasn't casting at least 90 percent of directing? This play was over before it began.

"Hello, everyone. I'm Bridie Hart."

The actors applauded, even cheered, for Leigh's mother, whose next line was "Leigh, sweetheart, you've taken bad posture to extraordinary heights, but now you can sit up."

But Leigh didn't sit up. She listened to her mother receive each actor and designer in turn. She replayed her Mrs. Robinson joke more than once, and got boffo laughs as usual. Leigh considered staying exactly where she was, exactly as she was, for the rest of the day.

It took a while, but eventually Leigh lifted her head so that she could search the production schedule for something resembling a solution to the casting problem, but the schedule held only tasks and their deadlines. She studied the calendar for a date where she could squeeze in time to repair this damage, but no such day existed. She looked around the room, and she knew she was stuck. She couldn't fire them. She couldn't direct them. She couldn't fix this.

* * *

The read-through began, despite Leigh's panic. James read the stage directions in a calm baritone. Leigh wanted to hate his stupid voice and his stupid, stupid sad eyes searching hers for forgiveness during each of Bridie's monologues. Leigh knew she was sulking as she reassessed her cast. They varied from subterranean bad to mediocre. She hadn't scheduled time for a good cry today, but she needed one. What was it she had figured out a few minutes ago? Oh, yes. She couldn't fire them. She couldn't direct them. She couldn't fix this.

They creaked through the reading, everyone trying to show how good they already were, before rehearsals even began. One of the actors actually surprised her with a bigger supply of charm than she had seen in his audition. The rest were, well, the rest. She couldn't fire them. She couldn't direct them. She couldn't fix this.

James called, "Blackout," and the actors applauded themselves, while Bridie nodded and took the applause for herself.

"Let's break for lunch, shall we?" Bridie decided. "And we can come back by two o'clock."

Now it was James who looked angry and confused. Leigh rose and said, "One o'clock. You will come back at one o'clock."

Bridie made a face that brought giggles from the cast.

Leigh bolted for the door.

· · ·

"Kendall. You have to come to rehearsal. I thought you were going to be here! Why aren't you here?" Leigh was in the middle of Times Square, shouting into her cell phone.

"It's just a read-through. Why? What happened?"

"I got the wrong cast. I keep hoping I'll wake up and it's all just a bad dream. I got the bottom-of-the-pile actors. The no-way-in-hell actors. I'm so fucked."

"Oh, shit. I'll be right there. What's your mother doing?"

"The usual."

"Well, goddammit, Leigh. Don't let her. What are you waiting for? Be in charge, already. You can sort out the casting thing later. Or not. But stop her now."

"Right."

"Now!" Kendall repeated.

· · ·

Leigh confirmed her diva status by returning late to the rehearsal, and bringing her bodyguard, Kendall Epstein. Most of the cast took notice, but Bridie didn't. She had pulled handsome young Maxwell into a side conference in the corner of the rehearsal room. She was directing him. "Remember that he's devoted to his mother, absolutely adores her. It's an Oedipal thing. And that mother-love, you should pardon the expression, it propels all of his actions and his conflicts. It's the key to the character, darling, the absolute core center of Maxwell."

"Thanks."

Leigh interrupted, which was her big thing for that day.

"Bridie? Sit down."

"In a minute, sweetie." Bridie never took her eyes off uncomfortable young Maxwell.

"No. Now." Leigh felt like she was acting as hard as she could.

"I'm explaining the character here. Maxwell is a sad, sweet boy who worships his mother. That's the real linchpin of the character."

"Sit down, both of you, or we'll start the second act without you."

Maxwell dashed out of the corner and back to the table. He was obviously relieved to escape Bridie, who lingered in the corner to have an extra-long glare at her daughter—no, at her *director*. She gestured insistently for Leigh to precede her to the table; that way she could saunter to her seat as if no one had rushed or threatened her, because Bridie Hart was, now and always, still in control.

Leigh sat and waited patiently for her star to decide it was okay to sit. Michael climbed into his seat and asked, "Leigh? Where did you go? Why did you just leave like that? I thought we'd have lunch together. I ate with your mom instead, and she thought you weren't coming back. This is the worst case of first-day jitters you've ever had, honey!"

Leigh decided that she could never tell Michael about the casting disaster, not unless she wanted to see him suffer a stroke. She smiled faintly. "First-day jitters," she replied. "That's me."

James called out from across the table, "Leigh? Do you want to say anything before we start the second act?" Leigh froze at the sound of his voice and refused to look at him or answer him. Instead, she tried to look each and every actor in the eye while she said, "Everyone? I'd like to hear the second act, okay?" She didn't manage to look at anyone, but she was aware that everyone noticed her inability to answer James directly.

During the second-act read-through, Leigh kept count of the number of times that Bridie had to be stopped from directing the other actors (twelve), the number of times she tried to tell a funny anecdote that the script reminded her of (four), and the number of times that she tried to speak when Leigh was speaking (seventeen). Kendall gave her urgent, pleading looks. But Leigh knew she couldn't confront her mother in front of a cast that already adored Bridie. That was a suicide mission.

When James read, "Blackout. Curtain," the actors beamed at one another and Michael rose and applauded them all. Despite her chilly beginning at this rehearsal, Leigh had hoped to make an encouraging speech preparing her cast for the tough road ahead. Instead, Michael spoke.

"Brilliant. You were all so brilliant. And, of course, my wife was brilliant for casting you all." That's right, she had been the one responsible for hiring them. Technically. Suddenly, the cast all seemed to like Leigh again. She saw a few smiles and nods around the table.

"You should probably know," Michael continued, "that this play is really personal for me. This is about my family and a real turning point in my father's life. He's my real-life hero. He still is, and I, I thank you all so much for doing this. You're so . . ." He couldn't finish. He was starting to cry. The cast rose and applauded him, and Leigh saw that several of them were teary as well. Maddie was choked up. The actor playing Maxwell hugged Michael. Kendall was hiding her face behind her script.

Bridie's voice sailed over the scene. "Thank you, Michael. And to you, my fellow actors, we have a powerful mandate here: to fulfill the promise of this script. I'm looking forward to taking this journey with each and every one of you."

How did she do that? She succeeded at looking everyone in the eye at the same time. This was the trick that made those *Mother Love* chats so successful. Leigh couldn't look at anyone, but looked at the floor instead. She was still looking at the floor when she asked Maddie to ask James to end the rehearsal. So far, asking James directly felt too challenging. She kept her eyes on the floor as she heard James announce, "Good night, everyone. See you tomorrow at ten o'clock."

Michael lifted Leigh in the air and swung her around. It was the most intimate touch she had known from him in so long, and it was intoxicating.

"You were right. I don't need to go to Florida. The play is wonderful, the actors are wonderful, you're wonderful. It's a wonderful life! Ha! We have to go out and celebrate."

Kendall was grimly shaking her head no. This was probably Leigh's big chance to pull wisdom from her mentor, and she couldn't miss it. Not to mention how little she felt like celebrating. Still, she hoped Michael would remember that he suddenly felt safe touching her again. Hold that thought.

"You go. You celebrate. I still have two more days of rehearsal here, and I have to get ready. Kendall and I are going to have a working dinner. Go. Have fun. You deserve it." Leigh reached up and kissed him before he could turn his head to one side, though he did try. She felt it.

Bridie's sly grin revealed that she might know what Leigh's real plans were. Still, she said, "Oh, now, Michael. A director doesn't have time to celebrate. She's got too much to do. We'll celebrate *for* her, won't we, dear."

Michael wasn't exactly happy, but he couldn't defy Bridie; so few could. Off they went. Leigh turned and saw that Kendall had hooked James and Maddie on either arm. She was bringing them along? How was Leigh supposed to talk about her awkward relationship with James if he sat at the table?

"I'm starving. And James says he can get us a booth at McHale's. Let's go," Kendall ordered. "And Leigh is buying dinner for us all. Isn't that nice of her? Now, let's go."

Maddie was shyly explaining to James that she was new to the world of assistant stage managing. He smiled and began to explain the job to her as they walked down the street. Kendall and Leigh fell behind and Kendall began her coaching.

"We'll talk about your mother and the cast when we get to the bar, but first I need to know: Why aren't you speaking to James? And how do you think you can direct a play without speaking to your stage manager?"

"I almost kissed him. I sort of told him I liked him. But he didn't like me back."

"Ah, yes, I understand. And wasn't it fun to be fourteen again? Isn't he just the cutest thing ever? Do you sit in homeroom writing 'Mrs. James McGovern' on your notebook? And then do you go crazy and write 'Mrs. Orlando Bloom,' and do you draw lots of hearts?"

"Hey. I don't have time for this much sarcasm," Leigh said in her best shout-whisper. "If I hadn't said anything to him, he wouldn't have screwed up the casting and I wouldn't be in this awful mess. This is all my fault. What should I do?"

"Grow up."

Leigh responded with a sigh loud enough for anyone to hear.

"I mean it, Leigh. Grow the hell up. You said something to this guy. It didn't work. Oops. Now move the fuck on. You don't have time to be embarrassed; you have work to do. You can't indulge in any of this 'oh, poor me' bullshit until after opening night. Got it? And besides, I think James did you a favor. The last complication you need here is an extramarital romance with Mr. Handsome Pants."

Leigh giggled in spite of herself and repeated, "Mr. Handsome Pants. Good one."

James and Maddie were half a block ahead of them, already heading into McHale's. Kendall stopped Leigh on the sidewalk and reiterated her point. "Put it in the past and move on. Put it all in the past. Can you do that?"

"Yes." And as she said it, it became true for her. Was that Kendall's magic or her own?

• • •

Leigh tiptoed into her quiet apartment. Michael was either fast asleep or barhopping with Bridie. Just in case he was sleeping, she slipped into the office noiselessly and wrote notes while the advice Kendall gave over dinner was fresh in her mind. She made notes about each member of the cast, and how to extract the best performances from them. She also wrote "This is your cast. Accept them" in the margin of her notebook seven times. Maybe that would be lucky.

Kendall's cast notes were so concrete and helpful. Leigh moved on to other thoughts.

OTHER MATTERS:

- Will Michael let me rewrite a bit? Must try to convince him.
- Have Maddie serve as a spy/mole among the actors. People always tell her things because she's so pretty. Keep a finger on the pulse of the morale.
- Don't ever ever ever say anything to James about what happened during casting. It never happened. He imagined it.
- Update Kendall ~~once twice~~ three times a week. More if necessary. Note—if she ever needs a kidney, you owe her one.

[7]

It was the afternoon of their second New York rehearsal. One more day, then they would go their separate ways and reunite in Jupiter, Florida. Leigh had been searching for the perfect moment to conquer her mother. She wanted a clean victory and she didn't want to wait for Florida. She needed to have it done and cleared away before they boarded the plane. Leigh had been expecting some sort of confrontation all day. It had been brewing since the morning, when Leigh interrupted Bridie's extended coffee break with the actor who played Maxwell. Whatshisname.

"Good scene," Leigh said to Bridie and the older actor, the guy with the hair transplant. "Very good, very clear. I think that once we get the lines down, we're really going to have to pay attention to the rhythm of this scene. Now—"

"The what?" Bridie demanded.

So, now it was time for Leigh to pretend to be twenty years older and wiser than Bridie, by saying, "The *rhythm*. You see, this scene has a lot of shifts to it, and they may require us to pay attention to the changes in rhythm or tempo as the characters become more agitated or more secretive. For example, it starts out as small talk, but Margaret has this whole loaded agenda, and then—"

"Yes, dear, I've read the scene, thank you. And I know what *rhythm* means. But why the fuck are you persecuting your actors with requests for *rhythm* when we haven't even learned our *lines* yet? We haven't even gotten on our feet. Hello?"

Oh, Christ, the actors were exchanging knowing looks. This was it. Use her strengths against her. Let her talk and talk and talk so that she wears out her welcome with the cast and annoys them with her passion for her own voice. It was against Bridie's nature to be concise. Leigh was 70 percent certain that this give-her-enough-rope approach would work, or she would never have said, "Really? Tell me more."

"Sweetheart, I love you. But none of us has any sense of your leadership, your vision, or your directorial style. What exactly are you waiting for?"

It was a classic sucker punch. Leigh stuck her chin out and Bridie walloped her. The cast was actually snickering and Leigh was truly, utterly speechless. So was Bridie, but her silence held sway over her director.

Leigh knew she needed to give some sort of answer, but she couldn't. Instead, she stared at Bridie, whose face beamed faux maternal love and concern. It was an expression she had perfected for the closing shot in her stupid *Mother Love* chats. Leigh knew that she mustn't cry, mustn't cry, mustn't cry. She had never cried at a rehearsal, not once; so she locked herself in a no-crying zone. It lasted for minutes, or maybe years. Would she ever be able to answer her mother?

The actors were studying her as if they could already tell that she had no clue how to direct this play or control its star. Did they think she was a total fraud? Probably. Could they tell that she was breaking out in a cold sweat? Definitely. Leigh was buried in silence.

But Bridie couldn't stay silent for long. She launched into a long speech about "*my* play, *my* scene, *my* role, *me, me, me,* and everything that *I want*" that was all that Leigh heard. And that seemed to be all that the other actors heard, too. She saw two actors exchange a meaningful look, so Leigh grabbed that lifeline and surfaced.

"Bridie. This isn't *Mother Love*. This is an ensemble piece. These actors, they're all in the same boat with you and with me. You are not the star."

Bridie inherited all of Leigh's panic.

"I never said—I never claimed—I never meant—you're twisting my—" Bridie choked on her words, while Leigh's confidence filled her up.

"We're going to follow the rules of the theater. That means that the actors will act. And the director will direct. You have to stop directing your fellow actors, stop contradicting me, stop making your own schedule. So make your choice right now: either step into the group with your fellow actors, or leave the show. I hate to rush you, but you have to decide now. We have two weeks before we go to Florida. That's just enough time to recast your role."

There were audible gasps around the table. Leigh hadn't planned to threaten her mother, but she suddenly knew it was the right thing to say. Her blood was pumping and she felt powerful. Bridie now looked shriveled and afraid.

"Bridie. Tell me now. Join the cast or leave the cast. Which will it be?" Now Leigh's voice was the one carrying across the room, firmly issuing the orders.

"Well. Really. You're just absurd. Of course, I join the cast, I just—"

"Good. Let's get back to work." Leigh cut off her now blabbering mother.

Bridie was trying to work up tears, but Leigh couldn't let her have that kind of victory.

"I really am glad you're not leaving us, Bridie. You're the best Margaret we could ask for. Thank you for staying." Bridie's surprise looked genuine. Leigh realized that she meant what she was saying. But the rehearsal was almost over, so she continued. "Does anyone else have any questions or problems?" No one even breathed during the silence here. "Okay. Well, if you think of any, my door is always open. For now, I think we can finish this act."

And Bridie Hart was obedient, cooperative, and absolutely wonderful for the rest of the rehearsal. Not a single interruption, not a trace of sarcasm, and she returned promptly from the last rehearsal break of the day.

The next day's rehearsal brought a Bridie who was subdued in both behavior and outfit. She was dressed down for the part of "fellow actor," and she was playing it, too. Leigh studied her for traces of fakery, even eavesdropped in the bathroom to hear gossip or sabotage from Bridie. Her search came up empty. It had taken her a lifetime to figure out how to subdue her mother, and here was the answer: Leigh had to resort to the big guns at the first attack. Of course. All those years of sulking and minor skirmishes did nothing to slow a tornado like Bridie Hart. But yesterday, she had jabbed her mother in her vulnerable underbelly—rejection. A public firing would be unacceptable; a public firing by her own daughter would be cause for suicide.

At the end of the rehearsal, James discussed the travel plans for January, and then the actors filed out, but Bridie lingered. It was a meaningful linger. She so obviously wanted to play a private scene with Leigh. Fine. Leigh was up and ready for any kind of scene Bridie had to offer. She rose and let Bridie lead her to the far corner of the room.

But what she heard her mother say was, "I'm so sorry. I had no idea I was behaving in such an unprofessional manner. Really, I'm appalled at myself. You've never worked with me before, Leigh, but I assure you, I'm a pro. This sort of misbehavior, well, it will never happen again. I promise."

On an ordinary day, Leigh might have dismissed this speech, but for one detail: Bridie didn't give her speech in front of an audience. There was no crowd to root for her. Did Bridie bother to blink without an audience or a camera? She may actually have meant what she said.

"Leigh? Are we going to be okay?"

That's when Leigh realized that she needed to answer her mother. "Of course we are." She studied her mother. Why did Bridie's voice sound so plain, so unadorned?

"It's just that, well, half the reason I wanted to do this play was to be with you. To work with you. Maybe if you could see how professional I am, you'll stop being mad at me for five minutes."

Leigh wished she hadn't let her mother put her in a corner. She looked longingly at the exit door as she said, "I'm not mad at you, Bridie." Now, if she could just crawl out of her skin and out the door, she'd be just fine.

"Well." Bridie sighed. "You give a good imitation of it." She paused.

"Look. This is just the way we are. It's the way we've always been." Leigh sighed. Her own voice had gone soft around the edges.

"I'm sorry that I'm not Mother Love," Bridie answered, after a pause. "You're the one person in the world who's so disappointed in me for that. Even more than that stalker boy. Remember him?" Leigh couldn't actually remember which stalker boy. There had been a few. Bridie looked so expectant. Was she waiting for Leigh to say more? To remember him?

"We'll be okay here." Leigh felt warmth rush into her voice. "I just needed to set some ground rules. You need to respect me, Bridie. I'm a professional, too. Don't worry so much. Okay?"

Bridie's whole face lit up, and Leigh realized that her own hands were wrapped inside Bridie's.

"Oh, thank God. You really scared the shit out of me. Honestly, I'd rather die than be fired by my own daughter."

"I understand," Leigh answered. Wait. Was Bridie more concerned about losing face than about losing her daughter? Should Leigh even pursue that question? Just then, Bridie hugged Leigh, who was so surprised, she let her own arms dangle at her side. Bridie left a lipstick kiss on Leigh's cheek and sped out the door without another word.

Was that real? Leigh was so confused, she forgot to have any hostility for James. She called out, "Hey, James, can you make sure that we have some prop hats to rehearse with when we're in Florida?"

James nearly dropped his script. She had taken him by surprise.

"Sure," he answered. Leigh struggled to keep herself from dancing around the rehearsal hall. She realized that she was humming "Everything's Coming Up Roses." She waved good-bye to James, who waved back automatically, still wearing a slightly stunned expression. She didn't realize that Maddie was waiting for her until she saw her in the doorway.

"Hey, Maddie. What's up?"

"How am I doing?" Maddie pushed off from the door frame and hovered over Leigh. "I mean, as an assistant stage manager? Am I making a fool of myself?"

It had never occurred to Leigh that Maddie needed reassurance. But there she was, large and looming, and asking for Leigh to prop her up.

"You're doing great. I don't know what we would do without you. You're great. In fact, you're supergreat." Leigh's script and notebooks were all packed up. Did Maddie need more?

"Really? Because I have a kind of embarrassing question for you." Leigh's least favorite kind. But today, she was fast becoming a superhero. She could handle anything Maddie threw at her, until Maddie said, "I really like James. And Rico made it sound like he'd be sleeping with any girl in Japan who'd have him. The bastard."

So far, all of Maddie's boyfriends were eventually declared bastards once they disappeared from her world. But today she liked James. James? Leigh's James? But no, not Leigh's James. Not really. Not ever. Maddie was gushing.

"I love his serenity. And his ass. But seriously, he's supernaturally smart about every topic you can think of, except technology. He's like a Puritan. And those eyes. Have you ever noticed those eyes?"

"No." Leigh hid behind her hands.

"That's because you're an old married woman. I'm telling you, this guy could be a matinee idol, except that he's better than that. Oh! And he gets this kind of Stan Laurel befummeled expression whenever I try to find out about his personal life. He's so cute it hurts."

Maddie had never used the word *cute* in her entire life. Not even to describe puppies. Leigh was absolutely certain of that.

"So what's the question?"

"What?"

"The embarrassing question?"

"Oh, God, here goes. Do you think he might like me, too? I mean, what's his story, anyway? Please tell me he's straight because I can't survive making that mistake again. And how long do I have to wait before I can say anything to him? Do I have to wait until we close? I hope not. I really, really hope not."

Leigh let Maddie splash around in her dewy embarrassment. She permitted herself zero thoughts about James and his eyes and his ass. Instead, she listened to Maddie describe what it would be like to paint a portrait of James. Leigh realized that she could take this moment to liberate herself from a decrepit old production crush that was lingering past the point where it was fun. Peel it off and give it to Maddie.

Leigh smiled then and said, "He's a wonderful guy. You two would be so happy together. I think it's beyond great—it's the best news I've heard since this play began. Go for it."

"Thank you."

. . .

A week later, Leigh and Michael exchanged Christmas gifts as they usually did. They sat on the floor of the living room in their pajamas, and Leigh forced herself not to think about children and Santa and stockings and children.

"Open this one first," she insisted, as she pushed a gift into Michael's hands.

Inside, he found a teeeeeeny, tiny iPod with all the accessories a runner might want, and then some. It would strap around his arm, weigh less than a fingernail, and probably connect him with the latest research from NASA. He was happy, surprised, and excited, in that order. She reached over to show him the tiny controls, but then found herself distracted by being so close to him so suddenly.

"Okay, now you open mine!" he said, pulling himself away from the sleek details of his gift, and from Leigh. He perched above her on the sofa while Leigh opened a laptop, as thin as a Communion wafer and fully loaded.

"I love it!" she declared. He urged her to play with this new toy while he made coffee. The rest of the gifts waited patiently while the coffee aroma took over the apartment, and Leigh cleaned up bits of wrapping paper.

For years, it had seemed to Leigh that she and Michael had invented Christmas. Bridie was always away from her daughters on Christmas. Always. When Leigh wanted to know why they didn't get a Hallmark Christmas morning with presents under the tree, Lilly explained that Bridie and Frank's wedding anniversary was Christmas Day, and that was supposed to excuse Bridie somehow. Of course, there was that infamous Christmas when Leigh got nothing, yes, nothing, because Bridie had simply forgotten about her. Leigh reminded herself that she was supposed to banish all thoughts of her mother on Christmas Day. It was a small gift, but it kept on giving.

Michael returned with two cups of coffee, and the gift giving continued, with Michael now perched on the arm of the sofa and Leigh adrift on the floor. It seemed they had indulged each other this year with pricier gifts than usual, all these toys for grown-ups. They opened cashmere, they opened music, they opened everything. It was all good, all catalog-shiny. But Leigh sat on the floor with all these things, waiting to feel happy, or at least full. The hard edges of the laptop gleamed and inspired her to clean up more paper bits, since they had to be finished opening gifts, but then Michael grinned at her.

"Wait. Stop." He took Leigh by the hands and sat her on the sofa. "We're not quite done. I have something really special for you. God, I still can't believe I kept it a secret all this time. Now, close your eyes." Leigh peeked through her fingers to see Michael dash off to the bedroom. What could it be? She closed her eyes tight, and for a moment she felt that tingle, that specialness, that the holidays were supposed to bring. Romance, secrets, magic. Here it was.

"This woman from Road Runners told me about this," Michael called out, "and it sounded so perfect for you. Open your eyes!"

He rolled a large purple vacuum cleaner into the living room.

"It's a Dyson!" he exclaimed. "Isn't it beautiful?"

Leigh smacked her forehead. She wanted to choke him, jump him, and slap him awake.

But she started laughing quietly while he explained the wonders of the Dyson vacuum cleaner. He talked about animal hair and carpet stains as if he were presenting a cure for cancer. Her laughter grew until he had to ask, "What? You'll love this. You like things clean. You like things just so. What's the problem?"

Animal hair? Things just so? Her laughter was out of control. She could barely hear him over her own voice. She felt like a Stepford wife. She felt like a character from *Women in Hats*. She felt like a fool. It was past time to talk to Michael about all this.

"Michael. Honey. I don't want a vacuum cleaner. Well, I mean, I do. I love it. Because I love you. And I want you. I want you back. Come here."

She reached for him, so he had to sit close to her, close enough for her to hold him.

"You've been so far away for so long, Michael. Where have you been?"

"Sorry. Well, the play has been a big deal, and I've taken on more patients to cover the loan and the—"

"No. When you're here, you act like I'm radioactive. You can touch me, I'm okay." She broke some sort of bubble by saying, "I had a miscarriage. Again. But I'm not breakable. Talk to me."

She could see that Michael so didn't want to talk, but she had him cornered. His face turned gray and angular for just a moment. He looked at the vacuum cleaner while he spoke. So did Leigh.

"I can't go through it again," he said "I know it mostly happens to you, but it happens to me, too. You have to promise me that you won't ever get pregnant again."

"Is that why we haven't had sex in three and a half months?" she asked. Maybe he hadn't done the math, but she had.

"Well. Yes." He was still avoiding her eyes; his shoulders were slumped uncharacteristically low.

"I'm sorry," she whispered, and waited for him to forgive her. Maybe he would say, "It's all right, as long as we're together." Or something similarly all-forgiving. She had deprived him of children, so she said it again. "I'm sorry."

He finally looked at her, and even dared to touch her face. "Please promise me you won't try to get pregnant again."

"Yes. I promise."

This was the role she would play for the rest of her life— Michael's faithful wife, the director, the one who couldn't have children. She reached out for Michael and hoped that she could play the part well.

· · ·

Leigh filled the postholiday days with reading and rereading the script. Tonight, she was letting Michael sleep while she curled up on the sofa to read that script for the 112th time. She didn't like to fall asleep when she was reading this play; whenever she did, the noisy character voices in her head would disrupt her sleep. Everyone spoke directly to the audience, everyone sounded bright and optimistic, even when they were in trouble. Come to think of it, so did Michael.

MAXWELL

Sons are always smarter than their mothers. That's a law of nature. I love my mother, but she has to be nuts if she thinks I'm going to spend all day selling ladies' hats. That's not a job for a man. Maybe she still sees me as a boy, but I guess I'll just have to show her. I'll become a dentist, and not just a good one, a great one. I'll make people smile. In fact, by the time I'm done, they'll want to smile about smiling. And then we'll sell this old hat shop and Mother can retire in style, and I'll send her to Paris every spring. And we'll all be so happy. Won't we?

Leigh wanted to answer Maxwell. Yes. You'll be so happy. You'll marry Sarah, even though her real name is Sylvia. And you'll have a very sweet son, but no grandchildren. Sorry.

MAXWELL

I'm done for. I'll have to quit dental school. She's got me right where she wants me.

SARAH

Oh, sweetheart, what happened?

MAXWELL

Mom's sick. Not really sick-sick. She's never been sick a day in her life.

SARAH

You mean—she's faking?
(*Maxwell nods vigorously.*)
Why?

MAXWELL

She says she has to stay in bed for a month. At least! And I have to run the shop the whole time. So I can't go to school.

SARAH

Are you sure she's faking? What if she's really sick?

MAXWELL

She just ate a steak dinner, baked potato, and ice cream sundae. Then she cleaned the kitchen from top to bottom. She's healthy, all right. But she knows I can't say no to her. And I know that she knows that I know *no* is not possible.

SARAH

Whatever you say. But why don't you just let me run the shop for you, while you go to class? I think it'll be a kick!

Leigh knew that Michael liked symmetry. He liked happy endings. He set up the relationships nicely, then started all the trickery in the second act:

(*Margaret enters through the back of the shop and sees Sarah, who is busily dusting the shelves. They both jump.*)

MARGARET

Who are you?

SARAH

Who are *you*?
(*Margaret needs a moment to think up a lie.*)

MARGARET

I'm, um, yes, I'm a customer. That's it. I'm a customer.

SARAH

Funny, I didn't hear the bell ring when you came in.

MARGARET

What a lovely hat shop you have here. Are you the owner?
(*Maxwell enters through the back of the shop, sees his mother, and ducks behind the register.*)

SARAH

I'm, um, well, I'm Sarah. Why not? Let me show you our new spring hats. They're newer than new. They're back here in the inventory room. Come see!
(*She guides Margaret to the side room where the spring hats reside. Once Margaret is offstage, Sarah signals to Maxwell that the coast is clear. He is peeking over the register, ready to leave, just as Ted enters through the front door.*)

TED

Where's my daughter? You! Have you seen Sarah?
(*Sarah runs into the side room, panicked. Maxwell tries to hide again, but he is too slow, so he pretends to be occupied with the cash register.*)
Hey. What are *you* doing here? I thought you were a dentist.
(*Maxwell seizes his white jacket from his bag and puts it on.*)

MAXWELL

> I am! I'm a dentist. See?
> *(They hear Margaret and Sarah offstage.)*

MARGARET

> *(Starting to enter)*
> Did a customer come in?

SARAH

> Ooh, look! Pretty ribbons!
> *(She pulls Margaret back, just as Grace enters.)*

GRACE

> Has anyone seen Margaret? Maxwell, why are you wearing that
> jacket?

Fun, fun, fun. By the end of that scene, Margaret figures out that Sarah is the one who is actually running the shop while Maxwell attends dental school. Margaret pretends she doesn't know a thing. But then her friend Grace has a scene with Sarah's father, Ted:

TED

> But she's running the shop for a good reason.

GRACE

> Ted. Stop. Don't say any more. Margaret's too upset to hear you
> over the drums beating in her head.

TED

> Why? Sarah's a very nice girl, and she was helping your son out.

MARGARET

I didn't want anyone to help him. I wanted him to run the shop. While I watched from upstairs.

TED

But how could he run the shop? He was in dental school!

Michael gave Margaret a long, long, long monologue (would he let Leigh edit that speech?) about how she felt deceived and defeated. But she was a good mother, and would do the good-mother thing. She would allow Maxwell to attend dental school and marry Sarah. When the time was right, she would sell her beloved shop. Bridie would do a choked-up half-cry for that part. Leigh could hear it in her head. And then came the big confrontation with Maxwell and Sarah:

SARAH

But why should you sell it? Last month, when you thought Maxwell was running the shop so brilliantly—well, that was *me*! I was the one actually running the shop. And I loved it. You can still pass the shop along to your son.

MAXWELL

But it'll be your daughter-in-law who runs it. You said yourself that the profits were up and the inventory was moving. Didn't you, Mother?

There would be hugs and kisses and tears. All of the couples were paired off. Just like life. A Jack for every Jill.

MARGARET

Ted? I think we've raised a couple of glorious kids here. Don't you?

TED

Why don't we discuss that in more detail . . . in Paris?

MARGARET

C'est magnifique!

CURTAIN. END OF PLAY.

Leigh put the script on the table and it nearly made an echo in the quiet apartment. Now that the character voices were silenced, she realized how still she had been all night.

Could she wake Michael up and ask him to come with her to her next doctor's appointment? Dr. Griffin finagled some time for Leigh the day before the flight to Florida to work out a birth control plan. Would Michael cancel patients and accompany her? Leigh gave him the benefit of her (slim) doubt. Yes, he had canceled patients for her in the past, but it was best to leave that scene in her imagination. If she woke him and asked him, he might alter her reality.

When the quiet blankness of the apartment was too much for her, she dialed Maddie. Of course. They had gone without their usual coffee date for a while, and Leigh needed a dose of Maddie's friendship. She could tell Maddie about the doctor's appointment, and maybe Maddie would come with her. And then they could talk about lighter things, and Leigh would feel better. She would tell Maddie about the silly production crush on James, and they could laugh about it. And then the two friends could work out how Maddie could start to flirt with James. This felt right. It felt honest and true, like something a better person would do. Maybe if Leigh always did what a better person would do, she'd be a better person herself. Maddie's phone was ringing, then clicked as she picked up.

"Hello?" James. It was James. It was James answering Maddie's phone at eleven o'clock at night. Leigh hung up.

Leigh decided to go to her doctor's appointment alone, and wasn't it better that way? She sat quietly while Dr. Griffin checked her clipboard and asked, "You don't smoke, right?"

Leigh didn't, because Bridie did.

"Good. I'll give you a few sample packs of the pill so you can start right away, then get your prescription filled."

Leigh accepted the plastic packs and studied the wee little pills, marked for the days of the week in wee little letters.

"When you get back from Florida, we can talk about some other options. But for now, let's see how you do with this."

Leigh studied the floor. She tended to study the floor a lot at Dr. Griffin's office. There were gallons of bad associations here for Leigh, so the floor was a safe choice. When was the last time Dr. Griffin had given her good news?

"Well," Leigh said as she rose to leave, "thanks for the freebies. I'll call you when I get back."

But Dr. Griffin wasn't ready to let Leigh go just yet.

"No, no. I'll give you a prescription, too. And I wanted to say that I know this is hard for you. I have to give you so much credit. You were given a raw deal, and you're moving on. I'm so glad that you're not going to try to conceive anymore. Really, you're doing the right thing."

The linoleum became hard to study. Suddenly she saw so many flecks and dents. Leigh nodded along with Dr. Griffin's speech. Finally, the doctor was getting out her pen and prescription pad. Good. Nearly done. Dr. Griffin's voice changed from compassion for Leigh to a tone that sounded more active.

"And I'll tell you this, I'd love to have ten minutes alone with your mother's ob-gyn."

Dr. Griffin sounded angry. That was the tone. Anger. The shadow line between her eyes might have been drawn with Magic Marker.

"Why?" Leigh asked.

Dr. Griffin stopped writing and looked at Leigh. "You're not the first child of DES I've treated. But you are the youngest."

"So?"

"Doctors knew about the dangers of DES as early as the fifties. By the time your mother was pregnant with you, the evidence against it was overwhelming. I think the FDA issued its official warning just a few months after you were born."

Leigh felt cold, unable to breathe.

"DES was still legal," Dr. Griffin continued, "but hey, any doctor with a grain of sense would have known better than to prescribe it. The evidence against it was enough to let anybody know it was too dangerous. I find it absolutely monstrous that someone gave it to your mother."

Leigh was piecing it together, frozen to the spot.

"What if the mother requested it? What if she were a big star and very persuasive? What if she always got what she wanted?"

"No. Even if your mother requested it, how could they have given it to her, *knowing* that they were putting the child at risk? I don't understand it. But I'd like to throttle her doctor. It's unforgivable."

Leigh didn't speak again for the rest of the day. She took her prescription and crushed it in her hand. She stepped out into the cold January morning where the air burned her lungs. She knew. Bridie knew. Leigh could picture the scene between poor, nauseous, pregnant, but selfishly determined Bridie and a doctor who never knew what hit him.

She would hold her palms in a prayer position. She would beg. "But doctor, please! I'm sick! How can you deny medicine to a sick woman!"

He would shake his head and try to be strong. "Have you tried changing your diet? Have you tried saltine crackers?" The poor sap.

She'd stop begging after a while and resort to bullying. "I'm a working actress! I'm a star! People expect me to be at peak energy one thousand percent of the time. How can I do that on a diet of crackers and ginger ale?"

He'd try reason and superior medical knowledge, not realizing that she valued neither. "There are studies about DES. There are very strong indications that it can harm the fetus." Maybe he'd go into detail here. Maybe he'd tell her that her daughter would sit in a gynecologist's office three decades and change later and curse her mother. Maybe he wouldn't get the chance.

She would need to calm his fears, so she'd assure him, "I took DES all through my first pregnancy, and my daughter is the most perfect child you'd ever hope to see. That sort of thing doesn't happen to me. I was born lucky."

But Lilly didn't live long enough to try to have children, so maybe Bridie damaged her the same way she'd damaged Leigh. Maybe she did. Fuck "maybe," Bridie *must* have harmed both of her daughters. But that thought wouldn't have stopped her from riding roughshod over that clueless MD. He'd start to crack, and she'd close the deal with, "If I can't get it from you, I'll get it from someone else. At least this way, you can monitor just how wonderfully well my pregnancy is going. Okay?"

She must have known. And she took the pills anyway. She knew.

Leigh crushed skulls in the snow as she walked all the way home. She needed to pack for Florida. She was ready for a change. She knew.

[8]

Michael and Leigh had breakfast at the airport, since they were massively early for her flight. He had given up his morning run and two patient appointments to be there for her. After a few minutes of silence, Leigh realized that they were having trouble making conversation with each other. They ate their bland food in the brightly lit food court. What if she told him about yesterday's appointment with Dr. Griffin? What if she told him what a villain her mother really was? What if she shared her mother's cruel selfishness? Did it matter that they were in the middle of a busy airport? Did it matter that she would be dropping this bomb and then leaving town? It would certainly give them something to talk about.

"Do you want more coffee?" he asked. "I know how you love your coffee!"

"No, thanks." Once again, they were quiet, and she felt a magnetic pull to hold her sad story inside. There was no way to tell him about Bridie. What she did. What she knew. Not today.

"Do you have your cell phone charger?" he asked. "You're gonna need it!"

"Got it," she answered. Oh, he looked so uncomfortable, studying the neon lights and all the carry-on luggage around them. Like he was on a bad date that needed to end soon. Maybe if she let him go early, he could still have a nice run.

"I think I should go to the gate now," she said as she rose. "I want to be there in case any of the actors show up early."

Michael smiled (was he relieved?) and told her, "You take such good care of them." He kissed his wife good-bye and waved as she took off her shoes for Security, then disappeared into the crowd.

*   *   *

The actors were not early. Leigh sat and waited for them, and sure enough, one by one, the sleepy actors joined her. She wondered what she would do or say the next time she saw Bridie, who wasn't going to be on this flight. She would be joining them later, in Jupiter, just in time for the first rehearsal the following Monday. She was booked to appear on *David Letterman*, promoting the release of *Mother Love* on DVD. Dave professed an undying passion for Bridie Love, and she always teased him mercilessly. It was nearly scripted. When Bridie finally did arrive in Jupiter, her limousine would bring her to the same moderately priced hotel where the rest of the cast was already settling in. Leigh anticipated a kind of culture shock for her mother, and she anticipated enjoying that shock, but not too obviously.

Over the holidays, Bridie had been present only in Leigh's thoughts. She had been having a wild holiday spree. Or something. Leigh hadn't seen Bridie in person since that last rehearsal. Her traditional framed portrait-of-self arrived in time for Christmas, and a bottle of champagne arrived at New Year's, but Bridie herself was absent, which was like an extra gift. Leigh must have been very good this year.

Leigh counted all of her actors and both of her stage managers. All present, all well, all wanting to chat with her. Leigh went off in search of a magazine.

Lilly. Leigh saw Lilly just ahead of her. That was her walk, graceful under any circumstances. That was the way she used to dance her hand against her side when she kept time to her music, maybe working out the melody on an imagined keyboard. Her hair was longer back then, but it was that color exactly, the color of dried blood. She was walking quickly, coming closer, and looking more and more like—

"Lilly!"

Not Lilly. Whoever she was, she didn't even look up. She was engrossed in her headphones and stopped suddenly when she encountered the wide selection of magazines at the newsstand. Leigh followed her for a few minutes, and then realized that this Not Lilly was about two inches shorter than real Lilly. Lost Lilly. Leigh froze and let Not Lilly buy a newspaper and drift into the crowd. Standing in the middle of all those people, Leigh started crying. She didn't want to, but there was no stopping it. She didn't pull herself over to the nearest restroom, and she didn't try to keep quiet. She cried out loud.

Her fellow travelers glided past her, and at least one of them snapped her picture.

When she was done, she reached easily for the tissues that were always stored in the same pocket of the black satchel she'd been carrying for years.

●   ●   ●

Three hours later, Leigh pulled her suitcase out of the airport, into aggressive Florida sunshine that shocked her. Was it always like this here? Were the palm trees lifted from a Dr. Seuss illustration? James had arranged a van service to transport the company to the hotel, where they would reside for the duration.

Leigh sat near the front of the van, and Maddie climbed in next to her. Leigh wanted so badly to ask, "Are you sleeping with James? Is it wonderful? Tell me everything," but she knew she'd never ask that.

"Leigh? Guess what? I need a favor. Again." Maddie was using a small voice. Her blond curls peeked out from under a baseball cap that supported the Anti-Art Art Gallery.

"Sure! Absolutely! What is it?" Did Leigh sound as convincing as her mother would?

"I sort of need a letter from you." Maddie didn't usually sound this shy. "It's for the IRS. I have to prove that I'm working and steady and how much I'm making and I can't believe that they think they're my mother or big brother or something. They're into everything. You wouldn't believe it."

"Oh, God, Maddie, of course. I can write the letter tonight at the hotel. Is that okay?" Leigh was a terrible person who didn't deserve friends like Maddie.

"This is so humiliating. Please don't tell anyone else. I mean, James knows, but none of the actors."

"James knows?" Be a good person. Grow up. "That's great. I'm glad that you two are getting along so well."

"Yeah. Only, Leigh, why didn't you tell me he was gay?"

"*What?*"

Leigh had to laugh, and it felt like a morphine rush. Maddie repeatedly insisted that she knew for a fact that he absolutely definitely was.

Leigh leaned in and spoke as quietly as she could. "I think he was married once."

"Who to? Liza Minnelli? Please. He's gay," Maddie whispered. It didn't feel true to Leigh, but she preferred this idea over anything that did feel true. Apparently, Maddie had flirted, teased, and, by her own telling, nearly thrown him onto her kitchen floor to have her way with him. There was no response from James, just a quick and embarrassed exit. It sounded so much like that late night in the casting office, the night Leigh had kept to herself.

"And that means that he's gay?" Leigh asked quietly.

"That's only happened to me twice before. And both of those guys are fighting for the right to get married in Boston even as we speak. They're gay. He's gay. I don't know how I missed it. I'm off my game."

James rose then and moved from the back to the front and center of the hired van to read out hotel information, rehearsal schedules, and per diem details to the cast. Leigh studied his hands. He was holding on to the back of her seat to steady himself through the bumpy ride. His hands were tan after four minutes in the Florida sun. Or were they tan all the time? She couldn't see the lines on his palms, and couldn't have read them anyway. She couldn't read him at all.

Which was fine, because Michael trusted her. He trusted her to be faithful, he trusted her to take kind and gentle care of his play. Leigh knew that she would do all those things, just as she knew exactly what she would eat for breakfast every morning, what colors she would wear every day, and which scenes in act 2 needed revision. In fact, it was Michael who reminded her to pack that laptop computer with her, "in case you get inspired to rewrite any scenes. I trust you." See? He said it in just those words. He trusted her, which is why she was so glad that James was (really?) gay.

⋅ ⋅ ⋅

Her hotel room wallpaper was electric blue, decorated with brutally large palm fronds and giant hibiscus flowers in a wide array of colors, none of which was found in nature. The polyester bed-spread matched the wallpaper. The bathroom was a difficult shade of Pepto pink and the table and chairs looked dyed to match, bridesmaid-style. The minirefrigerator was bright green, to match the palm fronds. Where did they ever find small green refrigera-tors?

Leigh stood in the middle of the room, wondering if she should unpack or ask for another room, wondering if the hotel had rooms in quieter colors or gentler decor. She smiled at the thought of ask-ing the front desk for wallpaper that didn't look like it would swirl to life during the night and strangle her. She started unpacking.

Most people unpack their belongings directly into drawers and closets, but Leigh knew better. She placed all of her clothes, toiletries, books, notebooks, and computer supplies into distinct areas, separated by function, on her large, busy bed. Only then could she properly organize her items into their temporary homes in the hotel room. She knew that it looked like an interim step, but she never had trouble finding what she needed during her stay at a hotel. She did this whenever she traveled. She felt that everyone should.

The cast had made plans to meet for dinner that evening at the hotel restaurant, and Leigh had enthusiastically called out that she would join them there. They may have been surprised, but they didn't show it.

For those first three days in New York, Leigh was incapable of learning their names. When she addressed them, she called them by their character names—Grace, Maxwell, Sarah, and Ted. In her mind, she referred to them as Hygiene Issues, Whatshisname, Blondie, and Hair Plugs. In Florida, Leigh was determined to ban-ish her offensive nicknames for them by finally getting to know them. She couldn't really direct them if she couldn't really talk to them. Here, in the world of Jupiter, minus her mother, she would get to know her cast or die trying.

She had packed their headshots and résumés, and when she was fully moved in to her tropical paradise, she sat at her pink table and studied their pictures until she was ready for a final exam on each of them. She knew that some of the roles they claimed to have played were actually roles that they wished they had played, but she accepted that as interesting and meaningful background information about each actor. In preparation for dinner with her cast, Leigh quizzed herself about their stage experience and scored a 95 percent. Not bad. She studied the personal details they revealed under "Special Skills" to help her think up questions to get to know each of them.

Jessica, were the cheerleaders in your school nice or bitchy?

Harmony, tell me about your latest craft project.

David, what's the secret to an excellent omelet?

Ben. So. French horn, huh?

Yes, it was a bit of a forced beginning, but she needed a jump-start. She needed to force these relationships into being.

And it worked. Dinner was a lovefest. Leigh started by sharing news Harry had given her just before they left: their Florida run was already 75 percent sold out. This locked-in success elevated everyone's mood. The actors laughed (even Ben, whose quiet demeanor in New York had seemed unbreakable) and told stories about themselves and their ambitions. Their specific aims may have varied, but they all just wanted to work at acting and nothing else. The ultimate dream was to drop any day jobs and live in the elite world of working actors. No one mentioned awards, limousines, or fame. And no one mentioned Bridie. Not until dessert, anyway.

Somehow, Leigh had made them all so comfortable, they now

felt that they could ask her all the personal questions they had been saving up since the first rehearsal. Leigh had promised herself that she would get to know them, direct them, be present for them, be with them. Now she realized that her promise included more than just finding out about them. She had to allow them to find out about her.

"Was Bridie a good mother?"

No. She's not a good mother, but she plays one on TV. The thing you have to remember is this: she's a star, and that means she's in a constant state of competition. Sometimes I think that maybe she's competing with me.

"Is that why you work in the downtown scene? To avoid the competition with her?"

No. I work there because it interests me, and I feel at home there. After my father left Broadway, he really pushed his artistic boundaries and tried new things. Lots of people have forgotten that part of his life, but I haven't. And that kind of work, well, that's what I like.

"Isn't this play too conventional for you?"

Yes. But I'm doing my best, and so are all of you. We can't judge the play and perform it at the same time. So, let's just do it full-out. My mother fell in love with this play before she even finished reading it. She saw a spark in there, and I think she was right. It's one of those diamond-in-the-rough situations.

"Does your mother want you to be more like her?"

What? No. Never. Maybe. I don't know. No. No way. She would never want me to be like her. . . . Wait. I'm not sure. I mean, she sort of made my sister want to be like her. You're weirding me out now. Can we change the subject?

"The tabloids make her sound so wild. What's the worst thing Bridie ever did?"

Please. Can we change the subject now?

And they did. A mass conversation about every topic imaginable ensued: Disney, e-mail, skin-care products, pop music, coffee, real estate prices. Leigh might not be their best friend, but she was part of their company.

Maddie raised her glass in a silent toast to her friend, and Leigh returned the gesture, then threw herself into the tangle of conversations around her.

*　*　*

Leigh was back in her hotel room, on the phone with Michael. "I had dinner with the cast and it was really wonderful. They're a good bunch." That was true.

"I'm so relieved," he answered. "I know something went sort of wrong with the casting, but I think they're terrific. Is that what was on your mind at the airport? You were so quiet. Or was it your mother?"

"Oh, it was Bridie." Leigh started pulling at a thread from her shiny polyester bedspread. Should she tell Michael about her mother knowing, *knowing*, that she harmed her?

"I know she's so, well, so Bridie." He sighed into the phone. "But in the end, she's still your mother. And she wants you to be successful and happy, just like her. That's all. She just wants you to have everything she has. Leigh, if you can make this work with your mother, it'll make everything better between you two. I really believe that."

It would have been appropriate to agree. Or, it would have been fair to tell Michael what she learned about Bridie, why it was therefore impossible to forgive her. Ever. For anything. Not for the time she sent ten-year-old Leigh away to summer camp despite her scarlet fever, because Bridie was launching a new affair and didn't want children underfoot. Not for the way she encouraged Lilly to quit school and join that rock band. And not for the way she made Leigh feel invisible at Lilly's funeral, and at Frank's. Not for that. Not for any of it. Leigh was lost in the past for a long, silent pause.

Her husband read her silence as understandable fatigue, and let her go for the night.

* * *

Leigh, Maddie, and James all converged at the door to the rehearsal hall well before any of the actors would be arriving.

"Are you excited? I'm excited!" a highly caffeinated Maddie asked.

James used blue tape to replicate the stage space on the floor, while Leigh and Maddie pulled chairs to the large vinyl folding tables in the middle of the room. Each chair sounded an echo as it clanged into place.

"I feel like we're in Wonderland," Maddie giggled. Leigh and James looked at her in disbelief. The fluorescent-bright, spacious room covered floor to ceiling in gold-flecked linoleum looked more like a suburban public school than that dark downtown theater.

"I mean the real Wonderland. Like Alice," Maddie explained. "I feel like we've stepped through the looking glass and we're in a place where everything's flopsy-turvy. Anything can happen here."

"The *real* Wonderland?" James was still working out that phrase when Leigh heard actors nearing the doorway. She heard Bridie over the others, as usual.

"Here comes the Queen of Hearts." Leigh tried to sound normal. She reminded herself that she couldn't kill her mother, at least not in Florida, where they have the death penalty.

"Greetings and salutations," Bride announced at the door. Her clothes were as loud as she was—pinks and greens that fought for attention. She first placed herself at the head of the large table, but she must have thought better of it because she moved herself to a side seat. Let the director sit at the head of the table, like a good little actress. But she continued her entrance monologue.

"Isn't this heat ungodly? Is everyone else struggling with their hair? I am!" She leaned in to David as if he were the most fascinating specimen of a man she had ever seen. "David, sweetheart, you have to share your secrets with the rest of us. Come on, give. How do you keep yourself so neat and coiffed?"

David paused, shrugged, and answered, "These are hair plugs, Bridie. See?" He parted the front of his hair to prove it. Which wasn't necessary.

"No! I would never have guessed! Now, you mustn't share *all* your secrets with us, David. Do keep something for your memoirs. Speaking of which, how is my darling child, the fruit of my loins?" Bridie was handing the spotlight over to Leigh, who didn't want it.

Leigh nodded and managed a half-smile, knowing full well that she was being rude, being curt, but deciding that she was letting Bridie off easy. Remember the death penalty. Don't kill her. Not here.

"I hear that our run is already ninety percent sold out!" Bridie announced, returning her attention to the rest of the cast. "Ninety percent. How fabulous! Comedies need good audiences. They feel safe enough to laugh if there are others in the house laughing. This is just the best news, isn't it?"

Everyone else was sitting around the table. Everyone else had their scripts open to page one. Everyone. Else. Leigh was waiting to see how long it would take Bridie to figure out that she wasn't talking to David Letterman. Was her I'm-such-a-professional act back in New York just a fleeting choice in the whirlwind life of Bridie Hart? Was she going to revert to her default diva status in Jupiter?

"Oh! So sorry, everyone, please do excuse me!" Bridie exclaimed as she opened her script and looked up at Leigh, all wide-eyed. Leigh managed a two-thirds smile this time as she nodded at her mother. But her smile expanded as she looked over her cast and her stage managers.

"Welcome to Florida rehearsals, everyone!" Leigh knew that she sounded like a tired cheerleader, but she didn't mind. She filled them in on rehearsal schedules, then let James fill them in on logistics, and Bridie didn't interrupt once. Leigh finished her opening speech with, "I'm excited about this project. We have solid rehearsal time to work on this, and, as you all know, our run here is almost seventy-five percent sold out."

Yes, she had told the actors over dinner, and yes, they had heard Bridie get it wrong. They waited to see how Bridie would respond to being contradicted in front of everyone. She did nothing more than a theatrical nod that projected an I-stand-corrected response.

"Let's not sit at the table anymore. Let's get on our feet," Leigh announced, and the actors milled about while Leigh toured them through the sections of tape that represented set pieces.

"And this is the exit to Margaret and Maxwell's apartment, and stage left we have the table with the cash register and such." Leigh flinched as she said it. Did Bridie realize that she'd spend most of the first act on the left side of the stage? That meant she would have to turn her head to the right, showing the audience her left side. Her bad side.

Leigh continued. "Okay, so the play will start with Margaret's entrance from the apartment, and cross down center."

Bridie complied, going through the required motions, but hey, she didn't have her script.

"Bridie? We're going to work through this scene. Do you want to go get your script?" Leigh asked, with zero hostility, absolutely none.

"Oh, no, I don't need it. I'm off book."

The other actors gasped. Bridie had more lines than anyone else, and here she was claiming to know them already. Leigh whispered to Maddie, "Can you be on book for Bridie? Follow along and feed her any lines, just in case?" Maddie jumped to it, opening her script and following each word that Bridie said, waiting for her to call out for the next line, but she never did.

Maddie sent wild, unsubtle signals to Leigh that Bridie's speech was perfect. But Leigh didn't need to be told; she would have heard any glitches. She would have seized on any pauses. Bridie did more than learn her lines; she got laughs and smiles from her fellow cast members. As usual, she was beloved by people who didn't know her very well. She was already inhabiting the character completely.

"Do you want me to stay down center or move around the set?" Bridie asked when she finished her letter-perfect speech.

"Which do you prefer?" Leigh didn't usually attend to such granular details at such an early rehearsal.

"Which do *you* prefer?" Bridie countered.

Somewhere in the room, an actor declared, "We're so lucky!"

*   *   *

For a whole week, nothing went wrong. Leigh's updates to Kendall, Michael, and Harry started to sound so bland. "Everyone's fine. Rehearsals are fine. I feel fine about it all." This last part was mostly true. When Maddie called in sick on Thursday, it provided minor drama, but Maddie pulled through and was well again by noon, so it didn't qualify as an actual problem, even when she relapsed the next morning. James could have run everything solo. With Maddie absent, Leigh felt free to touch his arm too much. He started touching her back.

Bridie set a standard for learning lines, and everyone in the room rose to meet it. Bridie's voice, when she was not playing

Margaret, diminished to a natural conversational tone Leigh had never encountered in her before. Her anger against her mother showed messy signs of thaw. Leigh couldn't deny that Bridie's presence was elevating this bottom-of-the-pile cast to a higher standard.

It looked so good on paper, Harry sounded delighted with each of Leigh's updates. He was already counting his profits. She didn't talk to him about the lingering, indefinable problem under the surface. She didn't know how to explain what felt wrong about the mother-son relationship in the play. She couldn't define what was missing from the character of Margaret. It nagged at her, but it wouldn't reveal itself.

"Kendall? It's me. Leigh."

"What? What's wrong? What is it? What did your mother do now?"

"I can't even describe it. She's being, what's the word . . . good. She's being a good girl. She doesn't contradict me, threaten me, or try to tell the cast what I was like when I was thirteen."

"I doubt you were much different."

"True." Leigh actually let herself smile at this. "But there's something wrong. Maybe it's in the script or maybe it's the way Bridie is playing her. There's something wrong with Margaret. I just can't put my finger on it. Bridie is missing something in the role. Something important."

"Leigh, sweetheart, maybe it's you. Maybe you need to stop thinking of her as your mother. She's an actor in a play. Try to lock that in or she's going to drive you—*beep*—then you'll miss the chance to enjoy this. If this were 1962—*beep*—your big break."

Leigh looked at the little display on her phone. She recognized her home phone number trying to break into her call.

"Kendall, my other line. It's Michael."

"That's my cue. Good night, Leigh."

She took a breath before she pressed the little button that would switch her conversation. Was it strange that she could picture their telephone and the table it was on, but was having more and more trouble picturing Michael himself?

"Hi, Michael. How's it going?"

"Great. Crazy. Exhausting. And you? Is Bridie still being good?" He had to ask every time he called.

"Yes, she really is. It's a first," she answered every time.

"This is such amazing good luck!" Michael gushed.

Leigh could give her mother credit for everything she could point to and name, but she did not, would not, would never, feel lucky to have her.

"I had dinner with Mom and Dad last night," Michael added. "They say hi, and want to know if they should see the show in Florida or wait till it comes to New York."

Leigh was only half listening because she thought she heard a faint knock at her door. But who would be coming to her room now? She pulled the door ajar and saw Maddie in the hallway, trying to hide her face.

Michael was saying, "Oh, did I mention that I'm trying to get into the New York City Marathon? One of my new patients can get me a number. What do you think of that?"

Leigh was opening the door all the way and waving Maddie in.

"Yes, okay, great. I gotta go. I'll call you again soon, okay?" Leigh said quickly as she saw that Maddie was hiccuping through the end of a serious crying jag.

"Okay. Good night. I love you," Michael called out, barely noticing that Leigh was cutting him off.

"Bye," Leigh said as she was dropping the phone.

Maddie sat on the bed and opened her mouth to speak, but instead she began wailing as she rocked back and forth. Leigh was at a loss. What could have happened between dinner and now? Had they run out of incredible good luck?

"Is it money? Is it the IRS? Maddie, I can help you. Just tell me."

Maddie was shaking her head. Leigh hugged her, soothed her, and brought her tissues and cool water. Eventually Maddie slowed herself down. She reached for her purse and retrieved a blue stick.

Leigh sat back at the sight of that stick.

Maddie was pregnant.

[9]

When Maddie was finally able to speak, she sorted through stray phrases. "I'm so scared," "Why is this happening to me?" and "I don't know what to do," she said a lot. She blew her nose loudly and said it all again, with a few more grains of calm. "I don't know what to do."

Leigh was scared, too, didn't know why this was happening, and didn't know what to do. But she struggled to quiet those questions and be present for her friend. "Oh, Maddie, honey, of course you don't know. Give yourself some time, give yourself a break. We'll work this out, I promise."

"How?" Maddie could barely speak, and was sobbing all over again, much too loudly to hear anything that Leigh had to say. Not that Leigh had any answers, but she was reaching through her entire body to find something that would comfort her friend.

"It's going to be okay, Mad. I promise." But Maddie was too far gone to hear.

"This is impossible," she may have been saying. "And I'm so so sorry."

"Why?"

"Because you're the one who wants to get pregnant." Maddie looked up at Leigh. "You're the one who *should* be pregnant. I have no business, I have no right. You wouldn't be quite so incompliment. I don't know what to do . . ."

"Slow down," Leigh said. "Slow down. Look at me." Maddie managed that, after another loud nose-blow. "I love you. Really. And I'm going to get you through this. I promise."

"How?" Maddie looked so hopeful.

"How. How? I can't lie to you here, I have no idea. But that's never stopped me before."

Maddie smiled for the first time all night, and Leigh tried to draw out more of a smile from her friend. But Maddie retreated back to tears so quickly, Leigh decided to stop trying. Let her let it out.

And she did. When Maddie couldn't cry anymore, she wandered through Leigh's questions. Rico was the father, but where the hell was Rico? Somewhere in Japan, somewhere unreachable, somewhere he didn't want to be reached. Was he ever coming back? Maddie didn't know for sure, but her gut told her that he wasn't. Should she keep the baby? Should she not? She broke down whenever she faced that question.

They reached no answers, no conclusions, no plans. Of course. They talked until Maddie's head was dropping to her chest. Clearly Maddie was drained, and she fell asleep quite easily, so Leigh did her best to cover her with polyester.

Leigh was wildly awake, pacing the room in silence. She was buzzed and flying as if she'd finished a double latte or twelve. She was trying to focus on Maddie, specifically on Maddie and motherhood. She tried to shape her thoughts in the air, but thoughts of Maddie kept shifting into Margaret. Margaret, the mother. The character who was missing something indefinable. And now that indefinable something offered itself in the air, and Leigh snatched it. She stood still and let her thoughts take root. She knew what she needed to do—for Maddie, for Margaret, for everyone. She had it.

Leigh left a note for Maddie, though it didn't look as if Maddie would wake up anytime soon, gathered her supplies, shut off the lights, and slipped quietly out the door.

· · ·

"Leigh? What are you doing here?" It was James, and he sounded like someone had woken him up. Leigh didn't look up from her laptop, which was resting on the hotel's bar. She reached blindly for her drink and got it every time.

"Hey, James."

The bartender answered for Leigh. "I'll tell you what she's doing here. She's keeping me from closing. Look, buddy, I'm not supposed to do this—I could lose my job over it—but I'll sell her a bottle of scotch to go, and she can keep computing in the privacy of her very own room." He leaned in close to Leigh and shouted, "But I gotta close this bar, lady! I'm tired!"

"Leigh? What are you doing?" James repeated.

"Rewriting the play," Leigh said to her glowing monitor.

"What?! You can't. It's not yours to rewrite." James was hitting high notes for someone so tired.

"Just let me finish this scene." She still wasn't looking up. "I'm so close. Talk amongst yourselves."

Their conversation faded into noisy wallpaper, which was something she was building up a tolerance to anyway.

Bartender: "*Blah-blah-blah* late."

James: "*Blah-blah-blah* under a lot of stress."

Bartender: "*Blah-blah-blah* don't care. *Blah-blah* cops. *Blah-blah-blah.*"

Leigh saved her work and rubbed her achy wrists. She had been pushing so much speed and pressure onto the computer, which was hot to the touch, she had initiated some sort of carpal tunnel cloud around her forearms. Well, it was worth it for this new first act. Maybe she could stay a little while longer and begin the new second act. She stretched out her wrists and her stiff fingers and noticed that these were the only body parts in distress. Her shoulders were low and relaxed, her face felt easy. She couldn't stop smiling. Everything was clear, everything was possible: Leigh knew what she had to do. She had known it about five minutes after Maddie fell asleep. She held on tight to this new— "Hey!" she cried as she realized James was shutting down her laptop, shutting down her work. He lifted the laptop over his head and said, "Come on, Leigh! Follow the laptop! You can do it!"

She followed after him, helplessly reaching for the one and only copy of the darkest, best, finally valid version of *Women in Hats*. What if he dropped it? What if he passed it by a behemoth magnet, thus erasing the contents of her hard drive? What if Bridie suddenly appeared and snatched it away?

"I can't go to my room. Maddie's sleeping there! James! Where are you going?"

• | •   •

Leigh was only half listening to James and his advice to put away the computer, to sleep it off, some *blah-blah* about too much excitement. Oh, he had no idea what excitement she had saved to that slim device. He opened the door to his hotel room and she opened the laptop again as she slid into a chair at his pink table.

"Can I work here? I'll be quiet. You can go to sleep. I need to finish the first act while the ideas are still so fresh in my mind."

"How can you finish something you were never supposed to start? Leigh. What happened?" James asked. "Why is Maddie asleep in your room, and why did you take over the bar?"

Leigh was almost tired enough to let slip about Maddie's condition, but not quite.

"Maddie was tired, she fell asleep. No big deal. But I had to work. The inspiration just landed in my head, and I had to set it down before I lost it. This is big. This is not just about the play, oh, no, it's so much more than that. And by the way, a bar is a great place to work. I never knew."

"Can I see what you've done?" James was, what, two inches taller than Michael? Three? There was just a bit of gray starting in his hair. More on the left than on the right. She had to stop staring at it because he was starting to laugh at her. So, she let him read the opening scene over her shoulder. Eventually, she switched places with him as he sank into the bright pink chair. His face looked like a tragedy mask, which wasn't the reaction Leigh wanted.

"Oh, no. Oh, shit. Does it suck?" she asked. "I'm too tired to have any objectivity. Please tell me."

"How do I read the next page?" His hands hovered over the keyboard until she showed him the key. She sat quietly while he finished the first scene. She stopped breathing from the moment he turned away from the glowing screen until the moment he said, "Wow." He shook his head as if he were giving bad news, but added, "It's wonderful. It's dark, but it's still funny. It's really scary, and I can already tell that it's building up to a battle royal between the mother and the daughter."

Leigh snorted. "You have no idea."

"It's actually kind of brilliant," he said, without moving his eyes from the screen.

Leigh restrained herself from kissing him. Just barely. "But you can't do this," he said quietly as he folded his arms against his chest and turned to look at Leigh. "Absolutely not. You can't switch Maxwell and Sarah. This is a completely different play, just with the same character names." Maybe this was why he looked so sad. He knew he was going to say this.

"And the same title. And I can change it. I did change it, at least for the first act, which, by the way, I want to work through a little more." She was up, up, up; she was making her pitch. "Because you see, now it's a mother-daughter play. Sarah is Margaret's daughter. Maxwell is her boyfriend, and he's still going to be a dentist, but nobody cares about that anyway." Leigh paced the room to outline the story she wanted to tell. She placed Michael's play on the left side of the air, but her own on the right side of the air, and much higher. "The story isn't about a hat shop versus dental school anymore, and it's no silly door-slamming farce. It's about a mother who wants her daughter to become her. She's going to relive her life through her daughter. She's going to consume her. But the daughter is fighting to escape." She moved as close as she dared to his face to say, "Now it's actually interesting."

Hah! He couldn't argue with that.

She was inspired, she was tapping into her inner genius, and she was kind of drunk. She stood toe-to-toe with him, trying not to notice that he was painfully handsome, so sleepy, tan, and slightly bristly. He was talking to her, but she just read his face instead. It said, "Come closer." So she did. His face worked so well to distract her, so did his shoulders. She shook her head and forced herself to look him in the eye, which was a fatal mistake.

"Don't you think your husband's going to kill you?" He was ending a long speech that she hadn't meant to ignore, but she had been so busy looking at him she hadn't heard a word. Did he notice that her eyes were traveling all over his face and body? Did it bother him? He was still lecturing her, so it couldn't bother him that much. "And how will you get it from the computer onto paper? How can you make that happen, exactly?"

She reached up and kissed him.

It wasn't a kiss to end an argument or to be cute. It was just an inevitable kiss. It was a kiss where Leigh and James belonged and remained for a good leisurely while. After they broke from the kiss, she stayed close, very close. In her fuzzy, drunken state, she remembered that she had tried something like that kiss once before, and she remembered how badly it had ended. If this were any other day of her life, she would have apologized and been thoroughly ashamed of herself. She would have panicked. But today, she breathed slowly, despite the three-dimensional drumroll in her heart. Why was it so easy to be brave now?

Why was he smiling back at her? Because this time, he was pulling her to him. He was kissing her. She indulged in that kiss until she absolutely had to tell him, "Um. Look. I can't have children." To her this was not a non sequitur, although James looked like he was expecting another kiss.

He said, "I'm sorry."

"Yes, well, me, too. I'm not sure why I just said that to you."

He didn't look like he minded her saying such irrelevant things.

"What happened to you?" he asked, and he pulled back a bit, ready for a long story.

"It's a long story. It ends with me not being able to have children."

He outlined her face very gently with his hand, and rearranged her hair out of her eyes. He was looking for something more from her, more information, maybe. She waited a few moments to see if she could kiss James again. She could.

She felt so safe kissing him, so she did it some more. If it was safe to kiss him, it was safe to tell him, "It's her fault. Bridie's. She did this to me." She gulped past that and needed water. James seemed to read her mind, and handed her a glass.

"I've had these terrifying miscarriages, these big bloody messes, and I think they're wrecking my marriage. But Bridie just keeps dancing through life with no punishment, completely unscathed. Do you think she got Letterman to propose to her again? I love that bit. Everyone loves that bit. Everyone loves Mother Love. Except me. She did this to me. And I had to write about it. Even though I couldn't actually write about it, exactly."

Leigh had to lie down, had to push Bridie out of her head, out of this room. She wanted to tell him how the first act ended, but she found herself talking about Michael.

"He said I could rewrite it if I needed to. And anyway, it still has a hat shop, so. There. I can still use the title. Right?"

James tried to hide his grimace, shielding his face behind those hands. "Oh, Leigh, Leigh, Leigh. This is going to cause you so much trouble. You can't do this." He stopped hiding behind his hands to find that Leigh wasn't relenting.

He stooped down next to the bed, took her hands, and suggested, "Save it for Wonderland, but don't just replace the play you were hired for with this . . ."

Leigh grinned and began singing the inane theme song from her mother's TV show.

"No one loves you any better than your M-O-Double-M-Y . . .
And if you start to cry,
She'll dry each tearful, make you cheerful.
No matter where you roam, your thoughts always stray . . ."

And James was kissing her.

· · ·

She opened her eyes. He looked good asleep. He didn't smile, he didn't let his mouth fall open. He looked like himself, but asleep. He was so comfortable and familiar, Leigh needed to stay connected to him. The sun was slicing through the floral/palm-frond curtains (how had she missed them before?), and maybe that was what woke her from such a secure sleep. She needed to burrow into his shoulder and hide from the sun, so she did. His arm draped around her slowly, but he kept his eyes closed. She closed hers, too.

James was probably awake, rehearsing a speech in his head: shouldn't have done this, big mistake, let's forget about it, and other phrases Leigh didn't want to hear. Let sleeping men lie. Let him keep rehearsing, and he won't be able to give the actual speech.

He rolled over and nearly crushed her. She tapped him on the shoulder.

"Excuse me. Need to breathe here," she whispered in his ear. He opened his eyes and gave a sleepy smile.

"Who are you?" he asked, and they quietly laughed in unison. Wasn't it kind of him to open the we-must-never-speak-of-this scene with a joke? Now Leigh was sorry she had let herself sleep so long; she had slept through so much good stuff. She wished she could have had more of this feeling. It was new, whatever it was. More.

James propped himself up on his elbow and looked ready to talk. Here it was: the ending was beginning. Fine. She could take it.

"So. What do you need?"

"For what?" She propped herself up to match him.

"For today. Before we get to rehearsal—whatever script we're rehearsing—what do you need?"

Leigh sat all the way up and knew exactly what she needed. "Coffee."

And just like that, James was ready to find Juan Valdez for the finest coffee in Jupiter, Florida. But then Leigh woke up a few more notches, realizing that she was in James's room. Maddie was asleep back in her room. And Maddie needed her.

"No time! I have to go! Now!"

He tried to stop her, but no one could.

"What's wrong? What happened?" he called out. But Leigh couldn't answer that. She jumped into her clothes, accepted the hopelessness of her wrecked appearance, and raced for the door. She stopped long enough to grab her laptop.

"I'll call you!" she promised.

He sputtered a few stray words before he said, "Leigh!" and she turned around, giving him exactly one and a half seconds to say more. He took too long to come out with "Just go," as he shook his head.

.   .   .

Maddie was like a caged tiger, pacing Leigh's room.

"Where the hell did you go? I woke up and you were gone. Just a stupid note, 'I'm at the bar.' Are you kidding me? It was like a bad one-night stand. Or a good one. One where the guy just gets the hell out before I have to see him in sunlight."

"I'm sorry. I didn't want to wake you. But I thought I'd be back before you woke up. How are you feeling?"

"Pregnant. I'm feeling very pregnant. I threw up in your bathroom, and, by the way, I'm getting good at it. All these years, I could have had a nice eating disorder. Too late now. Oh, God, I wish I had brought my paints with me. If I were painting, I'd feel like I could actually do something. And everything is clearer when I'm working with color. All I brought was that stupid sketch pad. I'm such a fucking idiot sometimes."

Leigh didn't know what else to do, so she brought her friend more tissues, but Maddie appeared to be all cried out.

"Maddie, I want you to have this baby, but maybe I'm being selfish because, hey, there'd be a baby, right? So, whatever you want to do, I'll support you, I'll help you."

Maddie sighed and studied her hands, so Leigh did, too. Such long, elegant fingers. The silence following that sigh lasted so long, Leigh reached out for Maddie's hand and sighed, too. Maddie asked, "Will you get me unlimited saltine crackers until this morning sickness is over?"

Leigh wasn't sure if Jupiter's morning sun was filling the room, or if she just felt overjoyed as she watched her friend make this choice.

Maddie's list of demands continued. "Will you help me choose a name for this kid? Because I don't think I could take the pressure. And will you change diapers? Because I know I can't do that. Ever."

Maddie was going to have a baby. Leigh let it sink in before she squeezed her friend a little too tightly around the ribs and said, "I will change every single diaper, if you want."

Maddie whispered, "We're going to have a baby."

. . .

Leigh found James in the hotel restaurant an hour later, eating some unidentifiable grain-and-seed type of cereal. He nearly choked when he saw Leigh, and stopped eating.

"I need to talk to you." She already sounded pressed for time, but he already looked frightened.

"It's not about that," Leigh reassured him. "I need more time. I need all the time I can get."

"For what?"

"For this rewrite. I want to finish it. I need you to cancel today's rehearsal. Maddie's still not feeling well, and why should we rehearse the wrong script, anyway? I want to do the new version."

"If this is what you want, I'll do it. I'm your stage manager, so I take my marching orders from you. But this could cost you a lot. Are you prepared to deal with that?"

Leigh smiled, and managed to contain a manic little laugh. Her mind thumped with energy born from the excitement of Maddie's baby and from the excitement of discovery and invention with this new play. Her synapses were firing too fast for her to explain herself, and there was no time to argue or discuss. She was looking around the restaurant for her actors. If they were among strangers, could she sidle up next to James for just a little while?

"So, I'll cancel rehearsal, but after that, what do you need?" James asked before she could get close to him.

"For what?"

"For today, for the weekend. To finish your rewrite. You only have three days until our next rehearsal, and you have a whole lot of work to do. What do you need?"

"Coffee."

.   .   .

Later that morning, Maddie moved back to her own room to be alone. She let Leigh know that she wanted utter privacy in case morning sickness resurfaced. Maddie didn't know how she was going to tell the others, but these bouts of nausea were not going to force her hand. Leigh understood perfectly, and was secretly grateful that Maddie didn't need her for a little while. Leigh was now free to spend the rest of that morning in her own room, sipping the coffee James had brought her and reading the new words she was going to give to her actors. There was so much more to do, but first she flipped open her phone and dialed.

"Kendall, I'm doing something that maybe I shouldn't." Leigh sounded so reasonable.

"Then don't do it. Duh." Leigh could hear Kendall shuffling papers while she talked.

"But I have to."

"Then do it. Or, here's a thought, tell me what it is." Kendall was always good at sounding impatient because she usually was impatient.

"I'm rewriting the play."

"Oh, my." The paper shuffling stopped.

Leigh disclosed everything. She described the new play in exquisite detail, and the anticipated reactions from Bridie, Harry, and, oh, yes, Michael.

"And who are you sleeping with? Not one of the actors, I hope.

Please let it be James. He's got that quiet, solid, baked-potato thing going on that could be useful for you. I approve."

"It's James. And how did you know?"

"You can't hear it, but I'm smiling here in New York. Now, as for the play, it sounds like a play *I* would like. Send it to me when it's done. And don't worry. I won't tell Harry or Michael."

.   .   .

Leigh worked through the morning, and worked through lunch. The day was flying by as she let herself get lost in the alternate universe she was creating.

"You should go outside," James advised when he returned to her room bearing more coffee and a supply of carbohydrates. "It's warm. There's this whole sunshine thing going on. You should check it out."

"Sunshine. Yes, I've heard of that. Maybe I'll give it a try." When she stood up, her entire body cramped and rebelled.

Leigh looked around at the crumpled pages she had shot to the wastebasket and missed. She saw the various stacks of pages around the room and had an urge to clean up the mess. But the midafternoon break sounded more important. James was right. Leigh knew she'd need James by her side through this whole adventure. With that in mind, she dashed to the front desk and requested a second key for her room. That way, James could bring her coffee or sunshine whenever he wanted to.

Was the clerk looking at her wedding ring? Did her messy look make him think she had just emerged from her bed? Should she care? She got an extra key for James. As she clutched her illicit key, she smiled seductively at the clerk. Let him think what he wants. Just as she relaxed into the freedom of her affair, her cell phone rang and she knew she had failed at hiding how badly it scared her. The clerk did just as bad a job at hiding his laughter.

"Hey, Leigh. It's me." Michael. Calling. Now. Shit.

"Hi." Her voice caught in her throat as she escaped all that clerk-smirk.

"You sound like you have a cold? Are you okay?"

"Yes. No. No, I'm not. I have a cold. I need to, um, rest." Her voice descended to gravel, which helped hide her lies from any clerks or stray actors who might be in the vicinity. What if James could hear her?

"You should stay in bed."

"Uh-huh."

Leigh had openly lied to her husband. She paused long enough to be shocked at her own behavior. But only for a moment. Of course, then she was shocked at the fact that she was only shocked for a moment. And that seemed to suffice. There was no more time or energy for additional shock, after all, because she was busy.

*   *   *

"Am I the reason you canceled today's rehearsal?"

Maddie may have been battling with guilt, but she was starting to get color back in her skin again. It had been only twenty-four hours since Maddie had announced her pregnancy, but the world as they both knew it had turned upside down. Now Leigh was taking an evening break to check on her friend.

"No, no, no. It's not you," Leigh reassured her. "I needed a little time to work on the script. So, I'm kind of holing up in my room for a while to do a little script cleanup." Yes, and Leigh was fighting the urge to clean up Maddie's room now. There were old takeout containers, snack bags, magazines, and bits of paper all over the room. Leigh lost the battle and started cleaning.

"You missed a spot," Maddie called out as she put her feet up on the bed. "Oh, and peel me a grape." Leigh guiltily dropped all of the trash in a not-neat little pile on the floor. She flopped herself onto the bed next to Maddie and put her feet up, too.

"This is weird," Leigh said, hoping she wouldn't have to explain what exactly was weird. She munched the stale potato chip Maddie offered her.

"Yeah?" Maddie said slyly. "Well, I'm pregnant. Now, *that's* weird."

. . .

For the next three days, James and Leigh settled into a routine. He started her day with a ridiculously large coffee. She would slide into her chair at the pink table in her room and set to work. As the day wore on, he brought her more than coffee—he brought food, water, treats. He rubbed her aching hands and shoulders. Leigh's visits with Maddie became an official midday break where the two friends could relax together while James brought Leigh's work to the hotel business center and fumbled his way through printing her new pages. When Leigh returned to her own room, James always greeted her with, "Ready to get back to work?" He held out the chair and gently pointed to his (windup) watch. She had precious little time to finish. They were paying the actors to sit around, not rehearsing, so Leigh had to get them all back to work by the end of the week if she hoped to open the play on schedule. But each evening, James would insist that she take more breaks for fresh air, for dinner with her cast, for sex with him. From time to time, Leigh wondered if she was hallucinating all this.

Each night, for three nights, he stayed with her. It was only three days, and Leigh would have sold her soul to keep them both there forever.

For three blessed days, her life in New York (husband, husband, husband) didn't exist, nor did her wicked mother. For three blissful days, she worked, she ate, she had a glorious time. So this was how it felt to have all she could possibly want. So this was how it felt to be full, to be happy.

10

Good morning, everyone. And welcome back to rehearsals. We have new scripts to work with, so if our stage managers would kindly . . ."

James seemed almost pleased as he handed out the thick scripts, while Maddie was downright tickled.

"Wow, I had no idea you had gotten so conspired!" Maddie was flipping through the new pages and smiling at Leigh as if she could see her naked in bed with James. Oh, shit. Did Maddie know? No, no, Leigh realized that Maddie just meant "inspired."

"Oh, I'm just trying something new." And she was.

"You're amazing. You're like a soul model for women everywhere." Maddie hugged her and went off to gather chairs around the table. The actors opened their scripts, and a few looked to Bridie for an expected volatile reaction.

"Live theater is full of surprises, isn't it," Bridie said with a twinkle in her voice. "I was once in a Broadway musical, directed by

Leigh's father, where I rehearsed one set of lyrics by day and performed another set for preview audiences by night. I ended up singing 'la la la' more than once, but I got through it." She rose and magnanimously put her arm around Leigh. "We'll learn our new lines and move onward and upward, won't we? We serve at the pleasure of our director."

Bridie must have sensed that her speech was running long. Although she may have wanted to say more, she sat herself back down and beamed up at Leigh. She was the apple-polishing, brown-nosing, ass-kissing kid who hungered for Teacher's approval.

"Let's just read it through first, shall we?" Leigh announced.

Bridie opened her new script, and seemed pleased that her act 1 entrance speech had grown longer. More lines – good, good. She launched them into the read-through in full voice.

MARGARET

My daughter is my immortality. Oh, the plans I have for her! I don't understand these mothers who let their daughters travel down the wrong road and call themselves wise. Why should children have to learn from their own mistakes? Can't my daughter learn from *my* mistakes?

That's why I built this shop. It's our fortress, our safe haven. This is where I'll keep her. Forever.

"Interesting. Really, really interesting, Leigh." Bridie's pleasure had transformed into simmering anger as she spoke.

"We're trying something new," Leigh coaxed her mother. "Just go with it." Leigh tried to be self-disciplined enough not to look up from her script, but she couldn't resist peeking at Bridie, who looked around the table, trying to make eye contact with the actors. But they were busy scanning the pages for their new lines. Bridie smiled like the good sport she would never be, and kept reading.

SARAH

Mother? Look at my latest painting. I'm so proud of it. What do you think?

MARGARET

Sarah, I've always said this: for the rest of your life, you'll be glad that you can paint so well. Everyone should have a hobby.

James read the stage directions. "Margaret kisses her daughter on the cheek and exits. Sarah addresses the audience."

SARAH

A hobby? I don't want it to be a hobby. It's going to be my profession. And I don't want to work in this prison of a hat shop for the rest of my life. I'm going to get as far away from that woman as I possibly can.

"It's very . . . different," Bridie interrupted to no one in particular. "Can I ask, what are the new relationships here?"

"Sarah is now Margaret's daughter. Margaret, as you can already see, wants to control her daughter and she wants her daughter to be just like her. But Sarah doesn't want to be anything like Margaret. And, in the next scene, Sarah is going to meet Maxwell, and—well, why am I giving it all away? Let's read, shall we?" Leigh tried hard to focus on the pages.

Bridie clapped her hands as she smiled. "Interesting. So now the mother is the villain of the piece. That's a bold choice. Most people couldn't make that work, but I'm sure you can."

"I didn't make Margaret the villain." And that was true. Mostly. Margaret was not a villain. She was a mother who made mistakes. Big, fat, repulsive mistakes. "She loves Sarah. She just wants her daughter to follow in her footsteps very, very closely. Why don't we just keep reading before we decide to hate it."

"Oh, just one little problem: Where will the paintings come from? You've already established them as a pivotal object. They're already so important. They'll have to be so good that—"

Leigh smiled at Maddie, who was radiating joy as she figured out Leigh's plan: Maddie would create the paintings to be the centerpiece of the play.

"Maddie? I was going to ask you later, but I thought that maybe we could commission the paintings from you? Of course, this would be a completely separate job from your work as assistant stage manager. We can go into the details later."

Maddie, who never blushed, was blushing crimson. Maybe it was hormonal warfare, but she was dangerously close to crying like a game-show winner. Leigh shouldn't have made the offer in front of everyone and embarrassed her like that, but Maddie would remain happy about this for quite a while. While Maddie nodded and choked back her sobs, Leigh tried to sound cool and efficient.

"Well. That's done. And I think we can count ourselves lucky to have such outstanding artwork available to us."

Harmony reached over and hugged Maddie. The whole cast knew that Maddie had been in some form of painting withdrawal here in Florida, and her obvious joy now informed anyone who had missed that fact before. Jessica was letting the tears fall. Both women turned to look at their new superhero, Leigh Majors. David gave Maddie an energetic two thumbs up, and Ben smiled. Ben actually SMILED.

SARAH

You're wrong about Maxwell. He loves me.

MARGARET

He's using me. I mean *you*. He's using *you*. I've seen it a thousand times. He needs someone to support him until he's through dental school. After that, he'll drop you like yesterday's news.

SARAH

He really loves me. I can feel it.

MARGARET

He's not worth all this fuss. And I'm not saying this because I think he's boring or not good enough for you—and by the way, he *is* boring and he is *not* good enough for you—it's because he doesn't really love you. No one loves you but your mother.

Jessica was reading beautifully, and Leigh quietly predicted good things for her career beyond musical comedy. But Bridie. Bridie was just marking it, stressing the operative word in each sentence but withholding anything more, anything better.

SARAH

He does. He loves me.

MARGARET

No. Not like I do. I'd lay down my life for you. It kills me that this hurts you, Sarah, but you have to break it off with him. Immediately.

James called out the lunch break and the cast burst into loud conversation immediately. They were excited for Maddie and her new paintings, excited for themselves and their new play.

"Maddie?" Leigh had to do this now in the correct, grown-up, businesslike style Maddie would appreciate.

"Yeah?" Maddie was pulling herself out of another hug with Harmony and Jessica.

"This is a lot of painting. And by 'a lot' I mean A LOT. It's really going to take over most of your time. The good news is it really is bigger pay—about four times what you were making as our assistant stage manager."

"Well, then, there can't be any bad news." She smiled back at her cheerleaders, Harm and Jess.

"Just a little: get started. You need to get paint, canvas, brushes, whatever you need—we'll reimburse you out of petty cash—and get to work. Here are some notes on the kind of paintings we'll need." Leigh made a mental note to let Harry know that she was about to spend all this money, but that note got erased while she walked Maddie to the door. "I was thinking about your painting style the whole time I was doing this. Can you do that? I mean, do you feel well enough to paint?"

"Painting is exactly what the doctor ordered."

Bridie stood a few feet away, regally summoning her daughter with her most imperious look. Clearly, she was not amused. Leigh waved at her mother and hurried Maddie along.

"Well, then, you're about to be so very healthy. We're going to need at least seven paintings. Seven great paintings. Can you do it?"

Maddie looked like she wanted to hesitate or negotiate for more time. But Leigh was trying to push one word into her friend's mind, and it worked.

"Yes." And with that, Maddie turned to the company and said, "Everybody! Your director is a genius and great broad. Just wanted to make sure you knew that. And now—I gotta go paint! Bye!"

Bridie was now combining a sneer and a glare in a way that seemed sure to cause a fire. Leigh watched Maddie dance out the door and immediately regretted sending her away. She needed her friend, her ally. Bridie was speeding across the room and right into Leigh's personal space.

"Leigh, sweetheart, this is a very good play you've got here. Really. And I think that it will be perfect for Wonderland and that very exciting, dark little world you have there." Her voice was still cheery, even though Leigh saw the hard set to her jaw. "But is this new play really right for Harry Greenwald? Is it appropriate for Michael's original intent? Is it?" Leigh took a deep breath while she searched for an answer, but then Bridie added, "And what would Michael say if he knew what was going on here in Florida?"

Leigh flinched. Did Bridie know about James? How? And how much? Leigh and her mother both turned to look at him while he pushed the cast to get to lunch while they still had time. "Go and eat!" he shouted. "The clock is ticking!"

James had given Leigh all the time she needed to work out an answer to her mother. "Mind your own business, Bridie. And go eat."

* * *

SARAH

I don't want to hate her. I love her. But she let me down. She let me down a lot.

GRACE

Honey, I've known your mother a lot of years. You have to talk to her. Tell her what you want.

SARAH

I've tried. But it's like she can't hear me. Or maybe she just doesn't want to hear me. Now she thinks I'm taking all these business classes to learn about accounting and inventory.

GRACE

You mean you're not?

(Sarah hands Grace a piece of paper.)
What's this?

SARAH

I got accepted at the Art Institute. And look—they even gave me a partial scholarship.

GRACE

That's fantastic. I'm so proud of you. But Sarah, how are you paying for the rest of it?

SARAH

With the money Mom gave me for business school. Please don't tell on me, Aunt Grace. Please!

"So, does that mean that the daughter is *stealing* from her mother? Isn't she being sort of unfair and a little bit mean to her hardworking but successful mother? Where did you get the idea for this daughter character?" Bridie had already interrupted the second act four times since the group returned from the lunch break. Leigh was keeping count.

"Let's keep reading," Leigh made a point of saying each time Bridie spoke out of turn.

TED

Son, don't stay where you're not wanted. If Sarah here doesn't trust you, then cut her loose. And little girl, you're making the mistake of a lifetime. This is a good boy.

SARAH

Please don't go. Max, you know I love you, and I trust you. It's just that my mother is . . .

MAXWELL

Crazy?

"Oh, please! That whole scene has to go!" Bridie's seventh interruption.

SARAH

Yes, she's crazy.

The cast was reading well, but they paused respectfully every
time Bridie interrupted. Was their allegiance shifting?

MARGARET

Don't do this to me, Sarah, please. You can't go. Not like this.

SARAH

This is good-bye.

MARGARET

Do you want me to beg? I've never begged in my life, not once, not
even when your father was leaving me. But I'll do it now.
(*She kneels.*)

"You've gone insane. You realize that, don't you?" Bridie's
twelfth interruption.

MARGARET

I'm begging you. Please. Stay here with me. I'll be good, you'll see.
Please.

SARAH

Good-bye, Mom.

When James called out, "Curtain," Leigh held her breath so that
she could hear even the faintest praise for her work. But no one
said anything. At least, not until Bridie spoke.

"I'm so sorry for all the disruptions. Let's put that behind us. But

Leigh, can we talk about this? Are you willing to listen to constructive criticism?" Bridie asked.

"Always." Leigh had never heard the similarities in their
voices before. The same notes, the same timbre. That couldn't be
good.

Bridie sat back as if she were waiting for the world to come to
her. But the actors didn't choose up sides. Eventually, they rose,
gathered their belongings, and started making quiet dinner plans
with one another. And off they went.

James remained in the room and went to Leigh's side. But he
said, "Leigh, I have to go to the business center and figure how to
get new contracts faxed over for Maddie. Are you going to be all
right here?" So he wouldn't be at her side for very long.

All the while, Leigh never took her eyes off her mother,
who was feigning serenity and doing a poor job of it. This was
an example of her deliberate bad acting, which was her way of
saying that she was rising above her emotional turmoil because
she didn't want you to see it, but, then again, she really did want
you to see it. Bridie was such an exhausting person to be around.

"I'll be fine. I have experience," Leigh reassured him.

James hesitated, then asked oh-so-quietly, "See you later?"
Leigh nodded, eyes on her mother-figure the whole time. It had
been years since she and Bridie had truly had it out. When was the
last time? Frank's funeral? Lilly's? Did it matter? Did it ever make a
difference? Back then, Leigh was always just a little bit afraid of her
mother. Bridie smelled the fear and always triumphed. Not this
time.

This was one of the worst times for Leigh's cell phone to ring,
but there it went. It sounded like a tiny bomb dropping in the middle of the room. Leigh had to look away from Bridie to find the
identity of the caller. Michael. Leigh shut off the phone without
answering and looked back at her mother.

"Mom, I've really come to expect you to behave better than this at my rehearsals." Mom? Why would she call this woman "Mom"? Shit. Bridie had put her expensive shoes up on the table, and Leigh was standing nearby like a useless waiter. She would have given anything to change the blocking on this scene.

"*Me? I* behaved badly? You took an adorable comedy and turned it into *Bridie Dearest*. And I won't have it. I won't. And just so you know, missy, there's a clause in my will that if you write a book about me after I die, my estate will sue you back to the Stone Age. Just wanted to make sure you knew that."

"This is not about you." Leigh threw her script and her notebooks into her bag, doing her own bad-acting version of fake-calm.

"The fuck it isn't." Bridie slammed her expensive shoes to the linoleum floor.

"Oh, of course. I forgot. Everything's about you. Silly me. Let's retitle the play *Bridie in Hats* or *Mother Love Live*. But whatever we call it, *this* is the script." She patted her heavy satchel bag as she threw it onto her shoulder, a little too hard. "This is what we're all here to do. So, you're either all in or all out."

"Fuck you." Bridie rose to throw the words right in Leigh's face.

"Hey, you signed a contract, Mom. Bridie." Shit.

"Fuck you." Bridie was leaning closer, trying to reach Leigh with her epithets. She missed.

"I'll see you at rehearsal tomorrow, okay?"

Leigh headed for the door while Bridie roared, "Fuck you!"

"Nice. You kiss your daughter with that mouth?" Leigh called over her shoulder, but never stopped moving.

• • •

Leigh found her cast gathered in the hotel lobby.

"We're all sick of the hotel menu, so we're heading out to explore Jupiter," Harmony explained. "Hey, that sounds weird. Anyway, you want to join us?"

Leigh did. She wanted to slow down her pulse from the Bridie drama and join them. But really, she should stay and check on contracts, paintings, rehearsal schedules, designers, oh, and Bridie. She should probably find Bridie and have a more civilized conversation with her as soon as they both cooled off. If she stood still for another minute, Leigh could probably come up with seven more reasons to stay at the hotel.

"I'd love to. Let's go."

After much discussion among the actors, they settled on BurrGrr, since it claimed to offer fare for both vegetarians and carnivores. Harmony and Jessica took the first cab, while Leigh, David, and Ben followed in the next

"One rule for tonight," David announced as their cab picked up speed. "No shoptalk. We can talk about anything—religion, politics, sex, you name it—but we can't talk about the play we're in. Especially when we've got the boss lady around."

It took Leigh half a second to realize that she was the boss lady.

"Good luck, buddy," Ben offered. "I mean, no offense to anyone here, but this is one of the weirdest productions I've ever been in, and I've been in some weird shit. I feel like I'm working on some bizarro family psychodrama. It makes me want to call in Dr. Phil."

"Me, too," Leigh chimed in.

At the restaurant, a teenage waitress brought menus for everyone. She had braces and bad skin. Bridie might have taken her aside to counsel her about a skin-care regimen, if Bridie ate at places like BurrGrr.

Jessica started to ask about the new script, but David cut her off. "We all agreed in the cab—no shoptalk."

Jessica shook her head and replied, "Yeah, well, I wasn't in the cab with you guys, and I think we can talk about our show if it comes up naturally, like, based on things we're already saying. Does anyone else think so?"

"No!" David shouted. "It's unhealthy. We are more than the sum of the parts we are playing."

"Hey. Are y'all actors and actresses?" The waitress beamed.

"Yes," Jessica replied. "We're in the show at the Greenwald Theater. It hasn't opened yet, so we're still in rehearsals." Jessica was so humble, so modest.

"Wow. Actors and actresses. Y'all look so neat. You must have such neat lives." She had given away all of her menus, but remained enchanted by the galaxy of stars in her section.

"We do have neat lives." Jessica sounded perfectly serious. "What's your name?"

The waitress pointed to her name tag, rather than say her name out loud. It said SHELBY.

"Shelby. That's a nice name." If Shelby had recognized one of the actors, she might have fainted.

"Ya know, my mom wanted to be a dancer, but then she got pregnant with me, and then the twins, and we all kind of ruined her figure, ya know? Y'all are so lucky. I hope ya know it. Y'all are the luckiest people alive."

"Yes, we are." Leigh surprised herself by being the one to say that. And from the way the entire cast turned to stare at her, she wasn't the only one surprised to hear her say it.

•   •   •

Once their food arrived, the cast dug into one another's love lives. It was endless drama, and Leigh wished she could take notes. Also, it would give her an excuse for remaining silent all night. She didn't know if anyone knew about James, couldn't remember how discreet they had been or hadn't been these last several days. She was too busy writing and being happy to watch over her shoulder. Maybe someone would ask her point-blank about James. Maybe not. She sat back while the cast took turns offering up romantic history.

David went through a nasty divorce a few years ago. "Believe me, they're *all* nasty." He was now living with a woman who was teaching him "how not to be a complete asshole." It sounded like he was taking his life lessons seriously. In fact, Leigh noticed that whenever she gave him a note in rehearsals, he was completely receptive, always saying "Thank you." So many actors were defensive at any public note, she had to wonder if his girlfriend had taught him to thank people who were trying to help him.

Ben believed that all romantic entanglements were codependent and rooted in the deep psychological scars of childhood. He quoted Freud and Jung, clearly impressed with himself. He made a good, if lengthy, argument against romantic love. He definitely scared Jessica, who may or may not have been carrying a small torch for him.

Jessica left her high school sweetheart behind in Michigan while she got herself settled in New York. He finally came to the city, but he lasted only a month. At the four-week point, he managed to despise everything about the place. He went back to Michigan, and Jessica learned that he got married a month ago.

"He swore up and down that I was the one, that he'd never love anybody else. But he married Andrea Lucas, who was a total slut in the eleventh grade and everyone knew it."

"Maybe that was what he wanted," Harmony said gently. Jessica was trying not to cry, and Leigh couldn't blame her. No one wanted to play a weepy scene at BurrGrr.

Ben reached across the table and took her hand. "He's marrying his mother. We all do," he said. To comfort her.

Harmony had been living with her partner, Christine, for twenty-three years. "It's not as exciting as it used to be, not after all this time. We're boring old ladies now, who occasionally go skiing. That's it. But I love her like crazy. That doesn't change. And the thing is, I haven't done a show out of town in so many years. And now, I can't believe how much I miss her."

Harmony seemed to be handing the conversation over to Leigh, who was also away from her spouse, who was also probably missing him. This was Leigh's cue to talk about her husband, their playwright, Michael. She didn't want to say his name or picture his face.

Leigh smiled and asked Shelby for a round of drinks for everyone. Before Shelby could leave, Leigh ordered a second round, "for a New York minute from now. Okay, Shelby?"

*   *   *

It was time to leave, and Leigh suddenly remembered that she had left her phone off all evening. When she brought it back to life, she saw three messages waiting, all from the same caller. Michael. She shut the phone off and stood up, feeling stupid and light. Why was she drinking manhattans, of all things? What was wrong with her? Now, yes, okay, she wasn't an actress, but she had been studying her mother for years, and that was akin to a degree from the Yale School of Drama. So Leigh decided to act sober. She suspected that she wasn't doing a great job, but she was doing better than David and Ben, who were stumbling and laughing out the door.

"You SUCK!" David was laughing.

"No, YOU suck!" Ben laughed back.

"You guys!" Jessica giggled.

Someone took Leigh's arm and said into her ear, "It's okay, Leigh. You're allowed to be drunk with us. We're safe." That sounded like Harmony. Oh, look: it was Harmony, who drank only water and green tea and stuff like that. Haaaarmony. What a great name she chose for herself.

"Haaaarmony. What a great name you chose for yourself."

"Yup. Let's go outside and get some fresh air."

This time, they all crammed into one taxi and giggled as they rode back to the hotel. Jessica began singing Rodgers and Hammerstein's greatest hits, despite Ben shouting, "Slow tunes! Oh the pain, the pain!"

• • •

Leigh opened her hotel room door and jumped when she saw James there. Yes, she had gotten him an extra key, she knew that, but hey, that was a lot for a girl to remember tonight. She stayed in the doorway, steadying herself thanks to the handy-dandy doorknob. Maybe he wouldn't notice that she was soooo drunk.

"Hey," he said. He looked serious, so she tried to look serious back, but she stayed connected to that doorknob. She was sober enough to know that she was more than a little wobbly. She struggled to focus on him.

"Maddie's all set," he continued. "My God, she's over the moon. Her hotel room is a big art studio now. Want to go see? I think she's just going to paint nonstop from now till opening. And listen, Harry called, and you need to get him soon. He's leaving for London on Friday. Did you know he has *two* shows he's trying to bring over to New York? Anyway, he didn't give me details about what he wanted, but it sounded like he was happy. For him."

"Hey." Leigh was finally answering that first "hey."

His grin was slow and steady and it won the race. He helped her into the room, helped her to bed. She needed the help.

"You had fun tonight, didn't you?" he was asking as she faded away.

"Mmm-hmmm."

. . .

Sun. Dear God, all that sunshine. It must be morning. Yes, morning. And Leigh was in Florida. Still. Jupiter, Florida. She looked over her shoulder and yes, that was James next to her, looking upsettingly warm and inviting on a morning when she felt like her head was filled with gravel.

Rehearsal. She had to go to rehearsal soon. And she had to *run* that rehearsal like a competent adult. She turned away from the vicious sun and held on to James, who seemed to like that.

Bridie. She was going to see Bridie today. Again. It was unreasonable to expect her to cope with Bridie every single day. She should have negotiated for hazard pay. She held on tighter to James, who seemed to like it even more.

Leigh may have had acting in her genes, but she couldn't act as if she were well. Not this morning. So she didn't. She groaned, almost weeping at the day before her.

"Are you going to be okay?" James asked very quietly, but still too loud.

"Eventually."

. . .

An hour later, Leigh quietly said, "Hi, everyone. Are you all okay this morning?" as the rehearsal began.

They weren't okay. It was a stupid question. Harmony was fine, but the rest of the actors were larvae under a rock that Leigh had just lifted.

"You're not fine. And that's okay. Neither am I. We overdid it—most of us—and now we're suffering. That's what—"

She was going to give them sage advice about that's what happens when you drink too much, so now let's just work through the pain, but James pulled her aside with an urgent message.

"No Bridie."

Leigh had to scan the room three times to confirm it: no Bridie. Where the hell was Bridie? She was usually proud of her hardcore, I-show-up-no-matter-what work ethic. Didn't she once perform in an episode of *Mother Love* when she had the Black Plague, or perhaps some other color plague? Didn't she always show up, even when you didn't want her to?

Leigh returned to her very quiet actors.

"Say. Does anyone here need aspirin? Or coffee? Or both?" That was an intentionally stupid question. "Go to the gift shop and get your aspirin, then go to the café and get your coffee. We're taking a little hangover break. We're back in half an hour. Make that forty-five minutes."

The actors were hers now. Forget about studying their résumés or breaking bread with them. She showed them mercy when they needed it most, and now they knew they could trust her. They stepped carefully out of the rehearsal hall. She called out, not too loud, "Get some for me, too!"

· · ·

Leigh and James began their search for Bridie at the hotel bar, and there she was. They soon learned that she had been there all night. The bartender looked weary, but relatively happy. It was a sharp contrast to how he had looked when Leigh tried to pull her all-nighter there.

Bridie had some sort of pastel laptop computer, covered with an array of colorful legal pads, and two copies of the script. She had pens and highlighters. She was a small office, plus wet bar. Her makeup was faded, but she looked steady and unreasonably healthy.

"There you are! At last! Where have you been, you two?" What, she had been expecting them? For how many hours? All night? "Leigh, this is Casey. Casey, this is Leigh, my daughter. The one I told you about, and her *friend,* James. Casey has been tending bar here for three years. That's stick-to-itiveness. That's what I call it. Three years!" She patted Casey's hand manically. "And when Casey here wanted to close the bar, we decided that Mother Love giving him a month's rent just to stay open for one measly little night was worth the minor fatigue in the morning."

Why hadn't Leigh thought of that? Bribe him, of course.

"Hi," Casey said as he wiped and wiped and wiped that bar. He might have said more, but a yawn swallowed him up. Bridie rose from her seat and embraced Leigh as if she were a long-lost plastic surgeon.

"Oh, honey, I'm so sorry. I'm really, truly sorry." Leigh noted that she didn't say what she was sorry for. "I know you did your very best with the script, and in the end, I have to admit that Michael's play did need a little fine-tuning. You were absolutely right about that! I should never have lost my temper with you when you were just trying to help." Bridie slid off the barstool, and Leigh realized that her mother must have shrunk at least an inch or two in the last few years. She hid it well with her expensive shoes, but she was now barefoot; her shoes were on the floor by the barstool.

"But honey, even Casey here looked at your version and he didn't like it as much as mine." She reached for two pink legal pads and handed one to Leigh, the other to James. She had written out a new play in longhand. "And Casey is the real deal. He's a real person, with real reactions and real feelings. He didn't like the play that made the mother the villain. I think that's valid and you should think about it. Now, just be open-minded, okay? Take a look at my version of the opening. It's so much better as a mother-son story. It's a hoot!" She pushed the pages toward Leigh's face, then posed casually by the bar, awaiting due praise.

MARGARET

> My son is my sun and he lights up my life. Despite any misunderstandings that may arise between us, I love him, and all of my actions, mistaken or otherwise, are based entirely on love. I am a good mother and I love him. I am loyal to him and I would never do anything against him. That's more than some people can say.

"See what I mean?" Bridie was borderline squealing as she clutched Leigh's arm, shaking the script past the point of any further reading. "How much do you love the son/sun pun? Don't say you don't because I know that you do. It was there in front of us all along and none of us saw it!"

Leigh wanted to argue that the mother in her version was not the villain, that she was more complex than that, but she was busy keeping up with Bridie's Bridieness. Leigh was dizzy, and wasn't that Bridie's intent?

"So, sweetheart, if we just pull all of these notes together, we've got it. The pink pages are about Margaret. The yellow are about Sarah and Maxwell. Get a secretary to type them up and we've got our script. It's got the complexity of your script, you'll see, but the dialogue is quite a bit sharper than what Michael created. Really, the best of both worlds here. This is the script that I feel I could perform." Leigh put the legal pad down. She had heard that deep alto tone in Bridie's voice right at the end there. That was the sound of an ultimatum.

"This is," Bridie repeated, "the *only* one that I'll perform."

Bridie gathered her pastel pages and placed them in Leigh's

hands. Leigh accepted them reflexively, but she didn't want them. Bridie said it once more, although she didn't need to. She almost sang it: "This is the only one that I'll perform."

Leigh took her mother's pages and laid them carefully on the bar. She wanted to be sure that there was nothing in the way as she said, "Mother. You're fired."

11

*L*eigh knew full well that it was a dream. After all, it took place on the completed set of *Women in Hats* and that set wasn't completed yet. And the costumes, which had arrived from New York that afternoon, had not yet been worn by the actors. But there they were. Jessica looked downright fetching in Sarah's pastel-pink twinset, her pencil skirt and bobby socks. Ben was dapper in his skinny suit and tie, like a young Elvis being a good boy for someone's parents. His sneer was perfect for Elvis; Leigh would have to find a way to incorporate some of that bad-boy aspect into Maxwell. Leigh looked down and saw herself in Margaret's tweed suit dress. It was itchy and didn't fit properly, and the pinchy shoes had spike heels that hobbled Leigh.

"Mother? Mother?" Sarah was calling to Leigh, who took a little while to answer her.

"Yes?"

"May I dance with Maxwell? Please?"

"Is that in the script?" Sarah and Maxwell both nodded, and

began dancing with or without Margaret's consent. A dance. That might be a nice romantic touch for the scene where they're alone in the shop. It would be easy enough to add that. Leigh hoped she could remember that when she awoke.

When she turned to watch the young lovers dance, she noticed that Maddie was painting the upstage wall in an imitation of the classic Andy Warhol celebrity portrait. Four color-drenched squares of the same face. It was Bridie's face times four. Didn't Bridie have an actual Warhol of herself? Yes, she did. And anyway, that was inappropriate for this set.

"Leave it alone," Kendall was stage-whispering from the wings. "Just get on with it."

"But I can't. That's all wrong. That's not what I wanted."

"Don't upstage yourself!" Kendall was gone and Lilly was in her place, shouting in full voice, despite the fact that the audience could hear her. Had the audience been there all along?

"Lilly? Is that you?"

"Duh!" Lilly laughed at her.

"What do I do next?" Leigh asked.

"Go! Be up there! " Lilly answered, pointing upstage.

Leigh crossed upstage. Maddie was putting the finishing touches on her faux-Warhol portrait, but it was not Bridie's face she painted. It was Leigh's. She bolted awake.

"What? Are you okay?"

She mumbled an okay, and squinted her way over to the pink table that served as a makeshift desk. She scribbled on her notepad: "Sarah and Maxwell dance act 1—v. romantic."

.   .   .

The front-desk clerk smiled discreetly as he handed Leigh three phone messages from her husband. She didn't even need to read them; weren't they all asking her to call him back? Probably. She crumpled them and left them on the counter. One fell to the floor, but she left it there as she zoomed into the hotel restaurant.

"Bridie's gone. She checked out of the hotel. And she cleaned out the minibar." James was trying not to sound breathless when he brought his news to the table where Leigh was having scrambled eggs with pancake syrup, a very messy meal she hadn't had since she was seven years old. It was an odd combination of tastes that didn't quite work together, but Leigh kept trying. Maybe the next bite would be better. Leigh had chosen a whole wheat bagel and nonfat cream cheese for breakfast every day for so many years. This was such a different way to start the day.

James looked a lot more upset about Bridie's departure than Leigh did.

"Well, she was fired, wasn't she?" Leigh asked. "Shouldn't a fired person leave?"

"Who's going to play Margaret? What are you going to tell Harry? Does Kendall know? Does this mean we're not going to open?" He braced his arms against the table, ready for battle.

"One time, I lost an actor in the middle of a run—in the middle of a performance. He was sleeping with his costar's boyfriend, and they got caught. They made it through the first act, but the guy was too afraid to do the big fight scene in the second act, so he left at intermission."

"What did you do?"

"Found a really ambitious guy from the box office. See? Actors can be replaced." And with that, Leigh returned to her sticky eggs. James seemed stumped, at least for the moment. She ate her ridiculous eggs and listened to James, who had a litany of sensible next steps.

"But Bridie Hart is not just another actor. She's a star." His voice was ratcheting up to a panic level that Leigh just couldn't understand. Was losing Bridie really a loss?

Leigh couldn't speak past her gluey eggs, so she shrugged an oh-well-who-cares response, which seemed to irritate James even more.

"You know, back in New York, when we were talking about understudies—and can I say a quick 'I told you so' on that—we all liked Christine Morris, but she was booked for that Shakespeare musical-adaptation thing. Well, they posted their closing notice, so we might actually be able to get Christine. It'd be a minor miracle."

Leigh ate and listened. Bridie had overruled an understudy because it was a limited run, and she was a pro. And the very topic of understudies often caused her to reenact the entire second half of *All About Eve*. Again.

Leigh was slipping into a trance, awakened by James telling her, "And by the way, Harry called again. You should call him back right away, before Bridie gets to him."

Too late. If Harry was calling, it was because Bridie already had him in her pocket. It was enough to stop Leigh from eating. James was still leaning and staring at her like he wanted something from her. Probably, he wanted instructions. Probably, he wanted to help the woman he was sleeping with.

"If you see David or Harmony, can you send them in to me? I need to talk to them both before rehearsal. I'll take care of the rest."

That didn't look like enough of a to-do list to reassure James, but he took it. He was two steps away from her table when she called out, "Hey! James!" He returned to her table and she kissed him. He looked stunned and didn't kiss her back. She couldn't blame him, as this was their first public display of affection. It still counted, even though there were only three customers in the restaurant, all of them strangers to Leigh and James. She kissed him once more, and this time he kissed her back, so she sent him on his way.

"It's going to be okay." She sounded like she meant it because she did mean it. Watching him leave the restaurant put her in a bit of a trance, which she broke with a request for a Bloody Mary. An anonymous waitress brought the drink, and Leigh took a massive gulp from it immediately. It burned her throat a bit and made her cough.

"Are you okay?" the waitress asked. Leigh looked up and saw her. Lilly. That was Lilly's face, her hair, her shape, herself. Lilly.

"I sort of think that I'm mostly okay, even though I'm taking a crazy chance here. But it feels sort of right. Sort of."

"Sort of," Lilly echoed. "I guess 'sort of' will have to be enough."

"What about you? Are you okay?" Leigh asked. "I've always wanted to know."

"Me? I'm great. You're the one starting her day with a Bloody Mary," Lilly answered.

Leigh blinked hard and realized that, of course, this wasn't Lilly at all. This was the waitress from the hotel restaurant, expressing concern about one of her customers. But, for a few seconds there, it really felt like Lilly was in the room.

. . .

"Harry? It's me, Leigh. You left a message for me."

"Yeah, kiddo, I did. Twice. Next time, don't take so long getting back to me. It makes me worry and my doctor says I already worry too much. I had Michael try and reach you, but that was a no-go, too."

"Oh. Sorry." Leigh remembered being the girl who would never have ignored all these calls and messages. How could she have let it get this far?

"I'm running out the door," Harry said. "So let's make this quick. First, how's it going?"

There was no way to answer that quickly, so she let out a small "Uh, um, uh."

"What the hell does that mean? Look, here's why I called. It looks like we got a Broadway house. It's a go."

When was he going to reach across the continent and kill her for firing his star?

"I wanted to wait and see the reviews in Jupiter, but I've been listening to you and it sounds like the rehearsals are going good. I like the script. And, hell, Bridie Hart can sell tickets any day of the week. At least, she'd better!"

It was time for another round of "Uh, um, uh" from Leigh. Her throat was closing.

"Okay, okay, it's a lot of shit to think about. Toss it around. Talk to your mother. Talk to your husband. Talk to Kendall. This could be the cash cow she's been wanting. Then talk to your cast, and talk to me. You don't have to decide today. We'll talk again when I'm back from London."

"Oh, good." Leigh felt cold and hot at the same time, which meant that this conversation was going to kill her if it went on much longer.

"I got about thirty seconds left. You got any new news for me?"

Tell the man you fired his star! "No." Coward! Chicken! Spineless wretch! "No news here."

She honestly had no choice. Of course, she didn't let herself think about that for more than half a second.

• • •

"How are you feeling, Maddie?"

Leigh was sitting at the foot of Maddie's bed, paying a late-night visit to her hotel room, which was, as James described it, now an art studio. Maddie had opened her windows, which made the air in the room surprisingly fresh, despite the fact that it was littered with canvases, sketches, paints, brushes, and rags. There was also a gross collection of room service dishes and plates with trace amounts of food stuck to them. Evidently, Maddie's appetite had returned. More than that, Maddie looked like Maddie again, not like the stricken, sobbing unwed-mother-to-be who had collapsed in Leigh's room just a few days ago. Of course, she looked appropriately tired while she painted and talked.

The tiny electronic bomb known as Leigh's cell phone began its warning cry. Here comes an explosion. It was Michael again.

"Hey!" Maddie pouted. "Don't answer it. Screen it and have a conversation with me. Okay?"

Leigh put the phone away, guilt-free since this was a favor to Maddie.

"Guess what I've decided?" Maddie asked while she fine-tuned something red on her canvas. "I've decided that I'm not really pregnant until we get back to New York. You see, as long as we're here in Jupiter, nothing is real. We're through the looking glass, so maybe this is all a dream. Wow, that sounds so much crazier when I say it out loud, but I'm sticking with it. After all, when I lie down, I can still zip up my pants. And I feel much better now that I'm drawing and painting." She looked away from the tiny detail to say, "Thank you."

"I'm glad you're feeling better." Leigh tried to steal a glance at the painting, but Maddie shifted her canvas to hide it from view. She taunted Leigh, who really should have known better than to try to see a work in progress.

"So," Maddie asked, "did Bridie find her inner nice girl again? Did you tame her?"

"No. She freaked out, wrote her own script, and told me that she had to perform her own version of the script. So I let her go. I had to. Harmony's going to play Margaret now. And we'll have to—"

Maddie was so stunned, she moved to cover her open mouth and nearly stuck a red paintbrush in it.

"No, you didn't! Holy shit. Please don't stop there." She abandoned her painting to sit next to Leigh on the bed.

"So she's gone. Back to New York, or somewhere. She didn't leave a note. And I think that Harmony can play Margaret really, really well. Of course, that means I have no one to play Grace, so I'm cutting some of her stuff and I'm giving the rest of it to David's character. We can lose Grace, and it'll all work. I think. I hope. Maybe."

"Holy shit. You are holy shit, Leigh. Really."

Leigh didn't feel like holy shit. All day long, she had been spinning plates, an activity that requires the plate spinner to remain calm and focused, so that was how Leigh had decided to feel. She had told herself that this was just another day at the office for her. She had plate-spun her way through the Bridie-free rehearsal. She had broken the news to the cast, who maintained world-class poker faces. She had sorted out having Harmony play Margaret, and having the cast cope with losing their star. But they all just kept rehearsing. It was business as usual. Or was it?

At the end of the day, Leigh had rewarded herself and the cast at Casey's bar. Yes, they were already hers, but now they were truly 100 percent hers. They would follow her into hell, which just might be where they were headed. Leigh wasn't certain of their destination. Knowing that she didn't know where she and her happy few would end up started to show in her face, and in the way she clutched her drink.

James was clearly impressed, however.

"They trust you," he had told her. "And they love you more than they loved Bridie. You're on the way to a really good production here. Do you think you can bring it home?"

That question had caused her to release her grip on her drink, pull him by his shirt collar, and kiss him right there in front of the entire cast and Casey the tired bartender. All through the kiss, she watched a movie in her head about plate spinning. She tried to shut it off, or at least slow it down so that she could enjoy the kiss and absorb the reactions. But all the while, she had to watch out for all those spinning plates.

"Leigh?" Oh. That was Maddie speaking. Leigh was still in the art studio/hotel room with Maddie. Right. Leigh realized that her breathing was rapid and shallow, verging on hyperventilation. She was feeling that hot-cold sensation on her skin again. She was in trouble here, wasn't she. Why did it feel worse to tell the tale of Bridie's departure than to live through it?

Maddie was rubbing Leigh's back and offering her a cool, clear glass of water. It looked like magic, so she drank it. It slowed her down, at least a bit, and that had to be good. Okay, okay, okay now. Breathe.

"Leigh? Can you tell me what's going on?" Poor Maddie, trying so hard to take care of Leigh, who didn't deserve it. Leigh tried to answer but her mind was a jumble. Michael. James. Harry. Kendall. Bridie. Michael, Michael, Michael. Leigh couldn't think in words or phrases anymore. She was spinning. She was dizzy.

"Long day. Big day," Leigh managed to say after a while. She looked at the mess around her and tried to dig her way out of it. She found one dirty dish, and then another, and began to gather them up.

"Um, Leigh, are you actually cleaning my room?" Maddie asked, half giggling.

"Just a little." Leigh didn't even look up as she spoke. She kept gathering bowls, glasses, and plates. Do this. Finish this. Clean up this mess.

"But you must be exhausted. Look, you don't have to do this." Maddie said a lot more, but Leigh couldn't make out the words.

She heard the sweetness in Maddie's voice and looked for more dishes. She found a plate hiding on top of the television, and somehow that seemed normal. Leigh reached for it, got it, and then it slipped through her fingers. The plate crashed to the floor and broke. The sound shook her body hard enough to let all of the plates and dishes in her arms follow. They broke into large pieces, but a few shards scattered and sliced through Leigh's ankle. They may have been inconsequential cuts, but they lurched her back into the room, into the here and now, with Maddie.

"Oh, my God!" Maddie cried. "See? This is why no one should ever do housework. It's dangerous. You're actually bleeding. Does it hurt?"

Leigh tried to shake her head, but Maddie's concern for her was overtaking her ability to be strong and grown-up. Maddie pulled her away from the broken dishes, sat her on the bed, and then disappeared for a minute or twelve. She reappeared with a cool, wet washcloth, which she used to clean the tiny little wounds on Leigh's leg. They were nothing, really. They certainly couldn't justify Leigh's feverish skin.

"What's going on?" Maddie asked. Leigh looked over at the broken mess she had created. She looked back at Maddie and took her friend's hands.

"I'm sleeping with James." Leigh finally said it. Her skin returned to a normal temperature, as if she had just removed something toxic. A secret.

She sat, half removed from herself, during Maddie's ensuing tirade, physically unable to listen to it word for word. She saw her stomp around her hotel room, wherever there was floor space. She heard the angry tone in Maddie's voice and a few stray phrases ("lying to me" and "how long" and "not right," and the words *friend* and *friendship* were repeated many times). Leigh tried to catch the heart of Maddie's anger, but it was elusive.

Leigh picked up the big pieces of broken dishes, but Maddie shouted out, "Leave it! You've done enough!" So Leigh obeyed.

"I'm sorry I hurt you, but please. I don't have time for you to hate me. Please move past it fast, okay? Please? I'll do anything," Leigh said in a clear, simple voice as she moved to Maddie's door. She looked down at the small cuts on her ankle. They had already stopped bleeding. "Some things have changed. Some things haven't," Leigh whispered. She walked back to the middle of the room and hugged Maddie. Maddie didn't hug her back.

. . .

Back in her own room, Leigh couldn't deny it anymore: she was in trouble. She had used up her entire store of false courage. She now felt sick as she saw herself in the mirror, afraid and out of control. Maddie knew the truth about James. So did the cast, and probably Bridie did, too. And soon the world would know, and Michael would, too. She turned away from her reflection, unable to continue watching herself crash and burn.

Leigh closed her eyes and watched her life run forward like a new play. The main character started out so stalwart and reliable, but was unraveling by the end of the first act, losing important friendships, relinquishing her last family relationship, sacrificing her marriage and her integrity. And for what? Act 2: Main character is lost, alone, and unable to pull off the artistic endeavor that has cost her so much. Curtain.

Suddenly, Leigh couldn't stop shaking. She gritted her teeth and stilled her hands long enough to dial Kendall's number, then everything would be okay. Kendall would tell her what to do.

"You've reached Kendall Epstein. You know what to do." Leigh heard the electronic beep and looked at the phone receiver.

"No. As a matter of fact, I have no idea what to do. I'm making a mess of everything, and I just want to put it all back in order. I have to put it back the way it was and I don't know how. I should never have agreed to come here. It's all my fault. Please tell me what to do."

Leigh jumped at the sound of James's voice.

"You're doing just fine, Leigh."

She still didn't trust herself to speak, so she didn't. He walked to her and helped her put the receiver down, which was taking her several tries. Her shaking was still there, but not as obvious. He was talking quietly, but she was studying his eyes more than his words.

"If I'm the problem here, I can go," he was offering. "If you want me to leave, just say the word. I can even hook you up with a top-notch stage manager. I'd make sure that you got the best. Just tell me. What do you want?"

What did she want? Excellent question. She touched his arm and she knew that she wanted him. But there was more. What was it?

"I want to direct this play."

When he smiled, it started in his eyes.

· · ·

Sticky eggs two mornings in a row. That couldn't be good for her cholesterol level, or any other aspect of healthy living. But this was what her appetite commanded, and she didn't have the strength to fight it. After another restless night of fever dreams (did she really dream about Lilly playing baseball?), she quietly slipped into her clothes, confident that she wasn't waking James, and padded her way to the hotel restaurant. It wasn't open yet, but the hostess gave her a copy of yesterday's *New York Times* to occupy her until it was officially six AM.

Leigh listened to the voice-mail messages that Michael had been leaving on her cell phone. He started out so sunny. "Hey, it looks like I missed you! Tag! You're it!" But he moved into a shadowy tone as the messages accumulated. "So. Me again. Call me, okay?" Leigh dutifully listened to each message, then deleted them all.

It was hard to read the paper with these ridiculous bangs in her eyes. She pushed them back and realized that they hooked behind her ears. After what—twenty years?—more?—Leigh had grown out her oh-so-classic bangs. Finally, with an unobstructed view, Leigh scanned the Arts & Leisure section for mention of Bridie, *Women in Hats*, or her own name. They weren't there. Jupiter was far off the *Times*'s radar. Good. Leigh pushed it aside and ate her nasty breakfast in peace.

"I'm sure she's here," James was saying as he scanned the restaurant from the entrance. With Maddie. Leigh put down her fork and pushed her plate away. She briefly considered hiding under the table, but James had already pointed at her, so really, that would have been too childish.

Maddie looked awful. Had she been to bed at all?

But it was Maddie who said, "You look like crap," without a trace of concern in her voice. "Didn't you go to bed last night? Or was it just another big night for you?" She sat down, clutching her arms around her middle, possibly protecting her baby from the bad friend across the table.

"Okay, so I'll leave you two to work this out," James was saying as he walked away. "Make sure you do."

Leigh tried to stand up and keep James there. Maddie wore an angry pout. What if Maddie tried to hit her? It didn't sound likely, but all sorts of unlikely things were happening lately. If they were to have a girl fight, Maddie could really hurt Leigh.

They sat in unbearably awkward silence until Maddie said, "What the hell are you eating?"

"Sticky eggs," Leigh replied as Maddie helped herself to a small taste.

"Not bad," she decreed.

"They're better when they're hot."

"Of course."

"Do you hate me?" Leigh lifted her head to look into Maddie's eyes.

"No. Although I could hate you for introducing me to this sticky-egg thing." Maddie was close to finishing the eggs, so Leigh pushed the plate over to her. Maddie pointed her fork at Leigh, which made Leigh freeze. "Leigh. I was mostly angry because you didn't tell me. How dare you not tell me?" She dropped her voice to a high whisper. "I told you I was pregnant, for Chrissake. You're the only one who knows. You lied to me. You didn't tell me about James, and that's like the sin of commission. Why?"

Leigh didn't have a good answer, so she didn't give any.

"You've changed. I can see it. For one thing, I don't think I've ever seen your hair like that. It changes your whole face."

Leigh knew that was true. She felt uncovered, but, more than that, she felt her line of vision had cleared enormously. But Maddie saw more changes than a mere hairstyle. "You're different," she continued. "And please don't get too different because I need my Leigh. More than ever. And in about seven months, I'm gonna need you so bad."

"I haven't changed."

"You even *look* different. And I don't mean looking like crap. I just said that because you look all messy and tired and I feel like so much crap. Maybe it's how much you're wanting things. You want things now. You eat big, disgusting meals. It makes you look—and don't take this the wrong way—it makes you look *larger*."

Leigh answered, "I've always wanted things. My whole life I've been wanting."

"Not like this. Not out loud." Maddie called out to the waitress, "Can I get a decaf here? And another plate of sticky eggs, please?"

"Thanks. I think." Leigh wasn't sure if she could say this part, but she gave it a try. "There was something else that I wanted, Maddie. I wanted you to be here. And I wanted you to be okay, and for us to go through this experience together. There's a baby on the way. And a play, too."

Maddie took another bite of eggs, then looked up, down, everywhere but at Leigh while she said, "I want things, too. I want you to listen to me. You were in outer space last night, so you didn't hear me, did you? Okay, so, listen up: right before you came by, the manager came by because the maid complained about what I was doing to the room. Anyway, I'll cut to the end: they have an upscale hotel in Miami, and he wants to buy a painting for their restaurant. The guy likes oil paintings. And he doesn't seem to have any idea how little money I usually make for my work. He's overpaying and I don't mind a bit." Maddie couldn't stop smiling, although she was trying so hard. "I'm gonna kill myself in Jupiter. All the paintings you guys want, and now this. And I want it. And I want to want it. But it means that I just can't take care of you right now. Not the way I'd like to. Shit. I didn't know getting what I wanted would be so exhausting."

"Me, neither." Leigh laughed as Maddie put the last bite of sticky eggs in her mouth.

.   .   .

Women in Hats was much darker now, as young Sarah struggled to escape her oppressive mother. Harmony and Jessica's final scene carried the weight of the entire play, and it wasn't quite working. All morning, they had been rehearsing that scene, with Leigh trying various gentle ways to nudge her actors further into the text. She took Harmony aside and asked her, "How does it feel to have your only family reject you? Because that's what she's doing."

Harmony shook her head and said, "Sorry. Stop right there. I don't go in for all that Method crap. Never liked it. Never worked that way."

"Okay. That's fair. What if I just gave you a simple objective to play through the lines." Harmony seemed open to that idea. "Convince her to love you" was the objective Leigh offered.

Leigh took Jessica aside and asked her, "So, Lilly. What if you really want to stay?"

"Who's Lilly?"

"What? I mean, Sarah. What if you want to stay?" Leigh stayed calm and focused.

"But I'm supposed to leave."

"Yes, but what if you're conflicted? What if you really don't want to leave? What if it hurts? What if you're frightened? What if you just want love? What if you want Margaret to talk you into staying? What if Margaret is right, and Maxwell will leave you in a few years? Can you convince Margaret to love you, Lilly—I mean, Sarah? Without changing one word of dialogue?"

Leigh didn't let her actors think about it for too long. She threw them into the scene, and all side conversations in the room stopped. The scene turned into a dagger. David was weeping openly as he watched it. Ben stood up and applauded when it was done. Victory.

·   ·   ·

Michael called Leigh in her hotel room that evening. "Hi, honey. Wow, I can't believe I finally got you. How are rehearsals going? I've been trying to reach you for ages now. Those first couple of weeks seemed so much easier, but now but you must be working around the clock."

"Yes. I am." Leigh turned away from James, who was perched on the bed beside her. She sat and waited for Michael to carry the conversation, and he seemed to take the cue. He talked about work, a big snowstorm in New York, and spoke longingly of visiting his wife in warmer climes. Michael visiting? She couldn't picture it, couldn't have it.

"What is it? What's the matter?" he asked. DON'T ANSWER THAT QUESTION. "Is everything okay with the play, honey?" Oh, that's a much better question.

"Well, yes. But, I've made some changes."

"It's okay, Leigh. I trust you."

She bowed her head in appropriate shame as he chatted away. He didn't mention visiting again, but he did call out, "Uh-oh! What did you drop?" at the sound of James getting the bathroom door unstuck.

Leigh kept her eyes closed, half hoping that she wasn't the girl having this conversation. Even though she was. She tried to focus on the play.

"So, the changes. In the play. They're mostly with Sarah and Margaret. I hope that's okay." Maybe the play wasn't a safe topic either.

"Is your mother cooperating?" Maybe there were no safe topics.

"Oh, you know Bridie. Bridie is Bridie."

"I miss you," he sighed.

After a few beats, she answered, "Me, too." She held her breath, wondering if Michael would read too much into that pause.

"Leigh? I know you're working, but you sound like you're a lot farther away than Florida. I'm getting a little tired of intruding on your rehearsals and your life down there." Leigh hid her face, dreading what Michael was going to say next. James tried to sit with her, but she waved him away with desperate energy.

"You're not intruding." Leigh knew she didn't sound believable. Why did she have to look directly at James while she listened to her husband's voice? Was that her way of making sure she was being punished for her bad behavior? Was it a variation on multitasking—listen and suffer simultaneously?

"That's how it feels from here." Michael's voice was so much stronger than Leigh's, so much stronger than usual. "And I'm really tired of it. You haven't called me once since you started rehearsals. Yes, you're busy. I'm busy, too."

She scanned her mind for a catalog of excuses and lies, yes, lies, comforting lies to give to Michael. If she just kept talking, she could overpower him, just as Bridie could. She clapped her mouth shut without speaking a word.

"Okay, then," Michael sighed into the phone, distorting his voice. "Let's not do this on the phone. I'll see you on opening night."

12

The set was a jewel. Leigh had sent her designer back to the drawing board three times to completely rethink the structure, and this final try was the best. The main set was a hat shop, but side walls fanned forward to reveal the Sarah/Margaret apartment stage left and Maxwell's home stage right. The colors moved from cool in the shop to warm in the apartment and hot in Maxwell's home. The furniture pieces were so perfect, they looked like they were lifted from a movie about furniture in 1962. Nothing rang false. Nothing was cheap or strung together with shoelaces. Nothing was built by cast members who threatened to sue over a splinter. This was Teamsters work all the way.

Leigh had the actors parade across the stage in their costumes. Harmony looked like she might have raided Jackie Kennedy's White House wardrobe. Jessica looked gorgeous in everything, she couldn't help it. David looked like a force of paternal seriousness and warmth. Ben looked like a star. How could she not have wanted these actors in the first place? Leigh couldn't imagine the play with anyone else.

. . .

Two days, then three, then seven rolled along, with no word from Bridie, no word from Harry, no word from Michael. Even Kendall had failed to return Leigh's incoherent late night call. And wasn't that for the best? Leigh was living in a near-perfect bubble that turned and repeated and renewed. Every morning, Leigh and Maddie had breakfast together. Leigh was rising early, while Maddie was ending her day, getting ready for bed. James would join them, followed soon by Ben, Jessica, and David. Harmony ate her own (much healthier) breakfast in her room, but joined the cast just to sit around the table with them. Eventually, James would have to herd them all into rehearsal, where Leigh would make everyone work hard. Then dinner together, then sleep, then get up and do it again.

Jupiter was heaven.

They were rehearsing on the actual stage now most of the time, but they moved to the rehearsal room on occasion, whenever the set needed more work. How could it possibly need more work? It was borderline embarrassing, but Leigh was actually overjoyed by the gorgeousness surrounding her little play. When her designers fussed over making things even prettier, more polished, more perfect, she sighed and accepted it as if someone were offering her one more delicious chocolate, one more sip of fine champagne. It was exquisite, and it was more than she had expected in the first place.

Leigh knew she had to tell them about Harry's Broadway plans for the play. There was a limit to how much one person could keep to herself, even when she had bionic powers.

"So, one more thing, and this is not a definite." Oh, tell them.

"Harry Greenwald has a possible opening in a Broadway house and he might *possibly* be interested in moving *Women in Hats* there. Possibly."

She could *possibly* them for years, all they heard was "Broadway-Broadway-Broadway." That was obvious. They were celebrating already. She need to tamp that down, for their own good. But before she could speak, Harmony rose and took the floor.

"You guys, I have to tell you the truth: when I first got the call for this job, I almost turned it down. I didn't really like the play, I didn't think it was such a great part, and, no offense, I didn't like the director. Then. But I needed the work to keep my Equity insurance going. I have this condition, it's called hyperhidrosis, and don't tell me you haven't noticed it, because it gives me enough of an odor that I can notice it myself, so *you* must have noticed it. Yes, you have, you're just all too nice to say anything. Anyway, I took the job for the insurance, but now I'm in love with this play. I can't believe I'm playing Margaret"—she was having trouble continuing over the catch in her voice—"and I love you all. I do. This has been a great journey. And now we're going to Broadway!"

Jessica hugged Harmony and eventually the guys joined them to form a group hug. It was lovely. And Leigh didn't want to ruin their moment of love. But she needed to be honest. With someone.

"Guys, listen up." She clapped her hands to get their attention. "Harry and Michael don't know about the changes that I made here in Florida. And they don't know that Bridie's gone. I mean, they don't know that I fired her. Once that news breaks, we could lose it all. But if you keep playing your parts as well as you have so far, I really believe we can overcome that. I think they'll see good actors in a good story. And that's all anybody wants."

There was a respectful pause as the actors took in Leigh's truth, but they refused to stop smiling, stop hugging, stop celebrating, so

Leigh smiled and hugged them, too. Let them enjoy their Broadway buzz. Yes, Broadway. And why not Broadway? These actors
belonged there. And so did Leigh. After all, did she have to remain
a not-for-profit baby all her life? Broadway. Yes, Broadway.

·   ·   ·

They were working through technical rehearsals, a time Leigh always approached with Zenlike patience at Wonderland. But this
wasn't Wonderland, this was Jupiter. And here in Jupiter, Leigh sat
in the house, quietly calling her notes, new cues, and changes over
a headset that actually worked and communicated her requests to
the booth, where James actually wore the headset and used it. Successfully. As she sat in the middle of all those empty red velvet
seats, she thought she heard her father laughing. This was where
he used to sit in a theater house, swearing at technicians who were
actually doing a tremendous job, then buying them all steaks and
drinks and hookers. Okay, so Leigh wasn't going to do that.

But Frank always liked to complain through those tech weeks.
Leigh remembered that last visit with him, how he leaned on Leigh
and confided in her. "The sound guy's getting divorced, so we're
cutting him some slack," Frank had whispered. "But not too much.
You don't need to baby these guys." Did he see her as a peer? As an
adult? She was a teenager, but he was including her, informing her.
Did he know she'd want to direct someday? Leigh tried to remember if she had ever told him that.

·   ·   ·

Jessica had been using large canvas squares as rehearsal props for
her paintings. But today, in the middle of tech week, Maddie and a
crew of Teamsters had appeared and begun parading a series of
paintings down the aisle of the theater, and settling them all in the
front row. It happened in the middle of lights being refocused and

costumes being pinned for minor adjustments and sound cues running over and over again to establish settings that would be just so. Leigh was giving all of her attention to the sound levels, since James was working with the lights, and the costumes didn't need any special intervention. All the plates were spinning and balanced. But when Maddie uncovered her first painting, everything started to slow and then stop.

The first two paintings were meant to be works in progress. The audience would see these two paintings in their early stages in act 1, then the finished products in act 2. So Maddie showed the not-finished canvases first.

Leigh could make out a pencil sketch of a woman walking out a door. There were shades of green and blue around her, but Leigh couldn't predict how the finished painting would look.

The next canvas showed swirled masses of red and brown, and a pencil sketch of a small figure in the front.

The costumers paused in their work to see the paintings. Even Leigh was curious to see how these two would develop. One of the prop men handed Maddie a draped canvas, which she uncovered with no ceremony. She hadn't spoken yet, but she placed the canvas in front of Leigh.

It was the green and blue painting, now in its finished state. It showed a well-dressed woman walking out the door of a shop, entering a busy street. The shop held the majority of the canvas, in braided shades of green and blue. The woman was not much more than a silhouette in a Cabernet red suit, her back to the store, and therefore to the audience, her brown hair pinned in a chignon, her matching red Grace Kelly purse dangling from her wrist. The woman was unrecognizable, but no one could fail to see that she had movement, she had purpose. She was leaving the dark shop for a world of luminous blues and yellows. The contrasts were startling, the colors saturated the canvas, saturated Leigh's eyes.

Maddie was just barely smiling. She had to know she had done good work here.

The sound cues stopped running, and the lighting technicians were craning around ladders to get a better view of the paintings. Maddie must have noticed this, because she lifted the first finished painting up above her head and slowly turned around, giving everyone a good look.

The actors and costumers sat down to watch the show. Jessica winced at a pin that stabbed her in the thigh, but her eyes never left the paintings.

The second painting showed a girl, maybe seven or eight years old, sitting on the sidewalk sidelines of something like a Macy's Thanksgiving Day parade. The girl, painted in shades of blue, sat on the ground, back turned to the parade, but facing the canvas. Her expression was enigmatic. Was she bored? Sad? Worldly wise? Content? Leigh couldn't settle on a definition for the child, but she was taken with her. Behind the girl, a crowd swirled in shades of red and brown. There were balloons, floats, stilt walkers strolling by, but all in soft focus. The enchanting child was the center of the picture.

Once again, Maddie lifted her work and gave it a slow turn for the population of their little world to see. The rest of the canvases were smaller, all of them portraits.

One showed Casey, the tired bartender, cleaning a glass.

The next showed Shelby, the teenage waitress, filling ketchup bottles.

The last portrait looked an awful lot like Leigh, sitting by herself in a restaurant that looked suspiciously like the hotel restaurant, and eating something disturbingly close to sticky eggs.

All of the paintings were in oil, and followed Maddie's signature style of old masters form for modern content. The portraits were all loving and deliberate. There was a calm to the brushstrokes and a feeling of wealth, of plenty, in the color choices. They were careful and complete. They were magnificent.

When Maddie lifted the last canvas for its display, Harmony started the applause, but everyone in the room picked up the cue instantly. Two lighting technicians were whistling their praise for Maddie's work. Her smile was endless.

She set down the canvas, but the applause continued. She covered her face with her paint-stained hands. Was she crying? Leigh hugged her, and yes, Maddie was actually crying. She broke the hug to wave her audience away, wrapped her arms around Leigh, and the two walked to the back of the house where Maddie could have a good, long, satisfying cry. The paintings remained at the front, where actors and technicians gathered around for a show. They let out audible oohs and aahs. Leigh saw that Maddie was catching each sound, savoring and saving it.

                         •   •   •

Leigh was running dress rehearsals in the evenings, and they ran almost like performances. The actors were almost ready, almost there. Their performances were still a little bit raw and sleepy. But each night, they were a few degrees closer to being fully awake in their characters. Nights ran quite late now, what with drinks and discussions with Casey or Shelby after the rehearsals. Soon, they'd begin previews in front of real live audience members. Strangers to their little world.

                         •   •   •

"Kendall? I have a little problem."

"Another one? Clearly, I should have called you back. Sorry about that, Leigh."

"We're about to have a special preview for an invited audience—a senior citizens' group. Harry arranged it. I don't know if they'll like this kind of play. But I do know that they're expecting to see Bridie Hart in the play, whatever it is. I fired her. She's gone, and I don't even know where she is."

"Okay, Leigh. Enough fucking around. You have to tell Harry what you've done, you have to own up to it. Do it before your mother busts your ass in *The New York Times* or something. And, by the way, I can't figure out why the hell she hasn't done that already. Do it before any audience sees this show. Get a press release out, get some signage. How long until your first preview performance?"

"Twelve minutes."

• • •

When the audience was seated and settled, Leigh stepped onto the apron of the stage, that small area in front of the curtain where she was most vulnerable to thrown tomatoes or other produce, and gave a brief curtain speech.

"Hi, everyone, and welcome to our very first public performance of *Women in Hats.*"

They applauded politely, well trained from years of television talk shows, no doubt. Leigh was smiling with fake confidence. She made sure not to look at any actual faces as she said, "My name is Leigh Majors, and I directed this play. I'm really proud of it, and I'm lucky enough to have a really talented cast here all the way from New York." The audience mumbled appreciatively. Maybe they were all relatives of Shelby, the waitress?

"Now, I know that some of you may be expecting to see my mother in the play today. Bridie Hart. That's my mother. But Bridie can't be here with us today."

Leigh had rehearsed a speech where she pretended that Bridie was ill, and Harmony, the understudy, was going out there a kid but coming back a star. This would evoke sympathy all around: be nice to Harmony, be nice to us all. But then she saw their faces. They were smiling, and it worked on her like truth serum.

"The truth is, I should never have tried to direct my mother. She's an impossible woman, and I had to fire her, and I'm not sorry. Do any of you have kids?" They were mumbling answers back to Leigh. "Can you imagine what it would be like if your kid tried to be your boss—in a business you've known since before your kid was born? Doesn't sound like fun, does it? In our case, it was a natural disaster."

And they laughed. Sympathetically! Okay, yes, a few people were talking among themselves, but nobody stood up and yelled at Leigh for being a rat. Nobody asked for a refund (it was a free performance). Nobody was going to disrupt Leigh's play because of Bridie.

Her smile switched from fake confidence to real joy.

"So Bridie's consoling herself in the nearest martini glass." Bigger laugh—this crowd must read the tabloids. "And we are here in beautiful downtown Jupiter, almost ready to open our play without her. Almost. You see, the actors and the technicians know their jobs, but you're our first audience. So you folks need rehearsal! We already know where the laughs are supposed to be, but we're going to need you guys to figure that out, and just make sure you have the best time. So, that said, please do bear with us if any technical problems arise. We're testing you to see if you're paying attention! So, sit back, relax, and have a wonderful afternoon. Thank you!"

Was this the same kind of rush that actors felt at the end of a performance? Leigh could have climbed Everest after that speech. She had infinite courage, infinite power.

James was smiling as he spoke quietly into his headset. "And go curtain."

The curtain rose, the stage was bathed in warm light. Harmony was center stage, adjusting the netting of her fashionable hat. She took her time, took in the audience. Leigh saw her breathe deeply and begin the scene. Margaret and Sarah, preparing to open the shop, while slipping in a little backstory. Sarah was smart and pretty. The audience liked that.

Okay, so sometimes senior citizen audiences converse during matinees. Sometimes loudly. Sometimes obnoxiously. A woman down front called out to another audience member, "Oh! So it's an autobiography! Did she say she wrote it?" But Harmony kept her rhythm and continued the play over that remark, and over the man wondering out very loud, "So is Bridie Hart in rehab? Is that why she's not here?"

The next interruption was a better one. It sounded like that same Calling Out Lady again, but this time she was saying, "Sarah doesn't want a hat shop! That's *your* dream!" Later, in that same scene, when she saw the first batch of Sarah's (Maddie's) paintings, she pronounced them "So nice!"

On any other day, Leigh would have wished for a Hannibal Lecter mask to lock over the Calling Out Lady's mouth. But today, that woman proved that it took less than ten minutes for the audience to forget about Bridie. It took just one scene to get them involved in Margaret and Sarah. It worked.

. . .

Halfway through the first act, Leigh figured out that Maddie was standing behind her. Had she been there all along? Maddie looked clean and well rested for the first time in days. Leigh wondered if she spied a little more roundness to Maddie's figure. They mouthed hello to each other, then Maddie signaled Leigh to join her outside. This was not a good time for a conversation. Leigh needed to stay by her actors, monitor the audience, take notes, though she hadn't come up with any so far. Couldn't this wait?

It couldn't. Maddie's signals were becoming more urgent. Leigh followed her as far as the stairwell to the dressing rooms, where they could talk quietly.

"Bridie's here," Maddie whispered.

"Where?"

"Back of the house."

"No, she's not."

"Yes, she is."

"No, she's not." Leigh's voice acquired a little too much heft.

"Leigh."

Both women darted back into the wings, where Leigh broke one of her cardinal rules: no checking the house. If you can see them, they can see you. But Leigh couldn't see far enough back to find any demons. Maybe Maddie was wrong.

*   *   *

Maddie was right. Leigh had sprinted out the stage door and into the lobby, then slowed down as she approached the doors to the theater. If she opened them, she could be turned to stone. But just then, the house manager, a bone-thin guy trying very hard to grow a mustache, answered Leigh's questions and confirmed the presence of Mother Love in the house.

Leigh went in. Bridie was sitting across the aisle from Leigh's reserved seat, dressed in magenta that was bright even in the dark. She turned slowly to bat her fake eyelashes at her daughter, then returned her attention to the stage.

Leigh tried to sneer, but it made her feel like she was thirteen. So she sat, fake casual, in her seat and prepared to take notes.

First note: *Bridie is shaking her head. Why?*

Second note: *Bridie is reading the program instead of watching my show. MY show.*

Third note: *Bridie is looking around the house instead of watching my show. MY show.*

Fourth note: *Stop watching Bridie.*

"So cute! They're going to fall in love!" Calling Out Lady called out as Sarah and Maxwell began dancing to the sound of Ella Fitzgerald singing "Prelude to a Kiss." Leigh stopped watching Bridie.

The first act was the tiniest bit slow, as the actors adjusted to having all those people in all those seats in the dark. But Leigh was sure that she was the only person who could have noticed that. She and James would see it. No one else. Not even Bridie.

When Calling Out Lady declared Margaret to be "a real piece of work!" Leigh smiled. She may have been interrupting, but at least she was getting it, enjoying it, and, okay, narrating it for everyone else. Leigh turned to give Bridie a smug grin, something regal rather than adolescent.

When did Bridie leave? Leigh looked around the house, picturing Bridie climbing onto the stage to give her own curtain speech. It was within her realm of crazy. But Leigh didn't see the bright dress anywhere. And was that good or bad?

The audience was blanketed in darkness as the first act ended. When the houselights pulled everyone out of the play and back into their lives, Leigh leaped for the door, confident that she would find Bridie at the bar.

And she was right. Bridie was drinking something brown and icy, and looking like she was about to kiss the uncomfortable bartender. She released his necktie when she saw Leigh.

"Pay the man, sweetheart. Can you take it out of my per diem?"

"Why would a fired actress still be on per diem?"

"And are you ready to apologize to your mother?"

"Why should I?"

"Do you really want to have this out in front of the blue-hair matinee?"

"Where should we go?"

"Do you think seniors approve of traitorous daughters?"

"Do you think they liked act one?"

Bridie toasted the end of their question marathon. She must have realized, long before Leigh did, that they had an audience. Leigh realized it only when she heard the Calling Out Lady call out, "Oh, so it really is an autobiography. What a shame." The audience had spilled out to the lobby for intermission.

Leigh urgently wanted privacy. She didn't want to play this out in front of an audience. What would they think of her? How much would this harm her image? For a flash, she wondered when she had acquired an image. Bridie began playing to the crowd.

"*I'm* supposed to be playing Margaret, and all of these good people would rather see me than that smelly old nobody you've got playing her. You should offer perfumed handkerchiefs to the first five rows, don't you think?"

Intermission might never end. Never.

"What kind of child fires her elderly mother?" Bridie was now asking her rapt audience, in her best glamorous-district-attorney style. "What kind of director rewrites a play to betray a playwright's vision? What kind of wife takes a lover while her husband toils to keep the family business afloat?"

Finally, Leigh found an opening.

"Me. I did all that and more. And I learned at my mother's knee." She was on a tightrope, with no net below. Did she just admit to all of Bridie's charges? Yes, that was how it felt. She still wondered how Bridie had figured out Leigh's affair with James so quickly and easily.

"You can't fire me. I'm your mother. I'm a star. And I haven't been fired from anything since 1958." Bridie stopped playing to the crowd and gave all of her enormous energy to Leigh. She growled, "Now, I cut you a break, sweetie, seeing as how you're like a daughter to me: I didn't call Harry and get *you* fired. So, say thank you for that, and put things right again. Give me back my part, and the old script."

"No."

"You're lucky that I'm your mother. That's the only reason I didn't go straight to Harry Greenwald and have him fire your ass."

"Lucky?" Leigh could barely manage enough breath to say the word.

"Leigh, I'm warning you: when this shit hits the fan, you'll be buried in it. I'm bigger than you, and I won't hold back." Bridie looked as feral as she sounded.

Calling Out Lady said, "Oooh, this is better than the play," which got some giggles from her fellow audience members.

"Tell you what." Leigh kept her eyes on her mother's face, as if a single blink would break the spell. "I'll pay for your drink"—she blindly placed a bill on the bar, praying that it was enough money—"but you're still fired."

The lights in the lobby blinked to signal the start of act 2. The audience seemed reluctant to leave the lobby show, so Leigh helped bring the scene to a close by walking into the theater. She wobbled like a newborn foal as she heard her mother call out, "This isn't over. When you get back to the real world, you'll find out what this misadventure is going to cost you! You can't be a wild woman, Leigh. You don't have it in you."

[13]

Opening night in Jupiter, Florida.

While it might not be a cultural epicenter, Jupiter was probably going to decide the fate of *Women in Hats*. And the night would include a visit from the producers, Harry and Kendall, and the playwright, Michael. Producer, Michael. Husband, Michael. Michael.

"You have to move out," Leigh told James. "Before Michael gets here. You have to go back to your own room. I'm sorry."

"I figured," he said as he found a stray sock amid the chaos in their/her hotel room.

From the time they arrived in Florida, James had grown from object of desire to essential person. She didn't think twice about asking him for help, advice, or faster sound cues. She didn't know when it happened, but his life became seamlessly blended with hers. She knew all about his crazy sister with five sons ("she'll keep trying till she has a girl"), his college years ("math majors were never popular"), and his apartment ("it slopes north to south and east to west, so it's a great place to play with Slinkies"). She tried to imagine a morning without him, without their choreographed morning routine, without James. But Michael would be in Jupiter soon. Would he even recognize Leigh or the chaos she was now calling home? The very thought of Michael clashed with the room. What would he say when he saw this mess?

"Look. My husband's only staying for three days, then he's got to go back to New York."

James nodded. That was, what, the fifteenth time she had said that since he started packing. But this time, he was done packing, so he finally looked at her sad eyes and asked, "And then what?"

"And then what—*what*?" She couldn't hold his gaze for more than a second. She looked for something to straighten or put away. There were too many choices. The room was a swirl of papers and unidentifiable plastic objects.

"I have never in my life just slept with a woman and then walked away. That's just not me. And if that's what I'm supposed to do here, you should have warned me. Or, at least, warn me now. Tell me. What do you want?"

If only she could have answered that. It might have changed everything.

· · ·

After James left, the room was unbearably quiet. But Leigh still didn't know where to put anything, or where to find anything except her scarf. Paper danced and did tricks. So did her other belongings and all those small plastic objects. She found his room key resting on top of her computer. She couldn't bear to look at it, and reached instead for her scarf.

The scarf had been a gift from one of the costume assistants. After the third (wonderful, wonderful) preview performance, everyone backstage seemed to be floating on air. One of the young costumers had a small box of fabric that was used for minor repairs. She pulled a long swatch of purple silk from the box. It was frayed at the ends, but Leigh commented that she admired the color, and on any other day that would have been that.

At intermission, Leigh was giggling with James over a near miss on a light cue when the young costume assistant approached her. "Here," she said. "You should be wearing this." She had finished off the frayed edges of the swatch, which was now a belt or a scarf or something.

"Oh, that's sweet of you. Thank you." But Leigh was never any good at wearing color or accessories. Still, she accepted the purple silk, already certain that she couldn't use the thing. So far, this young costume assistant had been too shy to introduce herself, or to have any conversations with the director. But today, she reached up (Leigh was inches above her) and tied the purple silk around Leigh's head. It framed her face like a heathen halo. It was petal soft, and brought color to Leigh's cheeks. She had hugged her anonymous costume assistant. She wore the scarf to the rest of the previews, and each time, the cast received a standing ovation at the end of the night. The lucky purple scarf became a staple of Leigh's wardrobe.

When the women of the cast went shopping for new opening night outfits, Harmony and Jessica swore that they would separate Leigh from her denim and black uniform.

"Good luck," Maddie laughed as they walked into the spacious dress shop known as Dressin' Gaudy.

"This lavender is so flattering to your skin tones," Jessica cooed over a cropped leather jacket. "And the yellow is so bright."

Leigh had never knowingly worn pastel colors in her life. But she walked out of Jupiter's Dressin' Gaudy shop with the lavender and yellow number that made her feel like a sexy Easter egg in a very short miniskirt.

"You've had those legs all this time and you didn't show them?" Harmony asked, outraged.

"You can't wear your work boots with this. You'll need shoes," Jessica instructed.

Maddie sat back and laughed. "Make sure everything matches her purple scarf! Matchy-matchy!"

And now these clothes were the only objects she could reliably find in the paper swamp that was her hotel room.

• • •

Kendall arrived first. As the only person in New York aware of the goings-on in Jupiter, she knew enough to check the lobby for the other players.

"They're not here yet. You're the first," Leigh let her know. She had posted herself in the center of the lobby as lookout, soldier, and general, all in one.

"I saw Harry and Michael at the airport, but I hid behind a newspaper," Kendall admitted. "Childish, I know. But I was saving my strength for you, sweetie." She touched Leigh's face gently and said, "You be strong tonight, you hear me? I've got your back."

Leigh hugged her, and then did something she had never dared to do in New York: she stayed in the embrace, soaking in Kendall's strength, courage, and any other prizes she could borrow for a night.

Leigh watched through the glass doors as Michael helped Harry out of a car and into the lobby. Harry didn't need any help, and slapped Michael's hands away. Michael was grim, in a gray suit, gray tie, and gray shirt.

"He looks like fog," Kendall said as Michael entered.

He moved awkwardly as he approached his wife. She wasn't sure of the correct protocol here, but neither was he. Eventually, he kissed her on the cheek.

"Hi," he said shyly. "Well. This is a big night, huh?"

Harry was humming Cole Porter as he hugged Leigh and said, "You nervous?"

"Oh. Yes," Leigh replied.

"Good. That means you care!" Harry declared. Leigh felt sick with fear. She knew her smile was unconvincing, but nobody called her on it.

"Is that new?" Michael was referring to the outfit. Leigh looked down at what little there was of her purple leather skirt, and nodded. "It's nice. And your hair is different. Wow. I almost didn't recognize you."

"Leigh. Don't you have something you want to say to Michael and Harry?" Kendall prodded her.

Leigh nodded and wished she had enough air in her lungs to speak. She would have asked for mercy. She wondered who would kill her first, Harry or Michael. Probably Michael. She was thinking through this scenario while everyone waited for her to say something, anything.

Kendall patted Leigh's back and said, "Leigh has made some changes to the play. Do you want to talk about those changes, Leigh?"

When had Kendall ever been so gentle, so careful? Leigh tried to thank her before she turned to her producer and her playwright/producer/husband to say, "I made some changes to the play." Silence. Okay, clearly they were all expecting her to say more.

"I don't really think you'll like what I did. But I do. I like it, I mean. I like the play. The changes. I'm happy with it. I'm hoping that you'll give it a chance. The play. The changes."

Harry was catching on, and Leigh held his gaze for as long as she could bear it, while he asked, "What exactly did you change, Leigh?" He didn't look nearly so small and frail anymore. And Leigh let it all leave her body, all the fear and tension. Just tell him.

"Everything. The first change was with the mother and—" That was as far as she got. She knew she was going to tell him everything. Start with the rewrite, end with firing his star, her mother. And she would have, but she saw, over his shoulder, the glittering blood-red ensemble that was draped over Bridie. Leigh watched her enter, greeting a few stray fans with her patented Mother Love smile.

"Good God, Leigh. You finally decide to dress up, and you look like a promiscuous bridesmaid." Only Bridie Hart could call that a greeting.

"Bridie. You remember Kendall. And Kendall, you remember my mother, Godzilla." Leigh wondered if she was a candidate for a heart attack. Surely her heart was assaulting her right now.

"Bridie? What the hell are you doing out here!" Harry bellowed. "Get backstage! Jesus, the play's going to start in about one minute. Are you trying to kill me?"

Michael was serious and instructive. "Bridie, please. Go get ready! Get in your costume!" He turned to Leigh and asked, "Is she drunk?" much too loudly.

Bridie's smile was carved in place. Leigh closed her eyes to it, and began.

"Bridie's not in the play anymore. I fired her. And please, give me enough time to explain." She felt Kendall holding her up, and she leaned into the support. "First things first. I changed the play."

The lights blinked a signal from James that it was time to begin. Friendly ushers began urging everyone into the house. "The show is starting! The show is starting!" they cried out, Henny Penny–style.

"It certainly is," Bridie purred as she led the way into the theater.

"I've got your back," Kendall repeated. Leigh grabbed her hand and squeezed it as they all filed into the theater, with Harry shaking his head and Michael looking grayer and more withdrawn than ever.

. . .

Harry refused to have an ugly scene at intermission. "An ugly scene" was how he termed it while they stood in an uncomfortable circle. He intimated that the ugly scene would still take place, but far from the public and the press. They stood in awkward silence for fifteen minutes, until they could return to their seats for the second act.

Leigh wanted the second act to last all night, but it didn't. It ended. Even though the power players behind this play looked grim during the curtain call, the audience insisted on being happy. For the fourth time since they had been in front of an audience, the cast received a standing ovation. Leigh took it in and owned it. It was her standing ovation. Kendall rose to join them, while Harry and Michael sat still, not even applauding.

And then, Bridie Hart rose to her feet. She applauded the cast as energetically as anyone could, and shouted out, "Bravo! Brava!" in a voice that sailed over the crowd and took the cast by surprise. Leigh's hands stalled in midclap, and she looked up at her mother. Bridie never looked down. She applauded, she shouted, she stayed on her feet.

Harry led his unhappy parade to a grand suite of rooms above the theater after the show. Leigh had never seen this space in all the time she had been rehearsing here. How was that possible? It was filled with curly antiques and lush Florida plant life. Harry sat behind the ample, glossy wooden desk. Michael and Bridie took one side of the room, while Leigh and Kendall took the other. Would Harry be judge and jury, and would he execute anyone? (This was still Florida, after all.)

Michael began, "You can't just do this to me. I'm talking about the play here. There must be about a thousand rules that say you can't just take my play and turn it into . . . into . . . that thing we saw tonight." After his voice cracked three times, he stopped trying to act brave. He was betrayed. He was miserable. He dropped himself into a Louis XIV chair, far from his wife.

Somehow, Leigh couldn't cross the great divide to embrace him. And even if she could, she doubted she could bring herself to touch him. Not anymore.

Judge Harry spoke up. "I like the new play." It stunned everyone into silence. "I do. It's not the commercial property I was looking for, but it's good. It could even have a decent run on Broadway. Every now and then, you need something like this play."

Michael hid his face behind one hand. Did he always give up so easily?

"Of course, the real problem isn't the script," Harry continued. "It's Bridie."

"Bridie is always the problem, believe me," Leigh sang out. "If there's a problem, she's somewhere at the heart of it. Plays, famines, global warming. It's all Bridie."

Leigh tossed this off, but Kendall touched her arm and said, "Hush. That's not helping."

Harry sat back in his chair, laughing. "Yeah, she's a handful. Why are you being so quiet tonight, Bridie? Come on, where's the Bridie Hart we all know and run away from?" But Bridie waved him away, refusing to speak. Yet. She parked herself on a window seat, so Harry returned to Leigh.

"I got some questions for you, kiddo. You ready?"

She was. She could answer anything, do anything. She was Leigh Majors, and she had bionic superpowers.

"Do you want to direct this play, whichever the hell play we end up with?"

Michael groaned as if he had a stomachache.

Leigh's voice rang out with a confident "Yes." And with that, Leigh and Harry were locked in a staring contest.

"You think you got the chops for Broadway, kiddo?"

"Yes." Kendall was backing away, no longer propping Leigh up.

"You think you got the balls to direct your mother—no kicking her out again?"

"Yes." She didn't blink, but she noticed that her mother was now standing taller.

"Can you direct the script your mother wants?"

Leigh took a moment to answer. "Yes." Kendall clucked and sighed, a painful sound, but Leigh would simply have to live with disappointing Kendall. And anyway, it was true: Leigh could direct either script, but she couldn't walk away from it all. Not now. She was the director and she would not be replaced. She broke away to look at Kendall and tried to explain it all with a look. But Kendall was shaking her head. Disappointed. Leigh returned to Harry's blue eyes, hidden behind dirty eyeglasses.

"I believe you," Harry replied. "And you did one helluva job here, Leigh. Your old man would be proud." And he blinked.

Leigh was now seventeen inches taller, and Bridie was a teeny little gerbil.

"This was a good night in the theater." Harry sat back, expansive and proud. "Better than I ever thought it could be," Harry was saying to everyone in the room.

From behind Leigh, Kendall added, "And let's face it, the credit goes to Leigh."

"True." Harry smiled as he agreed.

Leigh was now thirty-nine inches taller, and Bridie was a paramecium.

Harry continued. "But. But, but, but. But. This is Jupiter, my dear. And if you want to move this to the next level, to New York, to Broadway, you gotta have a name actress in the lead. You gotta have, oh, I don't know, Bridie Hart. You do. Believe me."

Bridie rose from her window seat now and said her first line. "Hey. Sweetheart. I know that change is hard, but you're so strong. I hope that you won't hold this change against me. Look at us. We're a family here, and we have to pull together if we're going to make this work—"

Leigh interrupted. "—'because after all, that's what a family does. A family of Love.'" Leigh laughed. "Jesus, Mother. That was from the series finale of *Mother Love*. Could you maybe say something original?"

Kendall was losing the battle to suppress her laughter. She snorted out a laugh that sounded like it must have hurt. Bridie rose and made an interesting diagonal cross from the window. Unnatural, but theatrical. But then her voice came out so diminished, Leigh didn't recognize it. "Harry, Leigh doesn't need me. This play would be successful just as it is. It's hers. And I don't want to work where I'm not wanted."

Leigh had to concede that Bridie was not acting now. She was actually defeated. Leigh wanted to feel happy, wanted to sew this all up and be done. Bridie was giving up and giving in. So why couldn't Leigh celebrate? Isn't that what her mother would have done, if the roles were reversed? It was Leigh's cue to speak, to stand up for her own dark little creation, but she couldn't manage it. She looked away from her sad mother and saw Michael. Oh, Michael. He kept his eyes downcast, not even watching the scene around him. She wondered if he knew how to fight for his play. Why wasn't he speaking up for himself?

Jesus, what had she done?

Kendall chimed in, "If we have a play that works, we shouldn't break it. Isn't that what you would say, Harry?"

"At this point, I don't care which play you do," Harry replied.

"But you're not going to open without a star. That's a deal breaker for me. So, Leigh, I think it's down to you, sweetheart. Get your mother on board, and we're a go. Leave her out, and we're done here."

Michael was still sitting in his expensive chair, pale and motionless, wrapped in sadness. He was broken, and Leigh had done it. She was a criminal, and she couldn't bear it another second, so she turned back to her mother.

Bridie had stopped angling her face just so, and Leigh could detect little splotches of red around her eyes, which were wet. Not that Leigh had ever trusted her mother's tears before tonight. But she knew what she had to do, and tapped her powers to get the words out.

"Bridie. Mom. We've all worked so hard, and now I think you should rejoin our cast. I think it's time we took this show to Broadway. Please?"

Bridie didn't answer, but she looked at Leigh as if she'd never seen her before.

"Okay. I'm sorry I fired you," Leigh added. Would that be enough to bring her mother back in?

"I'm sorry I made you fire me. It was my fault." Bridie said it so softly, Leigh barely heard it. But once she put the words together in her head, nothing made sense anymore. Maybe they really were through the looking glass.

"I'll come back," Bridie said through a catch in her voice. She cleared her throat, shook it off, and straightened up. "I'll come back," she repeated.

"Okay. So. Good." Leigh didn't know where to go next. But Harry urged them, "Kiss and make up. Come on, you two."

Their hug and kiss were painfully awkward, but they did it for its own sake. There.

"Good!" Harry sat back in his chair once again, all joy and delight. "Looks like we have ourselves a show. You keep running this version of the show and this cast in Florida. We'll update the whole shebang when you get back to Manhattan. Right? I'll need your stage manager to work out the fine details. And hey, do we keep the same set now that we're switching back to Michael's script?"

Michael was jolted back to life by Harry's words. *His* script! Yes! He just hadn't been following. His script and Bridie were a package deal. Leigh was too busy trying to decipher her mother's latest mood to join in Michael's celebration.

"We'll just need new costumes for Margaret," Leigh answered Harry. "And for Grace. There are some props that we'll need, but we can work that out with Ja—with the stage manager."

"Don't work out anything," Bridie said evenly. "You can choose either script. I'll do my job."

The room fell silent as Michael froze, watching his play slide away again. Leigh was dizzy. She didn't want to leave this evening wishing she had done any piece of it differently, but her superpowers were nearly drained. Kendall must have sensed it, because she stepped in for Leigh.

"Why does she have to decide everything right here, right now? She's putting her mother back in the show. Isn't that enough? Let her go enjoy her opening night. Jesus."

Leigh looked at each person in turn, until her eyes landed on Michael.

Michael was in agony. The sadness in his eyes pulled Leigh toward him. She had betrayed him, and he didn't deserve it. She had betrayed him despite his innocence and his kindness. She went to him, and she held his hands.

"We'll do Michael's script." Leigh thought she heard her mother sigh a tiny "Thank God," but she couldn't be certain.

Michael mouthed a silent "Thank you" to Leigh. She tried to tell herself that she was right back where she started, but she knew that was a lie. Same play. Same star. But everything was different now.

"Kendall's right!" Harry declared as he rose from his giant desk. "An opening night is an opening night. Our business here is finished, so let us retire to the party." He extended his arm to Kendall, who hooked on to his elbow graciously. He offered the other to Bridie, who tried to wave him away, but he wouldn't have it. She had to take his arm, so she did, and Leigh watched the most unlikely trio parade out the door.

Alone with Michael was scarier than everything that had gone before. Alone with Michael was too much. What if he could tell everything that she had been doing? Leigh braced herself for one more storm.

"So, Leigh. You don't look like yourself. Your voice is so big and different. What's going on? What happened to you in Jupiter? Wait. Don't answer that." His half-smile faded to sadness. A muscle in his cheek twitched as he said, "Whatever it was, you're not coming home, are you?"

"No. I'm sorry, but no. I'm not." She reached out for him, but he turned his body away from her.

"No. I didn't think so . . . no." His face was locked in a no-expression expression. Was he fighting hard to hold it all in? "I didn't deserve this."

"I'm sorry."

"That doesn't help."

14

"We'll be landing soon," James said quietly. Leigh nodded against his shoulder, almost tunneling into his arm. It was a good place to be, so she inhabited him as best she could. He looked down at her, pulling ever so slightly at the purple scarf in her hair. Leigh met his look and realized that she hadn't been taking care of him, not at all. She hadn't tended to his worries, his sadness, and there must be some. There must be a lot. She wanted to ask him about it, but the lure of his shoulder was too great.

Maddie was seated across the aisle, lecturing the entire cast about the political implications of childbirth. She had been reading up on pregnancy and child care since the run began. Once her pregnancy became impossible to hide, she became militantly pregnant. She was La Leche League and Dr. Spock rolled into one gorgeous, loud-voiced woman.

"Absolutely everyone should insist on having a female

og-byn," she declared. No one laughed anytime Maddie misspoke, not when she sounded so earnest.

Leigh returned her attention to James. They hadn't slept together since Michael's visit at the show's opening. Michael flew home right after the opening performance, but Leigh never explained why he left so quickly. And she couldn't explain her own paralysis around James. They had had such a small piece of time left in Jupiter. Why couldn't she take advantage of it, enjoy it, sleep with James? Leigh couldn't answer that question, not even for herself. She wanted him, that was undeniable, but she couldn't bring herself to resume the affair, even though it had already done its damage to her marriage. Still, she missed James more each day, and she wondered when she'd be able to move, to feel, to touch him again.

"I've missed you," she ventured.

"Me, too." He didn't pause or hesitate before he answered. "Can I ask you something?"

"Anything," she answered, but she hoped it would be an easy question.

"Why did your husband leave Florida so quickly?" Leigh lifted her head off James's shoulder. Husband conversations required a little distance. "Wasn't he supposed to stay longer?"

Leigh could have launched into a monologue to dazzle and distract him: changes in the show; troubles at home; busy, busy practice. But it felt and sounded too Bridie.

"He was sad. I think I made him sad," she answered.

James covered his face with his hands, rubbing a layer of regret away.

"Yeah," he said. "I can see that."

Why wasn't James angry? He looked older since their last flight. She saw a bit more gray in his hair, and the lines in his forehead worried Leigh. His voice went even softer when he asked, "I've been wanting to ask you this for days now: When we get to New York, where are you going to go?"

Leigh closed her eyes. "I don't know."

.   .   .

When Leigh landed in New York, she impulse-decided to go to her apartment. At least for a little while. She could slip in during the day, stock up on clean, warm clothes, and then find somewhere else to stay. She knew she couldn't stay with Michael, and she didn't think she should stay with James. The pit of her stomach nearly pulled her to the ground when she tried to define that "somewhere else." Her map of the world was bordered by Wonderland and home. As she navigated to new territories, she thought, *Here be monsters.*

"I'll call you," she whispered to James. She kissed him right there in the airport, in front of the actors and the baggage handlers. She kissed him as a public declaration of . . . something.

She tried to read *The New York Times* in the taxi, but it was giving her a headache. There was a minor blurb about *Women in Hats.* It was centered on money—ticket sales, investors, predictions—but they didn't mention any of the backstage drama. So Leigh put the paper away. Her headache expanded as they reached the city itself. Now the headache felt more like a squirrel had nested in her head, then experienced extreme nester's remorse and was scratching his way out. If only she could let him out. She made her way to the Upper West Side, and was a sixteenth of an inch away from unlocking her door when she heard him. Michael. Inside their apartment.

"[Something-something] plane landed two hours ago, but [something-something]. [Something-something] patients to [something-something]."

Michael. He was at home in the middle of a workday? For her? Was she supposed to know that? Leigh was not going to subject herself to a confrontation with Michael. Not today. She spun herself and her suitcase around, down the elevator and across the street to her coffee shop. As soon as she looked out the large front window, she saw him. Michael. He was walking to the corner, so pale and small. He was definitely shorter than James and his features didn't measure up to James's at all. His shoulders, his chin, oh, he looked so weak by comparison. Which was the wrong thing to do. Don't compare them. Try to be too mature to do that. He didn't walk well. Did he always drag his feet like that? Had he stopped running? Did she ever find him attractive? What could she possibly say to him today?

Leigh bought her coffee to go and headed for home, now that the coast was clear. She juggled suitcase, keys, and spilling coffee as she opened her front door. Home. Coming in from all that Florida sunshine made the apartment seem so blank, so plain. Yes, there was some comfort in all that simplicity. But not today.

Should she phone him? Which one? James or Michael?

Should she pack her clothes, some books, anything else?

Should she clean up the spilled coffee?

Leigh stood in the middle of her blank room for minutes. It was quiet, until she began to smile, began to hum, to find a song that Bridie had sung so many times. And now Leigh sang it out:

"*Sometimes I stand in the middle of the floor,*
Not going left.
Not going right."

She hummed a few lost lyrics, then belted out,

"*OR AM I LOSING MY MIND!*"

Coffee was pooling around the cup, and she knew she really should clean it up. That was a nice table and it was going to get stuck with a permanent ring. If only she had the strength to rescue it. Or not. She was rescued from her indecision by a convenient knock at the door. It was her father-in-law, Dr. Payne.

"I was hoping Michael would be here, too," he said as she let him in. "He told me he was going to meet you at home." He didn't want to take off his coat, although he looked red-faced. His forehead was damp, and his expression was sour. He was holding the *Times*, open to the blurb about *Women in Hats*.

"Is it true?"

She knew enough to wait until he was much more specific. Had Michael talked to his parents about his crumbling marriage? About the affair? Was she going to have to break that news to them?

"Is my son investing in this cockamamie show? No offense."

Leigh had never seen his face quite so red. Please don't let him have a heart attack. He was taking shallow breaths, so she got him a medicinal drink of water. He put it down on the table without taking a sip, and kept talking.

"You have to know, I love Mikie. I do. Jesus, I haven't called him Mikie since he was twelve and he made me stop. He's a good kid. You love him, too, right?" Rhetorical question. Hopefully. "But sometimes he doesn't have the sense God gave a bag of sticks. It was crazy enough to try and top his old man and write a play—but then he goes and puts the practice at risk? Everything I made? Everything I built? He just gambles it away? So help me, I never knew I raised an idiot." He swatted the paper against his hand. The cracking sound made Leigh jump.

"How did he try to top you, Dr. Payne?"

"My paintings. Which are good."

"Very good." Yes, they were. Of course.

"He wanted to be a big dentist *and* a big artist. Jesus. Can you get him out of this? I swear to God, if I'd known, I would have stopped him. I would have called the bank. I would have taken back the practice. He's a nice kid, when he isn't busy being an idiot." He was tugging at Leigh's arm like a child who wanted a treat so badly. "Look after him, will you? Protect him from his own stupid self. That's what a good wife does."

· · ·

"Maddie? It's me, Leigh. Buzz me in."

Leigh hoisted her suitcase up the many stairs to Maddie's apartment. Her friend was half asleep when she unlocked her door for Leigh, who wanted to be completely asleep. Thank God for Maddie. She didn't have to explain, at least not very much.

"Can I stay here?" Leigh asked breathlessly, already confident that Maddie would hug her and say yes.

"Yes." Maddie hugged her. Leigh finally realized that she was cold, so cold. She had been dressed for Florida humidity when she was walking around in sharp, nasty, cool New York pre-spring. Florida was over. She rubbed her arms hard, while Maddie brought her an itchy black sweater.

"You need to talk to Michael," Maddie advised. She didn't need to spell out any more than that.

"Eventually. But not tonight."

· · ·

Leigh stayed in the hazy cocoon of Maddie's apartment, waiting for rehearsals to begin again. Michael didn't call. Why should he? Maddie bumped into him once, when she ventured out on a food run to satisfy a serious craving for pepper jack cheese.

"He looked like a robot," Maddie said when she returned.

"What does that mean?"

"Like he's only moving around because his battery hasn't run down yet."

Back in the gray light of New York, Leigh saw her betrayal, no, *betrayals,* of her husband with laser clarity. She spent whole mornings studying them, if only to prolong the punishment she was inflicting on herself. Only Maddie could pull her out of that corner, by forcing her to talk about the baby.

"What if it's a boy?" Maddie asked, sitting cross-legged in a rickety old rocking chair. She swung her body forward and back to rock the chair. "How do I raise a boy without letting him know that his whole gentry has been cruel and unusual? On the other hand, what if it's a girl? How do I raise a girl without imprinting all these issues against men?"

"Maybe it'll be neither," Leigh suggested, and for some reason, Maddie was comforted by this thought. She let her feet drop to the floor.

"Should I move to the suburbs and learn to play soccer? I hate anything where I have to run."

"If you want to move, I'll go with you." And Leigh meant it. "We'll be a couple of crazy artist ladies and their adorably goofy baby. We'll be the next bad sitcom. *Subversive Suburbanites,* or something like that."

"You would go to the burbs with me? Really?" Maddie stopped rocking and put all of her energy into beaming at her friend. "Wow. I'm not moving, not if I can help it, but you would do that for me?"

She would.

* * *

James didn't call at all. Not once. Not that she was looking for his call. He was so maddeningly quiet and self-sufficient. She decided to call him, but the phone just rang and rang.

"Do you think he sees my number on his caller ID and he's screening me?" Leigh asked Maddie.

"James?" Maddie called from the kitchen, where she made her thirtieth variation on pasta with marinara sauce. "I think he doesn't have an answering machine. I think he has a rotary dial telephone. Or maybe just a tin can and string. Relax. You'll see him at rehearsal tomorrow."

* * *

Leigh, Maddie, and their stack of new old scripts arrived before anyone else. Leigh was wearing makeup and Maddie helped her do her hair. She combed and brushed and pulled and twisted until Leigh's hair became a complex topknot that fell apart as soon as Leigh turned her head. Maddie brushed it all back down, and wrapped it in that purple scarf. She had been living with Maddie for ten days, with not one word from James. Her purple scarf revived her.

"What are you going to say when you see James?" Maddie asked. She was much rounder now, and sought out chairs everywhere she went.

"What am I going to say when I see *Harmony*?" Leigh corrected her.

"Harmony knows Bridie's coming back. She took it really well, I thought."

"That was when she still had weeks and weeks to play Margaret. It's different now. Everything's different now."

"Are you trying to avoid James?"

And James walked in, almost on cue. Leigh felt her knees buckle ever so slightly. Her mouth was a little too dry to speak. Why did he have to look so much better than Leigh remembered? If only her legs worked, she could run across the room to him. If only.

Maddie roused herself from her chair and noisily made herself scarce with, "Gotta pee. Always gotta pee. I'm gone. Not even here."

James looked at the floor entirely too much, then he looked at the new scripts.

"The old scripts, huh. Here we go." He took the stack of scripts and began to thumb through his copy. How dare he be able to read at a time like this? She still couldn't speak, so dreadfully dry. But she couldn't hide her disappointment. He put his script back on the table, maybe he had only been pretending to read, and she took his hand with both of her hands, placed it over her heart. She wanted so much to speak, if only she could.

"Where have you been?" James asked quietly. Oh, she had never heard him sound so sad before. "Why didn't you call me?" he asked. "I tried to call you, but your husband answered and I kind of panicked and hung up."

"I was staying with Maddie. Oh, God, I never told you. I tried to, but you don't have an answering machine."

"I thought—"

Leigh didn't get to hear what James had been thinking. Just then, Ben and Jessica walked in together, holding hands. Leigh finally figured out that they were now a couple. A cute one. Ben brought a carton of Krispy Kreme doughnuts for everyone.

"Is Maddie coming? I made sure to get plain glazed for her. She's such a purist mama," Ben said.

"You are so thoughtful." Jessica was not quite gushing, but close.

"Hey, everyone. Oh, you're already getting your refined-sugar fix? So early?" Harmony smiled as she entered the room. Her Florida tan had faded, but she looked so serene, so rested. She clucked in disapproval at the doughnuts. "You know, these things are just poison for your system. So, I'll just take them all, and save you from yourselves." Harmony was grinning as she munched on a doughnut, hugging each person in the room.

David appeared, with a matching box of Krispy Kremes. He and Ben laughed and did the traditional man-hug/pat-pat before settling in and saying, "Ah, the new old scripts. So, we're starting a whole new ride."

"I get double doughnuts," Maddie called from the door. "Doughnuts for me and for the ingesting baby."

"That one almost makes sense," David said as he handed over the feast.

Leigh wanted to say something, anything, to her cast before Bridie arrived and changed the whole atmosphere. But Harmony spoke up first.

"Hey, everybody. I just want you to know that I had a blast playing Margaret. I hate letting it go, and that's why I came here today to quit."

Leigh couldn't stop herself from crying out, "No!"

"Let me finish," Harmony said, her trembling chin contrasting with her even voice. "I came here to quit, but I can't do it. We're connected here. We're a family. And you can't quit your family. Even if you want to."

She hid her face in her hands. This makeshift family circled around her until she was ready to lift her head. "See?" she said. "We really are a family."

And there was Bridie, standing in the doorway. How long had she been there? She entered, took center stage, and demurely lifted a script from the table. She looked at the cast with sad solidarity, as if she were one of them. Oh, wait. She was.

"I know that this is a big change for all of you, and I'm still not so sure we should be making this change. But here we are. That's all."

Bridie sat down. That was all? That was it?

James let his hand rest gently against the small of Leigh's back, and she wanted to tumble into his arms. She wanted to freeze time and hold this moment, imperfect as it was.

"So. Welcome to rehearsal, everyone." Leigh's voice was high and breathy. She didn't want to move too much and lose James's hand. "Technically, you're all early. Which is against Equity rules, but we'll let it go just this once!" It was a silly old joke, but the actors giggled at it anyway. Bridie didn't giggle. She was still quiet.

"Let's get to work."

They began reading the play, and damn, Bridie knew all of Margaret's lines, and damn, she read them well. Everyone rose to her level, and damn, it was good.

James called out, "Take ten, everybody," when they finished the first act. Harmony looked like she needed one more good cry. Leigh was ready to forego ten minutes of looking at James so that she could console Harmony, but Bridie got there first. She reached across the table and squeezed Harmony's hand.

"Let's go outside," Bridie whispered.

When they returned from the break, it was clear that both women had had a good cry. The friendship scenes between Margaret and Grace were suddenly so rich and believable. It all worked. It all contributed.

• • •

The actors were dismissed from that first rehearsal, and Leigh would finally have her opportunity to be alone with James. She lingered in the rehearsal hall, and so did he. She wanted some time just to look at him, to touch him, to talk to him, and she took it.

"Leigh?" James asked. Maybe he was thinking the same thing. She turned around to face him and he said, "Your husband is here."

James's shoulders crept up just a bit as he cleared his throat and pushed in chairs that didn't need pushing in. Leigh walked to Michael, who was stuck in the doorway.

"Hi," he said. He looked so sad, so tired, and several pounds thinner.

"Hey," she answered. "Come on in." Michael managed a few stingy steps into the room.

James left without a word. He waved to Leigh from the doorway, but she couldn't move to acknowledge him. If she looked directly at him, she might turn into a pillar of salt.

"I brought some of your things," Michael said. He had a large overnight bag, filled to bursting. He brought it to the table and set it down, like an offering.

"You didn't have to." Leigh tried to keep looking at Michael.

"Yes, I did. I wish I'd never written this play. I wish I'd never lost you."

"I'm sorry," she said.

"You should be. You really fucking should be. I'm trying not to be too angry at you, but what the hell? You deserve it." His voice still hadn't healed since Jupiter. It sounded raw and painful. But that didn't stop him from talking.

"So? Are you still with him?" he demanded, but Leigh didn't want to answer. Didn't want to mention James or her affair. "Come on, Leigh. Are you?"

"I don't know."

"Yeah. That sounds like you." Large patches of red surfaced on his face, and his breathing was rapid. Leigh felt afraid of him, trying to assure herself that Michael would never hurt her. But they were all alone, and this was always how Bridie's Lifetime TV movies began. "What do you want, Leigh? I'd really like to know one thing: Did you ever really want to be married to me? Did you?"

"I don't know," she replied softly, and Michael slammed his fist on the table, and it echoed horribly.

"Well, try, goddammit, try! Answer me. Did you wreck our marriage on some stupid whim? What exactly do you want?" Maybe he could hurt her. Maybe there was some truth behind Bridie's awful TV movies.

"I did. I wanted our marriage. I wanted you. But I can't lie to you, Michael, I'm stuck. And all I want right now is to direct this play and do right by you."

He slowed down. He nodded to himself, and almost smiled at Leigh.

"There. That wasn't so hard, was it?" If he had been about to cry or shout or hurt her, he breathed it all away now. "And, just for the record, I want you to do the best work you've ever done. You have to. Me, I'd pull the plug on this whole thing, but I can't. I'll lose the practice and pretty much everything I own. So, the show really *must* go on." He half-laughed. "And it has to be good. It has to be a hit."

"It will be." Leigh had no business making such a promise, but it seemed to console him, at least a bit.

"So. I guess I'll see you around."

"Opening night?"

"Right," he said as he drifted toward the door.

She heard his footsteps down the hall and the front door open. She opened the heavy bag immediately. He seemed to have defied the laws of physics when he packed this bag. It contained more than it could contain. But there, on the top, carefully bubble-wrapped, was the framed photo of Lilly, taken by her father.

• • •

Rehearsals ran like a study in perfect rehearsals. Bridie didn't put one toe out of order, and the actors accepted her into their ensemble. Bridie Hart was queen of the damn world. How did she do it? How did she go from fired, disgraced actress to beloved member of an ensemble of actors who had been doing perfectly fine without her, thank you very much? She was Bridie Hart. That was how.

Kendall watched an early run-through, and offered a sheet of notes to Leigh, most of which Leigh had predicted.

"Any personnel issues?" Kendall asked, and clearly she meant, "Has Bridie been misbehaving?"

"I just have one personnel issue," Leigh said evenly.

"What did she do?" Kendall settled in for a juicy story, but Leigh surprised her with her answer.

"It's James. He's been avoiding me since we started rehearsals again."

Kendall looked to the sky, as if asking for strength.

"Jesus Christ, Leigh, I'm here to help you with the play, not your love life."

"Right. Skip that. Everything's fine."

"But since you've got the play all tangled up with your love life, let me say this: own up to what you're doing. You don't want to play the part of the cheating wife, but guess what? You're playing it. Now get over it. Fuck around, if that's what you need to do. Make a mess. Get fat. Make mistakes. But who can blame the boy for protecting himself when he's involved with a girl who doesn't know how to want what she wants?"

"Kendall, I don't understand a word you're saying."

Kendall held Leigh's face in her hands and said, "You went to Jupiter and turned into your mother. Oh, well. Grow up."

Leigh felt as if she'd been kicked in a soft spot.

$$15$$

New York. Opening night.

This was the night that their Broadway run officially began, and the night that their reviews would be published. In the movies, theater critics came to opening night, then jotted their first impressions for publication the next morning. The cast was always gathered backstage for an emotional all-nighter as they waited for the early edition of the papers. But in real life, they held a press night a few days prior to opening, so that those early editions of the papers contained much sharper insults.

"It's a hit, I'm telling you," Harry insisted. "I can smell these things!"

"Don't say that, Harry. You'll jinx everything," Leigh said.

"Bullshit."

Kendall arrived wearing, oh my God, a dress. A vintage black dress with taffeta and tulle.

"Hey, even *I* like to play dress-up every now and then," she said to the stunned expression on Leigh's face.

Harry offered his arm and said, "Shall we?"

Kendall took one arm, but Leigh declined the other. She didn't want to go in. It was too soon, and it was all too sickeningly scary. Earlier in the day, Maddie had kicked into her best maternal mode, trying patiently to force Leigh to eat, but it was pointless. She couldn't look at food today, or even consider its existence.

Leigh paced the sidewalk outside at a frantic tempo. Her mantra switched from "Please, please, pleeeease let the critics like the play" to "Fuck them, why do they have so much power over me!" back to "Please, please, pleeeease let the critics like the play." She was also veering between weeping from the pressure and fear to laughing at herself for carrying on so, then she was angry at the power of the press, and then she went right back to weeping. She was Ophelia en route to the mad scene.

"Leigh? Are you okay?" It was Michael. Oh, Michael. She hadn't seen him since he delivered her belongings to rehearsal. But here he was, and he looked so good. So strong, so handsome, so warm. She wanted to run into his arms and complete her mad scene with a sympathetic soul.

"This is my friend Jennifer," he said before Leigh could go completely mad.

Michael had a date. And she was pretty. She smiled politely and reached out to shake Leigh's hand, which was shaking all by itself.

"This is kind of awkward, isn't it," Jennifer said. "Anyway, I'm really looking forward to the play. Michael tells me you're a great director."

Leigh managed the handshake and even a smile.

"Thank you. That's really very kind of you," Leigh was able to reply.

"My dad wouldn't come to the opening, can you believe it?" Michael exclaimed. "He's still upset about the practice and everything. Parents!" Jennifer gave him a sympathetic squeeze.

Michael took Leigh by the arm, and Jennifer stepped back to watch the opening-night crowd as it did its crowding.

"So, Leigh. I figured we could wait until after the play opened to start doing the whole lawyer thing."

"Sure."

"But I don't want to wait too long. I think I might be moving into Jennifer's place. Sooner rather than later. It's all happening really fast. I guess that's how it is when you know what you want. Anyway, that's not for tonight, right? We'll work it out later. Tonight's all about the play!"

He kissed her on the cheek and escorted Jennifer into the theater. They looked so right. Leigh wondered if they went running together every morning. Of course they did. Would they have children together? Of course they would. She waited a safe minute or two, then walked into the theater.

Leigh paced much faster now, to make up for any lost pacing outside the theater. She clenched her hands into fists and beat her sides while she made a variety of deals with God, Buddha, Vishnu, and whoever else was listening. She promised to give up swearing, junk food, and alcohol, if only this play would be well received. Her empty stomach growled and hurt.

Leigh waited until every audience member was seated, then stood at the back of the house. Darkness. Then light. Then Bridie. Applause.

· · ·

The opening-night crowd was there to have a good time, so that's exactly what they did. They laughed, applauded, and stood up tall for Bridie's bow. Leigh was drooping with exhaustion by that point, as if she had been carrying all of the actors on her back all night. She was ready to put them down. In another ninety minutes, the first reviews would be available. Leigh fingered her watch, hoping to accelerate time.

Backstage, she congratulated each actor, yes, even Bridie, and accepted congratulations from everyone. Harry was smiling as if he knew it would all end well.

"The advance box office is already good," he reasoned. "And we've got Bridie Hart. She is some hot shit. We'll be fine. Okay, if the critics really lay us low, that'll hurt. But they won't."

"How do you know?" Leigh hated the desperation in her voice.

"I don't. But they won't do that. It wouldn't be right."

"But the world is a strange and perverse place." Leigh's voice was espresso-quick. "Wrong things happen every day. And to very nice people who've worked very hard and just want a little taste of success, but it seems to be too much to ask for and they'll have to stay in a not-for-profit, shoestring-budget kind of world for-fucking-ever. It happens."

"Maddie?" Harry was calling Maddie over from a conclave of happy women who were touching her belly. "Your friend here needs some champagne. Can you grab a bottle from the stash I put in the booth? You two can toast your opening night, right?"

"Harry! I can't drink. I'm pregnant."

"Oh. I thought you were just getting fat. Can you get the champagne anyway? For Leigh?"

• • •

Leigh and Maddie were hanging back. Everyone in the cast and crew danced off to Tavern on the Green for an elaborate opening-night party. Leigh wished that Casey the tired bartender could be there, along with Shelby the happy waitress. If only she could fly to Jupiter tonight. Since she couldn't, the two friends lingered backstage for as long as possible, then started wandering toward the party on foot, champagne in hand.

They were so close to the party, maybe just a block or two away, but Leigh had to sit down. They sat on a bench on the edge of Central Park with the bottle of champagne between them. Leigh had lost track of the fact that Maddie wasn't drinking it. Maddie sat in a mama lotus position while Leigh hugged her own knees and moaned, "They're going to hate it. They're going to roast me on a spit. They're going to do one of those reviews where they really have fun hating me." She stopped moaning long enough to reach for more champagne.

"They won't. All the reviews in Jupiter were good," Maddie countered.

"Jupiter was another world. And another play. I threw away my stupid career for this stupid play. And I threw away stupid James because I'm so stupid, stupid. It's like he's waiting for something from me and I don't know what it is because I'm so . . ."

"Stupid?"

"You think so, too?" Leigh let her feet fall to the ground, and started bouncing them until Maddie made her stop.

Leigh had nearly killed the champagne. At first, she found it tricky to drink from the bottle, but she got surprisingly good at it.

A delivery truck for *The New York Times* rolled by, and Leigh felt as if some force of nature thrust her from the park bench, speeding toward the nearest newsstand. Maddie followed with much less speed and urgency.

Leigh searched the paper for the review, captioned with a glorious photo of Bridie. She scanned the text as quickly as she could in her diminished state. She found the words "genial comedy" and "family fare" in the first paragraph. Then two paragraphs described the plot with a dearth of adjectives. A paragraph on the joys of having Bridie Hart back on Broadway, a mention of the

mother-daughter relationship, and a nod to each of the other actors. All this was followed by a bionic joke. A bionic joke? No!

Early reports about the backstage dramas in the out-of-town
tryouts made the production look like Leigh Majors' bionic
bomb, or even a six-million-dollar flop. But the end result is a
throwback to the kind of plays everyone got excited about
back in Frank Majors' day. And it's fun to revisit that world
once more with *Women in Hats*.

That was it? That was the big review? Fun? Genial? Not a flop?
Leigh rolled the paper into a tight cylinder and tucked it under her
arm. She was damned by faint praise.

"Well. The big review is in and it's very, very medium. Let's go to
the fucking party," she said to Maddie.

"Yeah, remember that old eating something idea? You want to
give that a try?" Maddie responded.

Leigh was stomping her way through the park, speaking to
the world, the sky, the critics. "I'm an idiot. Fuck this play. Fuck
theater. I hate theater. I hate my life. I hate everything. Except for
you and your baby. You're cool. Everything else sucks."

"Leigh?" Maddie interrupted. She was having trouble keeping
up with Leigh's stomp-a-thon. "You're actually scaring me right
now. Please take a breath."

Leigh's version of taking a breath consisted of finishing the
champagne, just in time to pick up a lovely flute of bubbly from a
silver tray at Tavern on the Green. They had arrived.

Leigh looked to her right and saw a sea of unemployed actors in
black and white, carrying food to the employed actors, who were
wearing finery. Leigh looked to her left and saw that Michael and
Jennifer were seated at a table looking even happier than they had
looked earlier. The happiness had multiplied and divided some-

Judy Sheehan

how. Bridie was at a larger table, holding court. She looked twenty years younger, what with all her happiness.

James was nowhere. Maybe he left, tired of trying to decipher Leigh. And who could blame him? James was just one more thing she got wrong. She really was an idiot.

The champagne was good.

Leigh turned to her right and realized that she was facing down a clutch of reporters, cameras, microphones, and long skinny pads of paper.

"This is *Stage Talk* with Stacy Barber for CBS News. We're talking with Leigh Majors, who tonight made her Broadway director- ial debut with *Women in Hats,* starring the ever-wonderful, ever- effervescent Bridie Hart! Now, Leigh, there's more than just a working relationship between you and your star, isn't that right?"

For the moment, Leigh was the center of the known universe, and she just had to smile. The bright lights blinded her to the world beyond the cameras, and the microphones were fairly beg- ging for a response. Leigh leaned closer to the microphone than necessary to say, "That's right, Stacy."

Leigh pulled back, then realized that she needed to get close to the microphone once more to add, "She's my mother."

"Mother Love is your mother, and you're directing her in a play. I think we're seeing some Broadway history here tonight, don't you?"

Again, Leigh leaned in close to repeat, "That's right, Stacy," be- cause it worked so well the first time.

"Wow, Mother Love is your mother. You're so lucky!" Stacy said. She shouldn't have said it, but she did. Leigh took hold of the microphone before Stacy realized what was happening, turned to the cameras, and began.

"Lucky? I'm so lllllllucky? Hey, Stacy, did I ever tell you about

how she used to make me break up with her boyfriends for her because she was too scared to do it herself? I was nine years old and
saying, 'My mother thanks you for all the beauty that you brought
into her life, but now you have to go. Don't call. Don't write. But
remember, you'll always have Paris. Good-bye.'"

Stacy wasn't trying to get the microphone back. In fact, the
cameras and microphones were nosing closer and closer with
every word Leigh spoke. It was intoxicating. Leigh started gestur-
ing grandly, and let her voice grow big enough to match her body
language.

"But that wasn't so bad," Leigh continued. "Not as bad as the
year she forgot to get me anything for Christmas. Okay, that's so
unfair. She forgot to have her *assistants* get me anything for Christmas. There. And would you like to count the number of birthdays
she spent with me? How many thumbs do you have? 'Cause that's
all you'll need to count them."

Leigh was vaguely aware of a crowd behind her as she shouted,
"Bridie Hart SUCKED as a mother. She was—"

James was there, taking the microphone away from Leigh, taking Leigh away from the center of the universe. It had gotten very
crowded, so he had to push his way through the throng and out to
the dark, cool green of Central Park. Apparently, she wasn't safe
around electricity. They stood in the middle of the greenery, and
Leigh wished that it could calm her.

Now that they were far enough from the cameras and lights, he
said, "So, can I ask you something?" She sat on the grass, which
was slightly damp, and he sat down next to her. "What the hell is
wrong with you?" he asked. "I've been wanting to ask you that
since we opened. In Jupiter."

"I wish I knew," she answered. She was beginning to realize that
she was cold. "Hey?" she said. "Here's one thing I know I want: sit a
little closer." James pulled her close, and her head fit so nicely onto

his shoulder. She was still shaking, or shivering. Was there a difference?

"Tomorrow, when you wake up and realize what you said tonight, I hope you'll call me," James said, and then kissed her forehead.

"Why?"

"Because it was brilliant." Why was he laughing like that? He looked so calm, so relaxed, for the first time in ages. "How long have you waited to say all that?"

"Too long." And she started to catch his laugh. They laughed up at the stars. Leigh felt light and silly. She let the stars settle into the sky and then she said, "I was married. It was wrong. I just couldn't."

"I know," he answered.

She wanted to kiss him and walk off into the eventual sunrise. But then Leigh looked toward the twinkling Christmas lights that decorated the Tavern. Bridie was marching through the lights and toward Leigh with impressive speed. Bridie was so energetic, so youthful. She could really play any age she wanted.

When Bridie's silhouette shifted from decorative lights to the starkness of the park, Leigh stopped shivering. She kissed James as well as she could and whispered, "Save yourself." He took her hand. She bit his thumb as if it were her own.

She stood up and waited for Bridie to reach her. And there she was. James rose and said, "Maybe you two should wait until tomorrow to talk. It's been quite a night."

"Are you speaking as a stage manager, or as the man who is sleeping with my daughter?" Here was the old Bridie Hart, and in good voice, too.

"I'm speaking as the man who's in love with Leigh." And just like that, Leigh was warm and strong and up for anything.

"I love you, too." She kissed him once more and added, "But go. I have to do this alone."

"You make me sound like a dragon you have to slay," Bridie
snorted. "Which, by the way, is a step up from the way you described me *on television*."

"Are you sure?" James checked back with Leigh, but she was already pushing him away.

It was a full moon, and that was all the spotlight Bridie Hart
would get for this scene.

BRIDIE

What got into you? Why? And why would you say all those things
in front of reporters and cameras? Jesus, they'll be playing that tape
in my obituary, won't they. Jesus!
(*Bridie closes in on Leigh, who stands her ground.*)

LEIGH

This is all your fault.

BRIDIE

My fault?
(*Leigh waves the newspaper.*)

LEIGH

Did you see the reviews? The genial, okay comedy that we're
doing? Is that what I gave up everything for?

BRIDIE

Oh, that's what this is all about! You always have to be so special, so
important. The critics' darling. Honey, the critics hated *Cats* but it
ran and ran and ran. And so will we. Just ask Harry. What did they
say that was so bad?
(*She takes the paper and scans the review quickly, and likes what she sees. this
infuriates Leigh.*)

Leigh walked away, knowing that Bridie would follow, and she
did. She saw a group of business-executive types, holding up

their cell phones to photograph Mother Love. She turned back, and found a quieter spot in a green field away from adoring fans. Bridie clutched the newspaper as proof of her own personal goodness.

LEIGH

You made me direct this play. I had a perfectly fine life until you came along and messed it all up.

BRIDIE

Hey, hey, hey. I didn't make you have an affair with your stage manager.

LEIGH

Maybe not. But it wouldn't have happened if I'd stayed home in New York, and it wouldn't have happened if I were somebody else's daughter.
(Bridie is facing Leigh, ready to fight.)

BRIDIE

You want a different mother? I'll see what I can do.

LEIGH

Thank you for the stupid offer.

BRIDIE

This is about that Christmas, isn't it.

LEIGH

Don't.

BRIDIE

Come on, let me have it. Tell me my crimes against you.

LEIGH

(Letting her fury loose. Her voice tears open.)

You forgot about me—and not just on Christmas—any day of the week. You drank too much! You fucked around too much!

BRIDIE

(Talking over her)
Don't you talk to me like that!

LEIGH

(Continuing over her)
You still care more about your image than my life. I wish I could forget you. Why do you have to fucking haunt me? You're this weird confusing voice in my head that wants me to be you. I don't want to be you, but I don't know how to escape you.

BRIDIE

Are you done?

LEIGH

It's your fault I can't have children.

Bridie was ashamed. There was no other way to describe that look. Leigh had never seen such an expression on her mother's face. And now that she had shamed her mother, she didn't know what to do with it. Bridie faltered, but Leigh tried to stay strong. Don't let her off the hook, not tonight.

BRIDIE

I'm sorry. The doctors were always scaring people back then—

LEIGH

You knew. You knew. You and your pills. You knew.

BRIDIE

I only took them at the beginning. I didn't think anything bad would happen. There were lots of mothers who took them all the way through. I was so sick, and I had to work. I had to.
(Leigh doesn't want to forgive her mother.)

LEIGH

But it's still your fault.

BRIDIE

Yes. It is. I'm sorry. I never thought it would happen to you. You were always so lucky. You married a nice boy, you did the work you wanted to do. And then you got pregnant. Just like that. So I figured that meant that you were okay, and those doctors were all wrong. But then. Well. Everything pretty much went to hell. And it all started with me, didn't it.
(Pause. She caresses her daughter's hair. Leigh tolerates it.)
I'm so sorry. And I'm sorry about all the things I missed. I'd go back if I could. I'd fix it all up.

No! Don't let her off the hook. Didn't she always let herself off the hook? No. Make her earn it. Leigh might never get her mother alone on this playing field again. And Bridie was stranded in all that greenery. No scripted response to rescue her now.

BRIDIE

You hate me. You always have.

LEIGH

I don't hate you. I wish I could. I love you. But you let me down. You let me down a lot.

BRIDIE

I did my best.

LEIGH

Maybe that's just easy to say. Maybe your best sucked, and you can't go back and fix it.

BRIDIE

Then stop asking me to.

LEIGH

Shut up!

BRIDIE

And if it's all true? If I was a total fuckup? What next?

LEIGH

Shut up!

Bridie was closing in on Leigh, pulling her close with her hands, her voice, her face. Why didn't Bridie just walk away? Why didn't she override Leigh with one of her famous monologues, then storm off to the bar? What was she staying out here for? Bridie wasn't posing her aging face oh-so-carefully, wasn't pitching her voice just right. She wasn't holding in her stomach. Whatever she wanted, it must be big.

BRIDIE

What comes next, Leigh? Hmm? Maybe you still have to move on.

LEIGH

Shut up!

BRIDIE

Maybe it's time to grow up, Leigh!

LEIGH

I said, SHUT UP!!

BRIDIE

OKAY!
(Long pause. Silence. After a while, Bridie sits on the damp grass, still silent. Leigh studies her mother, confused. minutes pass. Bridie doesn't move a muscle, and Leigh would notice if she did. When she's ready, Leigh sits next to Bridie.)

LEIGH

(*Quietly breaking the silence*)
Thank you.

BRIDIE

Don't mention it. Oh, God, look at me: my dress is ruined.

LEIGH

Just wait till the paparazzi see you.
(*Bridie giggles. They sit for so long, so long. Leigh lets her head drop to her mother's. They look back at the restaurant, where the party crowd is still checking on them. Bridie waves, so does Leigh. They look at the stars. Leigh starts to feel the cold again, but Bridie keeps her warm.*)

Bridie smelled like Chanel No. 5, as always. That had been her scent forever. Whenever Leigh smelled it on a passing stranger, she thought that Bridie must be in the room. Leigh thought she saw a shooting star, or two or three. No, those were photographers, getting a strange shot of mother and daughter, stargazing. Look, another shooting star. Then the dark took over once again. The dark made everything so quiet, for so long. And then,

BRIDIE

You miss Lilly, don't you.

LEIGH

Mom, don't.
(*Leigh sits up. She doesn't want to have this conversation.*)

BRIDIE

It's okay. I miss her, too.

LEIGH

Stop.

BRIDIE

She was so beautiful.

LEIGH

She looked like you.

BRIDIE

She did

LEIGH

You shouldn't have pushed her. You should have let her be.

BRIDIE

I never pushed her. I never pushed either one of you.

LEIGH

You made her be like you.

BRIDIE

She *wanted* to be like me. She loved me. At least *one* of my daughters loved me.

LEIGH

She loved you so much she cut school and got in front of a rock band and got on a motorcycle.
(*Bridie is shaking.*)

BRIDIE

And she died. She left me. She was my baby. And I lost her.
(*Bridie tries to continue, but she can't speak for a while. Leigh wants to embrace her mother, but somehow she just can't. Bridie has to pull herself together in her own way, and it isn't easy.*)
She's gone. She's gone forever.

LEIGH

But that's the thing: she doesn't feel gone. She feels close.

BRIDIE

Yes, I know that feeling. I love that feeling—like she's a grace that stays with us. That part is forever.
(Lilly enters quietly. Bridie doesn't see her, but Leigh does. She watches her sister, but Lilly reveals nothing.)

LEIGH

I'm so tired.

LILLY

You're not used to this kind of high drama.

LEIGH

I think I'd like to be alone for a bit.

BRIDIE

Sure. We can pick up fighting in the morning.

LEIGH

And we will.
(Bridie walks away, ready to exit, but stops to look back at her daughter. The connection between them has changed forever.)

BRIDIE

Good night.

LEIGH

Good night, Mom.
(Bridie walks back and kisses Leigh, then exits. Leigh looks around and sees Lilly still standing there.)

Lilly. She was wearing that green dress, so gauzy and see-through, with gold bangles sewn everywhere. She looked like a gypsy. She looked like a park spirit. She wore that same cocky smile, contrasting with her sleepy, sultry eyes. She may have been dead, but she was still rock and roll. Leigh kept her cool, as if this were just another conversation with Lilly.

LEIGH

Hi.

LILLY

Hi.

LEIGH

(*Laughing*)
Can you believe the day I'm having?

LILLY

What are you going to do?

LEIGH

I have no idea.

LILLY

Good.
(*She takes Leigh by the arm and walks her to the top of the hill. There, Lilly wraps her arms around her sister, keeping her warm.*)

LEIGH

Give me a clue?

LILLY

Take good care of Maddie's baby. She's going to need you.

LEIGH

Okay.

LILLY

And be with James. And be in Wonderland. And be in the world.

LEIGH

You never used to talk like that.

LILLY

Hey, we all change. Oh. And give Mom a fucking break.

LEIGH

Ick. Do I have to?
(*Lilly pushes Leigh, who stumbles, then falls on the soft grass. They both laugh, but Leigh knows that she is losing her sister, has lost her sister. Lilly doesn't sit with her on the cool grass. She steps away. She is ready to leave.*)

LEIGH

Okay. I'll try.

The night had reached that point of darkness that felt irreversible. Now that Leigh had a chance to study her sister, oh, yes, she had changed. Her hard edges had softened, her eyes were content. She reached out for Lilly, who backed away one more step and said, "No."

(*Lilly moves away. Leigh can barely speak through her tears.*)

LEIGH

Lilly? Do we have to say good-bye?

LILLY

Yes.

LEIGH

No. Please don't go. I need you.
(*Leigh can cry as much as she likes.*)

LILLY

You'll be all right now. Mostly. But, ready or not, I'm going. It's time. It's the last scene.
(*Blackout*)

$$\left[\begin{array}{c} \text{Epilogue} \end{array}\right]$$

RECENT SALES

Maddie LeSage's recent show at the Aqua Gallery included a series of oil paintings of her infant son visiting characters in classic paintings. Her son has now crawled from *The Last Supper* to *Washington Crossing the Delaware*. While most of the paintings sold, the surprise sale was a pen-and-ink drawing of the child chasing Alice chasing the White Rabbit as they tumble into Wonderland. It was purchased by an anonymous collector for twice the asking price.

Newyorkart.com April 2007

LOST IN WONDERLAND

Six months ago, when Leigh Majors directed *Women In Hats*, it looked like she had gone commercial, and on a very grand scale. While critics gave the play a mixed reaction, audiences did not. They have flocked to see this comedy, despite the fact that Bridie Hart's contract with the show recently expired. Her replacement, Harmony Hecht, has experienced almost no downtick in the box office. Producer Harry Greenwald sums it up: "It's a good old reliable comedy. And a cash cow, believe me."

Majors disappeared from the New York theater scene until recently. When asked what she has been working on during this sabbatical, Majors replied, "I've been helping a friend with a baby. And it was so much fun, I'm starting the paperwork for an adoption."

Wonderland Theater has officially announced that Ms. Majors will be taking over as artistic director, following the retirement of the company's founder and artistic director, Kendall Epstein.

Majors has already appointed James McGovern as company manager, which shouldn't come as a surprise. Rumors that Majors and McGovern are an item have been swirling since Majors' divorce from her husband, Michael Payne, the author of *Women in Hats*.

When asked about Wonderland's upcoming season, Majors replied, "Kendall will still be consulting, advising, and generally having her say about everything we do at Wonderland. And we consider ourselves lucky to have her nearby. Our first project will be an alternate version of *Women in Hats* that will run at Wonderland. It may not be as popular as the Broadway version, but we want to give it a go. Meanwhile, I intend to take on the occasional commercial project to help fund my work here in Wonderland."

Such as?

"I'll be directing Bridie Hart in the *Mother Love Reunion* movie."

Of course.

We look forward to more wonders in Wonderland.

Theater in America September 2007

Acknowledgments

Writing this book was an adventure from start to finish. How lucky I am to have this page, where I can thank my fellow travelers. Since this isn't an Oscar speech (and none of you can mock what I'm wearing), feel free to turn the page while I just keep offering thanks until the orchestra plays me out.

Thanks beyond measure to:

Bob Gilbo, for everything. And for everything else.

Looking Glass Theatre, Justine Lambert, Kenneth Nowell. I wouldn't be writing a postcard without the firm push and loving support you guys have given me over the years.

Myra Donnelley, evil twins rule the earth.

Elizabeth Dennehy, Carrie Gordon, Ellen Hickey, Kathryn Kaufman-Seay, Karen Fleming, Diane Vecchiarello. I'm forever proud of my membership in the Senior Seven.

Fred Sullivan, my special love.

MaryAnne Beggs, and Jeanne LeSage, the real thing.

The DreamMoms, especially Pat Nealon and AnneMarie Gussman. What a long strange trip it's been.

Signe Pike and Allison Dickens, editors and artists who helped bring this book out of the primordial ooze where it began.

Dan Lazar and Simon Lipskar of Writers' House, for being the absolute best in the business.

My mother, who is gone, and my father, who is here. I am, and always will be, your daughter.

Finally, love and thanks to the little girl who is the true north and pure heart of everything I do: Annie.

WOMEN IN HATS

Judy Sheehan

A READER'S GUIDE

A CONVERSATION WITH

Judy Sheehan

Women in Hats gives us an exclusive peek into the world of show business as we are drawn into the story of Leigh Majors and her relationship with her famous mother, Bridie Hart. Author Judy Sheehan caught up with her old friend Elizabeth Dennehy to talk about the book, actors, writing, and life. Elizabeth's father is actor Brian Dennehy. Can the daughter of a famous actor bring us new insights to the story of Leigh and Bridie? Here is their conversation:

Elizabeth Dennehy: So, here you are writing about actors.

Judy Sheehan: Hey, they make good subjects. They supply their own drama, don't you think?

ED: Yes, I think I've seen a little bit of that. My father, my husband, me—we're all actors. As I was reading the book, I couldn't help but wonder: Are you maybe having a little fun at our expense? Do you have a sort of love/hate relationship with actors?

JS: You know that I started out as an actor—full disclosure time: you and I studied theater in college together and then we were in *Tony n' Tina's Wedding.*

ED: And our friendship survived all that!

JS: Thank God. Well, when I started writing plays, I switched to the other side of the audition table and got to see actors in a whole new light. It's an irrational business and it can easily bring out the crazy in people.

ED: Okay, I think I've seen a little bit of that, too. . . .

JS: It's true! The ones who are successful constantly worry that they aren't successful enough. And the ones who really are struggling—they have to be so emotionally resourceful just to keep going.

ED: At the start of the book, Leigh and Bridie are practically estranged. It was a very chilly relationship. But by the end, I felt like Bridie was really trying to connect with Leigh. Did you know that this would be the outcome when you started, or did you make it up as you went along?

JS: I worked from an outline that reads a bit like a choppy short-story version of the book. I didn't know every detail of the outcome, but I knew that Leigh had to forgive her mother, especially before becoming a mother herself. And Bridie had to make an effort to redeem herself as a mother; she had to help her daughter in a very real way. The unresolved anger and sadness that these two women carried could poison their lives if they let it continue. There is that old saying that holding a grudge is like taking poison and hoping that the other guy dies. That's exactly what's going on with these two.

ED: Bridie surprised me at times. She didn't raise a big stink when Leigh fired her in Florida, and then she actually stayed with her daughter all through that massive confrontation in Central Park. What's going on with her?

JS: She's trying to be a good mother, and she really does care what Leigh thinks of her. If Lilly had lived, she and Bridie might have ended up as best friends, and Leigh might have gotten left out. I like to think that Lilly would have worked to pull her sister into the family circle. But now Bridie needs to repair her relationship with Leigh—and she's doing this in her own slightly crazy way. She can't run to the producers and complain about being fired, because it was her own daughter who fired her. It's much too personal, and it's so humiliating.

When Leigh and Bridie have their big confrontation after the opening night, I think that's the moment when Bridie really steps up. She takes all of her daughter's anger. She doesn't hide or run away. What's more, she helps Leigh to accept Lilly's death. It's one of the few times in her life that Bridie is really putting her daughter's needs ahead of her own ego.

ED: I really enjoyed the way that Bridie's actions were always captured as stage directions, and you comment on her line readings. Why does that final scene turn into an actual play?

JS: I think that's part of how Leigh sees her mother—always performing. She always frames her mother in that context. In the big final confrontation, when Leigh is drunk and finally letting everything out to her mother, it's not an ordinary conversation. It's a scene. Leigh sees it that way in the moment, and she'll always remember it that way, so I wrote it that way. This is one of the aspects of the book that I didn't plan, you know. As I got into the emotional heat of that chapter, it just made sense to me to let it play as a theater scene. When I read it now, it still seems a little hallucinatory, but I think it really works.

ED: Speaking of hallucinatory, talk to me about Lilly coming back in visions to Leigh.

JS: I think that was a sign of Leigh starting to thaw, so to speak. She's kind of shut down and stiff at the start of the book. She isn't very accessible. That's one of the factors that destroys her marriage. She just can't be fully present emotionally. But Leigh's love for her sister runs very deep, and her grief is almost more than she can bear. When she starts to see Lilly—on the street or in her dreams—she is starting to unclench and open her heart.

In the end, I don't know if Lilly's presence in Central Park is real or imagined. I'm going to leave that up to you.

ED: Sometimes I got the feeling that Bridie was jealous of Leigh.

JS: Yes, she definitely was. When it comes to daily life, Bridie doesn't have to play by the rules because, hey, she's a star. She gets away with terrible selfishness and bitchiness. We get to see flashes of Leigh's childhood, and it really isn't pretty. Bridie has quite a mean streak. Sometimes the rules of common decency just don't apply to her.

ED: But it seems as though Leigh really lets go of the rules when she goes to Jupiter, Florida. She fires her mother, rewrites her husband's play, and has an affair. She really does become Bridie, if only for that moment. Is that the only way for her to understand and forgive her mother?

JS: Maybe it isn't the only way, but I think that Leigh's inner Bridie was bubbling under the surface for years, just waiting to get out. Once it emerged, she and Bridie could connect, minus all of the hidden resentment and scorn. She was so determined never to be like her mother, something finally had to give.

I don't know if we all become our mothers, but certainly a lot of us go down that road whether we want to or not. Sometimes I hear my mother's voice when I speak to my daughter, and I wonder, Who said that? But, of course, my mother was nothing like Bridie Hart. She was married to my father for over fifty years and never ever put a toe in show business. But she had twelve children (I was number ten), and I think that this made her larger than life. She wasn't just a person, she was a force of nature.

ED: Did you grow up wishing that your parents were famous?

JS: No, I grew up wishing that *I* could be famous. I had a lot of confidence in my acting ability, but the more I worked at it, the less I enjoyed it. Today, when I look at the actors whose work I really admire, I'm absolutely in awe of them. How do they do it? I haven't got a clue. And as for fame, boy, did I have a change of heart about that one. Today, I happily hide behind my books and have no desire for that kind of fame or recognition. It seems to be toxic, not to mention exhausting.

ED: But wouldn't it be fun to go to the movie premiere of *Women in Hats*?

JS: Oh, my, yes. But what would I wear?

ED: I'd loan you something.

JS: Thanks. You have beautiful clothes.

ED: But tell me, who would play Bridie?

JS: Meryl Streep. Why not dream large? And it would be sort of perfect, because Bridie has a touch of the Shirley MacLaine mother character from *Postcards from the Edge.* Meryl Streep played the daughter in that one. Can't she play the mother in mine?

When I was writing the character, I started out with a picture of Bette Davis in *All About Eve,* which is a wonderful movie. But somewhere along the line, Bridie became her own person, with her own voice and her own look. It's a little bit like seeing a picture develop. The pale outlines give way to specific detail.

ED: Could I play Leigh?

JS: Consider it done. In exchange for the dress you're going to loan me for the premiere.

ED: Okay, so let's get back to Bridie as a mother. She doesn't create a very good role model for Leigh, who will become a mother at the end of the book. Bridie has always put her own needs before everyone else's.

JS: And I'm a bit nervous for Leigh, that she'll go in the other direction. She might become a martyr-mother who is all about self-sacrifice. She'll have Maddie and James to keep her in check, and she can always look in on *Women in Hats* to remind her of all that she went through during that play. So, she should be all right.

ED: Do we always have to choose between what we want and what's best for our children?

JS: It's a balancing act, isn't it? The in-flight safety messages on the airplanes always tell us to put our oxygen masks on before we try to help anyone else. That's because we'd be pretty useless to our kids or any other people if we were unconscious. I think that this metaphor applies to life on the ground. We have to take good care of our children, but we have to model good self-care for them. Sometimes I really push the limits of my physical stamina so that I can work, write, and be a good mother. But I try—I really try—to ask myself if I want my daughter to grow up and treat herself the way that I am treating myself.

ED: All the good stuff in life is so challenging. You've taken on quite a few challenges, so could you compare them a bit? Is it more difficult to write a play, or a novel? And how does parenting compare to all this writing?

JS: Parenting doesn't compare at all. It's monolithic. Anyone who claims that it's easy isn't doing it right. It isn't supposed to be easy. It's all-consuming, relentless, and by far the most exciting, fulfilling adventure I've ever had.

Within the world of writing, I have to say that novels are the most challenging form I've ever encountered. Maybe I'm just looking at my playwright days through rose-colored myopia, but a novel is so much like creating a universe. A play allows so much more collaboration and contribution from actors, directors, designers, and the audience. But a novel puts the responsibility squarely on the author's shoulders. It's daunting, to say the least.

ED: You said that the first draft of this book was so bad, you couldn't even submit it to your editor. How did you prevent yourself from crawling into a cave in a fetal position and withering away?

JS: By the skin of my teeth. Remember, I'm starting to turn into my mother, right? Well, she could teach a master class in endurance and perseverance. So, I just got stubborn about it, and wouldn't let go. Once I understood the missing ingredient in the story, I rewrote the book from top to bottom.

ED: What was missing?

JS: In the first draft, there was no miscarriage, no DES, none of that. And really, that's the volcanic center of the anger Leigh has for her mother.

ED: I can't imagine the book without that element. How did you end up adding it?

JS: I happened to see a documentary about women dealing with infertility. The filmmakers followed a woman who had suffered several miscarriages due to a medication that her mother had taken during pregnancy. The woman was now bedridden for nine months, surrounded by very intimidating medical equipment, all in an effort to carry this pregnancy to term. The medical care was all paid for by the woman's mother. She looked like someone who might never recover from the load of guilt that she was carrying. She was willing to do anything to make this up to her daughter. Once I made the connection between that mother-daughter and the mother-daughter I was creating, all the pieces fell into place. The second draft was much better than the first. And the third draft was better than the second.

But Bridie is a very different kind of mother than the one in that documentary. She isn't forthcoming about the DES, and she isn't someone who likes to be seen in any kind of harsh light. She doesn't want to own up to any of the mistakes that she made as a mother, but this is a mistake that will haunt her.

ED: How did you know that the offspring of famous people are not all as lucky as one might think?

JS: I remember, years ago, you told me that when you were really feeling desperate at an audition, you'd say, "I'm Brian Dennehy's daughter," as if that would impress them enough to give you the job. I replied that when I was desperate at an audition, I'd say, "I'm Brian Dennehy's daughter's friend." Neither of those lines did us much good, I think. In the end, it didn't matter who your father was. You always had to prove yourself in every audition, and you still do.

I like to think that it all balances out for us: that the people who are the offspring of celebrities get the same mix of good stuff and not-so-good stuff, which is just an inevitable part of life. But fame itself just seems to be some weird viral factor that can't be controlled.

ED: Would you discourage your daughter from a life on the stage?

JS: I have to be honest here: yes. It's just too insane and scary. I'll admit to being an overprotective mother on this one. But I live in New York City, and this town eats actors up and then spits them

322 A Reader's Guide

into the Hudson. It's kind of awful. How could I let my kid face that kind of life?

On the other hand, I think that she's a mini-Renaissance woman. She's so good at so many things. She's smart, she's musical, and she's a really gifted artist. She's also gorgeous, sweet, funny, and kind.

ED: And you're being totally objective here, right?

JS: Right.

1. From early childhood, Leigh is determined to distinguish herself from Bridie. But are there early signs that she is her mother's daughter? What are they?

2. Bridie and Frank both made a lot of mistakes. They were self-involved and occasionally self-destructive. But ultimately, Leigh has turned out to be a substantial person living a full, creative life. Was Bridie truly a bad mother? Was Frank a good father? What does it mean to be a good parent or a bad one?

3. Michael realizes his dream of writing a Broadway play, but why does he offer this as a gift to Leigh? How might this characterize their relationship throughout the book?

4. Leigh's miscarriage devastates her marriage, but it takes her quite a while to accept this fact. If Leigh and Michael could go back and make new choices, could their marriage have been saved, or are there events that a marriage simply can't survive?

5. Leigh has created a surrogate family for herself, with Kendall as her mother and Maddie as her sister. In what ways have you created your own family?

6. At the airport en route to Jupiter, Florida, Leigh believes that she sees her dead sister, Lilly. She then sees Lilly in a dream, and in a restaurant. What is the importance of these sightings?

7. In Jupiter, Leigh betrays her husband's trust: she begins an affair with James and she turns Michael's play—his baby—into her play. What factors prompted this change in Leigh? And do you think this is an aberration, or has Leigh changed forever?

8. Is James the right match for Leigh? Will they be together ten years from now?

9. Why does the final confrontation between mother and daughter transform from a narrative into a play? How does it illuminate the scene or the inner lives of the characters? And why do you think Lilly is present in this scene?

10. Does Bridie help Leigh to accept herself and to accept her sister's death? Does Bridie redeem herself in the end? If you were in Leigh's shoes, what sort of relationship would you maintain with Bridie?

ABOUT THE AUTHOR

JUDY SHEEHAN is the author of . . . And Baby Makes Two. She started her career as one of the original cast members and creators of the long-running stage hit Tony n' Tina's Wedding. Currently Sheehan is the playwright-in-residence at New York City's prestigious Looking Glass Theatre, which produces her work every season. Excerpts from her plays have appeared in the popular anthologies Monologues for Women by Women and Even More Monologues for Women by Women. In 2000, Sheehan joined the growing ranks of adoptive parents when she traveled to China to adopt a ten-month-old girl. Judy and her daughter, Annie, live in New York City. Women in Hats is her second novel. Visit her website, www.judysheehan.com.